CHRISTMAS DISAPPEARANCES

Twenty hectic, nonproductive minutes later, I circled back past the photo booth once again. This time Bertie, Eli and Cooper were there. The photographer and his assistant were fiddling with their equipment. Bertie just looked annoyed. Hands on her hips, she was staring at Santa's empty throne.

"You look frazzled," she said as I approached.

"I *am* frazzled. We have a missing dog."

Cooper and Eli stopped what they were doing and glanced over.

"A very valuable dog," I told them. "A top show dog."

Bertie's eyes widened. "Not Kiltie?"

"I'm afraid so."

"Then you're probably not going to want to hear about our problem," she said.

I took a deep breath. "What now?"

"Santa Claus is missing, too . . ."

Books by Laurien Berenson

A PEDIGREE TO DIE FOR

UNDERDOG

DOG EAT DOG

HAIR OF THE DOG

WATCHDOG

HUSH PUPPY

UNLEASHED

ONCE BITTEN

HOT DOG

BEST IN SHOW

JINGLE BELL BARK

RAINING CATS AND DOGS

CHOW DOWN

HOUNDED TO DEATH

DOGGIE DAY CARE MURDER

GONE WITH THE WOOF

DEATH OF A DOG WHISPERER

THE BARK BEFORE CHRISTMAS

LIVE AND LET GROWL

Published by Kensington Publishing Corporation

The Bark Before Christmas

LAURIEN BERENSON

KENSINGTON BOOKS
www.kensingtonbooks.com

KENSINGTON BOOKS are published by

Kensington Publishing Corp.
119 West 40th Street
New York, NY 10018

Copyright © 2015 by Laurien Berenson
"A Christmas Howl" copyright © 2015 by Laurien Berenson

All Kensington titles, imprints and distributed lines are available at special quantity discounts for bulk purchases for sales promotion, premiums, fund-raising, educational or institutional use. Special book excerpts or customized printings can also be created to fit specific needs. For details, write or phone the office of the Kensington Special Sales Manager: Kensington Publishing Corp., 119 West 40th Street, New York, NY, 10018. Attn. Special Sales Department. Phone: 1-800-221-2647.

Kensington and the K logo Reg. U.S. Pat. & TM Off.

Library of Congress Control Number: TK

ISBN-13: 978-0-7582-8459-4
ISBN-10: 0-7582-8459-4
First Kensington Hardcover Edition: October 2015
First Kensington Mass Market Edition: October 2016

eISBN-13: 978-0-7582-8460-0
eISBN-10: 0-7582-8460-8
First Kensington Electronic Edition: October 2015

10 9 8 7 6 5 4 3 2 1

Printed in the United States of America

Acknowledgments

I feel incredibly lucky to be working with the wonderful team at Kensington Publishing. A heartfelt thank-you to Michelle Forde, Adeola Saul, and Alexandra Nicolajsen for promoting my books and ushering me into the world of social media with such grace and prowess, to Robin Cook, whose production skills make me appear smarter than I am, and to Louis Malcangi for my beautifully designed book covers. And a huge shout-out to my terrific editor, John Scognamiglio, whose expertise and ideas are always invaluable.

My deepest appreciation goes to my wonderful agents, Meg Ruley and Christina Hogrebe, whose boundless patience and support make this series possible. You are the best cheerleaders an author could ever hope to have.

Chapter 1

"Here," said Bertie, handing me a slicker brush. "Don't just stand there. Make yourself useful."

The directive involved a Poodle. Nothing new about that in my life.

This Poodle was a cream-colored Miniature puppy, sitting on a nearby grooming table. The puppy looked as though she'd recently been bathed and blown dry. Now she needed the dense hair on her legs raked with a slicker so that Bertie could scissor her trim. When I glanced her way, the Mini gazed at me with trusting brown eyes.

I can talk and brush a Poodle at the same time. I've been doing it for years. Sad to say, I could probably do it with my eyes closed. And since I'd shown up at my sister-in-law's house unannounced, interrupting her preparations for the upcoming weekend's dog shows, I supposed I deserved to be put to work.

Make yourself useful. It's my family's rallying cry. We have my Aunt Peg to blame for that.

Dog show aficionados know Peg as Margaret Turn-bull, breeder and exhibitor of some of the best Standard Poodles in the country over the past four decades. In recent years Aunt Peg has shifted her focus; now she's a much-in-demand Toy and Non-Sporting Group judge. But one thing hasn't changed a bit. Aunt Peg still has impossibly high standards and she blithely expects everyone in the vicinity—especially her relatives—to live up to them.

I've long since accepted the fact that Aunt Peg is always going to find my efforts wanting. But Bertie, bless her heart, she keeps trying. Maybe that's because she's a relative newcomer to the family. Married to my younger brother, Frank, Bertie is also a successful professional handler. She has a thriving business and a competitive string of dogs, several of which were currently in the process of being prepped for the weekend shows.

It was Friday, so I'd known that Bertie would be busy. Still, that hadn't stopped me from dropping by without warning. I needed someone to talk to. Someone with an impartial opinion who would either take my side and commiserate or else do exactly the opposite—tell me to grow up, stop complaining, and get to work.

Either way, I knew I could count on Bertie to talk me down off the ledge. She always had before.

So there I was, standing in Bertie's finished basement—which doubled as her kennel and grooming room—on that cold December morning. A French Bulldog was air drying in a crate with a towel draped over its back. Two Schipperkes, a Briard, and a pair of Toy Poodles were observing the activity from inside the long runs that lined the room's walls. Bertie had a silver Bearded Collie out on a second grooming table. It looked as though she'd been getting ready to grind the dog's nails when I arrived.

It was no wonder that I'd barely gotten my coat off before Bertie was already putting me to work. Tit for tat, Aunt Peg would have said.

I took the red slicker brush from Bertie's outstretched hand and raised the Mini puppy into a standing position on her tabletop. Lifting a hind foot, I began to brush upward through the plush leg hair with a sharp, practiced, flick of my wrist. Bertie turned on the Dremel tool and quickly shortened and shaped the eight nails on the Beardie's front feet.

Then she put down the grinder and said, "Well? You drove all the way over here, you might as well spit it out. What's the matter now?"

I didn't stop brushing, but I did angle my body in Bertie's direction. "Do you want the long version or the short version?"

She let her gaze drift around the room of half-groomed dogs. "It's not like I don't have time to listen. Tell me everything."

"You know I went back to work part-time, right?"

"Sure. You got your old job back at Howard Academy. Special needs tutor just like before."

By *before,* Bertie meant prebaby. My younger son, Kevin, had been born two and a half years earlier, and the single semester I'd taken for maternity leave had stretched to several by mutual consent. The school had been happy with the teacher they'd hired as my replacement and I'd been delighted to be a stay-at-home mom. It was a luxury I hadn't been able to afford when my older son, Davey, was born.

But over the summer my replacement had left and at

the start of the current school year, I'd found myself teaching once more. I loved my job; I always had. The kids I worked with were wonderful and it was enormously satisfying to know that I could make a difference in their lives.

For three happy months, I'd been juggling part-time work at Howard Academy with my family life at home. In fact, the transition had gone so smoothly that I'd agreed to step up to a full-time position when the new semester began in January.

Bertie reached around for a back paw. The Beardie lifted its leg obligingly. "So what's the problem?"

"The Howard Academy Christmas Bazaar." I snorted with annoyance. "That's what."

"If you want me to bitch and moan convincingly on your behalf," Bertie said, "I'm going to need more information than that."

"How much do you know about Howard Academy?"

"Pretty much just the basics." She paused, then added, "Considering that *my* child goes to public school." Bertie and Frank's four-year-old daughter, Maggie, was in her first year of preschool and enjoying every minute of it. "Exclusive private school in Greenwich, Connecticut. The kids that go there are all like Richie Rich, trust-fund babies getting started on the educational path that will take them straight to the Ivy League. Am I close?"

"Yes, and no," I told her. "That may be the school's history and its reputation but it's no longer entirely correct. Actually, Mr. Hanover would be very disappointed to hear his beloved institution characterized in that way."

"He's the Big Cheese, right?"

"He is indeed. Not that anyone would ever dare call

him that. Our headmaster is quite dignified, and very much aware of the significance of his position."

"In other words," said Bertie, "a prig."

I wished I could tell her she was wrong, but Russell Hanover II didn't just govern Howard Academy, he also shared the school's conservative ideology and its firm belief in its own importance. Fortunately, however, that was only one side of my boss. He was also a man who worked hard, played fair, and stood up for his teachers when they needed his support. All of which made me feel compelled to defend him.

"He may be a bit of a prig," I said. "But it's not on purpose."

Bertie shot me a look. "Is there any other way?"

I thought about my answer as I moved around the grooming table to work on the puppy's off-side legs. "Mr. Hanover honestly wants what's best for his school and for his students," I said after a minute. "He's aware that both he and Howard Academy are in a position to influence the next generation of this country's political and financial leaders. And he doesn't take that responsibility lightly."

"*Oh my God.*" Bertie swept the Beardie off his table and led him across the room to an empty run. "I can't believe you just said that. This Hanover guy must be turning you into a prig, too."

"Hardly."

Bertie cocked a brow. "Are you *sure?*"

"Be quiet," I said with a laugh. "And listen to what I'm trying to tell you. At one time, what you said about HA's student body would have been true. But things have changed dramatically in the last couple of decades. Now the byword in education is diversity, and that includes extending a helping hand to those less fortunate. In the current school year, nearly one third of Howard Academy's students receive either full scholarships or financial aid."

"So what? That place has the money."

"That's just it," I told her. "It doesn't. The endowment funded by the Howard family a hundred years ago when they donated their property and founded the school is pretty much gone. So every dollar that's given away in scholarships has to be raised, primarily through alumni donations and school benefits."

Bertie fastened the latch on the Beardie's pen, then straightened and stared at me across the room. "I thought we were going to be talking about you. Why is any of this *your* problem?"

"Normally it wouldn't be."

I sighed. Loudly. And mostly for effect. The Mini puppy who, like all Poodles, was attuned to the people around her, tipped her head to one side and cocked an ear in my direction.

"Let me guess," said Bertie. "We've finally worked our way back around to the Christmas bazaar."

"Bingo. It's one of the biggest fund-raisers of the whole year. Mr. Hanover called me into his office earlier today. Apparently you're looking at its new chairman. As of a few hours ago, I'm in charge of the whole shebang."

"That sounds like a big job."

"It is!" I wailed. "It's *huge*."

"And when does this happy event take place?"

"Next weekend. Saturday."

Her eyes widened. "*Eight* days from now? You must be kidding. How are you ever going to pull the whole thing together by then?"

"Well, there's good news and bad news about that."

"Shoot," said Bertie.

"The good part is, most of the advance planning has already been done. The committees were formed six weeks ago and everyone is already working on their assignments. The whole school has been buzzing about the event for the last month."

"Okay." She nodded. "So what's the bad news?"

"The woman in the middle of all that activity, a parent volunteer who was the former chairman, eloped to Cabo San Lucas yesterday morning. Apparently she tendered her resignation as chairman of the bazaar by e-mail. Mr. Hanover was *not amused*."

Bertie and I grinned together.

"Maybe you should follow suit," she said. "E-mail Hanover and decline the position."

"That's not an option," I told her. "The parent was a volunteer. I'm an employee. Mr. Hanover thought that giving me the position was a great idea. He said it would ease me back into full-time work before the next semester starts."

"Right," said Bertie. "Because that's what every mother wants before Christmas. More stuff to do."

I lifted my hands helplessly. "I didn't have a choice. Mr. Hanover steamrolled over all my objections. He said the event was already primed and all I had to do was step in and make sure that nothing went seriously awry."

"*Awry?* That's the word he used?"

"You betcha."

"Prig," Bertie said again. "With a capital P."

The Mini's puppy's legs were finished. I moved on to the rounded pompon at the end of her tail. "He's actually a pretty good guy," I told her. "You'd probably like him if you met him."

"Well, that's not going to happen," Bertie replied. She reached into a pen and scooped out a Toy Poodle. Then she turned and looked at me, her eyes narrowing suspiciously. "Is it?"

"I don't know," I said innocently. "Could be."

Bertie crossed the room and plunked the Toy Poodle down on the other tabletop. "Melanie Travis, what are you up to now? And what makes you think there's even the slightest possibility that I might want to be involved?"

I gestured toward the Mini, now brushed, and fluffed, and ready to scissor. "This one's good to go. Don't you want to work on her next?"

"If you think I would even dream of letting you change the subject, you must be delusional." Bertie retrieved a cloth case from a nearby shelf, unzipped it, and set a pair of Japanese scissors down on the edge of my grooming table. "Here you go. Your trims are every bit as good as mine. Have at it."

Aunt Peg would have disagreed with that assessment. Not me. I accepted the compliment with pleasure, and went to work.

The Mini Poodle was young, but she already knew what was expected of her. When I slid my fingers beneath her chest, lifted slightly, then dropped her front legs into a square stance, she raised her head and held the position. I picked up the scissors, ran the long blades lightly up the puppy's leg to lift the hair, and began to trim.

"I agreed to go back to work at Howard Academy as a teacher," I said. "Not a circus ringmaster."

"We're talking about a few booths in a school auditorium, right? How bad can it be?"

"Have you ever *been* to the Howard Academy Christmas Bazaar?"

"Heck, no. Why would I want to do that?"

"It's mayhem. Out-of-control chaos. A veritable zoo."

Bertie, busy popping the rubber bands that had held the Toy Poodle's long topknot hair up and out of the way, thought for a minute then said, "Luckily you're very good with animals."

"That's not funny," I grumbled. "But it does segue nicely into my next point."

"Which is?"

"One of the attractions is a Santa Claus and Pets Photo Booth. The school has hired a photographer and students have been encouraged to bring their dogs and cats to the bazaar to get their pictures taken with Santa. Mr. Hanover's secretary is already working on the arrangements but he wants me to help out, too. He thought it would be right up my alley."

"I can see that," said Bertie. She turned on the water in the big, utility sink and checked the temperature with her fingers. The Toy Poodle was about to have a bath.

"The pictures will be uploaded on the spot and parents will have the option of having them turned into Christmas cards," I said, raising my voice to be heard above the running water. "It's a great idea and I'm hoping that the booth will be a big moneymaker. I thought I'd walk around the shows this weekend and try to drum up business among the exhibitors."

Bertie wasn't the only one who'd be spending the

next several days driving back and forth to the "Big E" Exposition Center in Massachusetts. My son, Davey, had his Standard Poodle, Augie, entered in the dog shows as well. The big black dog had spent the previous five months away from the show ring, growing hair— enough to balance out his new continental trim. Davey was delighted that his pet was finally ready to make his adult debut.

"You'll be swamped," said Bertie. "Especially if you have to oversee that booth *and* everything else."

"That's what I'm thinking."

"You ought to tell Hanover that you need some help."

"I already did."

Bertie was bent over the sink. She had one hand covering the Toy Poodle's eyes. The other held the nozzle and directed the spray toward the loose top-knot hair. She looked back over her shoulder at me and frowned.

"No," she said firmly. "No way."

"It will be fun," I told her brightly.

"No, it won't. It will be chaos. You just told me as much. Besides, I'm busy next Saturday."

"No, you're not. I looked at the calendar. It's December. There isn't a decent dog show within two hundred miles."

"I'm sure I must be doing something."

"You're not," I said. "I even checked with Frank. He told me you were free."

"Frank's a traitor," Bertie muttered. "I wouldn't believe a word he says."

Funny thing about that. I'd felt the same way about my feckless younger brother for years. But meeting

Bertie was the best thing that ever could have happened to him. Not only had she become a steadying influence in his life, but it also turned out that Frank's desire to live up to his wife's expectations was the impetus he'd needed to finally outgrow his irresponsible ways.

"Come on," I said. "Give me a hand. It's for a good cause."

Bertie sighed. She was wavering, I could tell.

"Between the kids, and Santa, and the pets, there's going to be a lot going on. You know I'll need someone there who's really good with dogs. And the best person I could think of was you."

"Not Aunt Peg?"

I lifted a brow. "Can you picture Aunt Peg in an elf costume?"

"Wait a minute." Bertie spun around. "You didn't say anything about an *elf costume*."

"Umm . . ."

"Before you answer," she warned, "bear in mind that it's a deal breaker."

"Then no," I said quickly. "The costume isn't mandatory. Though I bet you'd look cute in a pair of striped tights."

That was an understatement. Bertie was gorgeous. She had thick auburn hair, killer cheekbones, and the kind of body that instantly rendered every other woman practically invisible. If anyone could pull off a forest-green tunic and pointy shoes, it would be my sister-in-law.

"Don't even think about it," she said.

"All right, you don't have to dress up. But will you come and help out? If I'm going to tackle a project this size—especially with Mr. Hanover watching—I'm going to need back-up I can count on. It's just for a few hours. And I'll owe you one."

"You're not going to let me say no, are you?"

Not if I could help it. I'd beg if I had to.

Bertie went back to bathing the Toy Poodle. Even though her back was turned, I heard her mutter, "Someone should have warned me before I married into this family."

"I tried to," I told her. "You didn't listen." *And thank God for that,* I thought.

"All right," said Bertie. "I'm in."

Chapter 2

Poodles are the greatest breed of dog.

You may be thinking that I'm a bit biased—and I am—but hear me out, because this is a breed with a whole lot to commend it. First, they come in three sizes—Toy, Miniature, and Standard—which makes it easy to find a suitable companion for every lifestyle from couch potato to serious athlete. And second, their temperament is beyond compare. Poodles are smart, they're silly, they're empathetic. They also have a terrific sense of humor. If you don't already know how to laugh at yourself, a Poodle will teach you—and she will make sure that you enjoy the learning process.

My husband, Sam, and I have five Standard Poodles between us. Six, if you count Augie, who belongs to Davey. Sam and I have been married for four years. Not surprisingly, we met because of a Poodle. My first marriage—over and done with more than a decade earlier—had been, among its many other problems, dog-free. The second time around, I'd chosen much more wisely.

Standard Poodles are the largest variety of the breed. It's easy to look them in the eye—and that's a mode of communication at which they excel. Poodles are thinking dogs. The only dumb one I've ever met is Sam's retired specials dog, Tar.

Big, black, and beautiful, Tar is a Gold Grand Champion with multiple Group and Best in Show wins. Fortunately what he lacks in brainpower, he makes up for in amiability. The big goof always means well. It's not his fault that he never has a clue.

Faith and Eve, the two Standard Poodles I'd contributed to our blended canine family, are a mother and daughter pair. Faith, who had come to me as a gift from Aunt Peg, was the first dog I'd ever owned. She'd entered my life as a young puppy, opened up a space in my heart, and wriggled herself right in. Our bond was immediate and all-encompassing.

Faith was well into middle age now and our connection had deepened and matured with time. Communication between us needed only a word, or a glance, or a gentle touch. I liked to think that I could read Faith's mind; I knew full well that she could read mine.

Though it was December, snow had yet to fall in southwestern Connecticut. Even so, it was cold. As I drove home to our house in North Stamford, a sharp wind rattled and shook the bare branches of the trees that lined both sides of the scenic Merritt Parkway.

By now, Davey would be home from school. He and Sam had clipped Augie the previous afternoon. Today they were planning to bathe him and blow his coat dry. Preparing a Poodle for the show ring is an exacting task, made even more so in this case since it was the first time that Augie would be making an appearance in his new adult trim.

For Poodle puppies that are destined for the show ring, hair matters from the moment they are born. Their coats are continuously pampered and protected, and maximum growth is encouraged. Up to one year of age, Poodles are shown in the puppy trim, with a dense blanket of hair covering their entire bodies. Once they reach adulthood, however, in order to conform to the breed standard, much of that hair must be clipped away.

Augie was now sporting the continental trim, which meant that a large, shaped, mane of hair covered the front half of his body, while his face, his legs and feet, and his hindquarters were all clipped to the skin. Rounded pompons adorned his hips and the end of his tail. In addition, he had bracelets of hair at the bottoms of all four legs.

Davey had turned twelve in September. Though he'd spent much of his childhood surrounded by Standard Poodles, Augie was the first dog that was truly his. Davey was old enough now to accept responsibility for a pet's well-being. Even better, he and Sam had decided to make finishing Augie's championship a joint project for the two of them to achieve together.

I couldn't have planned that better if I'd tried.

Our grooming room is located off the kitchen toward the back of the house. I knew that the loud, droning, whine of the blow-dryer would cover the sound of my arrival. My human family wouldn't hear me come in, but the pack of Poodles certainly would.

Faith and Eve were already there to greet me before I'd even closed the door behind me. Sam's two bitches, Raven and Casey, quickly followed. Tar, a chew toy dangling out of the side of his mouth like a cigar, brought up the rear. Five black dogs—all of them wearing the easy and convenient sporting trim—milled around the hallway, eddying around my legs like a comforting current.

It's hard to pat five dogs at once, but I was giving it my best shot when the Poodles' ears suddenly lifted. As one their heads swiveled away, their gazes turning back in the direction from which they'd come. A second later, I heard a high-pitched shriek.

"Momm—eeeee!!"

Alerted by the Poodle posse, I knew which way to look. Abruptly a two-foot-high, mostly naked child came barreling through the kitchen doorway and rocketing down the hall. Diaper bouncing, bare feet slapping on the hardwood floor, Kevin careened through the startled pack of Poodles and crashed into my legs. He wrapped his pudgy arms around my thighs, gazed upward, and aimed a loud, smacking kiss in the direction of my face.

"Mommy home!" he cried.

I reached down to pick him up but I was a moment too slow. Kevin had already spun away again. Eluding my hands, he bounced off of Eve and wiggled past Tar. Finding himself in the clear, he zoomed back down the hallway. Once he'd learned to walk, there'd been no stopping that child. The only pace he knew was a dead run.

"Hey, Kev," I called after him. "Where are your clothes?"

"Gone!"

Undressing himself was Kevin's new favorite game. There were mornings where he'd whipped off his socks and shirt before I even had a chance to pull on his pants.

He thought zippers were vastly entertaining, and buttons didn't deter his small fingers one bit. No doubt somewhere in the house was a bundle of discarded, pint-sized clothing. On other occasions, his sneakers had ended up in the garbage and his T-shirt was left floating in the dog's water bowl.

Aside from his chubby cheeks, the little fair-haired, blue-eyed, dynamo was the image of his father. Now he yelled out his reply without even bothering to slow down. Reaching the end of the hall at toddler-warp speed, Kevin shot through the doorway, angled left, and disappeared. The Poodles and I followed at a more sedate pace.

As we rounded the corner, Sam poked his head out of the grooming room. He usually wears his blond hair short, but he'd been busy lately and was in badly need of a trim. I liked my husband's current, scruffy look. It gave him a bad-boy vibe that I found compelling.

A lean, six-foot-two, Sam had to lean way down to brush a kiss across my cheek. "I thought I heard you come in," he said. "Did you happen to see Kev?"

"He blew by me a minute ago. Since he's not with you, I'm guessing he ended up in the dining room. That child does realize it's winter, doesn't he?"

"If so, he doesn't seem to care. I take it his clothes are gone again?"

"Yup. Wearing nothing but a diaper."

"Be thankful for small favors," Sam said with a laugh.

There was that. I'd already had to explain to Kevin that since the Poodles were housebroken, he needed to be, too.

Inside the small room, Davey had Augie lying flat on his side on a rubber-matted grooming table. A freestanding blow-dryer directed a steady stream of hot hair toward a section of hair that he was carefully straightening with a pin brush. Davey took his eyes off his task for a few seconds. He looked up at me with a smirk on his face.

"Did I do that when I was Kev's age?" he asked.

"No." I thought back, then added, "Never."

"I bet I was a model child."

"Not exactly. Your favorite game was hide-and-seek."

"What's the matter with that?"

"You were always getting lost. And usually at the most inconvenient times."

"I was exploring," Davey corrected with a grin. "I wasn't lost."

"To a parent, it all looks pretty much the same," Sam told him. "We like to know where our kids are."

"Yeah, well." Davey patted his pocket happily. "Now you can call me."

The personal cell phone was a new perk, one that made my son feel very grown up. For safety's sake, I liked knowing that he was only a phone call away. Typical twelve-year-old, Davey didn't care at all about that aspect. He liked the fact that the Smartphone made him feel cool, and that it gave him instant access to the Internet—a pair of benefits I could have happily done without.

"Speaking of calling," said Sam. "We've heard from Peg three times since Davey got home from school."

No surprise there. In fact I wouldn't have been shocked to arrive home and find that Aunt Peg had dropped in to supervise Augie's preshow grooming. She's a woman who likes to be in charge.

"What did she want?" I asked.

"Auggg-eeee!" Kevin squealed behind us.

Legs pumping, small hands fisted around Tar's chew toy, the toddler went racing across the kitchen with Tar in hot pursuit. I winced as the Standard Poodle skidded on the floor and sideswiped a chair. Hearing his name, Augie opened his eyes, lifted his head fractionally to have a look, then settled back in place. What a good dog. At least somebody remembered his training.

Kevin glanced our way but didn't stop running. A moment later, he and Tar disappeared in the direction of the hall.

I gazed after him thoughtfully. "He can't get the front door open yet, can he?"

The toddler's list of accomplishments seemed to grow daily. And unfortunately, sometimes when he'd mastered a new skill, I found out the hard way. Now I pictured him letting the dogs outside and all of them dashing madly around the front yard, accompanied by Kevin dressed only in his diaper.

Sad to say, one of my chief goals in life is to keep most of the chaos surrounding my family confined to a place where the neighbors won't see it.

"No way," said Sam. "The knob's too big for his hands, and it's too stiff for him to turn."

I waited a beat. Sam thought for a moment, then frowned. "I'll go check," he said.

"So," I said, turning back to Davey as Sam left the room. "You've heard from Aunt Peg?"

"Three times," Davey confirmed. He repositioned the dryer's nozzle and moved on to a new section of hair. "She wanted to make sure I knew that Saturday's judge likes a pretty head."

Connie Wilburn was our first judge of the weekend. Now in her late seventies, Mrs. Wilburn had been judging Poodles since before I was born. Her opinion on a dog was knowledgeable, impartial, and well worth seeking. The downside was that Mrs. Wilburn wasn't nearly as limber as she'd once been. Arthritis prevented her from bending down over a dog and really getting her hands on the body beneath the hair. She had always appreciated a Poodle with a pretty face; now that was just about all she could see.

"Augie's got a great head," I said. "Nothing to worry about there."

"I know. That's what I told Aunt Peg. But then she called back to say that she'd stop by the setup on Saturday to put in Augie's topknot for me."

"I hope you said no, thank you."

Handling Augie to his championship was Davey's second try at dog show competition. Several years earlier he'd been eager to try out his fledgling skills in Junior Showmanship. Initially he'd had a great time. He'd done pretty well, too—until Aunt Peg's overbearing coaching had managed to ruin his enjoyment of the sport.

This time around, Sam and I were both determined that things would be very different. Davey would be allowed to learn at his own pace, make mistakes without censure, and find his own path to success—no matter how long it took.

"I did." Davey sighed. "But she'll probably show up anyway."

"Who?" Sam reappeared, trailed by Raven and Faith. "Are we talking about Peg?"

"Of course, who else?" I glanced around behind him. "Where's the munchkin?"

"I got him settled in front of the TV with a cartoon

and a couple of Poodles for company. I think all that running around wore him out."

Faith sidled up beside me and pressed her muzzle into my hand. I curled my fingers around her lips and squeezed gently. She blew out a warm breath into my palm.

Every Standard Poodle in the house save Augie was a retired show dog. So they were all familiar with both the lengthy duration and the repetitive tedium of the grooming process. I knew that Faith was feeling conflicted. She was happy not to be the dog who had to lie perfectly still on the grooming table; but at the same time she was a little bit jealous that she wasn't the one receiving all the attention.

I squatted down beside her, wrapped my arm around her body, and gave her a hug. Faith leaned into me. Her tail waved gently back and forth. It was just enough to let me know that we were good.

"The third call," said Davey, "was Aunt Peg offering to give me a lesson in how to manage Augie's ears at the show. She wants me to be sure to hold them back so that Mrs. Wilburn can see Augie's length of muzzle and the chiseling under his eyes."

"I told her I'd take care of that part," said Sam. "And that all she has to do is come and watch."

"I'm sure that went over well," I said.

Aunt Peg was a doer, not a watcher. Having scaled back the extent of her own exhibiting due to the demands of her busy judging schedule, she now seemed determined to compete vicariously through her great-nephew.

"At least she hasn't called back again," said Davey.

"Don't worry, Sam and I will run interference for

you at the show," I told him. "Not only that, but I've got a brilliant idea. One that should keep her busy all day."

"Whatever it is, I already love it," Sam said. Davey nodded in agreement.

"Aunt Peg's a Howard Academy alum. I'm going to get her to walk around the show and encourage local exhibitors to support the Santa Claus and Pets Booth at next week's Christmas bazaar. Aunt Peg knows everybody. Not only that, but there's nothing she likes more than telling people what to do. So why not marry those two things together and put her to work on behalf of a good cause?"

"Good thinking," said Sam.

"That sounds a whole lot better than having her follow me around all day, telling me everything I'm doing wrong," Davey said glumly.

"Cheer up," I told him. "This is supposed to be fun. And you're not going to do anything wrong."

"I hope not," said Davey.

"I just hope Kev keeps his clothes on," I replied.

Chapter 3

Dog show exhibitors spend half their lives in cars, driving to far-flung locations. Or at least that's the way it feels.

Living in southwestern Connecticut, we were ideally situated dog-show-wise. Nearly every weekend of the year we were within easy driving distance of events in both the New England and the Mid-Atlantic states. The shows we'd entered that weekend were taking place at the Eastern States Exposition in West Springfield, Massachusetts.

Exhibitors often find themselves dealing with indoor venues that offer cramped conditions, bad lighting, and nonexistent parking. Compared to that, the Big E was a very welcome alternative. Dog shows held at that location are always a huge draw, and nearly everyone we knew would be exhibiting. There were major entries in all three varieties of Poodles.

Since we only had Augie to prep for the ring, our arrival was timed for midmorning. By then, the coliseum building was already crowded. Bertie, who had gotten to the show shortly after dawn with her whole string of dogs, had saved us a spot in the grooming area right next to her own setup.

We left our car in the unloading zone, and made our way across the huge room, looking like an itinerant band of gypsies. Sam dragged the dolly loaded with Augie's crate and grooming table, the wooden tack box, and various other dog show necessities. Davey had Augie on a leash. The two of them bounced up and down with excitement and ran on ahead to explore.

Kevin and I straggled along in the rear. Kev is endlessly fascinated by the world around him and when I'm not in a hurry, I love his artless curiosity. Now, however, life would have been happier with a less inquisitive child.

No matter how hard I tried to point the toddler in the right direction and keep him moving forward, he still managed to find a reason to stop every few seconds. Kev was intrigued by everything from a Saint Bernard wearing a drool bib, to a Dachshund navigating a broad jump, to a rolling ball of fluffy white hair.

By the time we reached the setup, Sam already had the dolly unloaded. He'd shoved the big crate in line next to one of Bertie's, then arranged the tack box and Kev's diaper bag on top of it. As we approached, he was setting up the grooming table in the middle of the aisle. He was also frowning.

"What's the matter?" I asked.

We'd just arrived. Surely something couldn't be wrong already.

"Bertie has some bad news."

"What?" I swung my gaze her way.

"There's a change of judge in Poodles. Mrs. Wilburn

had a fall this morning in her hotel room, and she was taken to the hospital. She'll be out of commission until after Christmas. Bartholomew Perkin is taking over her assignment."

"Who?"

I looked back at Sam. Like Aunt Peg, he's been involved in the dog show world for many more years than I have. He was often familiar with judges I didn't have the experience to know. Now, however, Sam just shrugged.

"Never heard of him," he said.

That wasn't good.

A great deal of time, effort, and expense is involved in getting a dog to the show ring. So exhibitors choose their judges with care. There's no point in taking a typey dog to a judge who only cares about soundness, or in showing a silver Poodle to one who favors blacks. Nor do owner-handlers waste their time showing under judges who are known to play politics. There are few things more frustrating than knowing you have the best dog in the ring, only to watch the judge hand the purple ribbon to one of the pros anyway.

An unknown quantity *might* turn out to be a decent judge. But since none of us had ever even heard of Mrs. Wilburn's replacement, I was pretty sure that the odds were against it.

"You all look like you've just arrived at a funeral," Aunt Peg said, coming up behind us. Standing a hair under six feet tall, she towers over me. It's a circumstance she's not above using to use to her advantage. "I take it you've heard about what happened?"

"Bertie just told us," I replied. "How much trouble are we in? Who is Bartholomew Perkin?"

"Good question."

That she didn't know either was really bad news. Aunt Peg is a steadfast member of the dog show community. She's spent the majority of her six decades devoted to the Poodle breed she adores.

While I'm the kind of person who is continually out of the loop, when it comes to dogs, Aunt Peg *is* the loop. She knows everything. She's on top of every new development.

If Aunt Peg didn't know who our new judge was, then he was clearly not worth knowing.

Kevin tugged at the hem of my jacket. Distracted by the conversation, I'd forgotten all about him. Quickly I leaned down and zipped him out of his parka. Kev unwound his scarf. I balled it up and shoved it down the empty sleeve of his jacket. With luck, we'd leave the show with as much clothing as we'd had when we arrived.

"Mr. Perkin's breed is Pekingese," Davey announced, finally arriving at the setup. He hopped Augie up onto the grooming table, slipped off his leash, then patted the rubber matted surface so that the Standard Poodle would lie down.

"How do you know that?" I asked.

"I ran into Crawford and Terry." Davey sketched a wave toward the other side of the ring. "They're grooming over there. Crawford isn't happy about the judge change either."

Crawford Langley was the busiest and most talented Poodle handler in the Northeast. He'd handled Standard Poodles to top wins at Westminster, Eukanuba, and our national specialty. Terry was Crawford's partner in life, his assistant at the shows, and the most talkative person I've ever met. He's my best buddy and I love him like crazy.

"Pekes," Aunt Peg said thoughtfully. "Maybe Mr. Perkin likes hair."

"Or maybe he likes short legs," Bertie guessed.

"Bite your tongue," said Sam. Even lying down, Augie's length of leg was evident. We certainly hadn't brought Mr. Perkin that.

Bottom line, it didn't really matter what our new judge wanted. Having devoted several hours to grooming Augie Poodle and a couple more to driving, we were already committed. Davey would take his Standard Poodle in the ring regardless.

Sam went off to park the car. I got Kev situated in a folding chair with a coloring book and a box of crayons. Davey opened up the tack box and began pulling out the tools of the trade. Making a row along the edge of the table, he lined up a slicker brush for Augie's bracelets, a pin brush for his mane coat and topknot, a greyhound comb for smoothing through the tangles, and a spray bottle for misting away static.

Meanwhile, Aunt Peg continued to mutter under her breath.

Bertie, putting the finishing touches on a Finnish Spitz, regarded her with amusement. "According to the catalog," she said, "Mr. Perkin comes from Arizona and he was hired to judge half a dozen Toy breeds."

"If he was available to fill in at the last minute, that means he didn't have a full slate," Aunt Peg replied. "That can't be good."

"This will be his very first Poodle assignment," Davey piped up. "Terry told me he just got approved."

"Lord save me from beginners." Aunt Peg rolled her eyes. "Well, there's nothing to be done about it now. I guess we're all going to find out what Bartholomew Perkin looks for in a Poodle at the same time."

While she was speaking, Aunt Peg sidled over and had a surreptitious look at Davey's line brushing. Augie was lying flat on the table. His eyes were closed; he was totally relaxed. Brushing quickly and smoothly, Davey was doing a great job of working his way through the dog's dense coat. Even so, I knew it was only a matter of time before Aunt Peg would begin to nitpick.

"Guess what?" I said. "I have a job for you."

"Oh?" Peg lifted a brow. "Do I need a job?"

I heard Bertie smother a laugh. I ignored that and said, "I know how much you like to stay busy."

"And so I shall. Davey needs my help setting Augie's topknot."

My son glanced up, caught my eye, and shook his head vehemently.

"Sam will do that when he gets back. And anyway, this is more important. I need your help."

"Well, that's nothing new." Aunt Peg gazed pointedly down her nose at me.

Bertie, that traitor, wasn't even bothering to hide her laughter now.

"But you'll like this job," I told Aunt Peg. "It's for the Howard Academy Christmas Bazaar. There's going to be a photo booth for people to bring their pets and have their pictures taken with Santa Claus. It'll be great."

For eleven months of the year, Aunt Peg is one of the least sentimental women I know. But as the Christmas holidays approach, all that changes. The mere sound of Christmas music is enough to turn her all mushy and misty-eyed. I was aiming for her soft spot and I knew it. With luck, I'd hit a bull's-eye.

"That's not until next week," Aunt Peg said. Sometimes I think she knows the details of my life better than I do.

"It's never too soon to start getting the word out," I told her. "And I can't think of a better place to find the kind of people who would want to take their dogs to visit Santa Claus than right here. I figured you could walk around the show and tell all your friends that they shouldn't miss it."

"That sounds like an excellent idea," Bertie offered from across the setup.

"It does," Aunt Peg agreed. She sounded surprised. "But I'm not sure why your job ought to be done by me. Why don't *you* walk around and spread the news?"

"I could do that," I said easily. "If you'd rather stay at the setup with the boys. Since you're going to be here anyway with Davey"—once again my son lifted his head and shot me an anguished look—"do you mind keeping an eye on Kevin for me?"

"Kevin," Peg said flatly.

"You know, the little boy? Almost three?" I pointed to a chair. "He's sitting right over there."

"Kevin," Aunt Peg said again.

Hearing his name for a second time, the toddler looked up. "What?" he inquired.

"I think you mean 'Excuse me,'" I told him.

Kev tipped his head to one side and thought about that for a moment. He didn't issue a correction, however. Instead he merely picked up his red crayon and went back to coloring.

"I don't do children," Aunt Peg stated.

"Kev's not *children,* he's family." I smiled sweetly.

"All the same—"

"You could help him color," I suggested. "Or maybe

read to him. Just don't let him start taking his clothes off." Slipping deftly between table and crate, I started to walk away. "And make sure he doesn't disappear. That's a biggie."

"But—"

"His diaper bag is on Augie's crate. And there's a changing table in the ladies' room. You know . . . just in case."

"I don't *think* so."

"Excuse me?" I stopped and cocked an ear, just like Faith would have done.

"*You* stay here," Aunt Peg said firmly. "And *I* will make the rounds of the other exhibitors."

I held my breath until she'd swept past me. Aunt Peg's long stride carried her quickly down the narrow aisle between the stacked crates. She went a good ten yards before she even slowed down. Then it was to stop and chat with a Bichon exhibitor. Aunt Peg never looked back once.

"That was masterfully done," said Bertie.

I was pretty pleased myself. "I guess I'm getting a little smarter as time goes on." I turned to Kevin and grinned. "Good going, kid. Thanks."

Kev looked up. "'scuse me?" he said.

Sam returned from parking the car. Bertie and the Finnish Spitz left to go to the ring. Davey finished brushing Augie's right side and turned him over. The left side—the one that faces the judge when the Poodle is in the ring—is always brushed last so that it won't flatten and lose its shape when the dog lies on it. Without Aunt Peg there to stir up trouble, things were remarkably peaceful at the setup.

An hour before the Standard Poodles were due in the ring, the Toy judging began. I was about to head over to get a look at our new judge when Sondra McEvoy, the mother of one of my students, passed by the setup. She was carrying her West Highland White Terrier, GCH Westglen Braveheart—informally known as Kiltie—tucked under one arm. Her other hand clutched a purple and gold Best of Breed ribbon, attesting to the fact that her recent outing in the show ring had ended successfully.

"Congratulations," I called.

"Thanks." Sondra angled her path my way. She was a slender woman in her early forties, with a pale complexion and wide-set blue eyes. Her short dark hair was styled in a chic bob. As she approached, Sondra blew out a relieved breath. "I was afraid I might not get him out of the breed today so I'm happy to have that behind me. The Group judge loves Kiltie. From here on in it should be smooth sailing."

From what I could tell, lots of judges loved Kiltie. The Westie was a regular competitor in the Group and Best in Show rings. Still, though the breed ring could sometimes seem like little more than a stepping stone for the big specials dogs, it didn't pay to take anything for granted. Every judge has a different opinion, and every dog is capable of having a bad day.

"Peg waylaid me when I came out of the ring," Sondra told me. "She's marching around the show like a woman on a mission."

"Good," I said. "That's just what I wanted her to do. She's supposed to be drumming up business for the Howard Academy Christmas Bazaar. Did she tell you about the photo booth?" I reached over and scratched underneath the Westie's chin. "Can't you just picture

Kiltie with a big Christmas bow around his neck? He'd look adorable."

"You don't have to sell me on the idea," Sondra said with a laugh. "Poppy already made me promise that I'd bring him." Poppy was Sondra's daughter, a quiet sixth grader who excelled at reading and harbored a fervent dislike of math. "Plus I volunteered to help sell raffle tickets. So we'll definitely be there."

"Excellent. Speaking of Poppy, where is she? Did she come to the show with you today?"

I knew that Sondra's daughter was one of Kiltie's most enthusiastic supporters. When Poppy came to my schoolroom for tutoring, we often began our sessions with five minutes of dog talk. Rehashing the recent show results and chatting about Kiltie's accomplishments had a way of making the math problems that followed seem slightly more palatable.

"No, she's with her father today." Sondra's gaze shifted away. "I don't know if you heard? My husband and I have separated."

I gulped, feeling like an idiot. That was one of the problems with being at Howard Academy only part-time; it was difficult to keep up with all the news. "I'm sorry," I said. "I didn't know. I didn't mean to put my foot in it."

"Don't worry, you didn't. These things happen. And in our case, it's been coming for a while. Jim and I are trying our best to keep things amicable. You know, for Poppy's and Kiltie's sakes."

"I'm sure that makes things easier for her," I said as Sondra turned to go. "I'll see you next week at the bazaar. And good luck in the Group!"

Augie, finally fully brushed, was now standing up on his table. Working under Sam's watchful eye, Davey was using a pair of curved scissors to smooth and round the hair on the Poodle's front puffs.

Sam glanced my way. "Toys must be almost finished by now. Why don't you go up to the ring and watch our new judge sort out some Minis? See what you think of him. I'll keep an eye on Kev."

"On my way," I said. "I'll pick up Davey's armband, too."

I hadn't even gone ten feet when Bertie came flying past me. Dodging between crates and tables she was racing back toward the setup with the hapless Finnish Spitz in tow.

"Quick!" she cried, gesturing toward a male Miniature Poodle, who was standing on one of her tables, prepped and ready to go to the ring. "Put him back in his crate. He's not here!"

"What . . . ?" Surprised, I turned around and followed her back to the setup.

Sam reacted more quickly than I did. In a single smooth motion, he swept the Mini off the tabletop with one hand and opened a nearby crate with the other. He tucked the dog neatly inside and turned the latch. Seconds later Sam was back at Augie's table, standing once more beside Davey and looking as if nothing unusual had occurred.

Totally confused, I looked back and forth between Bertie and Sam. I had no idea what had just happened.

Bertie had devoted an hour that morning to brushing, trimming, and spraying the Mini dog. I'd watched her do it. Tossed back into a crate like that, the dog's topknot would be knocked askew, his ear hair would get in his mouth. The Poodle would mess up everything—just before he was due to go up to the ring.

"But his topknot—" I started to protest.

"It doesn't matter," Bertie told me firmly. "He's not here."

"But—"

Sam caught my eye and shook his head. I took that to mean that he'd explain to me later what had been going on. But that did nothing to assuage my curiosity now.

Bertie, meanwhile, had slipped the looped collar off over the Spitz's head and walked him into a lower-level crate. She closed the door behind him, then straightened and gazed in the direction of the ring.

"Oh crap," she muttered.

Now what?

"Here comes Armageddon," Bertie said.

"I should hope not," I replied, trying to lighten the mood.

It didn't work. Bertie still looked rattled. Sam was staring at the ceiling. I got the impression he was trying to pretend that he was somewhere else.

Then I turned and saw Hannah Fort, a fellow Miniature Poodle exhibitor, striding in our direction. The expression on her face was thunderous. She hadn't even reached the setup before she lifted her arm and pointed her finger accusingly at Bertie's stacked crates.

"I saw that dog," she announced. "I know he's here. You have to show him."

"No, I don't," Bertie replied calmly. "And I'm not going to."

"He's on the grounds. He has to be shown!"

"There's a judge change. And I don't like the new judge. The dog is withdrawn."

Hannah's eyes narrowed. "Did you provide notice of your withdrawal to the show secretary?"

Bertie couldn't have, I thought. There wouldn't have been time. She'd only decided not to show the Mini two minutes earlier. And I still had no idea why.

"It doesn't matter," Bertie said. "The dog is not going in that ring, Hannah. And nothing you can say will change that."

"This isn't just about you! How dare you be so selfish and screw things up for the rest of us?"

Bertie shrugged. She looked unhappy. "I don't have any choice."

"I've been waiting four months for a major," Hannah snapped. Her cheeks were flushed, her lips drawn in an angry snarl. "Do you have any idea how much time and effort I put into making sure that there would be one here? The number today is spot on. And if you pull that dog, it will all have been for nothing."

Chapter 4

Uh-oh.

Well, at least that explained one thing. The Mini's withdrawal was still a mystery to me but now I knew why Hannah Fort was so angry.

In order to complete its championship, a dog must accumulate fifteen points in class competition against other non-champions. Half a dozen classes are offered, but three of those—Puppy, Bred-By-Exhibitor, and Open—usually receive the highest number of entries.

The classes are divided by sex and once they've been judged, the winners of each class go head to head to compete for the titles of Winners Dog and Winners Bitch. Only those two entrants receive points toward their championships; and the number of points they're awarded is determined by the amount of competition that they've beaten on the day.

A dog gets one point for beating a small entry and as many as five points for winning over a large one. Included within that fifteen point total, a champion must collect at least two major wins—meaning that he must defeat enough dogs to be awarded at least three points.

The rule is a good one. It prevents an inferior dog from completing its championship by simply piling up single points against lower-level competition. But the quest for majors can also become a sticking point. Variables like time of year, breed of dog, and even the weather can have an effect on entries. It's not uncommon for a deserving dog to "single out" and be stuck—and out of competition for several months or more—while he waits for a major entry to appear.

At times like that, frustrated exhibitors have occasionally been known to give fate a nudge. The practice is called building a major and it involves calling around and cajoling other breeders to help make up the numbers. Dogs that might not be quite ring-ready are pulled out of ex-pens and backyards and entered in the designated show. And on that day, one lucky owner— usually but not always the architect of the entry—goes home with a major win.

I sidled over to stand beside my sister-in-law.

"Bertie," I said softly. "What's the matter?"

"I stopped at the Toy ring to have a look at the new judge on my way back from Spitzes. Mr. Perkin was doing Open Dogs, and he's *measuring*."

"Damn," Sam said, but he didn't sound surprised. He'd probably guessed what the problem was five minutes earlier.

The Poodle breed's three varieties are divided by height, as determined by measurement at the highest point of the shoulder. Toy Poodles are ten inches or under. Miniatures stand between ten and fifteen inches. Standards are any Poodle taller than fifteen inches.

The height specifications aren't just a recommendation. They are written into the breed standard as a requirement. And any Poodle that doesn't fit underneath the wicket for its variety can be measured out by the judge and disqualified from competition.

Most experienced Poodle judges simply eyeball a dog's size. Breed experts often feel that attributes like type, conformation, and temperament are more important than an errant quarter-inch in height. And because bigger dogs stand out in the ring, exhibitors tend to show Toy and Mini Poodles that are "right up to size."

It's not unusual for a slightly oversize Poodle to finish its championship. Experienced exhibitors know which judges are sticklers for size and plan their schedules accordingly. But Bartholomew Perkin—currently wielding his wicket in the Toy ring—had been an unknown quantity. And now Bertie was stuck.

"It's not my fault that your dog is too big," Hannah said sternly. "The major is on the nose. If you don't show him, we're all out of luck."

"Think about it," said Bertie. "If the judge measures Doodle out, he'll be disqualified. Your major will break anyway. Plus Doodle will have a DQ on his record." Not a trifling consideration, since three disqualifications would knock the dog out of competition permanently.

"That's a chance I'm willing to take."

"Well, I'm not. The dog is staying in his crate."

Hannah pursed her lips in annoyance. She considered for a moment, then tried another line of attack. "We don't even know that Perkin plans to measure Minis. You might be giving away a major that *your* dog could have won. And how do you suppose his owner who's been paying your bills for months, will feel about *that* when he finds out?"

Bertie squared her shoulders. "Are you threatening me, Hannah?"

"Surely not," Sam said quickly. Ever the peacekeeper, he stepped between the two women. "Maybe we'd all like to take a minute to calm down and think about what we're saying."

Aunt Peg, whose nose for trouble is unerring, chose that moment to reappear. "I've just been at the ring," she informed us breathlessly. "It's a madhouse up there. Bartholomew Perkin is measuring Toys and the rest of his entry is scattering like leaves in the wind."

Fire, meet gasoline.

Five of us turned and stared. Only Kevin was oblivious. If there's one thing Aunt Peg always knows how to do, it's liven up the proceedings.

After all that, the judging itself was anticlimactic.

Aunt Peg took herself back to the Poodle ring to watch the drama unfold. Doodle remained hidden in his crate. Sam convinced Hannah to move along. He helped Davey put in Augie's topknot, and the two of them began to spray the Standard Poodle up.

Now that there seemed to be little point in checking out the judging for myself, I used the lull in activity to take Kevin for a spin around the coliseum. Even though we were in Massachusetts, I saw plenty of exhibitors from Connecticut and more than a few from Fairfield County. Whenever I spied a familiar face, I stopped and put in a good word for the Howard Academy Christmas Bazaar.

There's much to be said for being affiliated with an institution that's been around for nearly a century. Everyone recognized the name of the school. Some had even previously shopped at the bazaar. At least a dozen exhibitors promised to bring their dogs the following week for pictures.

Of course, occasionally I was laughed at, too.

"Greenwich?" a Puli exhibitor said incredulously. "That's all the way on the other side of the state."

"But it's a small state," I pointed out.

"Even so. I'm not driving two hours to go to a *Christmas fair*."

"It took you longer than that to drive here," I said.

"For points," the woman sputtered. "I came *here* for points!"

Other exhibitors in the vicinity nodded in agreement. Even I couldn't argue with her logic. Points are our Holy Grail. We would drive over mountains and through hurricanes if we thought some judge, somewhere, might give points to our dogs. Compared to that, a photo opportunity with Santa Claus wasn't nearly important enough.

"Hungry now," Kev announced. "Want lunch."

Heading back to the setup, he and I cut directly across the showroom floor. As we threaded our way through several rows of rings, I saw that the Minis were being judged in the Poodle ring. Bertie's Open dog was conspicuous by his absence. When she appeared at the beginning of the bitch judging and entered the ring for the Puppy class, Bertie received several dirty looks. By now, everyone was well aware that she was the one who'd broken their all-important major.

Head down, Bertie concentrated on the task at hand and pretended not to notice the angry glares. I hoped the other exhibitors kept in mind that they weren't the only ones who'd been hurt by Doodle's withdrawal.

With the change of judge, Bertie's dog had lost his chance at the major, too.

"PB and J," Kevin said, tugging on my arm when he decided that we'd lingered long enough.

He and I had just enough time to race back to the setup and rummage through the cooler I'd packed that morning. Sandwich and juice box in hand, we turned right back around and followed Sam, Davey, and Augie up to the ring. Aunt Peg was waiting for us near the gate.

"Forget everything I told you about showcasing Augie's head," she told Davey. "Mr. Perkin doesn't seem to give a fig about a pretty face."

"What *is* he looking for?" asked Sam.

Aunt Peg frowned mightily. I was glad that, for once, her annoyance wasn't directed at me.

"I have no idea," she said. "I've watched everything that man has done for the last half hour. And if he has a consistent thought in his head about what a Poodle ought to look like, it has not yet bothered to make itself known."

That didn't bode well for Augie's adult debut.

"In fact," Aunt Peg continued, "after Mr. Perkin is finished for the day, perhaps I'll step inside the ring and recommend that he might want to reacquaint himself with our breed standard."

"That will go over well," I said under my breath.

Aunt Peg has ears like a bat. "Nonsense," she replied. "Any judge who isn't willing to continue learning would do better to find himself another profession. I'm sure Mr. Perkin will find my remarks eminently useful."

"Or something," I agreed.

Sam watched the byplay with a small smile, but he

knew better than to get involved. Instead, he reached out and patted Davey on the shoulder. "It looks like today's going to be a wash. So just go in and have some fun, okay?"

"Sure, Sam." Davey grinned. The politics of exhibiting are meaningless to him. As long as he and Augie were together, he was having a good time.

Oh, to be twelve again, I thought. When life was just that easy.

Augie, now mature and ready to take on the best of the competition, had been entered in the Open Dog class. When the puppies were called into the ring for the start of the Standard judging, Aunt Peg produced a comb from her pocket. She leaned over and ran it lightly through Augie's ears to smooth them down. The rest of us pretended not to notice.

"Hey, doll," said Terry, coming over to stand beside me. His partner, Crawford, was handling a handsome, brown puppy in the ring. By my estimation, he would probably win the class.

I glanced at Terry over my shoulder. His look is an ever-changing, work-in-progress and I never know what to expect when I haven't seen him for a few weeks. Now Terry's hair was dark again. It was also gelled and marcelled into waves.

It was a style few men could carry off. Terry, however, has the panache to make anything look good. With his smooth skin, chiseled features, and baby blue eyes, he could have been a model. Luckily for all of us, Terry had opted for a career in dogs instead.

"What's new?" I asked.

That's my standard greeting for Crawford's assistant. Terry always has all the best gossip and he loves to share.

"Bertie's in the doghouse," he said in a low tone. "She broke the major in Minis."

"That's old news," I sniffed. "What else have you got?"

"Oh my." Terry reared back. "We're snippy today, aren't we?"

"You try being assigned to run a school Christmas bazaar on one week's notice, and see how cheerful you feel about it."

"No, thank you very much. I think I'd rather stick to Poodles." He turned an appraising eye on Augie. "He looks good."

"Of course he looks good," said Aunt Peg. In a round-about way, Augie was a product of her breeding program. "For all the good that will do him today."

"What do you mean?"

She lifted a brow. "Have you been watching the judging?"

"No. But we took the variety in both Toys and Minis," Terry said with a shrug. "Crawford was happy."

That pretty well summed of the life of a professional handler. As long as the end results were good, it didn't much matter how they'd been achieved.

"Mr. Perkin is all over the map with his placings," said Aunt Peg.

As if to prove to her point, the judge pulled a weedy apricot puppy from the back of the line and sent it up to first place. Even the puppy's handler looked surprised by that turn of events. Crawford and his handsome puppy ended up third out of four.

"It looks as though Mr. Perkin is spreading things around," I said to Terry. "And you already got yours in Toys and Minis."

"Better than not getting it at all." He favored us a cheeky grin and hurried away to help Crawford.

The Bred-By class, with its single entry, was done in a flash. Then it was Augie's turn.

"In you go," said Sam. He gave Davey a small nudge toward the gate.

The long line of seven, black, male Standard Poodles that comprised the Open Dog class filled one entire side of the ring. Standing among his peers, Augie looked great, I thought. But either the judge didn't share my opinion, or else he was so overwhelmed by the sight of so many large black dogs in his ring at once that he lost his place early on and never found it again.

Either way, it didn't seem to matter to the outcome.

The four of us stood outside the ring and watched the proceedings with an air of bemusement that gradually morphed into total confusion.

"I think he's having trouble telling them apart," Peg said in outrage when Mr. Perkin reshuffled the group of Standard Poodle dogs for the third time.

"He looks like he wishes he could pull out his wicket again and sort them out that way," Sam muttered under his breath.

Davey and Augie had started the class in the middle of the pack. By the end, that was where they remained. Augie placed fourth out of the seven dogs. He and Davey received a small scrap of white ribbon for their efforts.

"Well, I'm glad that's over with," Aunt Peg said as our pair exited the ring. "It was like watching a train wreck in slow motion. You know you should look away, but somehow you just can't make yourself do it."

Even though he'd been privy to our discussion before the judging, Davey still looked dejected. "I thought Augie was better than that," he said unhappily.

"He most certainly is," Aunt Peg told him. "And if Mr. Perkin couldn't figure that out, it was his fault not yours."

"Think of it as a practice run," said Sam. "There's always tomorrow."

Dog show exhibitors are optimists. We have to be. Knock us down one day and we still come back the next and do it all again.

"There's only one way to salvage this day," I said. "We'd better stop for ice cream on the way home."

I was happy to see Davey's eyes light up. Kev jumped up and down and landed my foot. It was nice to be the most popular person in the room for once.

The following morning found us back in West Springfield, preparing to repeat everything we'd done the day before. Despite the disappointing outcome on Saturday, Davey approached the second day's judging with renewed enthusiasm for his and Augie's chances. Our judge was the estimable Mr. Harry Hawkins, former Toy breeder and all-around Poodle expert. With luck, Sunday's assignment would proceed much more smoothly than that of the day before.

Things got off to a promising start when Bertie finally had the chance to get Doodle into the show ring where he promptly won the spot-on major in Mini dogs. To her credit, Bertie managed not to gloat when Hannah Fort—who was still grumbling under her breath—discovered that Mr. Hawkins didn't even like her Mini dog enough to award him the Reserve ribbon.

In deference to the other exhibitors, Bertie deliberately downplayed her dog's assets during the Best of Variety judging. That enabled the Winners Bitch to be named Best of Winners, thereby "sharing the major" and ensuring that she wasn't the only Mini exhibitor who went home happy. I hoped that counted for something in the court of public opinion.

Terry came swanning by the setup a few minutes later. Crawford was in the ring, showing his Toy special in the variety. Terry had a second Toy, who'd already shown and lost, tucked under his arm. We were just about to head up.

"Crawford's puppy is scratched," he told us. "He's running a temperature. I guess something yucky was going around last night. Anyway . . ." Terry gazed over at Augie. Davey had just hopped the big Poodle down off his table. He stepped back and let him shake. "I'd say that opens the door for your boy."

"I wish you wouldn't do that," I said. Aunt Peg is a great believer in jinxes and lately her superstitions have been rubbing off on me.

"What?" Terry asked innocently. "I just came over to wish you luck." He leaned down and said to Davey in a low tone, "Go get 'em, kid. Harry Hawkins should take one look at that dog and fall in love."

"I know," Davey replied. My child is fearless when it comes to competition. I have no idea where he gets that kind of confidence from. It certainly isn't from me. "Aunt Peg told me the same thing."

"Then it's a done deal," Terry agreed. "The Almighty has spoken."

Luckily for all of us, Aunt Peg was up at ringside. Otherwise we never would have heard the end of *that*.

When we arrived at the ring, the Standard Bred-By-Exhibitor Dog was being judged. Sam fastened on Davey's armband. I checked to make sure he had bait. Kev and Davey bumped fists for luck. Augie did his part: he stood there and looked gorgeous.

Davey entered the ring first when the Open Dog class was called and took Augie to the head of the line. It was a spot he never relinquished. Showing with poise and skill that belied his age, he deftly showed off all of Augie's good points and minimized his weaknesses. It helped, too, that dog and handler were best friends. Together they made a formidable team.

Standing beside me, Aunt Peg sighed. "He's got the touch. I could turn that child into a star."

"Not going to happen," I told her firmly.

"So you say. . . ."

The point wasn't worth debating. At least not now, when Mr. Hawkins was motioning the line of dogs around the ring for the last time and Augie and Davey were still in front. A minute later, Davey had stuffed the blue ribbon into his pocket and moved quickly back onto the mat to form a new line. The winners of the previous two dog classes reentered the ring and fell in behind him.

Mr. Hawkins gave this new group a cursory look. He already knew what he wanted. Quickly he sent the Poodles around the ring again. As he pointed to Augie, I leapt in the air and let out a whoop.

Davey is usually embarrassed by that kind of parental display, but now he was too happy about the win to care. When Augie sensed his handler's excitement and jumped up too, Davey caught the big Poodle in his arms. He hurried across the ring, and dropped Augie gently down beside the Winners marker.

"Davey winning! Davey winning!" Kevin cried. A quick move on Sam's part prevented the excited toddler from running into the ring to stand with his older brother next to the steward's table.

A moment later, the triumphant pair joined us outside the ring. Davey was clutching the coveted purple ribbon in his hand. He had a dazed look on his face.

"Did that really happen?" he asked.

"It did indeed," Aunt Peg told him. She took Augie's leash and moved the Poodle to one side so he wouldn't get messed up before the Best of Variety judging. "That was well done."

Praise from Aunt Peg was a rare and precious commodity. Davey flushed with pleasure and ducked his head to hide a jubilant grin.

Sam was studying the catalog. "Three points," he said. "The major held. That's your first."

"And it's only the beginning," Aunt Peg announced.

Fortunately I was too busy savoring the moment to argue.

Chapter 5

After the busy weekend we'd had, Monday morning came all too early.

Since rejoining the teaching staff at Howard Academy at the beginning of the semester, I had been working three days a week. My tutoring sessions were scheduled virtually back to back on Mondays, Wednesdays, and Fridays and I already felt like I was always playing catch-up. Now that the task of managing the Christmas bazaar had landed in my lap too, I was pretty sure that I'd be lucky to see daylight before the end of the week.

Howard Academy is situated on a hilltop just north of downtown Greenwich. The original school building, once the sumptuous, early-twentieth-century mansion of founding siblings Joshua and Honoria Howard, sits at the end of a long, meandering driveway. Constructed of stone and built to last, it has weathered the century well. Its public rooms house both the administrative offices and the classrooms for the younger grades.

The school's new wing, added in the 1960s to accommodate a growing student population, is a soaring vision of glass and concrete. Classrooms there, including mine, are big and bright. They feature every amenity that the wealthy parents who pay Howard Academy's hefty tuition bills, assume their privileged children should have access to. And in the case of my particular classroom, they also feature a Standard Poodle.

That would be Faith, of course.

Six years earlier when I began teaching at Howard Academy, I was a single mother and a recent convert to the joys of dog ownership. I'd petitioned for permission to bring Faith to work with me and Mr. Hanover had proven surprisingly receptive. Always eager to promote ideas that would set his school apart from the dozens of other private academies in Fairfield County, he'd decided that the presence of a dog in the special needs room would do much to foster the school's image as a child-friendly environment.

To our mutual delight, Faith had quickly become a valued member of the teaching team. Her calm demeanor and friendly temperament proved soothing to even the most recalcitrant students. The Standard Poodle's welcome presence had transformed my classroom from a place that students were assigned to report to, to one that they were instead eager to visit.

Indeed, when Faith and I had returned to Howard Academy the previous autumn, much of the student body had turned out on our first day to welcome us back with dog biscuits and chew toys. Watching Faith interact with the eager children, I'd gotten the distinct impression that my Poodle's absence had left more of a void in the school community than mine had.

I try very hard not to take that personally.

Driving around the main building, I pulled into the lot behind the new wing and found an empty parking space near the cafeteria door. Faith, who'd been riding shotgun, hopped out of the car with her head high and tail wagging. And why not? In her mind, Howard Academy was all laughing kids and biscuits. No one had assigned *her* to take over a multibooth, volunteer-staffed, bazaar at the last minute.

I got Faith situated in my classroom with a rawhide bone, a fresh bowl of water, and a promise to return shortly before heading down the main hallway to the teachers' lounge. Before the first bell rang each morning, the lounge was information central. Some teachers stopped by to grab a cup of coffee, others stashed snacks in the refrigerator or compared notes about school activities.

All were hoping to share the latest gossip.

I'd spent the previous evening on the phone with a dozen different parent volunteers. Each had assured me that the tasks they'd been assigned for the bazaar were under control, and that the loss of Virginia Highland to a beach in Cabo in no way impacted their readiness to go forward. That was all good news. Now I was really hoping that the teachers who'd been conscripted to work on the event would tell me the same thing.

I poured myself a cup of coffee from the ornate silver urn and added a dollop of thick cream from the china pitcher on the tray beside it. Also on the sideboard was a plate of fresh blueberry scones and a small bowl of whipped butter. The school kitchen sent up fresh pastries every morning and their scones were my favorite.

I was debating helping myself to one when a voice behind me said, "There she is now . . . *Madam Chairman*."

I counted to five under my breath, turned, and smiled sweetly. "Good morning, Ed. How are you today?"

Ed Weinstein taught upper school English. He was opinionated, outspoken, and altogether annoying. He also had a permanent chip on his shoulder—due, I suspected, to his tendency to weigh the state of his own finances against that of his students.

Over the years, Ed and I had butted heads on any number of topics. In the time that I'd been away from Howard Academy, he had grown a beard and given up smoking. The former was a change for the better: the beard had covered up his weak chin. I couldn't say the same for the latter, as nicotine deprivation had done nothing to improve his often-surly disposition.

"I'm fine," Ed replied. "Now that you're here." He was seated at the heavy wooden table in the middle of the room. Now he reached over and pulled out the chair beside him.

"Why is that?" I hadn't intended to linger in the lounge, but I supposed I could sit for a minute.

"I thought you might want to give us a status report on the Christmas bazaar," Ed said with a smirk. "You know, now that you're *in charge*."

I paused to blow on my steaming mug then said, "Right now, I'm still trying to get up to speed. I only found out that I'd be overseeing the event on Friday."

"That should have given you all weekend to get things figured out."

"It might have, except that I had other plans that couldn't be changed. Which is why I'll be working doubly hard all this week to make sure that everything proceeds smoothly."

"Don't mind Ed," said Louisa Delgado. A vivacious woman with glossy dark hair and a beautiful smile, Louisa taught math to the upper grades. She helped herself to a chair across from us at the table. "He's just mad that Mr. Hanover didn't make him chairman."

"Really?" I turned and stared at Ed. The notion that someone might have actually *wanted* the job came as a surprise.

"When Russell needed someone to step in and take over," he said, "the position should have come to me. I have seniority. Not only that, but I'm good at making sure that things get done right."

No one commented on Ed's use of the headmaster's first name, but a few of the teachers in the room rolled their eyes. We'd all seen Ed's obsequious act whenever Mr. Hanover was nearby.

"I'm sure Melanie will do a fine job." Ryan Duncan, who taught lower school social studies, raised his cup to me in a small salute. "She's a hard worker."

"She's a tutor," Ed grumbled, like I wasn't sitting right there. "Not even a real teacher. And she only works part-time."

"Which is probably why Mr. Hanover picked me," I said, striving for patience. "He probably thought that I'd have more time to devote to the bazaar than someone like you."

"Someone like me?" Ed's eyes narrowed. "What does that mean?"

Rita Kinney, a slender, quiet, woman who was my best friend among the Howard Academy staff, entered the lounge and caught the tail end of the conversation. She stood in the doorway and laughed.

"Melanie means someone who's already busy, Ed," she said. "You know, like you. Since you're always busy butting into everyone else's business."

"Now see here!" Ed shoved back his chair and stood.

Abruptly the other conversations in the room fell silent. All heads turned our way.

"Do sit down, Ed," Louisa said softly. "You know you don't want to make a scene."

I wouldn't have been so sure of that, myself. From past experience, I knew there was nothing Ed Weinstein enjoyed more than boasting and blustering until everyone else backed down and he got his own way. As both a teacher and a mother, I've had plenty of experience dealing with behavior like that. Now I knew just what to do.

"Ed, I had no idea you felt this way," I said. "Let's do something about it. If you'd like to take over as chairman of the Christmas bazaar, I have no objection." I stood up beside him. "Let's go right now and see if Mr. Hanover is in his office. You can make your case for being in charge and I'll be happy to bow out gracefully."

"Now?" Ed looked stunned. He clearly hadn't been anticipating this turn of events.

"No time like the present," I said cheerfully.

"I have class in ten minutes."

"We'll make it fast then." I skirted around the table and headed for the door. "Come on, let's go."

"But—" Ed stood beside his chair. He still hadn't moved.

"But what?" I paused near the doorway, next to Rita.

"I can't take on a project that big now. It's too late."

"Like Friday was a whole lot earlier?" Rita said under her breath.

Ed aimed a glare her way. "Friday would have given me the weekend to work on it. To bring everything together."

A glance around the room confirmed that I wasn't the only one who wasn't buying Ed's lame excuse.

"In that case, I guess you'll just have to hope that Melanie can get it all done this week," said Ryan Duncan. "I know I'm pulling for her. And I'm definitely glad that I don't have to do it myself."

"Me, too," Louisa echoed. Several other teachers also added their agreement.

Out in the hallway, the first bell rang: a warning to teachers and students alike that we had five minutes to get to our respective classrooms. Ed strode across the room and pushed past us out the door. With his departure, the level of tension in the room eased. People began to talk again. They started to gather up their things.

I looked around the lounge. Several teachers whose names were on my list of committee heads still remained. "Can we talk over lunch?" I asked. "Just a short meeting to make sure we're all on the same page?"

I was grateful to see everyone nod. Whether Ed recognized it or not, this wasn't just *my* job. We all needed to work together to make the Christmas bazaar a success.

My title is special needs tutor. Though I have my own classroom, I don't teach a specific age group or discipline. Instead, it's my job to ensure that every child at Howard Academy receives as much individual attention as he or she might need to excel—both in their class work and within the school community.

Howard Academy's curriculum is rigorous and exacting. The course selection is varied and sophisticated. Students are offered every opportunity to succeed. Even so, some still manage to slip through the cracks.

It's my job to catch them when they fall.

Most of the students that become part of my program are those who don't possess the scholastic tools or the academic drive that it takes to keep up in this unapologetically competitive environment. Identified early by their conscientious teachers, the children are sent to me before their small problems can become big ones.

In many cases all it takes to turn them around is some one-on-one oversight, coupled with focused tutoring targeted on their specific needs. As a group, my students are diverse, enthusiastic, worldly, and altogether delightful. They are also children with first-world problems.

Skiing trips interfere with their deadlines. Clinics with noted riding instructors demand their energy and attention. Late nights in the city at the opera or ballet leave them tired and listless in class the next day. Some have parents who are inattentive and mostly absent. Others have their every move scrutinized and analyzed by adults who demand that they achieve near-perfection.

Sometimes what I really want to do is gather them all in my arms, give them a big warm hug, and reassure them that everything will be all right. Sad to say, our new guidelines pertaining to teacher/student interactions expressly forbid such a thing from ever happening. Ever sadder, most of my kids are already so jaded that they probably wouldn't believe me anyway.

It's hard to be a teacher these days. And sometimes I think that it's doubly hard to be a child. That's why I want what I do to matter. If I can make my students' lives even just a little bit easier, then the effort that I expend is well worth it.

My first session of the day was with two sixth grade girls, Charlotte Levine and Quinn Peterson. Other than the similarity in their clothing—both were attired in the school uniform: navy plaid wool skirt, white button-down shirt, and navy blue kneesocks—the two girls couldn't have been more different. Charlotte was small, shy, and earnest. Quinn was blond, bubbly, and ever-talkative.

Both, however, currently shared a problem with science reports that were overdue. Their teacher had sent the pair to me in the hope that I could help them develop better study habits. Not to mention coming up with the missing reports.

As usual, Quinn came dancing into the room. She sketched a cheery wave in my direction, called out, "Good morning, Ms. Travis!" then went straight to Faith's bed in the corner to say hello to the Standard Poodle.

Charlotte followed close behind. Her books were clutched against her chest and her head was tipped downward over them. Dark bangs, too long for her small face, fell forward to obscure her eyes.

"Good morning, Charlotte," I said. "Are you ready to get to work?"

"Yes, Ms. Travis. But I already finished my science report. I worked on it over the weekend."

"Good for you." I walked over to the round conference table where Charlotte was taking a seat. "Can I see it?"

She handed over a narrow sheaf of papers bound inside a clear plastic cover. *How Does Mold Grow?* I read on the front.

Hmm. I hadn't the slightest idea. Science had never been my forte. I flipped through the pages. The report had pictures, and diagrams, and very wide margins. Still, it wasn't up to me to evaluate the project, only to make it appear. Mission accomplished.

"Quinn?" When I gazed toward the corner, the other sixth grader popped to her feet. She crossed the room to join us. "How's your report coming?"

"Just fine," she said with a sunny smile. "Almost finished."

"So you'll have something for me to look at tomorrow?"

"You don't work on Tuesdays," Quinn pointed out. She was an expert at evasive maneuvers.

"Usually I don't," I said. "But this week I'll be in and out every day."

"How come?"

"Mr. Hanover put me in charge of managing the Christmas bazaar."

"Oh right." Charlotte looked up and nodded. "I heard about that. Puggy was really bummed."

I didn't know Puggy. He wasn't one of my students. "He's bummed about the bazaar?" I asked, surprised.

"No, about his mother running off to Mexico with her lawyer."

"Oh." I swallowed. There wasn't much I could say to that.

"Hey, it's not so bad," Quinn said brightly. "New stepfathers can be fun. "It's in their best interest to get you on their side, so they give you stuff. Ask me how I know."

Oh my. On that note, a change of subject was definitely called for.

"Are you girls coming to the bazaar?" I asked.

"Of course," said Charlotte. "It's a school function."

"I wouldn't miss it." Quinn stifled a giggle. "I'm bringing my pony."

I'd misheard, I thought. I must have.

I tipped my head in Quinn's direction. "You're doing . . . *what?*"

"Scooter," she replied. "My pony. I'm bringing him to the bazaar. My mom said she'd hook up the trailer. Scooter's thirty years old. He used to be bay but now he's mostly gray all over. He never gets to go anywhere anymore so this will be, like, a big day for him."

"I must be missing something," I said. "Why is Scooter coming to the bazaar?"

"There's going to be a booth where you can get your pet's picture taken with Santa Claus." Quinn's tone implied that the answer should have been obvious. "I thought that sounded like a cool idea. Scooter's old for a horse. He might not have that many more Christmases left. So I figured I'd better get his picture while I can, you know?"

So much for thinking that I'd had things marginally under control. "Does Mr. Hanover know about this?" I asked.

Quinn shook her head. "No. Why would he? But I'm sure he'll love Scooter. Everyone does. He's very friendly, for a pony. And he even likes candy canes."

"I'm sure that's a plus," I said faintly. I made a mental note to be sure to have a pitchfork and muck bucket near the picture booth.

"I have a dog," said Charlotte. "She's a Cockapoo. Her name is Coco Lily."

"A Cockapoo?" Quinn echoed with interest. "She must be one of those new designer dogs."

For Charlotte's sake, I tried not to grimace.

Designer dogs. I hated both the term and the currently trendy product it described. Hype and false promises aside, how could it possibly be a good thing to take two nice purebreds and breed them together to create a purposely mixed result?

"I don't think Coco Lily is a real breed," said Charlotte. "I'm pretty sure she's just a mutt. But my mother thought calling her a Cockapoo made her sound special."

"I'm sure she's very cute," I said.

"She is." When Charlotte smiled, her whole face lit up. I was tempted to reach over and brush back the young girl's shaggy bangs. "And she's going to have her picture taken, too. Poppy's mom . . . Mrs. McEvoy . . . you know her, right?"

"Sure." I nodded. Poppy and Charlotte were best friends. "We both show dogs and we see each other at the shows."

"My mom is busy that morning so Mrs. McEvoy is going to pick me up. Poppy's bringing Kiltie, too. We might even get their picture taken together. Wouldn't that be fun?"

"It sounds like an excellent idea," I agreed.

"Mrs. McEvoy is going to bring a crate for Kiltie so he has some place to stay while she sells raffle tickets and Poppy shops at the bazaar. When she heard that I'd have Coco Lily, Mrs. McEvoy said she'd bring an extra crate for her, too."

Quinn thrust out her lower lip, redirecting our attention back to her. "It doesn't sound like nearly as much fun as a pony," she said.

"Neither does doing a science report." It was time for me to get the two girls back on track. "But it still has to be done."

"But it's *Christmas,* Ms. Travis." Quinn's voice was edged with a whine.

"Not for two and a half weeks," I said briskly.

"*Nobody* works in December."

Charlotte was laughing now. As well she could. Her report was done.

"That's where you're wrong." I slipped Quinn a wink, then opened up her science text and pushed it across the table. "Everybody works in December. Even us. Welcome to the real world, kid."

Chapter 6

I spent all morning running around getting stuff done and by lunchtime I was ready for a break. Like many things at Howard Academy the midday meal is a decorous affair. The setting alone is enough to remind us to watch our manners.

Students and faculty gather together in the large, high-ceilinged dining room. We sit at heavy, dark wood, refectory tables that are set with linen, and china, and crystal water goblets. The kitchen staff serves a hot meal family-style. The food is invariably delicious.

Each long table is joined by a teacher; we all take turns eating with the students. It's a job that can vary from exhausting to exhilarating, depending on the day. The remainder of the teaching staff usually dines at the two end tables under the leaded glass windows on the far side of the room.

I gathered my committee heads around me at one table and pointedly ignored Ed Weinstein when he brushed past us and sat down at the other. Coming in at the last minute, I hadn't had the opportunity to choose any of the teachers I'd be working with. Now, looking around the table, I knew I couldn't have asked for a better group of collaborators.

Rita Kinney, with her fashionable flair and eye for detail, was in charge of decorations. Barbara Blume, an ample woman in her midfifties who had been at the school for nearly two decades, headed up vendor relations. Tony Dahl, who coached our teams and taught physical education, would be overseeing setup and maintenance of the booths and facilities.

Listening to the detailed reports delivered in turn by each of my committee chairs, I found that they were way ahead of me when it came to the planning and execution of the upcoming bazaar. Never had I been more grateful and relieved to be part of such a great team.

"If you have any questions," said Barbara, "just ask away." One of the most popular teachers at Howard Academy, she was the perfect person to be in charge of a job that would require tact and diplomacy. "I'm sure I speak for all of us when I say that I know this was a lot to dump on you at the last minute. So think of us as your support team. We're here to help you any way we can."

"You guys are doing a terrific job," I said honestly. "You're already on top of everything. You have no idea how delighted I am to find out that my position is apparently superfluous."

"I wouldn't quite go that far," said Tony. His face creased in a smile. "But I think we're all happy to have someone competent back at the helm. Virginia meant well when she volunteered to help out. But as you might imagine, she's been a little distracted lately."

"Distracted?" Rita muttered under her breath. "The Christmas bazaar was the last thing on that woman's mind."

"My ex-husband was a lawyer," Barbara said with a chuckle. "Five dollars says she lives to regret that trip to Cabo."

A waitress approached the table with a platter of chicken cordon bleu. Quickly we all schooled our expressions into something more appropriately somber, but I doubt that she was fooled as to the nature of our conversation. There weren't many secrets within the school community.

"So you guys tell me," I said, as we dug into our lunch. "How can I help you? What do you need me to do?"

"Best thing you can do," Tony said, looking up from his meal, "is run interference for us with Mr. Hanover. Distract him, report to him, tell him everything's running smoothly, so that he's not always looking over our shoulders and getting in the way."

Barbara and Rita both nodded.

"Our headmaster is a wonderful man," said Barbara. "But he's a perfectionist. Sometimes it slows down the process, you know?"

I did indeed.

"I'll do my best to keep him in check," I said. "Anything else?"

Nobody could think of a thing. Amazing. Between my trio of teachers and the parent volunteers, it sounded as though everything was mostly under control. That's a rare occurrence in my life, and I wasn't about to push my luck by demanding more details or asking more questions.

We had cherry cobbler for dessert. It was the perfect ending to a highly satisfying meal.

* * *

That feeling of well-being remained with me for the next two days. It wasn't all smooth sailing as the date of the bazaar drew inexorably closer. But fortunately the problems that popped up were small, and for the most part easily dispatched. It was beginning to look like the Christmas bazaar might even go off without a hitch.

Wednesday afternoon, I arrived home from school to find a bright red Civic hybrid sitting in my driveway. I knew that car. It belonged to Claire Walden, a woman with whom I'd become friends the previous summer. Claire was now engaged to marry my ex-husband, Bob.

Claire had been busy in recent weeks, planning her upcoming wedding. I'd been busy at school. Now I couldn't even remember the last time we'd seen each other. I parked behind the Civic, and Faith and I entered the house through the front door.

Normally we would have been swarmed by Standard Poodles but that day the front hall was empty. Faith looked as surprised as I was. She gave a short, sharp bark. It sounded like a reprimand to her peers—as well it should have been. My watchdogs were falling down on the job.

That single bark was all it took to turn things around. I heard the sound of scrambling feet and a moment later the pack of Poodles came flying out of the kitchen and racing down the hallway. As all five jostled for position and eddied around us, Claire appeared in the doorway at the back of the hall.

"It's great to see you," she said, coming forward to give me a hug. Claire was tall and willowy with long, dark, hair that swung in a shiny curtain around her shoulders. "It's been way too long. While I waited for you to get home, your dogs and I have been playing a game of catch in the kitchen."

"Good place for that," I said faintly. Fewer breakables than the rest of the house, though outside in the backyard might have been better. I pulled off my coat and scarf and tossed them on a side table. "Where are Sam and Kevin?"

Wednesdays, Davey had basketball practice after school. I wouldn't expect him home for another hour. But Sam, who worked at home and who'd also been doing double duty watching over Kev while I was at school, should have been around. Especially since we had a guest.

Claire shrugged. "You were due back any minute and they had an errand to run. It was all very hush-hush. Maybe a little secret Christmas shopping? I certainly didn't want to get in the way of that! And besides, your Poodles have been keeping me entertained."

They were good at that, I thought. Especially when someone was willing to let them play ball in the house.

We walked together into the living room. Claire sat down in the middle of the couch and was promptly flanked by Tar and Raven. Casey, who had just missed getting a seat next to our guest, had to content herself with draping her body over Claire's feet. If Eve hadn't come and climbed into my lap, I might have felt seriously left out.

"I'm delighted to see you, Claire," I said. "But what are you doing here?"

"What do you *mean* what am I doing here? I can't believe you didn't call me! Bertie told me about your Christmas bazaar. As soon as I heard, I came right over.

You know what I do for a living. Why didn't you ask me to help?"

Claire had been a corporate event planner before finding her niche organizing children's parties. Managing a private school Christmas bazaar was the kind of thing she'd be great at.

"Because I know how busy you are," I said.

"Everybody's busy." Claire sniffed. "I could have made time for you."

"But that's just it. I didn't want you to have to do that. You're putting together your *wedding*."

Bob and Claire's wedding was scheduled for New Year's Eve. "Out with the old and in with the new," Claire had said in reference to their chosen date. I'd wondered whether I should take offense at that, considering that "the old" was me. Then it had occurred to me that there'd been yet another wife between me and Claire, and I decided to let it go.

"Oh that," said Claire.

"Yes, *that*. It's a big deal. Hopefully you'll only do it once in your life."

"That's the plan," she agreed. Then her brow furrowed. "Though Bob doesn't exactly have the best track record in that regard."

"Only because he didn't meet you first," I said firmly.

Claire started to reply. She opened her mouth, then closed it again. Her lower lip quivered slightly. "If you make me cry," she said after a moment, "I will rescind my offer of assistance. And then where will you be?"

"I'll be very sorry," I told her. "But not about the bazaar. Just that I made you cry."

"I'm not crying." Claire sniffled. "I hate to cry."

"So you always say. Your actions speak differently." I reached over and patted her arm. "I've seen documentaries set you off."

"It was about *whales,*" Claire blubbered. "And it was very sad."

I gave her a minute to regain control, then said, "Seriously, you and Bob make a great couple."

"Thank you for that." Claire drew in a deep breath and managed a smile. "And for . . . you know . . . not making things awkward."

"Bob loves you," I said. "And you're wonderful with Davey. I think we're all very lucky to be adding you to our family."

"What a lovely thing to say." Claire bit her lip.

I hoped she wasn't about to start sniffling again.

"You *see,*" she said earnestly. "That's exactly why I want to help with the bazaar. You and Bob and Davey and Sam, you're all my family now. And families should pull together when things get tough."

In my experience, families tended to fracture and fight when problems arose. And I was well aware that Claire's family had once done the same. But I loved the fact that she was trying to build better relationships than the ones she'd known in the past.

"I'm happy to be able to say that the bazaar seems to be in pretty good shape," I told her.

"Bertie mentioned that you might need help with a photo booth . . . ?"

"She's coming to assist with crowd control. We've invited kids to bring their pets . . . I'm pretty sure that a little pandemonium is a given. Unfortunately Bertie drew the line at wearing an elf costume."

"I could do that," Claire volunteered.

"Really?"

"Sure. I've worn worse at children's parties. I'd rather dress up like an elf than the Leaning Tower of Pisa or the back half of a Chinese dragon."

"I don't think I even want to know," I said with a laugh.

"Dragons are hard, elves are easy." Claire smiled happily.

And so it was settled.

Friday morning when I arrived at school, there was a note in my box asking me to present myself at Russell Hanover's office at my earliest convenience. Not surprisingly, communication among the staff at Howard Academy still relied on a system that had served the institution well since the early twentieth century. Mr. Hanover's secretary, Harriet, had both my e-mail address and my cell phone number. And yet I'd still received a handwritten message in my in-box. You had to love it.

The note hadn't sounded urgent, so I waited until I had a break midmorning before walking over to the main building where the headmaster's office was located. It's always a pleasure to stroll through Joshua Howard's former home. With its soaring ceilings, antique crown molding, and polished hardwood floors, the mansion still retains a great deal of old world charm despite its change in circumstance. The original front hall serves now as a reception area. Mr. Hanover's office, once a formal parlor, is just inside the front door.

Harriet was at her desk when I arrived. The headmaster is a busy man and I expected I'd have to wait. Instead, I was shown right in.

Mr. Hanover was seated behind his imposingly large desk when I entered the room. Like everything else in the room, it was a statement piece, chosen to convey a sense of tasteful prosperity and enduring dependability. Other rooms at the school might buzz with activity or hum to the insistent pulse of technology, but not the headmaster's office. His realm was an oasis of calm.

Russell Hanover II is well aware of the impression he conveys. His brown hair, now thinning on the top, is impeccably styled. His suits are custom tailored in England. The wire-frame glasses are a new addition; they lend his bland features a bit of distinction. Their look is slightly non-traditional. I think his wife, Bitsy, must have picked them out.

Immediately Mr. Hanover rose to his feet and came out from behind his desk to greet me. We met in the middle of the Aubusson carpet.

"Ms. Travis, welcome. I know you've been busy. Thank you for making time to see me." He swept his hand to one side, indicating a leather chair that sat beside his desk. "Please, have a seat. Everything is going well?"

"Very well," I said.

Considering the various scrapes I've gotten myself into at Howard Academy in the past, I'm not above shading the facts if I have to. This time I was happy I could answer the question truthfully. I sat down and folded my hands primly in my lap.

"We've had a bit of a wrinkle with regard to the bazaar," Mr. Hanover said. "And I thought it my duty to keep you informed."

"Oh?" I leaned forward in my seat. "What happened?"

"I think we can both agree that the presence of Santa Claus at a Christmas bazaar is a necessity. An intrinsic requirement, you might say."

"Of course," I said. "Go on."

"First thing this morning, I was made aware of a message that had been left on the school's answering machine overnight. It seems that the Santa Claus hired by your predecessor had a sudden change of plans, forcing him to cancel his engagement."

Well, crap, I thought. My favorite thing about the entire bazaar was the photo booth. Not only that, but it was sure to be a popular attraction. And now, a mere twenty-four hours before he was due to appear, my Santa Claus had gone AWOL?

Abruptly I sat up and squared my shoulders. The bazaar was my responsibility. There had to be a way to fix this.

"I'll get right on it," I said quickly. "I can make some calls."

"Harriet spent most of the morning doing just that," Mr. Hanover informed me. "As you might imagine, two weeks before Christmas, anyone with even a passing resemblance to Saint Nick is already booked up."

A burst of adrenaline propelled me to my feet. "I'll find somebody," I told him. I'd slap a red suit and a white beard on Sam if I had to. "I promise I won't let you down."

"I admire your dedication to duty, Ms. Travis. But a mere ten minutes ago, the situation seems to have resolved itself."

I had started to head for the door. Now I stopped and slowly turned around. "How?"

"With what appears to be a rather large stroke of

luck. A man named Chris Tindall called and said that he'd heard we were looking for a Santa Claus. He was free tomorrow to appear at our bazaar and I hired him on the spot. Thus I'm happy to report the Santa crisis has come to an end."

"That's wonderful," I said with a touch more enthusiasm than I actually felt. The unexpected good news almost felt like a letdown. "Do we know anything about this new Santa Claus?"

"Only that he's available," Mr. Hanover replied. "Under the present circumstances, I should say that seems like quite enough."

"It's certainly a start," I said. I couldn't help wondering why—with Santas currently in such short supply—this particular one was ours for the asking. "Assuming he actually shows up. And is capable of doing the job."

"Ms. Travis, I am well aware of your penchant for asking questions."

The headmaster's flat statement shut me up. As I was sure it was intended to do.

"I'm every bit as cynical as the next person," he continued. "However, it would be hard to imagine that our Mr. Tindall wouldn't be up to the task. Especially as I'm of the impression that the ability to impersonate a jolly mythical personage does not require anything in way of superior acting skills."

"No, of course not," I agreed hastily.

Mr. Hanover was right. We'd been in need of a Santa Claus and now, fortunately, one had appeared. Who was I to question how that had come about?

The headmaster's expression softened. "I know the circumstances seem a bit unorthodox, Ms. Travis, but surely if I can bring myself to go with the flow, as the younger generation says, you can manage to do the same? It is the holiday season, after all. Perhaps you can join me in believing in a little Christmas magic?"

Mr. Hanover never ceased to surprise me. Christmas magic indeed.

Ho, ho, ho, I thought. Whatever worked.

Chapter 7

Saturday morning I was up with the sun. Okay, it was mid-December so that wasn't saying much. But still.

In the last few days, I'd come to the realization that Davey and Kevin were almost as transfixed by the Howard Academy Christmas Bazaar as I was. Kev's excitement I could understand. At his age, he thinks Christmas is the best day of the year, and anything that has to do with his favorite holiday is wonderful by association.

Davey, however, is several years past believing in Santa Claus. And while he enjoys getting and giving presents, singing carols, and eating Christmas cookies, he's a typical boy when it comes to shopping. So I hadn't thought that a day devoted mostly to the acquisition of Christmas swag would rank high on his list of things to do.

It turned out I was wrong.

Having stayed late at school on Friday evening to oversee the final stages of booth setup and decorating in the auditorium, I had nonetheless planned to be back at Howard Academy by eight A.M. Saturday morning. That would give me a full two hours before the doors opened at ten to talk to the vendors as they unpacked their wares, introduce myself to the extra maintenance crew that Tony would have on hand, and to iron out any last-minute glitches. Sam would be bringing the boys over later in the day once the bazaar was in full swing.

When I passed through the kitchen on my way out the door, Sam was still upstairs in the shower. Davey and Kevin, both early risers, were seated together at the kitchen table. Davey had made a stab at putting out breakfast. He had a bowl of Cheerios and a glass of orange juice. Kev, who was perched in his booster seat, was gnawing happily on an apple that was much too big for his hands.

Through the windows at the back of the room, I could see the Poodles running around outside in the fenced backyard. Left to his own devices for too long, Tar is apt to start a hair-pulling game. I made a mental note to make sure that everyone was back in the house before I left for the day.

Kev's head whipped around as I came through the doorway. "Time to go!" he cried excitedly.

The toddler scrambled down out of his chair, wiggling his body handily between booster seat and tabletop. My little escape artist. Still clutching his apple, Kev came flying across the room. Apparently the fact that he was still wearing his footie pajamas was not, in his mind, an impediment to imminent departure.

I caught Kev and swung him up into my arms and

smacked a kiss on his nose. "The bazaar isn't even open yet. You guys are coming later with Dad. Besides, you need to get dressed first."

"Dressed *now,*" Kevin insisted.

I plopped him down on the countertop, opened a drawer, got out a knife and sliced his apple into several long wedges for easier eating. Then I reached over, opened the back door, and whistled the Poodles inside.

As usual, Tar led the way. He likes to think that he's the leader of the pack and he's lucky that the bitches are gracious enough not to disabuse him of that fallacy.

Running full tilt across the deck and through the open door, Tar hit the hardwood floor and went sliding past me. Feet scrambling for purchase that wasn't there, the big Poodle careened into the water bowl on the other side of the room. The bowl has a weighted base but it wasn't enough to withstand that kind of onslaught.

Bowl and dog both went flying. Tar bounced off the wall as water sprayed out over the floor. Watching the unexpected show from his perch on the counter, Kevin squealed in delight.

Meanwhile, the remaining Poodles were still standing in the open doorway letting a draft of frigid air into the house. They'd been savvy enough to anticipate trouble and wise enough to want no part of it. When I waved the crew inside and quickly shut the door, Raven, Casey, and Augie scooted past me and disappeared down the hallway.

Eve picked her way daintily across the kitchen floor. She wrinkled her nose at the small flood and carefully avoided stepping in any puddles. Faith just stood and stared reproachfully at Tar.

"What do you think you are?" I said to Eve as I grabbed a handful of paper towels and began to mop up the mess. "A cat?"

"A cat!" Kevin chortled happily. "Eve thinks she's a cat." He flicked a piece of apple into the air. It was headed in Eve's direction but Tar leapt up and caught it on the fly.

"Hey," I said. "No feeding dogs from the kitchen counter."

"Not a dog," Kev corrected me. "Eve's a cat."

Davey looked up from his cereal and shook his head. "You're going to regret starting that," he said.

"Tell me about it," I grumbled.

Over by the sink, the empty water bowl had finally rolled to a stop, still resting on its side. Tar followed the dish, staring at its unfamiliar configuration with his head tipped to one side in confusion. After a moment, he reached out a front paw and batted it. The bowl spun in a small circle, then wobbled briefly before dropping flat on the floor. Amazed by his accomplishment, that big silly Poodle leapt up in the air and barked.

Breakfast at the Travis/Driver household. On good days, it's a zoo. On bad days, you don't even want to know.

I lifted Kevin down off the counter and set him on the floor. "Your clothes are on your bed," I told him. "Go upstairs and get dressed."

"Already dressed," Kevin argued. He pushed out his lower lip in a pout. "Ready to go."

"You can't go to the bazaar in your pajamas." I walked the toddler to the kitchen door and gave him a nudge toward the stairway. "Dad's upstairs. He'll help you."

"I can help him," Davey volunteered. He was already dressed. He picked up his glass and bowl and dumped them in the sink.

"Thanks. That would be great. I want to get to bazaar early. You know, before anything has a chance to go wrong."

"At Howard Academy?" Davey wasn't facing me, but I saw his shoulders stiffen. "Nothing ever goes wrong there."

"What do you mean?"

"Isn't that the perfect school? Where the perfect kids go?"

Davey started to follow his younger brother from the room. I laid a hand on his shoulder and stopped him.

"Wait," I said. "Stay here a minute and talk to me."

Kev was already gone. The toddler raced down the hall, rounded the banister, and began to scramble up the steps. Reluctantly Davey turned back to face me.

"What?" he asked.

"Something's the matter," I said. "Tell me what it is."

"Nothing."

"Like *that's* going to work." I waved him into a chair.

For the first eight years of Davey's life, it had been just him and me. Our relationship had always been close, not because it had to be, but because we truly enjoyed each other's company. He and I had always been able to talk to each other. We'd shared the things that were bothering us.

Now as he approached his teenage years, I could feel Davey pulling away. He'd grown reticent and he valued his privacy more. I knew that what I was experiencing was the natural progression of a mother/son relationship. It was time for Davey to begin testing his wings—and to push against the boundaries that I'd always set.

But this disgruntlement sounded like something different. And I wanted to know what. I grabbed a seat across from him.

"Talk to me," I said.

Davey frowned. Brown eyes, so much like his father's, stared at me across the table. "What do you want me to say?"

"I want to know what's bugging you."

"It's nothing."

"I don't think so," I said. "Tell me what's up."

"Don't you have to go? I thought you wanted to get to the bazaar early."

"The bazaar will wait." I reached across and squeezed his hand. "Or it won't. Either way, the world won't come to an end. I always have time to talk to you."

"That's not what it seems like," Davey mumbled.

Aha, I thought. Now we were getting somewhere.

"Does that mean you weren't happy when I went back to work?" I asked.

"No. It's not that. You always worked."

Yes, I had. As a single mother, I'd had no choice. When Davey was young, I had been employed as a special ed teacher at his own elementary school. Later I'd taken the job at Howard Academy. Davey had never seemed to mind my job before.

"So what is it then?"

"Kids talk," Davey said. He was still frowning.

"Your friends, you mean?"

He nodded.

"What do they talk about?"

"About your school. You know, Howard Academy.

About how all the kids who go there are stuck-up snobs with fancy cars and their own Lear jets."

"Lear jets?" I echoed faintly.

"And yachts, too."

"Yachts," I repeated. My son probably thought I sounded like a parrot.

"That's right," he said defensively. "Isn't it?"

"Some of the kids at Howard Academy do come from families with lots of money," I told him. "But not all of them. And having that money doesn't mean that they live perfect lives, or that they're happy all the time. In fact many of those kids have the same kinds of problems that you and your friends do."

Davey looked up. "A mom who's always getting into trouble?"

I choked on an unexpected laugh. "Okay, maybe not that problem. But some of them come from broken homes. Or have absentee parents. Or have parents who would rather give them stuff than sit down and spend time with them."

"That last part doesn't sound so bad to me."

I was pretty sure he was teasing. At least I hoped he was.

I wished I was sitting next to Davey so that I could wrap my arms around him. Even though I knew he'd protest.

"Think about it this way," I said. "Remember how happy you were last year when you got Augie?"

"Yeah, sure."

"That was a big thrill for you, wasn't it?"

Davey nodded.

"Some of the kids at Howard Academy will never feel that kind of excitement. When you already have everything handed to you without working for it, or even asking for it, none of it means much. It's just there."

"I guess," said Davey. He didn't look convinced.

"Are you jealous of those kids?"

He didn't reply right away. After a minute he muttered, "Maybe a little."

"Because they have things that you don't?" I paused, watching his face carefully. "Or because your mother spends so much time with them?"

"Both, I guess. I mean, you spend all day with those perfect kids, listening to them talk about their great lives, and then you come home to . . . us."

That *did* propel me out of my seat. I slipped around the table and gathered my son in a hug. If he didn't like it, tough.

"Yes, to *you*," I said firmly. "To the two best kids in the whole world. To exactly where I want to be."

I felt a warm jolt of pleasure as Davey wrapped his arms around me and hugged me back. "Are you sure?"

"I'm positive." I leaned back and looked him in the eye. "Are you kidding me? I'm *beyond* positive."

"Okay." Davey laughed. "I get it."

"Good." I pulled away and stood beside his chair. "Those friends of yours who talk . . . do you want to bring them over here this week after school and I'll set them straight?"

"No. Definitely not." He paled at the thought. "None of my friends need a lecture from my *mom*."

"You're sure?" I teased. "Because I'd be happy to oblige."

"No way," Davey replied. "I'm fine. Really."

I heard Sam and Kevin coming down the stairs. The clatter of sixteen Poodle feet accompanied them.

"Fine about what?" asked Sam. He'd heard the end of our conversation.

"Everything," Davey assured him. My son and I shared a look.

"Eve is a cat!" Kevin announced gleefully.

Sam looked around the room. "Did I miss something?"

I gave him a quick kiss and grabbed my coat. "The boys will fill you in," I said.

It was time for me to run.

There's a sign just inside the Howard Academy gateposts announcing a ten-mile-per hour speed limit and advising visitors to watch out for children. Most days, I try to obey the rules. That morning I didn't even come close. Instead, keeping a careful eye out for icy patches, I sped up the driveway, whipped around the back of the school, and parked in the first empty space I saw.

A number of vendors had come in the evening before to unload and set up their booths. Those who hadn't were busy getting everything moved into place now. The double doors that led to the auditorium were standing open, and Tony's crew was helping the latecomers bring in their wares.

Before I'd even reached the building, I could already hear the Christmas carols that were being piped into the auditorium by the school's sound system. Holiday music always makes me smile. The soaring notes of "Joy to the World" put an extra bounce in my step as I strode across the parking lot and hurried through the doorway.

I meant to get right to work. Instead, once inside, I

couldn't help but pause for a minute and simply admire the vista before me. Our plain, functional auditorium had disappeared. In its place was a Christmas wonderland.

Rita Kinney had outdone herself with the decorations. Everywhere I looked, I saw fresh pine boughs and garlands. Huge, shiny,ornaments, strung on red satin ribbons, dangled from the ceiling. A pathway, lined by glittering Styrofoam candy canes, directed children to the photo booth where Santa Claus would be waiting. The air smelled wonderful: like evergreen, and cinnamon, and warm apple pie.

Just inside the door, I saw concessions offering face painting, caramel apples, penny candy, and toys and games. Beyond them were booths selling ornate wreaths, and watercolors, and handcrafted Christmas ornaments. The local crafting community had come out in full force. Their stands were lined with homemade quilts, needlepoint Christmas stockings, wooden puzzles, and hand-knitted scarves. Stocking stuffers were everywhere.

Even though I'd watched the room come together piece by piece, the finished panorama before me still made my breath catch in my throat. The bazaar looked incredible, far better than I'd had any right to expect. Now I could only hope that our efforts would be rewarded by a huge turnout of parents and customers, and that they'd all be eager to shop and spend.

"I said no and I meant *no!* Didn't you hear me?"

Whoever the woman was, half the room must have heard her, I thought as I turned to see what the commotion was about. A middle-aged woman, beautifully dressed, perfectly coiffed, wearing four-inch heels that would have made my feet beg for relief, was standing just inside the double doors, shaking her finger in Tony Dahl's face. Under other circumstances, the woman might have been attractive. Now she just looked furious.

I hurried over to the pair. "Excuse me," I said. "Can I help?"

"I should hope so! This . . . *man* . . . is trying to tell me that my homemade jellies and jams have been relegated to an inferior booth at the back of the room." She flung out an arm dismissively, indicating the direction she'd been sent to set up. Luckily Tony ducked, otherwise she might have hit him in the nose. "That is simply *un*acceptable. I want to speak to the person in charge!"

"That would be me," I said, holding out my hand. "I'm Melanie Travis. And the man who's been trying to help you is Tony Dahl, our head coach and phys ed teacher."

"I don't care if he's Father Christmas," the woman snapped. "He's wrong!"

I withdrew my hand, unshaken, and tried out a smile instead. It probably didn't look very sincere because Tony—who'd prudently removed himself from the line of fire—winked at me from behind the woman's back.

"I doubt that," I said. "Tony's very good at his job. But let me have a look. I'll check and see where you belong." I thumbed through the papers attached to my clipboard and took out the final diagram of our floor chart. Barbara had given it to me the night before. "Your name is?"

"Madeline Dangerfield." The woman's toe began to tap. "I spoke with somebody about my booth. Somebody *important!*" She peered at me through narrowed eyes. It was clear she didn't think I measured up.

"Was it Barbara Blume?" I asked. Scanning quickly

through the chart, I didn't see Madeline's name on a booth near the front of the room. In fact I didn't see it listed anywhere.

"How should I know? It was more than a month ago. Right after Halloween."

"It couldn't have been that long ago," I said, looking up. "Barbara confirmed with all our vendors within the last ten days. Didn't she call you?"

"Maybe she did. Who knows?" Madeline's shoulder rose and fell in a careless shrug. "I don't answer the phone every time it rings. Half the time, it's telemarketers."

"Barbara would have left a message for you." I was sure of that. "Did you return her call?"

"Why should I have had to do that? I'm here now. That ought to be good enough."

That explained the problem. Barbara must have stricken Madeline's name from the main list when she hadn't been able to get hold of her.

"Yes, but—"

"Are you in charge or not?" Madeline demanded.

Fervently wishing that I could answer no, I nodded instead.

"Then do *something!*" The foot was still tapping. I was tempted to reach over and place my boot on top of it.

"I'm afraid that since Barbara didn't hear from you, we don't have any space available right out front. But the booths over by the windows are lovely. They're light and bright and they'll get lots of foot traffic."

Tony, hearing his cue, set his crew in motion. Before Madeline even had a chance to reply, her boxes had already been picked up and whisked past us on their way to the other side of the room.

"Instead of standing here arguing," I said, "I'm sure

you'd rather get your jellies and jams set up and your booth ready for business. We'll be starting the bazaar in less than an hour."

"You're lucky I'm in an accommodating mood," Madeline sniffed. "And I certainly hope you don't plan to *charge* me a rental fee for being stuck in that inferior location."

I wasn't about to make any promises on that score. "I'll send Barbara over later to talk to you," I told her.

"I pay tuition, you know. I have two daughters here. Do you *know* how much it *costs* to go to this school?"

Actually I did, pretty much to the penny. Which was why, even though I worked at Howard Academy, my child went to public school.

"I'll see what I can do," I said with a sigh.

"Of course you will. I'd expect nothing less." Madeline turned her back and walked away, heels tapping across the floor.

What a way to start the day, I thought. But things could only get better from there, right?

Chapter 8

Claire and Bertie arrived soon after that. They walked into the building together, talking and laughing, and looking remarkably cheerful considering that I'd not only gotten them up early on a Saturday morning, but also planned to put them to work for the remainder of the day. Claire, dressed in jeans, was carrying a garment bag slung over her shoulder.

"I didn't know if you'd have a costume that would fit me," she said, when I hurried over to greet them. "So I brought my own."

"You have your *own* elf costume?"

"I borrowed it for the day." Claire grinned. "Trust me, I'm a woman of many resources."

"I never doubted that for a minute. And thank you for thinking of it because it suddenly occurs to me that I forgot all about costumes."

"No problem," said Claire. "I've got you covered."

I gave her a quick hug. "I think you just saved my butt."

"Hey," said Bertie. "Claire's not the only butt-saver around here. What's a girl have to do to get a little attention?"

"With your looks, just stand there," Claire said. "That should do it."

Bertie growled something inaudible under her breath as I turned her way.

I didn't even ask. Instead I said, "You're going to be my chief animal wrangler. Between the kids, the pets, and the parents, you're going to have plenty to do."

"Easy peasy," Bertie replied. "I'm on it."

"Let me introduce you to our photographer, Eli Wolichek." I led the pair over to the candy-cane-bordered path. "He's at the booth getting set up."

"You also need to direct me toward a place where I can get changed," said Claire.

"Sure, the ladies' room is right through those doors—"

"Ms. Travis! Hey, Ms. Travis, wait!" I turned and saw one of my favorite students, Poppy McEvoy, skipping in my direction.

Skinny, freckled, and with a head of bright red hair that tended to go its own way, Poppy was small for her age and often shy in social situations. A voracious reader, she preferred to spend time with books rather than with kids her own age. The eleven-year-old had entered my room with obvious reluctance for our first tutoring session three months earlier, but once she'd seen Faith we'd quickly established a rapport.

"You guys go on ahead," I said to Claire and Bertie. "I'll catch up in a minute."

Poppy wasn't alone. Her hand was clasped firmly in that of a man dressed in creased blue jeans, designer sneakers, and a dark corduroy shirt with the cuffs rolled back. I'd seen him around the auditorium earlier, un-loading boxes and helping to re-hang a decorative curtain that had begun to sag. He'd appeared to be part of Tony's volunteer crew. But now, seeing him with Poppy and noticing that they shared the same small, wiry build and copper-colored hair, I realized that he must be her father.

Jim McEvoy quickly confirmed that impression with an introduction. "Sorry to bother you, Ms. Travis," he said, "I can see that you're busy. Poppy wanted me to come over and say hello. You're her favorite teacher. She talks about you all the time."

"It's a pleasure to meet you, Mr. McEvoy. Poppy's a wonderful girl. I really enjoy working with her."

"Please, call me Jim. Unless that's too informal for a school like this? I know how Howard Academy likes to keep up appearances. That's one of the things Sondra likes about this place."

"Dad-deee!" Poppy wailed. She rolled her eyes and the subtext was clear: *Don't embarrass me in front of the teacher.*

I just smiled and said, "I see Tony has conscripted you to be part of his crew. Thank you for coming by to help out."

"That was Poppy's doing." Jim glanced down at his daughter. "She wanted me to spend the day with her at the bazaar, but unfortunately I have other plans. I told her I could fit in a couple of hours early this morning though, so she signed me up."

"We appreciate your efforts," I said. "Every little bit helps."

"Kiltie's coming later with Mom," Poppy told me. She was clearly excited about the prospect. "I'm going to have his picture taken with Santa Claus."

"I'm sure that will be fun," Jim said with a tight smile.

Suddenly I remembered Sondra mentioning at the dog show that she and her husband had separated. I wondered if Jim's "other plans" were merely his way of ensuring that he and his wife wouldn't both be at the bazaar at the same time.

"Speaking of which," I said, "I need to go check on the photo booth. It was nice to meet you, Jim. And once again, thanks for your help. Poppy, I'll see you later, okay?"

"Sure, Ms. Travis," Poppy said happily. "I'll be here all day."

All was running smoothly at the photo concession. The photographer, Eli, and his assistant, Cooper, obviously knew what they were doing. Everything was already set up and ready for business. Bertie and Claire had introduced themselves, then Claire had gone to change her clothes. She returned to the booth dressed in a short green tunic, yellow and red striped tights, and a pointed cap sporting a jaunty feather.

"Don't you dare laugh," Claire said, correctly reading the expression on my face as the cap's long feather swooped from side to side, then dipped down over her eyes. She pursed her lips in annoyance and blew upward to chase it away. "Seriously, do not."

"You look great," I said, biting back a smile. "You fit right in with the décor."

"Better you than me," Bertie said happily.

"Every Santa has to have at least one elf." Eli peered out from behind his tripod. He had a round face framed by a pair of Clark Kent glasses, and the kind of cheerful demeanor that children would naturally gravitate to. "And speaking of which, where is your Santa Claus?"

Good question.

I glanced down at my watch. "It's only a little past nine. He's not late yet. I'm sure he's on his way."

At least I hoped he was. The prospect of a Christmas bazaar without a Santa Claus didn't even bear thinking about.

"Ms. Travis, do you have a minute?"

It was Danny, the school janitor, with a question about an electrical hook-up and a blown fuse. That was followed by a complaint from one of the vendors about a neighboring booth that was burning incense. Then a food concession worker tipped over a tub of ice, turning the other end of the auditorium into a skating rink.

As soon as one problem was solved, another quickly popped up to take its place. I spent the next forty-five minutes putting out fires—only metaphorically, thank goodness—and running from one crisis to the next. I also kept my eye on the door. Surely our Santa Claus would be putting in an appearance soon.

As the minutes ticked by and the bazaar's start time drew ever closer, my chest grew tighter and tighter as though a vise was pressing around my ribs. It was never a good idea to question Mr. Hanover's judgment but maybe I should have pressed a little harder for details anyway. Or I should have gotten Chris Tindall's phone number from Harriet and called him myself to confirm his appearance. . . .

"Ho! Ho! Ho!"

People stopped what they were doing. Heads swiveled around. All eyes in the room were drawn to the doorway by that magic greeting.

A six-foot-tall Santa Claus wearing the requisite red suit, shiny black boots, and fluffy white beard, stood just inside the open entrance. His feet were braced wide apart. His hands were fisted on his ample hips. He smiled like a pirate as he looked around the auditorium.

"Santa Claus is here," he announced in a booming voice. "Is everybody ready to get jolly?"

Indeed, I thought. More than ready.

I blew out a relieved breath and hastened across the room.

"You must be Mr. Tindall," I said as I drew near.

"No." He stared at me reproachfully. "I'm Santa Claus."

Great. We had a method actor.

The man's beard was so big and bushy that I could barely see his face. And although he filled out the big red suit admirably, this Santa Claus carried himself with the ease of a younger man. No matter. I was sure the children would be pleased by his appearance and I was just happy that he'd shown up.

"Santa Claus, of course," I apologized. "Are you ready to get to work?"

"Ho, ho, ho," he replied. "Just point me in the right direction."

I did better than that. I walked the big man down Candy Cane Lane and introduced him around. Santa barely gave Eli and Cooper a passing glance. But he stopped to smile at Claire and then leered at Bertie, who was setting out the trays of candy canes and dog biscuits that would be handed out to visitors.

"What a chump," Eli muttered under his breath.

"Last-minute replacement," I replied in a low tone. "Kind of like me."

"You seem to be handling things pretty well."

"So far, so good. Keep your fingers crossed for me

that it stays that way. And don't worry about Bertie. She'll put him in his place if she has to."

Ten minutes later, the double doors connecting the auditorium to the school's main entrance were thrown open. The Howard Academy Christmas Bazaar was officially in business. I'd worried that things might be slow to get started, but my fears were unfounded. As soon as access was granted, the first wave of customers came streaming into the big room.

"Brace yourself," said Rita. I'd taken up a position next to the stage, it was a great vantage point from which to observe the proceedings. She came over and stood beside me. "Here they come."

Ed Weinstein, striding past with a box of fruitcakes in his hands, paused in front of us to have a look. "Last year's opening crowd was bigger," he announced.

"It's barely ten o'clock," I said. "We've got plenty of time before we have to start worrying about the numbers."

"You'd better hope so." Ed smirked. "It would be a real shame if your big event fell flat."

"Shut up, Ed," said Rita. "Isn't somebody waiting for those fruitcakes?"

"I'm on my way. You know me—always happy to do my bit." Ed spun around and walked away.

"Don't pay any attention to him," Rita told me. "He hates to see anybody else succeed."

"Let me guess," said Louisa, coming over to join us. "Are we talking about Ed?"

"Who else?" I sighed. "Was last year's opening crowd really bigger?"

"I wouldn't know." Louisa shrugged. "I wasn't here first thing in the morning."

"Me, either," said Rita.

I looked at them both in surprise. "How come?"

"Because last year's chairman didn't ask us to show up early," Louisa replied. "So we didn't."

"I thought all the faculty got involved on the day of the bazaar," I said.

"Would you?" Rita asked with a laugh. "If you'd had a choice?"

"Well . . . no."

"See? That's how we all feel. The bazaar is a lot of extra work for everybody. I do the decorating so I get my part done ahead of time. Then I usually take the day of the bazaar off."

Louise winked. "Once the date for the bazaar has been announced, I've been known to arrange to be out of town."

"But . . ." I sputtered looking at the two of them. "You're both here now."

"Sure." Louisa nodded. "Because ever since you got put in charge, you've been running around the school bursting with enthusiasm and rallying the troops. How could we resist?"

"Oh no," I said with a low moan. "Are you saying that you both changed your plans to be here? You must hate me now."

To my surprise, Rita smiled. "You don't get it. If we hated you, we wouldn't have come to help out. It's because we *like* you that we're here."

"We all want to see you succeed," said Louisa. "So we turned out to help make sure that it happens."

"Oh." In the moment it took me to process that, I realized it was pretty great. Rita and Louisa had shown up to lend a supportive hand. Bertie and Claire had done the same. I had the best friends in the whole world.

"Wow," I said. "Thank you."

"Don't mention it." Rita braced her fingers against my shoulder and nudged me toward the ever-growing crowd. "Just make it worth our while. Go back out there and get to work."

I spent the next two hours walking slowly around the auditorium, browsing from booth to booth, and checking in with the vendors to make sure that they had everything they needed. Every single one had shoppers checking out their wares. Some vendors were too busy to even stop and talk to me.

Business was brisk everywhere I looked. The Christmas-related items—wreaths, stockings, personalized ornaments—were flying off the shelves. By eleven o'clock, a line had already formed at the food concession. As lunchtime approached, the gift wrapping booth was so crowded I couldn't get within ten feet of it. Ryan Duncan was taking a turn there. He simply lifted his hand to motion a quick thumbs-up and waved me on my way.

Early afternoon, I stood off to one side and observed the photo booth for a few minutes. As I'd expected, Bertie and Claire had everything under control. Though the concession drew plenty of interest, the line for pictures never had a chance to get too long.

Claire was wonderful with the children. Bertie was equally adept at managing their pets. Our Santa Claus, seated on his gilt-covered throne, seemed to enjoy interacting with his audience. He was both affable and accommodating as the kids and their pets were perched upon his ample lap.

I'd meant to stop only briefly but the photo booth was so much fun to watch that I found myself lingering. I watched Santa Claus handle Kiltie, and Coco Lily, and a young boy's Gila monster, all with equal aplomb. Eli framed and shot his pictures with swift precision and Cooper was a wizard at producing the finished Christmas cards quickly and efficiently.

I sensed Mr. Hanover's presence behind me a moment before he spoke. "I'd say our Santa Claus is working out rather well, wouldn't you?" he asked.

"Absolutely," I agreed. "He's doing a great job."

The headmaster paused to let his gaze slip with satisfaction around the room. "I might offer the same congratulations to you."

"Not yet." I held up both hands, fingers tightly crossed. "We still have several more hours to go."

"I have every faith in your abilities, Ms. Travis. I trust that you'll manage to stay on top of things."

"Thank you, I—"

A medium-sized, blue-and-white, canine missile came hurtling past my legs, nearly knocking me over. Mr. Hanover started to reach out his hands to steady me but my reflexes—honed by years of dog ownership—had already kicked in. I swooped down and snatched up the end of the long leather leash that was whipping across the floor in the blue merle Aussie's wake.

"Memphis, darn it! You're a bad dog! Come back here."

The Australian Shepherd didn't seem at all inclined to heed his owner's frantic calls. But he had no choice but to respond to my hand at the end of his lead. Captured, he spun around and circled back, then sat down with his long pink tongue lolling out of the side of his mouth. Dark eyes twinkling, the playful Aussie looked like he was grinning at me.

"I'll leave you to manage this, shall I?" said Mr. Hanover.

He melted away into the crowd, just as the dog's owners appeared. A small boy, looking shamefaced by his error, ran past me and threw his arms around the Aussie's neck.

"Sorry about that," said the boy's mother. She took the leash from my hand and wrapped it around her fingers. "Eric was supposed to be holding on tight but Memphis likes to play and he got away. We were on our way to see Santa."

"Memphis led you right to him," I said.

"I bet he smelled the biscuits," Eric guessed.

The Aussie now had his nose tipped up in the air. He'd risen to his feet and he was looking longingly in the direction of Bertie's trays of treats.

"He'll get one after he has his picture taken," I told them as I walked the trio to the back of the line.

"No, he won't," Memphis's owner said firmly. She gave the leash a sharp snap. "He's a bad dog."

I reached down and gave the Aussie's head a pat. The dog gazed up at me happily. "If you don't mind my saying so he won't make the connection. You're mad at him now because he embarrassed you—"

"No, I'm angry because he didn't come when I called."

I'm always amazed by how many people—who've never taken the time to teach their dogs a good, solid, recall—nevertheless expect those dogs to come when summoned, even under the most trying circumstances. If Aunt Peg were there, she'd have given the woman a stern lecture on dog training.

Short on time, I merely said instead, "Memphis will be much more likely to come when you want him to, if you don't yell at him and call him a bad dog."

The woman looked at me like I was daft. "It's not like he understands the actual *words*."

I left the trio at the end of the line, sidled up to the front, and beckoned Bertie over. "Keep an eye on the Aussie," I said. "He's a pistol."

"So I saw," she replied with a chuckle. "I love a dog with personality. Don't worry about us. We'll be fine."

"Everything else good?"

"Perfect," said Bertie.

It was exactly what I wanted to hear.

Chapter 9

As the afternoon passed, the crowds grew steadily larger. I continued to make my rounds, keeping a constant eye out for anything that might require my attention. I resolved a complaint about an ornament that broke right after a customer bought it, found Danny the janitor and got him to reset the fuse box again, then mediated an argument between two children, both of whom were determined to purchase the same Christmas stocking.

By midafternoon, I'd begun to breathe a little more easily and smile a lot more often. I greeted countless students and their parents and saw numerous dog show exhibitors who'd heard about the bazaar from Aunt Peg and come to shop. Sam showed up with the boys and I took time out to watch them get their faces painted before heading back to work. Sondra McEvoy and I crossed paths several times, both of us circulating around the large room. I stocked up on raffle tickets and signed Davey's and Kev's names on the stubs.

Quinn Peterson arrived with her pony, Scooter, and caused a minor sensation when she blithely led the aged Shetland in through the auditorium's back door. The pony seemed somewhat bemused by all the activity, but was otherwise impeccably behaved. He quickly became a kid magnet as the pair waited in line for their turn with Santa Claus.

"Ho, ho, horse!" Santa boomed in a jolly voice.

Wherever he'd come from, I thought, this guy was a find. Nothing the kids threw at him seemed to faze him.

Confronted by the lights, the camera, and Santa Claus himself, Scooter merely blinked his eyes and flicked his gray-tipped ears back and forth. He graciously allowed himself to be maneuvered into position. As a reward for his good behavior, Bertie treated the Shetland to two candy canes. He nibbled them both with quiet dignity while the group of children now gathered in a semi-circle around the booth, pressed in closer and watched wide-eyed.

"Can I have a pony ride?" asked one.

I started to step forward, but Quinn had everything under control. "I'm afraid not," she said. "Scooter's too old to be ridden anymore. But you can give him a pat if you like. Scooter likes it when people pat him."

One by one, the children stepped forward to run their small hands through Scooter's long shaggy coat. Eye to eye with many of them, the Shetland gently nuzzled their pockets looking for treats. He stood patiently until everyone had had a turn.

"Time to go," Quinn said finally. "Was that okay, Ms. Travis?"

"That was perfect," I told her. I escorted the pair

back to the door where the trailer was waiting. "I hope you love your pictures."

Quinn flashed a sunny smile. "I'm sure I will. See you Monday!"

With Scooter's departure, the level of excitement in the room seemed to drop. I wasn't the only one who was getting tired. By now the bazaar had been open for five hours. Just three more and I could call it a day. I couldn't wait.

Sam brought the boys by so that I could check out their purchases before they headed home. Davey appeared to have satisfied his curiosity about my workplace. And Kev had worn himself out running from one booth to the next, eager not to miss a thing. Both boys had enjoyed their time at the bazaar thoroughly.

Sam, who'd managed it all, was my hero. Nothing new about that.

"You'll get your reward later," I told him in an undertone.

"I can't wait," he replied. He wasn't the only one.

As my family left and I turned back to the room, I thought I heard a dog bark. Despite the number of pets we'd hosted throughout the day, the bazaar had been remarkably free of canine commotion. I knew I had Bertie to thank for that. Now I paused near the stage, lifted my head, and looked around.

"What?" asked Rita, coming up beside me.

"I thought I heard a dog bark."

"Only one?" She laughed. "That's a miracle, considering."

"Yeah, I know."

Together we both looked toward the photo booth. In the time since I'd last paid attention to the concession, the line of kids had disappeared. A thick velvet cord had been draped across the end of Candy Cane Lane. A sign on Santa's gilt throne read BE BACK SOON. "There he is." Rita pointed across the room. Our Santa Claus, his arms cradled around his ample belly was heading out the door. "Look at the way he's holding his stomach. I wonder if he ate too many candy canes."

"I don't think that's his problem," said Claire. Careful not to trip in her pointy shoes, she walked over and joined us. "I'm guessing he's desperate for a smoke. When you stand right next to him, he kind of reeks."

I wrinkled my nose and hoped fervently that Santa would have the good sense to walk around a corner of the building—and out of the sight of any children—before pausing to light up a cigarette.

"You guys have been doing a great job with the photo booth," I said to Claire.

She smiled and nodded. "I can't believe how busy we've been all day. We never even got a chance to stop for lunch. Santa Claus was getting kind of peeved about not having a break, so we all decided to take one now."

"Where is Bertie?" I asked.

"She, Eli, and Cooper went to check out the food concession. I'm on my way to join them."

"Lunch is on me," I told her. "You guys have earned it."

Rita and Claire went their separate ways. I took a deep breath and headed back into the fray.

"Melanie?" Tony Dahl waved me over to the gift-wrapping booth. "A little help?"

"Sure. What do you need?"

"A customer told me there's a loose dog running around over by the wooden puzzle booth. It's jumping on people and being a bit of a nuisance. I thought you might want to check it out."

"Thanks for telling me," I said. Our second loose dog of the day. "I'll go take care of it."

The puzzle booth was at the far end of the room. I started to head in that direction. A small shriek redirected me.

"I've been attacked!" Madeline Dangerfield screamed from inside her jam concession. "It's a rat!"

Well, *that* got everybody's attention.

"It's not a rat," I said quickly, raising my voice so that everyone around us would hear me. "There are no rats in here."

As I was speaking, a small, fluffy, gray dog came scooting out from behind the booth: Charlotte's Cockapoo, Coco Lily. I'd met her earlier when she was having her picture taken. I leaned down as the little dog came barreling toward me and Coco Lily ran straight into my arms.

"Good *girl,*" I crooned. The Cockapoo seemed relieved to have been caught. She licked my chin and wagged her long, plumed, tail. Tightening my arms around her wriggling body, I rose to my feet.

"Look," I said, turning in a small circle so that everyone could see. "It's only Coco Lily."

"Coco Lily." Madeline sniffed. "What kind of name is that for a dog?" At least she had the grace to look embarrassed by her outburst.

To my relief, several people began to laugh about the mix-up. Everybody resumed their shopping. Crisis averted.

Still holding the Cockapoo in my arms, I gazed around the big room. I wondered where Charlotte was and how Coco Lily could have gotten loose. Earlier, I'd seen both her and Kiltie tucked safely into their side-by-side crates behind the raffle table. Both dogs had appeared to be sleeping.

At the time—with Sondra walking around the bazaar selling tickets—the booth had been untended. I wondered whether she'd returned to the table since then. Taking Coco Lily with me, I headed in that direction. With luck, I might find Charlotte along the way.

It was almost four o'clock and the crowds in the auditorium were finally beginning to wane. Even so, it took me a few minutes to make my way across the room to the raffle table. As I drew closer I saw that Helen Baker, another parent volunteer, was currently manning the booth.

"Come to buy some raffle tickets?" she asked with a bright smile. "We have plenty of great prizes."

"No, thanks, I got my tickets from Sondra earlier. I've come to return a wandering dog. Coco Lily is supposed to be locked in one of those crates in the back of the booth. You didn't happen to see how she got out, did you?"

Helen shook her head. "Sorry, I have no idea. When I got here a few minutes ago, both crates were empty. Just like they are now."

Both crates?

I dodged around behind the table and had a look for myself. Helen was right. Both Kiltie and Coco Lily's crates were sitting open. And neither one was occupied.

Maybe Poppy had taken Kiltie outside for a walk, I thought. Might she have accidently let Coco Lily loose as well?

As soon as the thought crossed my mind, I quickly discarded it. Poppy McEvoy was a conscientious and responsible child. She would never have released Kiltie from her crate without first looping a leash securely around the Westie's neck. And if Coco Lily had somehow gotten away while she was there, Poppy would definitely have gone chasing after her.

"Is something wrong?" asked Helen.

"I don't know," I said slowly. The hair on the back of my neck was beginning to tingle. I leaned down, slipped the Cockapoo inside her box, and fastened the latch. "I think I'd better find Sondra."

"I saw her over near the food stand about ten minutes ago," Helen said helpfully.

"Thanks, I'll start there. Could you keep an eye on Coco Lily for me? And if Charlotte Levine shows up, would you keep her here until I get back?"

"Sure," Helen replied. "I can do that."

By the time I reached the food concession, Sondra was nowhere to be seen.

"She was here a few minutes ago," Bertie told me. She, Claire, and Eli were just finishing their late lunch. "Try over near the stage. And while you're looking around . . ."

I'd started to go. Now I stopped and turned back. "Yes?"

"If you run across our Santa Claus, send him back inside. He's been gone for at least twenty minutes. We thought he'd come and grab some food with us, but we haven't seen him. Now we're ready to get back to work."

"He's probably out there puffing away and lost track of time," Eli grumbled. The two men had not hit it off.

"If I see him, I'll let him know," I said. "But first I really need to find Sondra."

"Then don't worry about us." Bertie waved me on my way. "I can run outside and reel our Santa back in."

I looked for Sondra near the stage, and then along the row of booths beneath the windows. I even stuck my head in the ladies' room. It was frustrating to realize that with both of us on the move around the auditorium, we could very conceivably just keep missing one another.

Then, for the second time that afternoon, I heard someone shriek.

"What now?" I muttered, spinning in my tracks.

And there Sondra was, standing beside the raffle table. It looked as though she'd sold most of her tickets and returned to the booth to replenish her supplies. Poppy was standing next to her mother. The young girl looked stricken. Helen appeared to have removed herself a prudent distance away.

As I hurried through the crowd to get to Sondra and Poppy, I suddenly realized that the most important thing about the scene was what *wasn't* there. Mother and daughter were now both accounted for. But Kiltie was nowhere in sight.

"What do you *mean* you don't know where he is?" Sondra demanded of Helen as I approached. Sondra's voice was sharp enough to make my ears sting.

"Why would I know anything about your dog? I just volunteered to sit here and sell raffle tickets." Helen gazed past Sondra and sent me a pleading look. "Here comes Melanie. She was looking for you. Maybe she knows something."

"Thank God you're here." Sondra whirled around to face me. "Where's Kiltie?"

"I have no idea." I was out of breath and the words came out in a rush. "That's why I was looking for you.

I saw that his crate was open. I was hoping that you had him."

"Why would *I* have him? I've been busy all day. That's why I brought a crate. The last time I saw him was several hours ago when Poppy took him to have his picture taken."

"She and Charlotte were together—" I began, but Sondra wasn't listening to me.

Instead, she'd rounded on her daughter. Her expression was thunderous. "Poppy Louise McEvoy, *what did you do?*"

Quailing beneath her mother's glare, Poppy seemed to shrink in size. She clutched her arms tightly across her chest. Her shoulders slumped and her lips began to quiver. A tear slipped down her cheek, followed quickly by another.

"I didn't *do* anything," she said, her voice scarcely louder than a whisper. "After Charlotte and I got the pictures, we brought Kiltie and Coco Lily right back here and put them in their crates, just like you told us to. I latched the door. I know I did."

"Don't you *dare* lie to me." Sondra bit out the words. "If you had fastened the door to his crate correctly, Kiltie would still be here."

"It's not my fault," Poppy wailed. "I was careful. Charlotte was here. Ask her!"

"Let's all take a deep breath," I said firmly. Stepping forward, I deliberately wedged myself between mother and daughter.

Poppy quickly retreated backward. She seemed relieved to have a barrier placed between her and her mother.

I glanced over at Helen. "Do you know Charlotte Levine?"

She nodded. "I know what she looks like."

"Do you think you could find her for us?"

Helen didn't even answer. Happy to have an excuse to escape the escalating scene, she simply turned and walked away. I was sorry I couldn't go with her.

"Now let's talk about this calmly," I said to Sondra.

"*Calmly?* You must be kidding. Maybe you don't understand what's going on here. My dog is *missing!*"

"Yes," I replied. "Right this moment we don't know where Kiltie is. And because of that, you've reduced your daughter to tears. Which isn't helping anything."

I heard Poppy sniffle. She wiped her nose on her sleeve. The young girl's distress made no impression on Sondra, however. She still looked mad enough to kill.

"Poppy," I said, shifting my attention to the sixth grader, "when was the last time you saw Kiltie?"

"A few hours ago," she answered in a small voice. "Right after the photo booth."

"You never came back to the raffle table after that?"

"No, not after I put Kiltie in his crate. I knew he'd be safe there, just like he is at a dog show. Charlotte and I wanted to enjoy the rest of the bazaar."

I heard Sondra growl under her breath. Pointedly I ignored her.

"So you were with Charlotte for most of the day?" I asked Poppy.

She nodded.

"Did Charlotte come back to the raffle table for any reason?"

"No. Why would she?"

"What does it matter where Charlotte was?" Sondra demanded. Her eyes narrowed. "Do you think *she's* responsible—?"

"No," I said sternly. "I don't. But it matters because shortly before I discovered that Kiltie was gone, I found Coco Lily running loose in the auditorium. So your dog isn't the only one who got out."

"What do you mean 'running loose'?" Sondra's voice rose. She snapped an impatient finger in the direction of the closed crate. "That silly little Cockapoo is right there. While my valuable show dog is missing!"

"I understand that," I said. "And we'll all help you look for him. Kiltie must be here somewhere. I'm sure he hasn't gone far."

"He shouldn't be gone at all." Sondra glared at her daughter who was staring at her feet.

"Don't blame Poppy," I said. "This can't have been her fault."

"It can't?" The girl looked up hopefully.

"No," I told her. "Think about it. Somehow, both crates got opened. Even if you didn't latch Kiltie's door securely, that wouldn't explain how Coco Lily also got loose."

"Hey, that's right," Poppy said. "I never even touched her crate."

"I don't have time for this," Sondra snapped. "We'll get that part sorted out later. Right now, I'm going to go look for my dog."

"We will, too," I said. "The more people searching for Kiltie, the faster we'll find him. Poppy, do you think you can grab some of your friends and mobilize them to join in the search?"

She nodded eagerly. "I have a picture of Kiltie on my phone. I'll send it to everyone I know and tell them to start looking."

"Great idea," I said. "Go to it."

Poppy hurried away. Like Helen, she seemed happy to make her escape.

When she was gone, I turned back to Sondra. "I'll alert the rest of the staff and they can help us spread the word. And I've seen a lot of dog show people here today. Let's recruit them, too. They'll all know what a Westie looks like and that will make things easier."

"It doesn't mean they'll help," Sondra muttered. "I bet a couple of them would laugh out loud if they knew Kiltie was gone."

"What are you talking about?"

"Jo Drummer's here, I sold her some raffle tickets. She has Border Terriers. And I saw Chip Michaels, too. You know, the Skye breeder?"

"So?"

Sondra looked at me as though I was stupid. "So if Kiltie goes missing, their dogs will move up in the group."

Oh man, I thought. Was that really the way her mind worked at a time like this?

"I don't think you're giving your fellow exhibitors enough credit," I said.

"Maybe things are different in Non-Sporting." Sondra's tone was lofty. "But Terriers are an extremely competitive group."

Yeah, right. That was how it worked. *My* group was easy.

"They're all dog lovers," I said shortly. "Trust me, they'll pitch in."

And they did. In no time at all, we had searchers peering into booths and checking under tables in every quadrant of the room. Teachers, kids and exhibitors all helped look. Vendors who were too busy to stop what they were doing, nevertheless promised to keep an eye out for the small white dog. Shoppers did the same.

The first thing I did was post volunteer guards at both doors. Assuming that Kiltie hadn't left the building, he wasn't going to be allowed to do so on my watch. My next stop was the photo booth in case Kiltie had gone there looking for the company of other dogs. To my surprise, however, the booth was deserted. Evidently it was still on a break.

On an easier day, that would have concerned me. I would have done something about it right away. Now it was just one more problem to be dealt with as soon as I got the chance.

Twenty hectic, nonproductive minutes later, I circled back past the photo booth once again. This time Bertie, Eli, and Cooper were there. The photographer and his assistant were fiddling with their equipment. Bertie just looked annoyed. Hands on her hips, she was staring at Santa's empty throne.

"You look frazzled," she said as I approached.

"I *am* frazzled," I said. "We have a missing dog."

Cooper and Eli stopped what they were doing and glanced over. Nobody seemed very impressed by my news.

"A very valuable dog," I told them. "A top show dog."

Bertie's eyes widened. "Not Kiltie?"

"I'm afraid so."

"Then you're probably not going to want to hear about our problem," she said.

I took a deep breath and asked, "What now?"

"Santa Claus is missing, too."

Chapter 10

I must have misheard her, I thought.

"What do you mean *missing?*" I asked.

"Gone," said Bertie. She flicked a hand through the air. "Vanished. Poof!"

I looked over at the guys. "Where did he go?"

"If we knew that," said Eli, "we wouldn't be having this conversation."

He had a good point.

"He went on a break," I said stupidly. "You all did."

"And the rest of us came back," said Bertie. "Santa disappeared."

I looked around the small, unhappy group. "What about Claire?"

"She's still looking for him," Cooper told me. "We already tried that. Eventually we gave up. But that Claire, she's an optimist."

Yes, she was, I thought. Good for her.

"She's wasting her time," said Eli. "Even at a Christmas bazaar, it's difficult to misplace a Santa Claus."

Yet another good point, unfortunately.

A thread of hysteria bubbled up within me. On top of everything else, this could *not* be happening now.

"But . . ." I stammered. "He can't be gone. You can't run the booth without a Santa Claus."

Eli nodded. "That's why we're packing up. If that guy's left we might as well call it a day, too."

"It's only four o'clock!" I said. "The bazaar doesn't end for two more hours."

Eli shrugged. "Not our fault. Tell that to your Santa Claus."

There were several things I'd like to tell our Santa Claus, I thought grimly. If only I could find him. And our missing Westie. And maybe a few quiet moments to myself in which to have a peaceful breakdown.

"Problem?" asked Mr. Hanover.

Damn! How did he always manage to do that? The headmaster had an unerring ability to find me whenever I least wanted to see him.

"Um . . " I said, stalling in the hope that something brilliant came to mind. Nothing did. I might as well just blurt out the news. "Our Santa Claus seems to have disappeared."

The headmaster nodded gravely. "Is that all?"

"*All,* Mr. Hanover?"

"I see a number of young people running around the room opening up boxes and peering beneath tables. Surely they're not looking for Santa Claus?"

"No," I admitted. "We also have a missing dog."

"A very valuable dog," Bertie added helpfully.

I could have kicked her.

Mr. Hanover sighed. "And here it seemed as though everything was going so well."

"It was going well," I said. "And I'm sure we've

raised lots of money for the school's scholarship fund. Now we just have a few minor glitches to deal with."

"Minor glitches," Eli chortled under his breath.

I aimed a glare in his direction. *Really*? Could *nobody* help me out here?

"Under the circumstances, I suggest we announce that the photo booth is closed for the day," Mr. Hanover said.

I nodded in agreement.

"That done, you might apply yourself to finding the very valuable dog."

"That's next on my list," I told him.

"Should our Santa Claus reappear, please send him to my office."

"Will do," Bertie volunteered.

"One more thing, Ms. Travis . . ." said Mr. Hanover. "About the dog?"

"Kiltie," I supplied. "He's a West Highland White Terrier."

"I'm afraid his breed affiliation is immaterial to me. What I would like to know is, to whom does he belong?"

"Sondra McEvoy," I said.

"Poppy's mother."

It wasn't a question. I nodded anyway.

"Lovely girl," the headmaster mused. "Reminds me of Pippi Longstocking."

Six hundred students in the school and Mr. Hanover knew every single one on sight. I'd never managed to trip him up yet. Not that I tried, mind you.

"Mrs. McEvoy is not only a Howard Academy parent," he said. "She is also a generous school alumna."

"Oh," I said aloud. *Ouch,* I thought to myself.

Mr. Hanover brought his thumb and forefinger together and pinched the bridge of his nose, just below where his glasses rested. "Oh indeed. Are we in any way responsible for her dog's disappearance?"

"I can't imagine how," I told him.

"Good. Let's keep it that way, shall we?"

"I'll do my best."

Mr. Hanover left us. *Oh my God,* Bertie mouthed as he walked away. "Is he *always* like that?"

"Like what?" I asked.

"I think the word you're looking for is *scary,*" said Cooper.

"I heard that," Mr. Hanover called back over his shoulder.

We stared at each other in horror. Fortunately the headmaster kept on walking. We waited in silence until he'd disappeared into the crowd.

I don't know about the others, but I was holding my breath. When I let it out, it was as if a burst of pent-up tension went with it. Unexpectedly I began to giggle.

After a moment, the other three joined in. There was nothing even remotely amusing about the situation. Maybe that was why we couldn't seem to stop laughing.

"What's so funny?" asked Claire, reappearing suddenly on the other side of the booth.

She was still wearing her elf costume, right down to the pointy shoes and the stupid feather in her cap. I had started to sober up, but the sight of her set me off all over again.

"Nothing," I finally managed to gasp a minute later when I'd caught my breath. "Nothing at all." I bit my lip to tamp down more giggles and tried for a serious expression. "No sign of Santa Claus?"

"None," Claire said unhappily. "And I've looked

everywhere. Even in this crowd a guy like that would be hard to lose. He's not here."

"Santa has *left* the building," Cooper intoned.

That wasn't funny. Or even slightly helpful.

Sensitive to the change in mood, Eli grabbed his assistant. The two of them went back to packing up.

"I heard you lost a dog, too," said Claire.

"Who told you that?"

"Some woman over by the raffle booth. She's throwing a pretty good hissy fit."

"That would be Sondra," I said with a sigh.

"And," Claire added, "she's threatening to sue someone."

"Not me, I hope," I muttered.

"Nah." Bertie reached over and patted my arm comfortingly. "You're only a teacher. You're off the hook. People who want to sue always go for the deep pockets."

"I've got news for you," I said. "Sondra and Jim McEvoy *are* the deep pockets. If Sondra's upset enough to bring legal action, it won't be because she needs the money."

"Whose fault is it that her dog is missing?" Claire asked.

"I have no idea," I said. "Still, I'd better go see what I can do to smooth things over."

I found Sondra at the raffle booth. She was just standing there, staring at Kiltie's empty crate as if she expected the Westie to magically reappear. She was so upset that she was shaking.

"Sondra," I said quietly. "I am so sorry—"

"You should be!" She spun around to face me. "This is all your fault."

In the face of her outburst, I felt myself growing oddly calmer. "Why would you say that?"

"Because if you hadn't come up with the idiotic idea for that Santa Claus and Pets Booth, Poppy would never have wanted to bring Kiltie to the bazaar in the first place. And now he's disappeared!"

The booth hadn't been my idea, I was only a last-minute substitution. There didn't seem to be any reason to point that out, however.

"We still have people looking—" I began.

"For all the good that's doing!"

"Tell me what I can do to be of assistance," I said. "Do you want me to call your husband?"

"Are you *kidding* me?" Sondra cried.

Oh crap, wrong again. Why hadn't I stopped to think before opening my mouth? If, as I'd suspected earlier, the McEvoy parents had arranged their participation in the bazaar to avoid seeing one another, there was nothing to be gained by *that* suggestion.

"Jim doesn't care in the slightest about Kiltie," Sondra snapped. "He never has. He thinks dog shows are a waste of time and money. Kiltie is *my* dog. Mine and nobody else's."

Thank goodness Poppy wasn't there to hear that, I thought. Judging by our conversations, I was quite certain that the girl cared for Kiltie every bit as much as her mother did.

"I can't just stand here," said Sondra. "I need to do something useful. I'm going to go down to the police station and file a report."

Aunt Peg had tried to do that very same thing once herself—when her stud dog, Beau, had gone missing in the middle of the night. The police had brushed off her concerns and referred her to animal control. Half a dozen years had passed since then. I hoped for Sondra's sake that her complaint received more attention from the authorities than Aunt Peg's had.

"That's a good start," I said. "But you'll also need to widen your search. You should make up flyers and post them in all the local schools and businesses. And call every vet in Fairfield County. Maybe Westchester, too. You'll also want to check with all the animal shelters."

Sondra paled at the thought of Kiltie in a shelter. But I could see her thinking things through and stiffening her spine.

"Kiltie is microchipped," she said. "That will help. And I'll offer a big reward for his return. Someone must have seen him. Maybe somebody's already picked him up. All I have to do is make it worth their while to bring him back."

I could only hope that the situation would resolve itself that easily. There was nothing that worried me more than the thought of a lost dog. Poodles don't roam, they prefer to be where their people are. Nevertheless, we had a secure fence around our two-acre backyard and I checked the gates daily. The mere thought of losing one of our Poodle pack made me go all hollow inside.

Sondra opened her purse, took out a piece of paper, and scribbled down her phone number. "Call me right away if you hear anything."

"Of course." I nodded.

She reached behind the booth and picked up Kiltie's empty crate. The second crate, where Coco Lily was now confined, was hers as well. Neither one of us mentioned it. Sondra walked past me and began to leave.

"Wait!" I called after her. "What about Poppy?"

Sondra barely paused. Distracted, deep in thought, she repeated her daughter's name back to me as though it meant nothing to her. "Poppy?"

"We should find her," I said. "Don't you want to take her home with you?"

Still walking, Sondra didn't even bother to turn around. She gave her head a dismissive shake as if she couldn't be bothered to think about anything that might delay her quest to find her dog.

"Poppy can catch a ride with someone else," she said. And then she was gone.

Taken by surprise, I simply stood and stared into the jostling throng of people where Sondra had disappeared. Holy crap on a cracker. Had that really just happened? Did Sondra actually intend to leave her daughter at the bazaar without even bothering to tell her that she needed to find her own way home?

I waited several seconds for Sondra to reappear. It didn't happen.

Wonderful. Now someone needed to find Poppy and tell her what was going on. Once again, it looked as though that job had fallen to me.

I found her at the food concession with Charlotte. Poppy was showing the man who was running the grill the picture of Kiltie that she had on her phone.

"Sorry," he said. "I haven't seen him."

"If you could keep an eye out for him, I would appreciate it," she replied politely. As she and Charlotte turned away, Poppy saw me heading toward them. Her face lit up. "Did you find Kiltie?" she asked.

"No," I told her gently. "I'm afraid he's still missing."

"Oh."

A wealth of disappointment was contained in that single syllable. Poppy looked so small and fragile that I wanted to reach out and hug her. Then I amended that thought silently. I wanted Poppy's *mother* to be there to hug her.

"I came to tell you that your mother had to leave," I said.

Poppy looked up. "Without me?"

"She wanted to go to the police station and file a report about Kiltie." That sounded every bit like the miserable excuse it was. "She thought you could find a ride with someone else?"

"Don't worry," said Charlotte. "My mom will take you home."

"Thanks," Poppy replied with a small smile. "That's very nice of her."

I looked at the two of them. "Does that happen often?" I asked Poppy.

Her slender shoulders rose and fell in a shrug. "Sometimes. My mom gets busy, you know?"

I got busy too, I thought crossly. But I never forgot where my children were, or who they were with.

"So you two girls are good?" I asked.

Both of them nodded.

"Charlotte, I never got a chance to ask you earlier . . . you know that Coco Lily got out of her crate this afternoon, right?"

"Yes," she replied in a small voice.

"Do you have any idea how that happened?"

"No, I don't." Charlotte looked up imploringly. "Honest, Ms. Travis, I would tell you if I knew. Mrs. McEvoy asked me the same thing. She thought I did something clumsy . . . or stupid. But after we put Kiltie and Coco Lily in their crates, I wasn't anywhere near them. And neither was Poppy."

Charlotte looked at her friend who nodded in confirmation. "We were together all afternoon. You have to believe me."

"I do believe you," I told her. "Whatever happened with those two dogs, I don't see any reason to think that you girls had any part in it."

"Tell that to my mother," Poppy said unhappily. "If she doesn't get Kiltie back . . ."

I waited but she didn't finish the thought.

"What?" I prompted. "What will happen if she doesn't find Kiltie?"

"Everyone will be sorry," Poppy whispered. "My mother will make sure of that."

Well, that was a depressing note on which to end what otherwise looked to have been a reasonably successful day. The event was finally in its last hour and now that it was nearing its conclusion, I realized how exhausted I was. Since eight o'clock that morning I'd been on my feet and running around, senses on high alert and humming with the need to detect and respond to potential problems. Now I couldn't wait to go home, kick off my shoes, pull a Poodle into my lap, and close my eyes for a few minutes.

Alas, it wasn't to be just yet.

The auditorium was beginning to empty. After a full day's work, the vendors and other volunteers were just as eager to be on their way as I was. So when Mr. Hanover's secretary entered the big room through the main door and paused for a quick scan around, she had no difficulty spotting me.

Harriet wasn't the kind of woman who moved quickly. Seated behind her desk outside the headmaster's office, she projected a pleasant, placid, demeanor that school parents found wonderfully reassuring. Beneath that un- ruffled exterior, however, was a smart, sensible woman who had the tenacity of a Pit Bull when it came to pro- tecting her boss's interests.

When she caught my eye and immediately began to hurry toward me, I knew something was up. I also knew that it probably wasn't good. I crossed the room and met her halfway.

"Mr. Hanover wants to see you in his office," Har- riet said. "Right away."

Out of breath, she lifted a hand and pressed her palm against her chest, as if to calm her pounding heart. That action was somehow even more alarming than the mes- sage she'd conveyed.

"I'll go right now," I told her. "Do you know what it's about?"

Harriet leaned in close as if she wanted to be sure that we wouldn't be overheard. Even though there was nobody near us, I found myself doing the same.

"The police are here," she whispered in my ear.

I drew back in surprise. "Already?"

The secretary looked shocked. "You were expecting them?"

"Not this quickly."

It couldn't have been more than half an hour since Sondra had left the bazaar. And while I'd always known that there were Howard Academy parents who pos- sessed the kind of power and connections most people could only dream of, I still had to wonder what kind of clout the McEvoys could bring to bear in order to roll out a police response this swiftly over a missing dog.

"Oh my word," said Harriet. Her hand fluttered to her chest again. "Do I even want to know?"

"Probably not," I told her. "Though I'm sure you will soon enough."

Unfortunately I was pretty sure it wouldn't be long before we would *all* find ourselves swept up in whatever kind of retaliatory maelstrom Sondra McEvoy chose to create.

Leaving Harriet behind to follow more slowly, I hurried out of the auditorium and down the well-lit passageway that connected the school's two buildings. I was feeling a bit breathless myself when I reached the mansion's front hall and paused outside the closed door to Mr. Hanover's office. Nerves probably.

I smoothed down my hair, straightened my blazer, then knocked lightly on the door.

"Come," said Mr. Hanover.

I pushed the door open slightly and peered around it, into the room, before entering. Not that I wanted to appear hesitant—that was always a bad strategy when dealing with our forceful headmaster—but in the past I've found myself involved with Detective O'Malley of the Greenwich Police Department on several occasions. From my perspective, our interactions haven't always ended well.

Mr. Hanover was standing by the window. In the middle of the room was a tall, well-built, black man whom I didn't recognize. That was good. Maybe I could start with a clean slate for a change.

"Ms. Travis?" Mr. Hanover sounded impatient, and I realized that I was still hovering in the doorway. "Please come in and close the door behind you."

I quickly did as I'd been told.

"Detective," said the headmaster, "this is Melanie Travis, the woman who's in charge of our bazaar. Ms. Travis, let me introduce you to Detective Raymond Young of the Greenwich Police Department."

We shook hands and took one another's measure. Detective Young had a firm grip and piercing brown eyes. O'Malley had always reminded me of a Chow: bulky, and a bit fluffy around the edges, but fierce underneath. Detective Young was more of a Doberman Pinscher: all muscle and focused intensity.

If anyone could locate Sondra's missing Westie without delay, this had to be the man for the job.

"I'm very pleased to meet you," I said.

"And I'm sorry to tell you that I've come with bad news," the detective replied. "I'm afraid your Santa Claus is dead."

Chapter 11

"*What?* No . . ." I frowned, then shook my head. The news was so unexpected that I couldn't seem to process it. "Santa Claus isn't dead. He's just missing."

"I'm afraid not," said Mr. Hanover.

He walked out from behind his desk and guided me to a chair. My legs felt suddenly boneless and I sank into it gratefully.

"But how . . . ?" I sputtered. "What happened? Where was he?"

Young's lips thinned into a straight line. "O'Malley warned me you would ask a lot of questions."

So much for my clean slate.

Grateful to think about something else for a moment, I said, "How is Detective O'Malley? I haven't seen him since last summer."

"He's enjoying the sunshine in Florida, and happy to be there. All in all, he's doing a whole lot better than your Santa Claus."

Just as I'd suspected, Detective Young was a man who knew how to focus. I took a deep breath and gathered myself together. Then I looked back and forth between the two men.

"Would somebody please tell me what happened?" I asked.

Mr. Hanover ceded the floor to the detective. Rather than telling the story, it appeared that the headmaster preferred to hear it again himself. Though you'd never know it to look at him, I was sure that Mr. Hanover was just as shaken by this unexpected news as I was.

"Half an hour ago, we received a call to nine-one-one," said Detective Young. "The caller said there was a man dressed like Santa Claus lying on the ground next to a car in Union Cemetery, and that he didn't appear to be breathing."

Union Cemetery was only about a mile away from Howard Academy on the other side of the Post Road. It was a small burial ground, containing mainly older graves dating from the nineteenth and early-twentieth centuries. This time of year, I would have expected the cemetery to be mostly deserted.

"Under the circumstances, the dispatcher thought at first that maybe we were being pranked," Young continued. "But unfortunately that wasn't the case. The officers who responded found just what the caller had described. EMTs arrived shortly thereafter and the man was pronounced dead at the scene."

"In the cemetery," I murmured. There was a certain irony there. I looked up and asked, "Do you know how he died?"

"It appears that he was hit by a taser at fairly close range and died as a result of that assault. We will know more after an autopsy has been performed. But right now we're guessing that the intent was to disable your Santa Claus, not to kill him."

"Why do you keep calling him *our* Santa Claus?" I asked. "This time of year, there are Santas everywhere. What makes you so sure that the man you found in Union Cemetery is the man that appeared at our bazaar?"

"I'm not yet certain of that," Detective Young replied. "But on the front seat of his car, the officers found a flyer for your Christmas bazaar with this address circled. It seemed logical to assume that this was where he'd been. And now that Mr. Hanover has informed me that your Santa Claus disappeared unexpectedly in the middle of the afternoon, I think we're on the right track."

"The man we hired was named Chris Tindall," said Mr. Hanover.

Young consulted his notes. "According to his driver's license, the man in the cemetery was Jerry Platt."

Mr. Hanover and I shared a look. It was hard to tell which one of us was more relieved.

"So that's good," I said. I braced my hands on the sides of the seat and stood up. "The man you found isn't our Santa Claus at all."

"I'd like to be sure." Detective Young pulled out his phone. "Do you mind if I show you a picture?"

"Is it horrible?" I asked.

"No, he just looks like he's sleeping."

Mr. Hanover walked over to join us. Together we looked at the screen. The man I saw there had closed eyes and slack features. He didn't appear familiar to me at all.

"Well?" Young asked after a long moment had passed and neither of us had spoken.

"I don't know," I said truthfully. "I never saw our Santa Claus's face."

Mr. Hanover shook his head as well.

The detective looked at us incredulously. "*Neither* of you saw him?"

"He was Santa Claus," I said with a shrug. "He had on a big, fluffy beard. And a red hat that came down low over his brow. I think his eyes might have been brown . . . maybe."

I looked at Mr. Hanover. He had nothing to add.

"Let me get this straight," said Detective Young. "You hired this guy to come to your school and interact with your children but you never bothered to meet with him ahead of time?"

"It's rather a long story," said Mr. Hanover.

The detective crossed his arms over his chest. "Go on."

The headmaster and I gave the detective a condensed version of the previous week's activities, beginning with the original Santa Claus who'd been hired well in advance and canceled at the last minute, and ending with the eleventh-hour phone call from Chris Tindall the previous morning.

"At that point, our choices were extremely limited," Mr. Hanover said. "Had we not agreed to hire Mr. Tindall, we would have had to give up on the idea of our Santa Claus and Pets Photo Booth."

"Pets?" Detective Young repeated. He regarded us with interest. "What kind of pets?"

"Whatever kind the kids wanted to bring," I said. "It was mostly dogs and cats. But we also had a ferret and a parrot. And one girl brought a pony."

"A *pony?*" Mr. Hanover swung his gaze my way. "I must have missed that."

"Don't worry," I told him. "Scooter was amazingly well-behaved. All the kids loved him."

"Wait a minute. Back up," Detective Young broke in. "There were *dogs* here with your Santa Claus?"

"Sure," I said. "That was the whole point. Kids brought their pets to have their pictures taken with Santa."

"Could be that explains something," the detective said thoughtfully.

"Yes?" Mr. Hanover lifted an inquiring brow.

"Along with the flyer for your bazaar, we also found a photograph on the front seat of Platt's car. It was a picture of a dog."

"What kind of dog?" The question popped out before I'd even had time to think. Aunt Peg would have been proud.

"Small . . . white . . . fuzzy looking," Young said vaguely. "You know, a dog."

My stomach dropped. "Damn," I muttered.

I walked back to the chair I'd recently vacated and sat down again. It was beginning to look like we might be there a while.

"What now?" asked Mr. Hanover.

"Kiltie," I said.

"What about Kiltie?"

"He's a West Highland White Terrier. He's small, and white, and fuzzy looking."

The headmaster made the connection. His face fell.

"A West Highland *what?*" asked Young.

I already had my phone out and was searching for a picture. Then it was my turn to tilt a screen the detective's way. "Like that?" I asked.

He squinted uncertainly. "Yeah, I guess that looks the same. I'm not much of a dog person. The little ones all look alike to me."

"Kiltie's a show dog," I said.

"Like Westminster?" Young asked. "My wife watches that on TV."

"Exactly like that."

"And that dog was here, at this school, earlier today?"

"He was," I confirmed. "His owner's daughter brought him to the bazaar to have his picture taken. He was here until sometime after lunch when he went missing."

"The dog had his picture taken," Young repeated, as if he wanted to be sure that he had his facts straight. "And that would have been with Santa Claus?"

"That's right."

"And then he disappeared?"

"Right again," I agreed unhappily.

Mr. Hanover had turned his back on our conversation. Once again, he was staring out his window. I'd known him long enough to realize that was a sure sign of his agitation.

"The same Santa Claus who's now lying dead in Union Cemetery?" said Detective Young.

I winced. "It's beginning to look that way."

Slowly Mr. Hanover turned around. "Why is it, Ms. Travis, that whenever I hope your information might simplify things it always ends up doing the opposite?"

I shrugged helplessly. There was no good answer to that.

"This Jerry Platt person," Mr. Hanover said to the detective, "who now appears to be the man we thought was Chris Tindall—who is he and why does he have two names?"

"Platt's a small-time crook who's pretty well-known to the authorities in Fairfield County. He's been in one kind of trouble or another since he was in high school, and it's not unusual for him to operate under different names."

"Small-time," I said. "What does that mean exactly?"

"Petty theft, criminal mischief, drunk and disorderly, things like that. Platt seemed to have an aversion to making an honest living, especially when he could find a way to get by outside the system. He didn't appear to be much of a thinker. If he was offered something that looked like an easy job, he usually took it."

"And this is the man whom we introduced to our students." Mr. Hanover closed his eyes. I thought I might have heard a small moan.

"Not your best choice," Young agreed. "Even under the circumstances."

"We didn't know," I said.

"Of course not," Mr. Hanover said briskly. "Had we been aware of Platt's background, we would have handled things very differently."

"The little dog that went missing," said Detective Young. "Who does it belong to?"

"A Howard Academy parent named Sondra McEvoy," the headmaster said. He didn't look pleased. "Will it be necessary for you to speak with her?"

"Possibly. I'd like to keep my options open. Can you get me her contact information?"

"You won't need it," I told him. "Sondra left the bazaar an hour ago. She was on her way to the police station to report that Kiltie was gone. And speaking of which . . ."

"What?" asked Detective Young.

"You found Platt's car and a picture of a Westie."

"That's correct."

"But no dog?"

"No," the detective replied. "But the car door was

open. If Platt had your missing pooch, he probably jumped out and ran away."

"Let me get this straight, Ms. Travis." Mr. Hanover's voice sounded like a low growl. "Are you implying that Kiltie didn't just wander off? That you think he might have been *dognapped?*"

Usually our headmaster is quicker on the uptake that that. With his job, he has to be. Now I suspected he'd known where I was heading all along even as he'd tried to deny it to himself.

"That's what it sounds like to me," I said.

"I've never heard of dognapping." Detective Young shook his head. "But petty theft fits the profile. It's the kind of criminal activity we'd expect from Jerry Platt."

"It's unlikely that Sondra McEvoy will think of Kiltie's disappearance as petty theft," I told him.

"What do you mean?"

"Kiltie is a very successful show dog."

The detective looked at me blankly. "Is that a good thing?"

"There are lots of people who would think so."

"With a name like Kiltie"—Young shrugged—"he doesn't sound like much. Those dogs on TV have fancy names."

"Kiltie has a fancy name, too," I assured him. "It's GCH Westglen Braveheart."

"Gee cee aitch," he repeated slowly, sounding out the letters. "Is that some kind of title?"

"It stands for Grand Champion. It means that Kiltie has beaten a lot of other good dogs over the course of his show career."

"At Westminster, right?"

He sounded so pleased with himself that I hated having to correct him.

"Westminster is just one dog show," I said. "There are hundreds of others held all around the country every year. Dogs like Kiltie compete in shows nearly every weekend. When they win, they pile up points toward year-end awards."

"Hundreds?" Young was surprised. "I thought there was just the one."

"Not even close. Westminster is the pinnacle of the sport in the U.S., and it's our most famous dog show. But you might want to think of it as the tip of a very large iceberg."

"So it sounds like this dog show thing must be a pretty big business."

"In some ways it is," I said. "There are a number of supporting industries where money can be made: professional handlers, photographers, advertising, things like that."

"And this Kiltie dog, when he wins at dog shows he rakes in a lot of money to pay for all that?"

"Well . . . no," I admitted. "Dog show exhibitors don't actually make any money. In fact, it's the opposite. Campaigning a top level dog can be incredibly expensive."

"So why do people do it?"

"Because they love it," I said simply.

Young didn't look impressed by my answer.

"Dog shows are fun, and exciting, and interesting on all sorts of different levels. Exhibitors love their dogs and they love the competition. And the satisfaction you feel when a good judge—a person whose opinion you really respect—says that your dog is the best one, that's what makes it all worthwhile."

I hadn't meant to give such an impassioned speech but the words had just come pouring out. The dog show world was stimulating, perplexing, and ever-fascinating.

I hoped my explanation had helped the two men begin to understand that.

No such luck.

Mr. Hanover, who'd been content to listen silently for the last several minutes, now glanced over at the detective with a dubious look on his face and said, "I guess it's like owning a boat."

"Yup." Young nodded. "If you have to try and explain the thrill, it's just not there."

Well, that put me in my place. Too bad Aunt Peg wasn't in the room. She would have made sure they felt the thrill. Or else.

"So with all that going on," said the detective, "how much is a dog like Kiltie worth?"

I thought for a moment, then went for the easy answer. "To Sondra McEvoy, I'd imagine he's priceless."

"How about to someone else? Jerry Platt, for example. What would he do with a dog like that?"

That was a tough question. It was also one I'd been pondering myself.

When Aunt Peg's stud dog was stolen, the thief's intent had been to substitute Beau for a lesser Standard Poodle and use him to revitalize his entire bloodline. In the intervening years, however, much had changed in the world of dog breeding and genetic research. Now the American Kennel Club did DNA testing, which would make such a switch impossible. So how *would* someone benefit from Kiltie's abduction?

"Maybe they'll hold him for ransom," I said. I was only half joking.

"A dog," Young said. His tone was flat.

I wondered if he'd been listening to anything I'd said.

"A show dog," I corrected.

"Maybe someone wanted to remove Kiltie from competition," Mr. Hanover said thoughtfully. Obviously *he'd* been paying attention. "A disgruntled competitor perhaps? Someone who might have been tired of losing to him—?"

Detective Young cleared his throat. "Excuse me," he said. "I think we're losing sight of the main objective here."

Not me. I thought we were right on point.

"The important question is why did Jerry Platt die this afternoon in Union Cemetery?" Young said firmly. "Your missing dog is, at best, an insignificant side issue."

I didn't agree. If Jerry Platt had left the Christmas bazaar with Kiltie in his possession, how could their two fates not be inextricably intertwined?

One look at the implacable expression on the detective's face was enough to stop me from mentioning that, however. I've learned from past experience that disagreeing with the police gets you nowhere. Cooperation is always a better tactic.

"Speaking of the cemetery," I said. "Who was the person that called nine-one-one? Did you talk to him?"

"The first officers to respond interviewed him and ran his ID. It all checked out. The guy was bringing a poinsettia to place on his grandmother's grave. He had no connection to the scene. All he did was happen upon it."

"Did the officers ask him if he'd seen anything unusual in the vicinity?"

I was wondering if the caller might have noticed a small, white dog running around. But obviously Detective Young's mind didn't work the same way mine did. He was done thinking about Kiltie.

"Aside from a dead Santa Claus, you mean?" he asked dryly.

"Yes." I lifted my chin. "Aside from that."

"I'm sure they did, Ms. Travis." The detective gave me a long look. Long enough that I began to wonder what else Detective O'Malley might have told him about me. "Let me assure you that we know how to do our jobs."

"Of course," I agreed.

"Thank you for coming by, Detective," Mr. Hanover said briskly. "Is there anything else we can do for you?"

"No, I have everything I need. At least for now. If you think of anything else I should know, you'll contact me, right?"

The headmaster and I both nodded.

Detective Young exited the office. He left the door ajar behind him. I rose from my chair and started to leave as well.

"A moment, Ms. Travis?"

Damn. I'd almost made a clean getaway. Now, unfortunately, I had no choice but to return and listen to what Mr. Hanover had to say.

I could think of several possibilities and none of them was good. Hopefully he wouldn't blame me for bringing trouble to his doorstep once again. Or lecture me on my inability to avoid being on hand whenever problems arose.

Then I gulped as another unwelcome thought struck me. Surely Mr. Hanover could see that none of this was my fault. I loved my job at Howard Academy. And I really hoped the headmaster wasn't about to fire me.

"Yes?" I said softly. Slowly I turned in place.

For an unbearably long moment, Mr. Hanover just stood and stared at me. I was holding my breath when he finally spoke.

"You will be careful, won't you?"

"Yes, sir," I replied.

"Good." His hand lifted and waved me on my way. "That's all."

Chapter 12

Late afternoon had turned into evening by the time I left Howard Academy and the rest of the night passed in a hazy blur. Kev and I were both tired enough after the long day to head to bed not long after dinner.

As I undressed and slipped into my pajamas, I filled Sam in on much of what had happened since we'd parted company earlier that afternoon. I could see that there were questions he wanted to ask but instead he tucked me into bed and turned off the light. Already half-asleep, I promised him a full explanation in the morning.

If I hadn't been so exhausted, I probably would have realized that Sam wouldn't be the only person who was eager for answers. No surprise that egregious omission was remedied by Aunt Peg herself. By the time I got up on Sunday morning, she was already there. In fact, she was letting herself in the front door when I came meandering down the stairs in search of coffee.

An icy blast of cold air accompanied Aunt Peg into

the house. Standing at the foot of the steps in my pajamas and bare feet, I wished I'd taken a minute to put on a robe. And maybe a pair of warm, fuzzy, slippers.

Then again, bearing in mind that it was just past seven A.M. I hadn't been expecting company. I'd intended to quickly run downstairs for a cup of coffee, then rejoin Kevin who was waiting for me in Sam's and my bed. He had one of his favorite books with him and we were going to read it together.

Now it looked as though that plan had been scrapped.

Aunt Peg pulled off her coat and scarf, stuffed her gloves inside her pockets, then handed the whole ball of winter clothing to me. Hands free, she knelt down to say hello to the pack of Poodles who'd come running to the door to welcome her. She spread her arms wide and gathered the mass of warm, wriggling bodies into them.

Note that I had yet to receive a similar greeting myself.

I opened the closet door and tossed her coat inside. With luck, it might have landed on a hook. I slammed the door shut and said, "That didn't take long."

Waiting for a reply, I crossed my arms over my chest for warmth. A Standard Poodle would have done the job admirably, but they were all clustered around our visitor. Even Faith, that traitor.

"*She gave you away,*" I muttered in Faith's direction. "Think about that. That's how I got you in the first place."

Finally Aunt Peg spared me a glance. "What are you mumbling about?"

"Nothing," I replied as she placed a hand on her raised knee and levered herself back up. "I didn't expect to see you here so early."

"It's not as if I had a choice." Peg paused and peered at my sleep-bleary face. "Goodness, you didn't think I was here on your account, did you? Certainly not. Sondra McEvoy called me."

Of course. I should have known.

"It's a sad day when I can't count on my own relatives to give me the breaking news firsthand."

"So it is," I agreed. Aunt Peg operates with the same relentless persistence of the Borg. I learned a long time ago that resistance is futile.

"But you can make up for that now," she said briskly. Peg gazed around the empty downstairs. From our vantage point in the hallway, she could see most of the rooms. "Where is everybody?"

"You do realize it's only seven-fifteen?" I said. "On a Sunday morning?"

"Certainly." Peg sniffed. "Otherwise I'd have been here sooner."

Twenty minutes earlier Sam would have been the one dealing with her, I thought wistfully. He'd come down to put the Poodles outside and start the coffeemaker. Then he'd dashed out front to bring in the Sunday *Times,* let the Poodles back in, and gone up to take a shower.

In fact, now that I thought about it, this was all Sam's fault. He was the one who'd left the front door unlocked. Otherwise Aunt Peg would have had to ring the doorbell and I could have pretended that I wasn't home. At least until the Poodles gave me away. That group of conniving canines was just one opposable thumb away from being able to open the front door themselves.

"Aren't you cold?" asked Aunt Peg.

"Yes," I replied. I wondered what had clued her in. Maybe it was the fact that my toes were turning blue.

"Then why aren't you dressed?"

"It's barely light out—" I began tersely.

"Aunt Peg's here!" Kevin shrieked from the landing at the top of the staircase.

Clearly he'd grown tired of waiting for me to return. Now his small face peered down at us through the spindles in the banister. Delighted by the prospect of an early-morning visitor, Kev came racing down to join us.

Aunt Peg scooped him up into her arms. "You're wearing pajamas, too," she said, tickling his footie-clad toes. "What's the matter with this family? Is nobody dressed in real clothes?"

"That would be me," Sam said, coming down the steps.

Freshly showered and shaved, he looked devastatingly handsome in a pair of dark jeans and a corduroy shirt. Not only that, but he was holding my robe and slippers in his hands. My hero, yet again. That was getting to be the theme of the season.

"Pancakes for breakfast," I said. If I didn't get this show moving toward the kitchen, I was never going to get my coffee. "Who's in?"

"Meeeee!" cried Kevin. When he began to wiggle in her arms, Aunt Peg leaned over and set him down carefully on the floor. Just like she would have done with a puppy.

"The first one's yours," I said to Kev. "But before that I need you to do something for me."

The toddler tipped his head to one side. "What that?"

"Go upstairs and get Davey, okay? Tell him it's time for breakfast."

"Time for pancakes," Kevin crowed. "Tar come with me."

The two of them scrambled up the steps. The rest of us headed for the kitchen. I poured two cups of coffee for Sam and me, and started the kettle for Aunt Peg's tea. While I got out a mixing bowl and the ingredients for the pancake batter, Sam heated up the griddle and set the table.

The first rays of the weak winter sun fell across the kitchen floor. Faith and Eve settled, side by side, in their path. Augie sat down next to Aunt Peg and rested his head in her lap. Automatically her fingers began to thread their way through the Poodle's long neck hair, checking for mats.

"Don't keep me in suspense," she said. "One of you had better tell me what happened yesterday at the Christmas bazaar."

"Not me," said Sam. "I only know the bare bones of the story. I want to hear the rest, too."

I took a deep breath and started at the beginning. "There was a photo booth at the bazaar where kids could bring their pets to get their pictures taken with Santa Claus."

"I *know* that," Aunt Peg said impatiently. "Skip ahead to something interesting."

"Like what?" I added the last of the ingredients to the bowl and began to stir. "Coco Lily getting loose? Kiltie disappearing? Our Santa Claus making a run for it? Chris Tindall turning into Jerry Platt and ending up dead in Union Cemetery? Where would you like me to begin? What did Sondra already tell you?"

"Not a single blessed thing about anybody dying," Aunt Peg replied in a shocked tone. "Who are Chris

Tindall and Jerry Platt? And what do they have to do with Kiltie's disappearance?"

"Chris and Jerry are apparently one and the same person," I said. "And he has everything to do with what happened."

Sam crossed the room and gently removed the bowl and the whisk from my hands. Abruptly I realized that I'd been whipping the batter into a lather. It was a good thing I'd promised Kevin the first batch of pancakes. He wouldn't know the difference if they turned out flat and rubbery.

Come to think of it, neither would the Poodles.

"I'll do that," said Sam. "You talk."

So I did.

It seemed like a good idea to get most of the story out of the way before the kids returned. I took my coffee mug and joined Aunt Peg at the table. She and Sam listened in silence as I quickly related the previous day's events.

By the time I was finished, the kettle was whistling, Sam was sliding the first batch of pancakes onto a plate, and Davey and Kevin had arrived to take their places at the kitchen table. I hopped up to fix Peg's tea and pour a couple of glasses of milk for the boys.

Usually when I'm trying to talk, Aunt Peg interrupts constantly. Her questions are good ones though, always incisive and to the point. And they usually help me to clarify my own thinking. So now, having rushed through the part about the dead Santa Claus in the cemetery—something I wouldn't have wanted to mention in front of the boys—I was ready to hear what she had to say.

"Well?" I prompted as I set the mug of Earl Grey tea down in front of her.

"Coco Lily." Aunt Peg sniffed. "What a ridiculous name for a dog."

Of course she would start with the canines. I'd have been disappointed by anything else.

"*Coco Lily!*" Kevin chortled, his mouth full of pancakes.

"Swallow first, then talk," I told him, then turned to Aunt Peg. "The name suits her. She's a Cockapoo."

Aunt Peg rolled her eyes. When it came to designer dogs—especially ones that were part Poodle—we shared the same opinion.

Sam had split the first serving of pancakes between the boys. Now the second batch came to Peg and me. We both dug in with gusto.

"Who does the Cockapoo belong to?" Aunt Peg asked after a minute.

"A sixth grader named Charlotte Levine. She's Poppy McEvoy's best friend. That was how the two dogs came to be crated together behind the raffle booth."

"While Sondra was busy selling raffle tickets," said Aunt Peg.

"Yes, but she wasn't sitting at the booth all day. For much of the afternoon she was making sales by walking around the auditorium."

"And leaving Kiltie unattended, apparently."

Sam joined at the table with his own plate of pancakes. I nudged the butter dish and the syrup in his direction, then got up to start the next batch. Davey and Aunt Peg were both looking like they were almost ready for seconds.

"That's no different than what everyone does at the shows," Sam pointed out. "We've done it ourselves. Nobody gives it a second thought."

Aunt Peg nodded, conceding the point.

"I'm guessing that Coco Lily was let loose to serve as a distraction," I said from beside the stove. "While Platt made his getaway with Kiltie."

"Or maybe Platt opened the wrong crate first by mistake," said Sam. "Once Coco Lily was out, it's not as though he was going to waste time chasing her down."

"What are you guys talking about?" asked Davey. Seated next to Kevin and trying to pilfer his little brother's pancakes, he hadn't been following the adult conversation. Now he tuned back in.

"A dog was stolen yesterday afternoon from the Christmas bazaar," I said.

Davey glanced at our dogs who were draped in various poses around the room. "A Poodle?"

"No, a West Highland White."

"Was it Kiltie?"

"Good guess." I looked at him in surprise. "How did you know that?"

Davey shrugged. "I saw him last week at the show when you were talking to Mrs. McEvoy. He's the only Westie I know."

"If you're only going to know one," said Aunt Peg, "that's the right one. That dog will be one of the favorites in the Terrier Group at Westminster."

I groaned softly under my breath. I hadn't thought I could feel worse about Kiltie's disappearance, but now I did.

I stacked the last batch of pancakes on a platter, and rejoined everyone at the table. As I sat back down, Aunt Peg looked at me pointedly. "So in case you hadn't thought about it, that means you have a deadline."

"Not me," I said. "Sondra. She's the one whose dog is missing."

"She's under the impression that that's your fault."

I choked on a bite of pancake.

Davey handed me his glass of milk across the table. Gratefully I took a long swallow.

"How does Sondra figure that?" Sam asked while I was incapacitated.

"Kiltie disappeared from Melanie's school, during her Christmas bazaar, when he was there for the express purpose of having his picture taken at her photo booth." Aunt Peg lifted a brow. "Need I go on?"

"What about personal responsibility?" asked Sam. "Sondra was the one who took Kiltie to the bazaar. She's also the one who arranged to have a crate there for him. I think she'd have a hard time arguing that the dog was ever in anyone else's custody other than her own."

"That may all be true," said Peg. "But Sondra doesn't want to think about things logically. All she knows is that her dog is missing and she's looking for someone to blame. She wants Kiltie back immediately, if not sooner."

"I can sympathize," I said. "In her place, I'd be worried sick."

Kevin's brow furrowed. "You sick?" he asked.

"No, honey." I reached over and patted his arm. "I'm fine."

"She told me last night that she plans to talk to her lawyer," Aunt Peg said ominously. "She intends to sue the school."

"Well, crap," I said.

"Indeed," Aunt Peg agreed. Howard Academy was her alma mater, too.

Sam shook his head. "That's nothing more than a nuisance suit. It won't get very far."

"Even so it will cost Howard Academy a lot of money," I said glumly. "There will be legal fees, and maybe a payout if the school settles."

"A quite substantial payout in that case," said Aunt Peg. "Sondra has set Kiltie's value at one hundred thousand dollars."

It was a good thing my mouth was empty. Otherwise I might have choked again.

"Seriously?" I gasped. Sam looked similarly shocked.

"In the right circles, Kiltie is quite famous," Aunt Peg pointed out.

"Even so," I said. "There's no way that dog can be worth that much money."

"Mrs. McEvoy can ask for whatever she wants," Davey piped up. "It doesn't mean that the judge will give it to her."

I looked at him in surprise. "How do you know that?"

"I watch *Judge Judy.*"

"You *do?*" That was news. "When?"

"Sometimes in the afternoons after school. When I'm bored."

I smothered a frown. The things a mother doesn't know.

"You'll go talk to Sondra," Aunt Peg said firmly.

It wasn't a question. And I'd been around this block enough times in the past to know that Aunt Peg's request had the ring of inevitability.

"I suppose I can do that," I said.

"Today?"

Though he tried to hide his chagrin, Davey's face fell. Beside him, Kevin jutted out his lower lip. Both knew that we'd made other plans.

I reached over and ruffled Kevin's hair. There was no way that I was disappointing those two. "No, not today," I told Aunt Peg. "We'll be busy."

Unaccustomed to having her schemes thwarted, Peg's tone was frosty. "Doing what, might I ask?"

"We're going Christmas tree shopping," Davey informed her.

"Christmas tree!" Kev echoed.

"Pish," said Aunt Peg. "How long can that take?"

"You try shopping with a two-and-a-half-year-old," I told her. "See how long it takes you."

"Then we have to set up the tree and trim it," said Sam. He and I had hardly seen each other over the last week. The boys weren't the only ones who were looking forward to a family outing. "I'm pretty sure that will be an all-day project."

"Maybe even longer than that," Davey added cheerfully. Twelve years old, he was already wise to his aunt's manipulative ways. "Maybe Mom can find some time for you next week."

Aunt Peg straightened her shoulders and glared around the table. By her estimation, this was mutiny in the ranks.

The four of us gazed complacently back. I even managed a small smile. It felt good to be on the winning side for a change.

"You people," she announced, "are ganging up on me."

You people. Did you catch that? She'd demoted us from family. Too bad it wouldn't last.

"No," I said easily. "We're just acquainting you with our schedule."

"Then I shall get out of your way and let you get on

with your busy day." Aunt Peg pushed back her chair and stood.

"Bye-bye!" Kevin trilled. He lifted his hand in a cheery wave. That child needs some work on his social cues.

Aunt Peg stalked from the room. Her departure was so sudden that even the Poodles were caught by surprise.

I got up and hurried after her. Just as she had known I would.

Fortunately I reached the closet first. That saved me the ignominy of having Aunt Peg find her coat on the floor. I picked it and shook it out before handing it over.

Peg retrieved her scarf from inside the sleeve and wound it around her neck. "I told lots of exhibitors about your bazaar last week in Springfield," she said. "Did any of them show up?"

"Quite a few. You did a great job. The bazaar was a big success."

"Were any of them terrier people?"

I thought back, remembering that Sondra had singled out several exhibitors. "Jo Drummer was there. Sondra said that she has Border Terriers. And maybe a guy named Chip Michaels?"

"Skyes," Aunt Peg said thoughtfully.

There's no point in asking how she does it. Aunt Peg knows everybody.

"And Sondra pointed them out to you?"

I nodded. "It was after we discovered that Kiltie was gone. She said that those two would laugh about her misfortune if they knew."

Aunt Peg pulled on her coat. "Sondra might be right

about that. You should talk to Jo and Chip. Maybe they know something."

"You don't have a very high opinion of your fellow exhibitors," I said.

"Oh please," she replied. "It has nothing to do with my *opinion*. I'm a realist."

Aunt Peg always manages to have the last word.

Chapter 13

After breakfast, we all piled into Sam's SUV and went looking for the perfect Christmas tree. Davey wanted to bring Augie with us. I decided that meant Faith could come, too. The result of that decision was that Davey and I spent more time talking to other shoppers about our "giant" Poodles and Augie's funny trim than we did looking at Christmas trees.

Fortunately the other two members of the family had the process well in hand. Sam's approach to tree selection meant engaging in a serious debate with the tree salesman over the merits of Scotch Pine versus Blue Spruce. Kevin simply raced around the large lot, pointing at every tree that was taller than he was and yelling, "That one!"

Apparently, my younger son is not a connoisseur.

"Look, Mommy, that dog is wearing Christmas ornaments in its hair!" I turned and saw a little girl pointing at Augie across the lot.

"Those aren't ornaments," her mother replied firmly. "They're earrings."

I smiled and led Faith their way. "What you're seeing is colored wrapping paper," I told them. "It's banded around Augie's ear hair to protect it and keep it out of his way."

The woman frowned. "Wouldn't it just be easier to cut it off?"

"Sure. But then he couldn't be a show dog."

The little girl looked at Faith and reached out a tentative hand. "Can I touch?"

"Faith would like that," I said, "She's very friendly."

Faith stood like a statue as the small fingers touched the smooth, plush hair on the side of her neck. The girl giggled softly. Faith's tail began to wag.

"She likes you," I said.

Bolder now, the child moved in closer. "I like her, too," she said happily. "Maybe Santa Claus will bring me a puppy for Christmas."

"I don't think so," her mother said quickly. "I think Santa Claus knows that we live in an apartment."

Luckily Sam chose that moment to call me over to check out a tree. I grabbed Faith and we made our escape.

The tree in question was medium sized and densely packed with branches. Sam spun the Blue Spruce around on its trunk so I could see what it looked like from all sides. With three votes already in favor, I figured my opinion was superfluous but I gave the tree an enthusiastic thumbs-up anyway. While I settled the bill, Sam and the boys fastened the evergreen to the top of the SUV.

Faith took that maneuver in stride. This was her sixth holiday season. She'd seen it all before.

Augie, however, was obviously perplexed. The previous Christmas, he'd been living in a kennel where he'd been exposed to a great deal less mayhem than was considered normal in the three-ring circus that was my family. Now he stood beside the SUV, staring upward and barking ferociously.

"It's the same tree that was right down here a minute ago," Davey said patiently. "You didn't mind it then. So what's the problem now?"

"Wait until we bring the tree into the house," I said. "He probably won't like that either."

Luckily Augie, like all Poodles, was a quick learner. Or maybe Faith had a quiet talk with him while we were riding home in the car. But by the time we'd gotten the Christmas tree situated in a corner of the living room, the big Poodle had decided to stop protesting. Instead he threw himself into the remaining festivities with all the joyous abandon that was typical of his breed.

Sam strung the lights. Davey placed the star on top. Kevin hung all the ornaments he could get his hands on at his own eye level. When we were finished decorating, our tree looked a little bottom heavy. And somehow all six Poodles had ended up with tinsel in their hair. But when I plugged in the lights, and we all stepped back to have a look, the effect was magical.

"Santa come tonight?" Kevin asked hopefully.

"No," I told him. "Not for two more weeks."

Davey took his brother's hands in his own to illustrate. "More days than all of your fingers," he said.

Kev looked down at his digits and sighed. "Long time."

From his point of view, I knew the wait seemed endless. From mine, I could only hope that I'd have enough time to get everything that was on my to-do lists done before the holiday arrived.

Monday morning, I got to school early. Stashing Faith in my room with an extra large peanut butter biscuit, I hurried over to the main building to see Mr. Hanover. Even though there was still half an hour before the first bell would ring, Harriet was already seated at her desk outside the headmaster's office.

"Is he in?" I asked in a hushed one. Joshua Howard's imposing front hall always has that effect on me.

"Since seven-thirty. He's on his third cup of coffee." Harriet didn't look pleased. "That's a new record."

Not the most promising start to the day.

"Did you find the little dog yet?" asked Harriet.

"Not that I've heard. I'm planning to talk to his owner this afternoon and see what else we can do."

"Ahem."

I looked up. The headmaster was standing in his doorway. I guessed the whispering hadn't helped.

Mr. Hanover lifted a brow. "Are you here for me?"

I nodded.

"Come."

It was a command, not a request. I scurried into the office. Mr. Hanover shut the door softly behind us.

"I hope you've brought good news," he said.

"Not exactly."

The headmaster took his seat behind his desk. "Be more precise, Ms. Travis."

"Unfortunately I don't have any news at all," I told him. "But I do have a couple of questions."

"Questions with regard to the weekend's lamentable occurrences, I assume?"

Was it just me or did the man sound like a thesaurus when he spoke?

I replied in words of one syllable. "Yes, that's right."

"Before we begin, I feel compelled to point something out."

"Yes?"

If he was about to tell me that Detective Young had already solved Jerry Platt's murder, I was going to jump up and down with glee. Right there in the headmaster's office. Decorum be damned.

"As you might imagine," Mr. Hanover began, "I devoted quite a bit of time yesterday to pondering Saturday's unfortunate events. You probably did the same."

A nod seemed required. I was happy to supply one. There was no way I was going to admit that I'd devoted a large chunk of the previous day to something as frivolous as selecting and trimming a Christmas tree.

"And I came to the realization that only twice in Howard Academy's long and illustrious history has even a whiff of scandal been permitted to cross our doorstep."

I winced slightly. It wasn't hard to see where this was going.

"Would you like to know what the common link was on both of those occasions?"

"Not really," I said softly.

"I shall tell you anyway. It was you, Ms. Travis."

I started to reply. Mr. Hanover held up a hand. My mouth snapped shut. It wasn't as if I'd had a good excuse.

"Before you speak," he said, "let me just say that I am mindful of the reality that we live in. In my position, one cannot afford to be an isolationist. Nor to stick one's head in the sand. No matter how attractive that alternative might seem on occasion."

"Yes," I said. I knew the feeling.

"A long time ago, I came to terms with the fact that one cannot live one's life in fear of the possibilities. As a thoughtful man, I must also accept that the world around us is ever evolving, perhaps more quickly now than at any previous time in history. It is our job as educators to adapt to those changes. And to deal with them as best we can."

"Yes, sir," I murmured.

Mr. Hanover's third cup of caffeine seemed to have rendered him quite philosophical. I wondered if we were still talking about me. Not that I was about to ask.

"Bearing all those things in mind," he said. "I have decided to be grateful."

I looked up. "Grateful?"

"As bad as these current events appear to us now, they could have been much worse. Nobody brought a gun into our school and started shooting."

"Certainly not," I agreed vehemently.

"We don't have drugs on campus, nor an epidemic of student suicides. There are no naked pictures on the Internet, nor instances of alcohol-fueled wild behavior. Our children remain safe, do they not?"

"Yes, they do," I replied. Compared to those potential problems, the thought of a missing dog suddenly seemed less terrible than it had.

"Quite so." Mr. Hanover nodded. "And that is what I will choose to focus on as we go forward. The only lamentable lapse in judgment was my own. Obviously a man of Jerry Platt's caliber should never have been allowed to come to this school, and I deeply regret that error on my part."

"That's very commendable," I said quietly.

"We will deal with this situation and then put it swiftly behind us," Mr. Hanover stated. "And now we begin to do just that. I believe you had some questions for me?"

I expelled a long breath. "Yes, I do."

The headmaster steepled his fingers in front of his chin. "Go on."

"You were the one who hired Jerry Platt to appear at the bazaar," I said. "I'd like to know more about how that came about."

"I'm sure you recall the circumstance. We were in a bind and Jerry Platt—then known to me as Chris Tindall—volunteered to fill in."

"He called you?" I asked.

"Yes, that's correct."

"Did you happen to ask him *why* he had called you? Thinking back now, I'm wondering how he knew that Howard Academy was looking for a Santa Claus."

Behind his glasses, Mr. Hanover's eyes widened. "Frankly the thought never crossed my mind. We needed a Santa Claus and suddenly one appeared. I was in no position to look a gift horse in the mouth, Ms. Travis."

"I realize that," I said. "But in light of everything that's happened since, doesn't it seem like a huge coincidence that our previous Santa Claus backed out of his commitment at precisely the same time that Jerry Platt—who clearly had an ulterior motive for his presence at the bazaar—called and offered his services?"

"Put that way, it does indeed," Mr. Hanover conceded. "It sounds as though you believe that Mr. Platt had something to do with our original Santa's abrupt defection."

"That would be my guess."

"Do you think he knew what Jerry Platt was up to?"

I shrugged. I had no idea.

"I'd like the opportunity to ask him," I said. "Sondra McEvoy has approached my aunt."

"Ah, yes." Mr. Hanover permitted himself a small smile. As Aunt Peg was one of the school's benefactors, she and the headmaster were well acquainted. "The inimitable Margaret Turnbull."

"Aunt Peg wants me to see what I can do to get Kiltie back."

"Mrs. McEvoy is quite distressed by the loss of her dog," Mr. Hanover said solemnly. "And by extension, so are we. The McEvoy family does not deal lightly with adversity. We have heard from their lawyer."

"Already?" I gulped.

The headmaster waved away my concern. "So far, it's only a preliminary overture. But as you might imagine we, too, are anxious for Kiltie to be located and returned to the warm and caring bosom of his family."

"Have you heard anything more from Detective Young?" I asked.

"No, and I cannot say that I'm distressed by that. I'm sure the police are continuing their investigation into Mr. Platt's demise. However I would hope that after questioning us on Saturday, Detective Young concluded Howard Academy's part in their inquiry."

"I agree," I said. "But it occurs to me that they might be as interested as I am in talking to our original Santa Claus. Maybe he knows something that would help the police in their investigation."

Mr. Hanover nodded. "I'll make sure that your thoughts on that subject are passed along." He reached out and touched the intercom button on his phone. "Harriet, would you bring me the information for the first Santa Claus that was hired to appear at the Christmas bazaar? Yes, the one who canceled his engage-ment rather precipitously."

I would have expected it to take a few minutes for Harriet to locate and copy down the necessary details. In half that time, the secretary was letting herself into Mr. Hanover's office. She carried a small sheet of paper in her hands. Either Harriet is amazingly organized or—as I've long suspected—she has the headmaster's office bugged.

Mr. Hanover took the paper from her, glanced at the paper briefly, then handed it to me.

"Hal Romero," I read, scanning the address and phone number I'd been given. "He lives in Glenville." I folded the note and put it in my pocket. "I'll stop by and talk to him tomorrow."

"I'll be interested to hear what you learn."

"So will I," I said.

My morning classes flew by. At lunch, it seemed as though all everybody wanted to talk about was the Christmas bazaar and what a huge success it had been. Mostly I sat in silence and let the conversation eddy around me.

The other staff members knew only that the event had drawn huge crowds and received enthusiastic re-views from shoppers and school parents alike. They weren't yet aware of how badly things had gone awry late in the day.

Jerry Platt's death had been reported in the Sunday edition of the local newspaper. The article had called the circumstances surrounding the petty thief's demise suspicious, but had not revealed that he'd died while dressed in a Santa suit. Apparently none of the other teachers had made the connection between the body found in Union Cemetery and the flight of our runaway St. Nick. Grateful not to have to deal with a barrage of questions, I had no intention of spreading the unfortunate news.

Though I had a good look around the dining room, I didn't see Poppy McEvoy anywhere. Later, her absence from school that day resulted in the cancelation of my last period tutoring session. That enabled me to grab Faith and skip out early.

The Standard Poodle seemed to sense that we were playing hooky as she and I ducked out the back door that led to the parking lot. Often I take her for a walk around Howard Academy's spacious grounds when the school day is over. That afternoon, I handed Faith straight into the car.

We coasted quickly down the driveway and out through the stone gateposts. As we made our getaway, I let out a delighted whoop. Faith hopped up and barked in reply.

Even though I'm all grown up, the thrill of skipping school never gets old.

Chapter 14

The McEvoys lived in Deer Park, a scenic mid-Greenwich neighborhood just ten minutes from school. I called Sondra from the road and asked if I could stop by.

"It took you long enough to get around to me," she said petulantly.

Sondra and Aunt Peg were two of a kind. Both were strong-willed women, accustomed to having people jump to do their bidding. And neither was above riding roughshod over anyone who didn't.

"But I'm on my way now," I replied.

"I'll be waiting."

Her tone conjured up a vision of fingers drumming on a tabletop. As if she'd spent the last day and a half waiting for me to appear. Seriously, how did other mothers do it? I wondered. Was I the only one whose life seemed to be consumed by the holiday season?

The McEvoys lived in a large, neoclassic-style home on a spacious, wooded, corner lot. Gravel crunched beneath the Volvo's tires as we approached the house. Before I'd even turned off the car, Faith was already on her feet and ready to go. She's always happy to participate in an adventure, and it's rare that I leave her to wait for me in the car. But Sondra obviously had dogs of her own and she'd already sounded prickly during our short conversation on the phone. I didn't want to risk upsetting things further by showing up with an uninvited canine visitor.

I told Faith she had to stay put and assured her that I'd be back soon. Then I locked the car and turned to gaze up the wide stone steps that led to the home's portico. To my surprise, I saw that the front door was already open. Hands propped on her hips, her stance radiating impatience, Sondra was waiting for me in the doorway.

I wondered if she'd been waiting there since she'd hung up the phone.

Sondra looked past me into the car. "Is that one of Peg's Standard Poodles?"

"Aunt Peg bred her," I said. "She's been mine since she was a puppy."

"Well, don't leave her sitting out there in the cold. Bring her inside."

I certainly wasn't about to turn down that invitation. Nor was Faith. As soon as I opened the car door, she jumped out and scampered past me. Trotting up the home's wide steps, the Standard Poodle easily beat me to the top.

"Hello, pretty girl." Sondra bent down to greet Faith before acknowledging me. Among dog people, that's pretty much the norm.

"Her name is Faith," I said.

As the three of us entered the house, I unbuttoned my coat. It was whisked from my hands almost before

I had it off. The maid's approach had been so silent I hadn't even heard her coming. Coat in hand, she disappeared just as quietly.

"Faith," Sondra repeated. "I like that. Did you show her?"

"Yes, she was my first. She's a champion, although it took us a while to get there."

"Owner handled?"

"Of course," I said with a laugh. "Aunt Peg wouldn't have allowed me to do it any other way."

"I'm sure you're right," Sondra agreed. "Come this way. We'll talk in the library."

Faith and I followed her across the hall. The room we entered was bright and sunny and lined with shelves. Though Sondra had called it a library, there were very few books in evidence. Instead the shelves held a vast collection of framed win pictures from dog shows. Many had Group and Best in Show rosettes displayed beside them.

Most of the photographs in the front of the room appeared to be of Kiltie. Farther back, other pictures highlighted earlier generations of Westglen West Highland Whites. In every photograph, Sondra posed proudly beside her small white terrier and smiled for the judge and the photographer.

All those pictures of Sondra with her dogs, I thought, and I had yet to see a single Westie in the house. It seemed decidedly odd. At least that explained why Sondra had allowed Faith to come inside. Apparently there weren't any other dogs in residence who might object to her presence.

I sat down in a leather chair and was immediately swallowed into its soft, pliant depths. Beside me, Faith turned a small circle and lay down on the carpet. She looked happier about her choice than I was about mine. I was half tempted to join her on the floor.

"Sorry," Sondra said, watching me struggle to regain my balance. "That was my husband's favorite chair. I've been meaning to get it replaced."

"It's very comfortable," I said politely.

"It should be." Her voice sharpened. "That's Jim all over. He likes everything around him to be comfortable."

I was probably supposed to be reading between the lines, I thought. And possibly even offering a sympathetic ear. But that wasn't why I'd come. Sondra could grouse about her marital difficulties on her own time. I was there to talk about Kiltie.

"Your show pictures are wonderful," I said. "But where are your dogs?"

"Outside in the kennel." Sondra lifted a hand and waved toward a wide picture window in the back of the room. "You can see it from there."

Any excuse to get out of that chair. I levered myself up and went to have a look.

The McEvoys' backyard was expansive and beautifully landscaped. A flagstone patio bordered by a low stone wall, led from the back of the house to a kidney-shaped swimming pool, now closed and covered for the winter. Beyond the pool was a medium-sized building whose architectural style matched that of the house.

"Jim didn't like having the dogs underfoot," Sondra said with a sigh. She came over to stand beside me. "After a while we both got tired of fighting about it and it just seemed easier just to move them out there."

And yet, I thought, Sondra had told me that she and

Jim were separated. So why were the Westies still living in the kennel?

"Jim loved that pool," she mused, gazing out over the yard. "It was probably the main reason why we bought this house."

"Are you a swimmer, too?" I asked.

"Hardly." Sondra laughed. "I hate to swim. Which is why it gave me such pleasure to take over the pool house and convert it into a kennel."

Ouch. I sneaked a peek at Sondra out of the corner of my eye. Clearly Kiltie's owner was not a happy woman.

"I put in every luxury and amenity I could think of," she said. "I'm sure the dogs are happier out there than they ever were in here."

Interesting notion. My Poodles don't care about luxury. They just like to be wherever I am.

"How many Westies do you have?" I asked.

"Five, including Kiltie." Sondra nailed me with a hard stare. "When he's here."

So much for chitchat. Apparently it was time to get down to business. I was more than ready for that.

I turned away from the window, walked back into the room, and chose a different seat. Faith lifted her head and stared at me reproachfully. After a few seconds, she got up and walked over to where I was now sitting, repositioning herself back at my side before lying down again.

I reached down and gave Faith a pat. Then I turned back to Sondra. "It's been almost forty-eight hours since Kiltie disappeared. What's happened since the last time we spoke?"

"As you might imagine, I've been busy," she told me.

"I alerted the animal hospitals and shelters. I called the grooming shops and pet supply stores. I posted flyers everywhere I could think they might do some good. There's even a doggie daycare facility in Stamford. Did you know that?"

"Yes," I said. "I've been there. What about online?"

"I have Kiltie's picture and information prominently displayed on several pet finder sites. Also Facebook, Twitter, and Instagram."

Sondra had covered a lot of bases very quickly. There was one thing, however, that she hadn't mentioned.

"And you also spoke to the police, right?"

"Twice, actually." Sondra gave me a look I couldn't quite decipher.

"You went to the police station on Saturday," I said slowly. "Right?"

"I did indeed. It probably won't surprise you to hear that the desk sergeant wasn't terribly interested in my 'missing pet.' Peg told me that she once had a similar experience with the authorities herself. I had every intention of having my lawyer raise holy hell until— much to my surprise—a detective showed up here yesterday afternoon with some rather startling information."

"Detective Young?" I asked.

"That's the one. Of all things, he wanted to ask me what I knew about your Santa Claus. The one you hired to appear at the Howard Academy Christmas Bazaar."

Damn it, I thought. The denial was swift and automatic. Platt hadn't been *my* Santa Claus.

"I'd read in the paper that there'd been a death in Union Cemetery," Sondra continued. "But it never crossed my mind to connect that story with Kiltie's disappearance. Not until Detective Young told me that Platt had spent the early part of the day at the bazaar *and* that he had a picture of a dog that looked like Kiltie in his car when he was killed."

"His information adds a whole new wrinkle to the story," I admitted.

"Of course it does," Sondra snapped. "I thought the fact that Kiltie got away was an accident. That *someone* hadn't been careful enough to fasten his crate properly."

She didn't have to name names. We both knew whom Sondra was talking about.

"But now I have to wonder if something else entirely happened."

"It seems to be a possibility," I said. "But I don't get it. *If* Kiltie was taken from the bazaar deliberately . . . why would someone do that?"

Sondra stared at me across the room. "How many reasons would you like?"

"As many as you have," I said mildly.

"You know who Kiltie is, right?"

"Sure. GCH Westglen Braveheart." I motioned toward the wall of pictures and awards. "Top dog."

"You're being flippant," Sondra accused.

"No, I'm being honest."

She wasn't appeased. "You're supposed to be a dog lover, too. I thought that you, of all people, would understand."

"*Supposed* to be?" I echoed. Now I was growing annoyed.

"Sorry, I didn't mean that." Sondra paused and sucked in a breath. Her lower lip began to tremble. "It's just that . . . you have no *idea* . . ."

"I think I do," I replied quietly. "I know how attached you are to Kiltie. I feel the same way about Faith."

Hearing her name, the Poodle lifted her head and cocked an ear in my direction. I slipped my hand down and scratched beneath her chin.

"If I didn't know where Faith was, or what was happening to her," I said, "I would be frantic with worry."

"I feel as if my whole world is crumbling." Sondra sighed. "And I don't know how to stop it from happening."

"You take it one step at a time. You've already made a great start. In a short amount of time, you've done a whole lot of things right."

She shook her head unhappily. "If Kiltie is lost, maybe those things will help. But if he was taken deliberately, nothing I've done will make the slightest bit of difference."

"You don't know that. Maybe whoever has him will turn him in to collect the reward."

"Don't be naïve," said Sondra. "The reward is a pittance compared to what he's actually worth."

"Yes, but—"

"You still don't get it."

"Get what?" I asked. The annoyance was back.

"You with your cute Standard Poodle that took a long time to finish." Sondra flicked her fingers dismissively in Faith's direction. "You don't understand what it's like when a dog like Kiltie comes along. A dog that's truly important, one that has an actual *career*."

Over the years, Aunt Peg had had a number of very good dogs. Tar, with Sam handling, had been a multi Best in Show winner. Maybe I'd never shown at Westminster myself, but I could well imagine the experience—and the dedication and talent it would take to get there. I didn't have Sondra's longevity in the dog show world, but I wasn't the uneducated newbie she assumed me to be either.

Sondra rested her head on the back of her chair. Suddenly she looked exhausted. "Having Kiltie gone right now? The timing couldn't be worse. This ruins everything."

"Is it because of points?" I asked. "Or year-end standings?"

"No, those are already sewn up."

"Then what?"

A minute passed before Sondra answered my question. Long enough for me to think that she wasn't planning to do so at all.

"I've been fielding a couple of offers," she said finally.

That came as a surprise.

"You were thinking about selling Kiltie?" I asked.

"No, not selling. At least not entirely. I'm going to form a syndicate, and take on a couple of partners. Kiltie is young for a dog who's already had this much success. Next year he'll be fully mature and at the top of his game, and I want to pull out all the stops. Kiltie deserves a shot at the big time and I intend to give it to him."

"I thought you already had," I said.

"This?" Sondra's gaze slid around the library, taking in the visible reminders of her success. "Sure, this is great—for an owner-handler with a family and other obligations. It's an enviable local record, considering that I can't travel all over the country and make sure that Kiltie gets to all the biggest shows."

Specialing a dog—competing with a finished champion in the Group and Best in Show rings—was a huge commitment, one that involved a significant outlay of both time and money on the part of the dog's owner. Single-minded focus on the final prize helped, too. In recent years, there had been very few owner-handlers who had managed to take a dog all the way to the top.

Sondra stood. She began to pace around the room. "This may look like a lot to you," she said, "but for a dog of Kiltie's caliber, it's only the beginning. There's so much more he can accomplish. He deserves to have backers with clout of their own. And a top professional handler. Someone like Todd."

Todd. The name seemed to hang in the air between us. I imagine it glittering with all the gaudy sparkle of a neon sign.

Todd Greenleaf was the rock star of the dog show world. A man so well known in the canine community, so well respected as a fierce and tireless competitor, that he went by just one name, like Madonna or Britney.

Todd's prices were sky-high, but his results more than justified the expense. He was offered many more dogs than he could possibly add to his illustrious string. I'd heard that there was a six-month waiting list to engage his services. Exhibitors vied just to get their dogs in line.

"You're giving Kiltie to *Todd?*" I said in a hushed tone.

"That's right. He's going out with him just after the first of the year. It's a done deal. We've already set up a huge advertising blitz to announce our new association. Once Todd and Kiltie start winning, I'll be able to reel in any partners I want. The only thing I had left to do was to break the news to Poppy. I'm going to tell her over Christmas break."

Abruptly I felt my stomach lurch. *Poppy.* I'd forgotten all about her. And it sounded as though Sondra had, too. Or at least that she'd neglected to factor her daughter's feelings into her grand plans. Poppy and I had discussed Kiltie on numerous occasions. She didn't see the little terrier as a top show competitor, but rather as a beloved pet and a treasured part of her family.

How could Sondra have overlooked such an important part of the equation? I wondered. She had to know that sending Kiltie out for a career with Todd would mean putting the dog on the road for the next twelve months. Or possibly even longer.

"Oh no," I said on a softly exhaled breath. "Poppy will be devastated."

Sondra looked over sharply. "She'll deal with it."

Her dismissive tone stung. "Yes, but—"

"It won't be forever. Just until Kiltie's had a chance to leave his mark on the record books. Poppy's a big girl. She'll understand how things have to be. She's known all along that Kiltie was special."

Yes, she had, I thought sadly. Except that Poppy's definition of special had been very different from her mother's.

"Speaking of Poppy, is she all right?" I asked. "She wasn't at school today."

"She's fine. As you can imagine, she had an upsetting weekend. I told her it was okay if she wanted to take the day off."

Brooding about Kiltie's disappearance wasn't going to help, I thought. Poppy would have been better off at school, surrounded by her friends, and keeping herself busy.

"Don't worry. I'll make sure she's back at school tomorrow." Sondra gazed at me from across the room. "And in return, you will find my missing dog for me."

I might have argued the inequality of that quid pro quo but, really, what was the point? Considering the conversations I'd had with Aunt Peg and Mr. Hanover, and now with Sondra, I was pretty sure that my searching for Kiltie's whereabouts was already a foregone conclusion.

"I'll take a look around and ask some questions," I said.

"Of course you will," Sondra replied. She strode toward the door.

Having served my purpose, I was clearly being dismissed. Faith and I hopped up together and followed.

The maid was waiting in the front hall with my coat. I wondered how she'd known we were coming. Surely she hadn't been standing there for the entire half hour that Sondra and I had been closeted in the library? Maybe the whole world was bugged and I was the only one who didn't know about it.

"I need Kiltie back no later than the end of December," Sondra told me firmly. Perhaps she felt she hadn't yet given me enough instructions. "Talk to the other exhibitors. Find out which one of those lowlifes snatched my dog and who I have to pay to get him back."

Faith scooted through the door as soon as the maid opened it. I followed her without stopping to look back. My Poodle and I were both happy to make an escape.

Chapter 15

Dressing a child to go outside in midwinter, especially a child who doesn't like wearing clothes in the first place, is a chore. First you have to locate the jacket, the mittens, and the boots. Then you have to wrestle them onto wiggling arms and legs. Finally you have to hope that in the time it takes you to put on your own coat and pick up your purse, phone, and car keys, the boots haven't been kicked off and the mittens aren't already on the floor.

Tuesday morning, the Standard Poodles sat in the kitchen and watched the dress-the-toddler show with interest and amusement. I didn't have school on Tuesdays and Thursdays, and Kevin and I were due in downtown Stamford for a Gymboree class at ten. Unfortunately we were running late.

Kev loves Gymboree. He participates eagerly in the singing, the dancing, and the games. Plus he gets to hang out with kids his own age. From his point of view it's a win/win. So I've never understood why it's so difficult to get him out the door on time.

"Tar come with us," Kevin announced as I set him down beside the door that led to the garage and grabbed my own coat out of the hall closet.

Tar pricked his ears. That silly dog doesn't know much, but he recognized an invitation when he heard one.

So did the other Poodles. They figured that if Tar was getting to go for a ride in the car, they should, too. So now they all came scrambling over to join us. Within seconds, I had six Standard Poodles jostling for position next to the door.

Somewhere in the midst of that rambunctious group was the little instigator. I knew Kevin was fine. I could see his red knit cap bobbing up and down among the dark bodies in what looked like my very own canine/toddler mosh pit.

"Sorry, guys, you're not going," I said firmly.

"Not going?" Kev wriggled his way to the edge of the group. Quickly he started to unzip his jacket so he could yank it off.

"Not you. I was talking to the Poodles." Reaching out a hand, I grabbed him while I had the chance. "You're coming with me to Gymboree. But the rest of you"—I swept my gaze around the Poodle-packed hallway—". . . are staying here."

Six pomponned tails drooped. Six pairs of dark eyes regarded me with desolation. As if the communal canine disappointment was simply too much to bear.

"*Really?*" I sighed.

"Really," Kevin agreed happily. He likes to echo what people say, even when he doesn't have a clue

what it means. I am hoping he outgrows that trait before he's old enough for it to get him into trouble.

I bent down and swept the toddler up into my arms.
Then I ran to the pantry and handed out six peanut butter biscuits. My car keys were in my pocket; my purse
was over my shoulder. While the Poodles were busy
munching, Kev and I slipped out the door and made a
run for it.

By the time class was finished an hour later, Kevin
was pleasantly drowsy and I was feeling energized.
Thanks to MapQuest, I had directions to the address Mr.
Hanover had given me the day before on the seat beside
me. It seemed like a perfect time to pay Hal Romero a
visit and find out what he might have known about our
last-minute Santa switch.

Glenville is a small, historic, neighborhood that was
originally a mill town on the western edge of Greenwich. Even as everything has grown around it, the area
still manages to maintain much of its quaint village
charm. I followed the directions to a quiet street not far
from the fire station.

Hal Romero lived in a narrow, two-storey, house
that looked as though it dated from the middle of the
previous century. The dwelling had originally been a
single-family home, but now it was subdivided into
several, smaller apartments. A gaudy plastic Christmas
wreath adorned the house's front door. Strings of mul-
ticolored lights had been over several low bushes in
the small yard.

I parked the Volvo on the street beside a sturdy-
looking oak tree whose naked branches snaked upward

toward a gray, midmorning, sky. Kevin and I walked up the short driveway, across an even shorter walkway, and climbed two steps onto the front porch. When we reached the door, I had my choice of three doorbells. The one in the middle had Hal's name listed above it.

"Want to ring bell," Kevin said imperiously.

I already knew that. Doorbells are one of my son's favorite things. And I'd learned a long time ago that the push-the-button game is much more enjoyable when Kev plays it on those occasions when it's actually necessary, rather than when we're at home and it's not.

I lifted him up and showed him which of the buzzers to press. Kev applied his index finger to the small button and pushed firmly. We both heard chimes sound inside the house.

Thirty seconds passed. Nothing happened.

"Again!" said Kevin.

We gave it another try. Still nothing.

The toddler looked up at me. "Nobody home," he said with a shrug.

"Maybe Hal Romero is coming," I said. "Maybe he's just slow."

Okay, so I was grasping at straws. But I really didn't want to have made the trip to Glenville for nothing. Sure, I could have called Mr. Romero first. But in my experience people who don't have any reason to want to talk to me, are much more likely to do so when I'm standing right in front of them, than they are when I give them advance warning of my intent.

"We'll give it one more try," I said, hoisting the toddler up again. "Last chance."

This time, the door opened fractionally almost before the chimes had even stopped ringing. A woman who looked to be in her fifties, with slippers on her feet and a scowl on her face, peered out at us through a gap that was less than six inches wide.

"Help you?" she said, sounding none too pleased by the prospect.

"I'm looking for Hal Romero," I told her. "Did we ring the wrong bell by mistake?"

"No, you got the right bell," she said with a windy sigh. "You just rang it so many times I figured if I didn't come out here and open the door you'd never shut up."

"Oh," I said. Oops.

"Ring bell!" Kevin cried gaily. "One more time."

To my surprise, the woman looked down and smiled. "I thought you were just being rude," she said with a chuckle. "But now I see what happened."

Delighted by her amusement, Kevin began to laugh with her. As his small body pumped up and down with giggles, the woman pulled the door open, stepped aside, and waved us through the gap.

"My son, Danny, used to love to ring the doorbell, too," she said. "Drove me crazy, that kid. Step inside for a minute. It's too cold to stand out there on the porch."

I was happy to comply. Bracing a hand between Kev's shoulders, I scooted him forward, then quickly followed. We entered a cramped hallway that held only two doors and a narrow staircase leading up to the second floor. The door on the right was closed. The one on the left stood ajar.

"How old is Danny?" I asked. I've never met a woman who doesn't like to talk about her children.

"Thirty on his last birthday," she said fondly. "And long gone from here now. He's married with a family of his own."

"We have Poodles," Kevin announced. He hates to be ignored.

Looking down, I saw that he already had his jacket off. His mittens, clipped to his cuffs, dangled from the ends of the empty sleeves.

"I like dogs," the woman told him. She obviously liked children, too. Then she lifted her gaze to me. "So you're looking for Hal. Are you a friend of his?"

"No, actually we've never met. My name is Melanie Travis. I work at Howard Academy."

The woman nodded. Not surprisingly, she'd heard of the school. "Beverly," she said. "I'm Hal's landlady." She nodded toward the staircase. "He has the apartment upstairs."

"Mr. Romero was hired to appear as Santa Claus at our Christmas bazaar this past weekend—" I began.

Kev tilted his head upward. "Santa Claus?" he said with interest.

Too late, I realized my mistake. And it was a doozy. Quickly I hunkered down to Kevin's height so we could talk eye-to-eye.

"Not the real Santa Claus," I said. "We're talking about one of his helpers."

"And he lives *here?*" Kev's eyes grew wide.

"Sometimes. But only when he's not at the North Pole."

"Wow." He gazed around the small hallway with fresh appreciation.

As I rose to my feet, Beverly gave me a sympathetic wink. Then she said to Kevin, "I've got the TV on in my apartment. Have you ever watched *The Price is Right?*"

Kev shook his head. He still looked slightly dazed— as if he was half expecting Santa Claus to pop out of the woodwork at any moment.

I am *such* an idiot.

"Do you like flashing lights and screaming ladies?" Beverly asked.

Kevin considered for a moment, then shrugged.

"Why don't you go have a look? Your mom and I will be right here, having a little chat."

"Okay."

He left without even checking with me for permission. Another time, that might have bothered me. Now I was just grateful to Beverly for rescuing me.

"I should have seen that coming," I said, shaking my head.

"Don't beat yourself up. We've all done it. Good save with the Santa's helpers line. They always fall for that one."

"I hope so," I replied, appreciating her attempt to make me feel better.

"Now back to Hal," Beverly prompted. "What did you want with him?"

"Like I said, he was supposed to work at our Christmas bazaar last weekend. But then he canceled at the last minute and left us in the lurch."

"That doesn't sound like Hal at all. He's usually very reliable. Dressing up and entertaining kids is how he makes his living. He's been doing it for years and he gets a lot of gigs. This time of year, it's all Santa Claus. But Hal also does a clown and a vampire. He has a magician act, too. He's the kind of guy who likes to keep busy."

"I was hoping I could talk to him about why he didn't keep his commitment to us," I said. "But I'm assuming he isn't here."

"No, he's not. He hasn't been around since last week."

"Thursday?" I guessed.

"Yeah, that's right. How did you know?"

"Some time that night he left a message at the school, canceling his appearance. The headmaster found out about it on Friday morning and had to scramble around to replace him."

"That doesn't make sense," Beverly said thoughtfully. "Hal would never want to disappoint kids like that."

"Do you have any idea where he went?"

She shook her head. "I didn't see him before he left. I just noticed he was gone and figured he must have gone off somewhere for the holidays. You know, visiting family or something?"

"Is that what he usually does this time of year?"

"I wouldn't really know. It's not my place to keep tabs. Hal's a good tenant. He's neat, he's quiet, he pays his bills on time. I've never had a single cause for complaint. He's a nice guy, but it's not like we get in each other's business."

"So I guess you wouldn't happen to know where his family lives?"

"Nope," said Beverly. "Not a clue."

Briefly I debated mentioning that the Santa Claus who'd taken Hal Romero's place had ended up dead. Then I quickly decided against it. I was pretty sure that the police would want to talk to Beverly as well. It was probably better if I let them break the news. And maybe I'd get lucky and Hal's landlady wouldn't mention that we'd already spoken.

"Thank you for talking to me," I said instead. "I appreciate it."

"Sorry I couldn't be more help. You want to give me a card or something? When Hal comes back, I can have him call you?"

"That would be great." I fished a piece of paper out of my purse, wrote down my name and phone number, and handed it over. Then I leaned around and stuck my head through the open doorway to Beverly's apartment. "Kev, honey, it's time to go."

I expected to see him sitting in front of the television but Kevin had bypassed the screaming ladies and flashing lights and found something better. He was standing beside a large aquarium, tucked into an alcove at the end of the room. Eyes wide, mouth slightly agape, Kev was staring in fascination at dozens of brightly colored fish swimming back and forth behind the glass.

No wonder I hadn't heard a peep out of him.

"Mommy, come see," Kevin cried. "*Pretty fish!*"

I'd already retrieved his jacket from the floor in the hallway. Now I carried it with me across the room. "The fish are beautiful. Please say thank you to the nice lady for letting you look at them."

"Thank you," Kevin mumbled.

Still utterly entranced, he didn't even turn around to acknowledge us. I reached down, slipped his arms into his sleeves of his jacket, and zipped him up. Then I gave his hand a little tug.

"Honey, we have to go now."

Kev planted his feet. "Like to see fish."

"I know they're nice. But they're Beverly's fish. And we have to leave."

"Not going," Kevin insisted. "Want fish."

A sudden inspiration struck. "Christmas is coming," I said. "Maybe Santa Claus will bring you a goldfish."

Kev gestured toward the aquarium. "And water, too," he said seriously.

"Water, too," I agreed. "And probably a fish tank."

I saw Beverly biting her lip. She was trying hard not to laugh. I was guessing that her son, Danny, had liked fish, too.

This time when I tugged on Kevin's small hand, he allowed himself to be moved. Beverly walked us to the door.

"I just thought of something," she said, when we'd reached the hallway. "You said you worked at Howard Academy, right?"

I nodded.

"Do you know a guy there named Tony? Big, friendly guy, African-American? Has a nice smile?"

"Sure," I said. "That's Tony Dahl. He's the head of the athletic department. Do you know him?"

"I met him here last summer. He's a friend of Hal's."

What an interesting coincidence. I paused next to the outer door, waiting to see if Beverly had more to add. Happily she did.

"Hal and Tony were out in the backyard grilling some brats one day," she told me. "It smelled pretty good so I went out to see if they had any leftovers. Hal introduced us and I remember Tony saying that he worked at your school. Could be he knows where Hal's gone off to."

"Thanks for the tip," I said. "I'll check into that."

All the way home, Kevin talked about fish. Waving his hands in the air, he sang about red fish and blue fish and counted their numbers on his fingers. When he reached the end of his impromptu song, he squealed with delight and started over again.

There was definitely going to be an addition to that child's Christmas list.

While Kev occupied himself counting fish, I kept my eyes on the road and pondered the unlikely circumstance that the school's coach and their missing Santa Claus had known one another. Then I thought of something else. When Coco Lily had been running around causing havoc at the bazaar, it was Tony who'd known about the disturbance and who had brought me the news.

Another coincidence? Possibly.

But now I found myself wondering what else Tony might happen to know about that afternoon's events.

Chapter 16

"Who would want to kill Santa Claus?" asked Bertie. "That's just perverse."

"Tell me about it," I said unhappily.

I'd brought Kevin back home, fed him lunch, and put him down for a nap. Sam had been out, meeting with a client, but he was due back shortly. While he held down the fort at home that afternoon, I planned to try and talk to a couple of the dog show exhibitors who'd been at the Christmas bazaar.

Sondra had already given me several names. But I wanted to get Bertie's take on the day's events, too. She had seen and dealt with everyone who'd brought dogs to have their pictures taken with Santa Claus. So she not only knew which dog people had been on hand that afternoon, she might also be able to give me some insight as to whether or not any of them had been acting suspiciously.

As soon as Kev was asleep, I carried my phone into the living room and sat down on the couch. Tar hopped up and draped himself across my lap. Augie turned a small circle and lay down on my feet. I dialed my sister-in-law's number and settled in for a long chat.

"It's really too bad how things turned out," Bertie said now. "And kind of hard to reconcile what you've told me about that Santa Claus with the guy I met on Saturday. Because he seemed like a nice person. He was good with the kids and mostly patient with their pets."

"*Mostly* patient?" I asked.

Bertie chuckled. "He really hated having that squirmy Gila monster in his lap."

I shuddered lightly. I would have felt the same way.

"Did you see Poppy and Kiltie when she brought him over to have his picture taken?" I asked.

"Sure, Claire and I both did. I recognized Kiltie right away. In that crowd, he stood out like a sore thumb."

I had to agree with her assessment: the Westie would have been hard to miss. Aside from his obvious quality, Kiltie's precise, stylized, trim would have set him apart from the rest of the children's pets.

"Poppy looked familiar, too," Bertie said. "I guess I've seen her around the shows with her mother. When she came to the booth she had a friend with her. The girl with the Cockapoo."

"That was Charlotte and Coco Lily. Did you notice anything out of the ordinary while they were there? Did anything unusual happen?"

Bertie thought for a minute before answering. "Nothing struck me at the time," she said finally. "As you know, we almost always had a long line of kids waiting. So we were moving pretty fast with each one. I remember Santa saying hello to Poppy and asking her what kind of dog she had while Claire was maneuvering Kiltie into position for the picture."

"Was it just normal chitchat?" I asked. "Something he asked all the kids?"

"Pretty much. Santa used a little small talk to put the kids at ease. He didn't treat Poppy any differently than anyone else. She gave him a big smile and told him that her dog's name was Kiltie. Poppy and that Westie were adorable together. I'm sure their picture turned out wonderfully."

Not that anyone would ever care, I thought with a pang.

"And Santa didn't pay any special attention to Kiltie either?"

"Not that I noticed," said Bertie. "The only ones he spent extra time with were the tough ones, the dogs who might have needed some socializing. There were a few who didn't like his beard, or his padded belly, or were just pretty damn sure that they weren't going to be sitting in some fat stranger's lap without putting up a fight."

"Wow." I exhaled softly. "I had no idea." Every time I'd checked in at the photo booth everything had appeared to be running smoothly.

"It was no big deal." Bertie brushed off my concern. "We managed. And Claire was great."

"I'm glad," I said. "I really like her."

"Even though . . . ?" Bertie let the thought dangle.

I was pretty sure I knew what my sister-in-law was getting at, but I couldn't resist teasing her. "Even though what? That she was running around all day in that silly elf costume? I wasn't going to say anything, but since you've asked . . . I'll have you know that I gave Claire extra points for that."

"Points," Bertie muttered darkly. "If I'd had to wear

that costume, you would have had to give me extra pay."

"Oh?" I laughed. "Was I paying you?"

"Not nearly enough apparently. And don't try to change the subject. You know that wasn't what I meant. New Year's Eve? The wedding? Your ex-husband? Does any of this ring a bell?"

"Bob," I said, even though we both knew his name.

"Yes, *Bob*. I know you guys want everyone to think that it's all copacetic between you now. But doesn't it bother you even a little bit that your ex-husband is getting remarried?"

"No," I replied honestly. "Why should it?"

"I don't know." I could picture Bertie's frown. "It's just what women do."

"That's a depressing thought," I said. "*Really?*"

"Really. Facebook. Go there. You'll be amazed by what you see."

"No, thank you," I replied. "I don't need that kind of drama in my life. I'd rather be happily oblivious. As for Bob, he and I have been divorced for years. And *I'm remarried*. What kind of a moron would I be if I didn't think Bob should be able to do the same?"

"Gawd," Bertie said vehemently. "I hate it when you act like a grown-up."

"Don't worry," I told her. "It doesn't happen often."

"Listen, I'm sorry not to be able to be more help about Kiltie," Bertie said. "If I'd realized that something wonky was going to happen later, I'd have paid more attention."

"We all would have," I said with a sigh. "That's the beauty of hindsight."

Discomfited by my tone, Tar opened his eyes and

gazed up at me. I wrapped an arm around the big Poodle's shoulders and gave him a reassuring hug.

"Sondra McEvoy is convinced that a fellow exhibitor is behind Kiltie's disappearance," I told Bertie. "She said she saw Jo Drummer and Chip Michaels at the bazaar. Do you have any other names for me?"

"Sure, that's easy," Bertie replied. "LouLou Barrington came by with one of her Samoyeds. Rick Stanley brought a Cairn. Jane Brew and her partner had a pair of MinPins."

"Thanks." I jotted down the names. "That'll definitely get me started. If you think of any more, let me know."

"I'll do that." Bertie paused, then added, "I want you to know that I feel really bad about what happened. I'm sorry that Claire and I didn't do a better job of staying on top of that guy. That we didn't prevent him from sneaking out of the building with a dog—"

"Stop right there," I said firmly. "None of this is your fault. So don't even *think* of apologizing. The only reason you were even at the bazaar is because you were doing me a favor."

"Yeah, but I still feel guilty—"

"Don't," I told her. "You and Claire did a great job all day. There's nothing for you to feel bad about at all. Besides, I'm going to find Kiltie and bring him home. And then this whole mess will all be over and done with."

"I hope you're right," said Bertie.

Despite my show of confidence, she didn't sound entirely convinced.

* * *

Considering that it was Tuesday—the best day of the week for catching dog show people when they might have time to spare—it was disappointing that my next three phone calls turned up nothing useful. I left messages for Jane Brew and Rick Stanley, asking them both to please call me back. And I had a very brief conversation with Chip Michaels.

I didn't know Chip personally, but the fact that he was acquainted with Sondra made me hope that he'd be willing to talk to me. Not only that, but throwing Aunt Peg's name around usually pries open any dog-related door far enough for me to wiggle through. Not this time, however.

He'd only stopped in at the bazaar for a short period of time, Chip told me in an aggrieved tone of voice. Though he'd later learned of Kiltie's disappearance, it had nothing whatsoever to do with him. He had seen nothing. He had heard nothing. End of discussion. Chip ensured that last part by hanging up the phone while I was still talking.

"That man needs better manners," I muttered, seriously annoyed by the brush-off.

Faith, who was lying beside the couch, lifted her head and cocked an ear inquiringly. I looked down at her over Tar's back.

"Don't worry," I said. "Your manners are great."

I had more luck with my next call. Jo Drummer lived in Waterbury and bred and showed Border Terriers. Like Chip, she had only a very vague idea who I was. Unlike Chip, she was happy to talk.

Even though I got the impression that she was only hoping to pump me for information about Kiltie and Sondra—the duo currently starring in the hottest dog show gossip—I could hardly complain. After all, I was hoping to do the same to her.

"I'm in my car," she said. "I'm taking a couple of puppies to handling class this afternoon in Trumbull. Why don't you meet me there?"

Trumbull was closer than Waterbury. I could be there in half an hour. That made the decision easy.

"It's a deal," I told her.

Sam returned a few minutes later. I gave him a quick status update—kids, dogs, dinner, Kiltie, in that order—then hit the road. The address Jo gave me led me to a recreation center attached to a church on the outskirts of town. When I arrived, Jo was already in the parking lot unloading her minivan.

Now that I saw Jo, she looked familiar. We'd probably crossed paths at the shows dozens of times. I pulled the Volvo into an empty space and parked beside her.

Jo had the minivan's side door open. As I got out of my car, she was leaning into her vehicle, unlatching the door to a wire crate. When she straightened up and turned around, Jo had a puppy in her arms and a smile on her face.

"You must be Melanie," she said. "Here, have a puppy."

"Excuse me?"

It wasn't the greeting I'd been expecting. Even so, I found myself holding out my hands. The gesture was automatic. And fruitful. Next thing I knew, I did indeed have a puppy.

"Her name is Bella," Jo told me as she went back into the van. "She's a sweetheart. You'll love her."

The Border Terrier had wiry tan hair and a mischievous look on her face. Five to six months old, I guessed. Bella was already making herself comfortable in my arms. Her pink tongue came out to lick my hand. She was adorable. How could anybody *not* love her?

"This is going to work out great," said Jo. She backed her body out of the minivan for the second time, once again holding a puppy to her chest. With ease born of practice, she lifted her knee and used it to slide the van door shut. "These two are litter mates and they both need socializing. Before you called, I was going to do half the class with each. But now that you're here, I'll handle Edward and you can take Bella."

"Um," I said uncertainly. "Okay."

Jo was a stocky woman in her fifties with short, iron gray hair and a weathered face that was make-up free. Her gaze was direct and to the point. Apparently someone who'd never been unsure of anything in her life, Jo seemed baffled by my uncertainty.

"*What?*" she said. "You show dogs, right?"

I nodded. "Standard Poodles."

"Good. That's close enough." She fished a flat show lead out of her pocket and looped it around Bella's neck. "There. Now you're good to go."

Who could argue with confidence like that? Certainly not me.

Cradling the puppy in my arms, I followed Jo into the rec center. The main room was already crowded with dogs and people. Most were standing in small groups talking while they waited for class to start.

A big, rectangular-shaped, ring had been set up in the middle of the room. The organizers of the class were finishing rolling out the wide rubber mats that covered the floor to give the dogs traction. Somewhere in the building, Christmas music was playing. The carols, piped into the room through a loudspeaker, gave the setting a festive air.

As I shrugged out of my coat, Jo waved at some people she knew and went to settle with the cashier. By the time she returned, handlers were already beginning to file into the ring. Jo tossed her jacket onto a fold-up chair and gestured me toward the back of the line beside her.

She leaned toward me so I could hear what she was saying above the music. "We're just here to play around and introduce them to the concept today. I want these guys to see other dogs, walk around on a leash, and get the idea that going to shows is fun. If she's squirmy on the table, or she sits down when she should be standing up, don't worry about it." Jo nodded downward toward Bella. "Do you think you can make sure she has a good time?"

"I don't see why not," I said.

It sounded like my kind of assignment. Good behavior was hard, fun was easy. And Bella, standing on the floor beside me and gazing around avidly, already appeared to be having a ball. She'd touched noses with the dog behind me, investigated the curling edge of the mat, and was now mesmerized by a Saint Bernard on the other side of the ring.

The instructor started the class by having us all gait once around the ring. Bella handled the commotion and the mats with ease. In no time at all, Jo and I found ourselves right back where we'd started.

The bigger breeds had gone to the front of the line and there were more than a dozen dogs ahead of us. It would be at least ten minutes until it was our turn for an individual examination. In the meantime, we could play with the puppies and talk.

Jo sat down on the mat, crossed her legs, and pulled Edward into her lap. "So," she said. "What's up?"

I dropped to the mat beside her. "I know you've heard about what happened to Kiltie."

The Westie's call name was used liberally in his advertising as a nod to his breed's Scottish roots. Which meant that everyone who was anyone in the dog community knew GCH Westglen Braveheart by his more informal moniker. And that included Jo. She didn't miss a beat.

"Are you kidding?" she said. "*Everybody's* heard. Who has their dog stolen by Santa Claus, for Pete's sake? Trust me, a story like that made the rounds at warp speed."

No surprise there.

"You were at the Howard Academy Christmas Bazaar, too," I said.

"Sure I was. Along with several hundred other people. I took these guys"—Jo's hand spread across our laps to indicate the two Border puppies—"to get their pictures taken with Santa. They're like kids, you know? They grow up too fast. I wasn't about to miss an opportunity like that."

"Sondra thinks that another exhibitor, maybe one who was present that day, took her dog."

Jo's eyes narrowed. "She does, does she?"

Hands playing with the active puppy in my lap, I settled for a nod.

"Well, that's an interesting theory. If you don't mind my asking, what's it to you?"

"I work at Howard Academy," I said. "I was in charge of the bazaar."

"No shit?" To my surprise, Jo started to laugh.

"What's so funny?" I asked.

"Because . . ." Jo stopped to catch her breath. "Because I thought you were going to tell me that Sondra had offered you some fabulous sum of money to track down her missing dog. And now I find out that all you really do is *work for a school?*"

"Howard Academy is a very good school," I said. I may have sounded a little miffed.

"Sure. Whatever. No offense meant."

"The fact is," I told her, "Kiltie was lost on my watch. So I promised Sondra that I would do whatever I could to find him."

"Okay. I get that. I guess." Jo tipped her head to one side. "So because I was at your bazaar, you think that makes me a suspect?"

"I think that makes it worth my time to hear what you have to say about the situation."

Jo lifted Edward out of her lap and set him down on the mat. She stacked the puppy, let him hold the pose for a few seconds, then released him. "I don't know that I have much to say at all."

I followed suit with Bella, stacking the puppy briefly on the mat, then tried another tack with her owner. "You have a Specials dog that competes against Kiltie in the Groups. He must be a very good dog."

"That's Gusto." Jo nodded. "He's these puppies' sire. And he's a terrific Border Terrier. But even so . . ."

When I released the puppy from her stack, Bella skipped to the end of her leash and pounced on her brother. Gently I hauled her back to my side.

"Even so, what?" I prompted.

"Gusto shows against Kiltie in the group but it not like

he's ever going to be a real threat to him, competition-wise. I'd have to be stupid to even think that he might be."

"Does Gusto ever beat Kiltie?" I asked curiously.

"He did once." Jo allowed herself a small smile. "Kiltie was off his game. Gusto was third in the group and Kiltie was fourth. Sondra was madder than a wet hornet."

I could picture that. From what I knew of her, Sondra was not the kind of person to take being beaten lightly.

"But if Kiltie is gone," I said, "Gusto moves up, right? That's got to be a good thing."

"Sure. But it's not nearly enough. The Terrier group is one of the toughest there is. Some might even call it cutthroat."

I nodded. I knew that.

"Borders, even really good ones, are a hard sell in that kind of competition. Judges like the flashy breeds, the ones that fly around the ring and really stand out. Compared to the Wires and the Kerries, we're just a little too plain for the big leagues."

Now that she'd pointed that out, I knew she was right. Judges did tend to favor breeds that were showy and eye-catching. It was one of the reasons that Poodles did so well in the Groups and Best in Show.

"If my goal was to do well in the group," said Jo, "it would be smarter for me to get another breed than to try and eliminate one of my competitors."

Right again, unfortunately.

Growing bored with the inactivity, Bella nipped at my sleeve. I disentangled her small teeth and set the Border puppy back on the mat. Jo and I both stood up. The line was moving forward.

When we stopped again, she leaned in close and

said, "The idea that someone like me would care that much about Kiltie, or his whereabouts, is laughable. But then Sondra has always had a highly inflated sense of her own worth. If someone really is out to get her, she only has herself to blame. Because if Sondra has a target on her back, she's the one who put it there."

Chapter 17

Cutthroat indeed, I thought. The Terrier group sounded like just the right place for Jo Drummer and her scrappy little Borders.

Despite the efforts she'd made to proclaim her innocence, Jo didn't appear to be at all sympathetic to Sondra's plight. I've never been able to resist poking against a sore spot. Now I decided to prod a bit more and see what kind of response I might be able to provoke.

"Kiltie is going out with Todd after the first of the year," I said casually. "Had you heard about that?"

Jo's reaction was immediate and gratifying. She reared back in surprise. "No! I had no idea. Are you sure about that?"

"Sondra told me so herself."

"I heard that Todd was going to be debuting an important new dog next year, too," Jo replied. "But not Kiltie. It's an Afghan Hound. One that's coming from England."

Normal people gossip about singers and movie stars. Exhibitors talk endlessly about the top dogs. Who has what dog. Who had beaten what dog. And where they were all going to show up next.

Still, this information came as a surprise. With two new "big dogs" arriving at Todd's kennel at the same time—and both obviously vying for top dog status— even a string as extensive as Todd's was going to feel a little crowded. Afghans were part of the Hound group, I thought. Westies were in the Terriers. That would help some.

"Two different groups," I mused aloud.

"Yes," said Jo. "But the whole point of playing at that level is to make it into the Best in Show ring. And then what? Todd may be a miracle worker, but even he can only handle one dog in the ring at a time."

I couldn't argue with that logic.

She turned away from me as the line moved up again and she nudged Edward back into position. As Bella and I followed along behind, I considered what Jo had told me. It would be interesting to hear what Aunt Peg had to say about the situation. She often understood nuances about the dog show world that went right over my head.

But in the meantime, I couldn't help but wonder. Was Todd setting himself up for an inevitable conflict between two of his clients? Or was it Sondra who'd misunderstood the situation?

Then it was Jo's turn to pick up Edward and place him on the table to be examined. The class instructor, playing judge, ran his hands swiftly over the puppy's body. When he was finished, he gave the Border an encouraging pat. Jo gaited Edward out and back across the mats. They even managed a brief free bait at the end.

When they were finished, it was my turn with Bella. The puppy wiggled on the table. She leapt and bounded on the floor. It wasn't a polished performance by any means. But the entire time she was in the spotlight, Bella's enthusiasm never diminished. When we went to join Jo and Edward at the end of the line, I was pleased to see that she looked happy with both her puppies' performances.

"One last question," I said to Jo.

The loudspeaker was blaring out a jazz rendition of "Little Drummer Boy"and once again I had to stand close to make myself heard. All that nonstop Christmas cheer was making me itch to get my fingers on the music's volume button.

Jo shrugged. I decided to take that as acquiescence.

"You go to a lot of shows," I said. "You know most of the terrier people. Can you think of anyone who might have wanted to hurt Sondra?"

"That's a pretty broad question," she replied. "You know how Sondra is . . . she can be difficult. When she's unhappy, she wants everyone else to be unhappy, too."

I thought of the scene that Sondra had caused at the bazaar when she'd discovered that Kiltie was missing. She'd lashed out in all directions at once. Even at her own daughter.

"I only know Sondra from what I see at the shows," Jo continued. "But she's miserable to be around when things aren't going the way she wants them to. And nobody *ever* wants to get on her bad side. Because Sondra's the wrong person to pick a fight with. I don't think I've ever seen her back down, or even reconsider her opinion. You know what I mean?"

I nodded, encouraging her to keep talking.

"Rumor has it that Sondra got her panties in a wad over something that happened at her local Westie Club. I heard she got a couple of novice breeders thrown out of the club for doing something that she took exception to."

"Do you know what they did?"

"I do not." Jo shook her head. "But you know how affiliate clubs can be. There's often enough infighting and jostling for position among the members already without someone purposely stirring things up."

Each breed of dog is overseen by a national club that's responsible for that breed's welfare and promotion. The club's hardworking members write the breed standard, marshal support for research into genetic problems, provide breeder referral and rescue services, and hold a national specialty show.

The affiliate clubs are regional offshoots of the parent club. They do many of the same things, but on a local scale. And since their members tend to live clustered in a single area, they also hold frequent meetings that often double as social gatherings. In a club with a varied and active group of breeders, it wasn't unusual for things to become contentious.

"Do you know which club it was?" I asked.

"I'm pretty sure it was the Tri-State West Highland White Club. I know they're down in Sondra's area. I heard that by the time she was finished throwing her weight around, she'd managed to tick off more than a few club members."

We all gaited once more around the ring and practiced a second individual examination. By that time, the two puppies were beginning to grow tired. Pleased with how well they'd handled things, Jo decided to quit while everyone was still having fun.

We walked out to the parking lot together. I waited as she loaded Bella and Edward into their crate for the ride home.

"Thanks for talking to me," I said. "I appreciate your input."

"I hope it helps," Jo replied. "At least for Kiltie's sake, anyway. He seems like a nice dog. I'd hate for something bad to happen to him."

"Me, too," I agreed.

"It's not his fault that he got stuck with such a crappy owner."

I couldn't top that sentiment. I didn't even try.

I wanted to talk to Aunt Peg. Unfortunately it had to wait.

Wednesday I had school again. Especially now—with the holiday season upon us—it was a real inconvenience when my job interfered with all the other things I would rather have been doing. And judging by the number of absentees among the students, apparently I wasn't the only one who felt that way.

When my ten o'clock tutoring session was canceled because the eighth grader whom I was supposed help study for postbreak finals, turned out to have already left on a ski trip with his parents, I used the unexpected free period to go looking for Tony Dahl.

I found him in his office on the ground floor. The small room was sandwiched between the gym, the locker rooms, and the cavernous space that housed the indoor swimming pool. As none of my regular duties ever brought me to this part of the building, I was unprepared for the smell that wafted through these lower corridors. It appeared to consist of equal parts chlorine, adolescent sweat, and wet feet.

The front wall of Tony's office had a wide bank of waist-to-ceiling windows. As I approached, I could see that he was on the phone. By the time I'd reached his closed door, however, Tony was already hanging up and signaling me to enter.

"I hope I'm not interrupting," I said.

"Not at all. I was just doing a little Christmas shopping. Come in and have a seat, and tell me what brings you all the way down here to the bowels of the building. Nothing too serious, I hope."

Against the long wall of the office, a faded couch sat perpendicular to Tony's desk. It was bracketed on either side by shelves filled with many decades' worth of trophies and team photos, some dating back half a century or more. Resisting the urge to stop and have a look, I walked over and sat down instead.

"I just wanted to ask you a few questions, if that's all right."

"Shoot," Tony invited. "Until girls' basketball in fourth period, I'm all yours."

"I'm looking for a lost dog," I began.

"Not your big Poodle." He immediately sounded concerned.

"No," I said quickly. "Faith is fine. She's upstairs. The dog I'm looking for is a little white terrier named Kiltie."

"The dog from the bazaar." Tony nodded in recognition. "I didn't realize he was still missing."

In the four days that had passed since the bazaar, the

buzz about Kiltie's disappearance had been superseded by fresher, more alarming news. The previous day, the tidbit that the man found dead in Union Cemetery was the Santa Claus from the HA Christmas Bazaar, had spread through the school like wildfire. A missing dog was nothing compared to that.

"Yes, he's still gone," I told him. "Kiltie belongs to a Howard Academy alum who's very upset about his loss."

"Poppy's Mom," said Tony.

"That's right."

"I heard some of the commotion she made on Saturday." He shook his head. "Is she still threatening to sue the school?"

"It's a possibility. That's one of the reasons I'm looking for him."

"I wish I could help you," said Tony. "But if I had any idea where that dog was, I would have done something about it on Saturday. It seems to me, the way dogs run, that little guy could be just about anywhere by now."

"But that's just it," I said. "Kiltie didn't run away. He was stolen."

"*Stolen?*" That got Tony's attention in a hurry. "By whom?"

"Our Santa Claus."

"For real?"

"I'm afraid so."

"The guy who ended up dead?"

I nodded. "It appears that way."

"That's just nuts," said Tony. "Who would bother to steal a dog when there are plenty you can have for free?"

"Kiltie isn't just any dog," I said. "He's a valuable show dog."

Tony shook his head again as if he was finding the entire conversation baffling. "People sure are crazy."

I was in no position to argue with that.

"What does that have to do with me?" he asked after a minute.

"You have a friend named Hal Romero, right?"

"Sure. Good guy."

"Do you happen to know where he is?"

"Home, I guess." Tony reached for his cell phone. "Do you want his number?"

"No, thanks, I already have it. Were you aware that he was the person originally hired to appear as Santa Claus at the Christmas bazaar?"

"I should be," said Tony. "I'm the one who told him to apply for the job. After he got it, he called and said thanks for the tip."

Well, that explained away the first coincidence.

"So Hal was happy to have the job," I said. "And yet he canceled his appearance at the last minute. And apparently he's since disappeared."

"I was too busy on Saturday to stop and think about the fact that he wasn't there," Tony said. "And what do you mean he's disappeared?"

"I stopped by his apartment yesterday. His landlady hasn't seen him since last Thursday."

"I wouldn't worry about that," Tony told me. "Hal works for himself. He's the kind of guy who likes to come and go on his own schedule. Maybe he took a few days off to go fishing."

"In December?" I said skeptically.

"Oh yeah, I didn't think about that." Tony still didn't sound perturbed. "So maybe not fishing. But he could still be just about anywhere."

"Here's the thing," I said. "When Hal canceled, that opened the door for Jerry Platt to be hired as his substitute. And that gave Platt his chance to steal Kiltie."

"Wait a minute." Tony sat up straight in his chair. "Are you telling me that if Hal had shown up and done his job like he was supposed to, he might have ended up dead like the other Santa Claus did?"

"Not at all," I corrected quickly. "Not unless Hal was involved in the dognapping scheme, too."

"No way. Hal wouldn't have had anything to do with something like that. But from what you're saying, it sounds to me like he might have been someone's unwitting dupe." Tony stopped and sighed. "So I guess things aren't looking too good for me either, are they?"

"What do you mean?"

"All I was trying to do was help a friend. And because of that, everything ended up in a big mess. I suppose I should be glad that you're the one talking to me instead of Mr. Hanover. How much trouble am I in?"

"None that I'm aware of," I told him. "Nobody blames you for what happened. I just wanted to talk to Hal and find out why he bailed on us. Somebody must have put him up to it."

"It sounds like that guy Jerry Platt was the one who did that."

"Possibly," I conceded. "But maybe Hal has another name for us. And if he does, I'd like to hear it."

"I'll try and find him for you," Tony offered. "Call around and see if anyone knows where he is."

"Thanks. I appreciate the help."

"Believe me, I'm happy to do what I can. This whole thing hits a little too close to home, you know?"

I did indeed.

On my way back up the stairs from the lower level, I ran into Madeline Dangerfield. She was headed in the other direction, carrying a small bundle of clothing in her arms. With our recent interaction fresh in my mind, I had no intention of stopping. With luck, Madeline might not even remember me.

But as we passed on the steps, she paused, and said, "You're Melanie, right? We met at the bazaar? I'm glad I ran into you."

What now? I wondered.

"Yes, I'm Melanie," I admitted. "Is everything all right?"

"Sure, I'm just delivering my son's gym clothes to his locker. After he left in the car pool this morning, I found them on the kitchen counter. That child has a selective memory when it comes to things he doesn't want to do. Like anything resembling physical activity."

"I just saw Tony," I said. "I'm sure he can point you toward the right locker."

"Oh, trust me, I've been here before," Madeline replied with a small smile. "I know just where to go. Listen, I want to apologize for my behavior last Saturday. There's no excuse. I was having a bad day and I'm sorry I took it out on you. Especially since you went out of your way to be helpful."

"Don't worry about it," I said. "The bazaar can be pretty stressful. Everybody's trying to get a lot of stuff done in a short amount of time and that kind of pressure adds up. I hope your booth worked out well for you."

Madeline nodded. "It turned out that being over by the windows was great. "I had shoppers coming by all day. I sold all the stock I had with me and took a bunch more orders for stuff to send out by Christmas."

"That's terrific. I'm glad your day was a success."

I went to move on, but Madeline wasn't finished.

"Say," she said, "did you ever find that dog that ran away?"

The question stopped me in my tracks. "No, not yet. Why do you ask?"

"I saw all the commotion at the time. Plus, you know—it was Sondra. Everybody always notices what's going on with her."

"They do?"

Madeline reached up and patted my shoulder. "Honey, you must be new around here if you don't already know that. But when I found out what had happened, I did feel bad for her. Sondra really seems to be going through a rough patch right now. First she lost Jim. And now her little dog is gone, too."

"She lost Jim?" I repeated. That seemed like an odd way to refer to a marriage that was breaking down.

"You know," Madeline said in a confiding tone, "he was stepping out on her with someone else."

Oh. "I didn't know that, actually. I just knew that Sondra and her husband were separated."

"It's Jim's wandering eye that got them there. Sondra tried to overlook what was going on for a while. But then she finally decided she'd had enough and kicked Jim out of the house."

"I don't blame her," I said.

"Me either. Especially since rumor has it that the woman has kids in this school."

"*Here?*" That caught me by surprise. "At Howard Academy? Who is it?"

"I don't know," Madeline replied. "I don't even think Sondra knows. Somebody around here must be pretty good at keeping secrets."

"Not me," I said. This conversation was turning out to be quite illuminating. I hoped that Madeline would keep talking. "I like hearing all the gossip."

Madeline just shook her head. "It's a shame that she has to deal with all this crap now, right before the holidays. But you know Sondra. She's a survivor. She'll get everything sorted out to her satisfaction if it's the last thing she does."

Speaking as one of the people currently being sorted, I never doubted that for a minute.

"I hope you have a great Christmas," said Madeline. She was ready to move on. "If I'd known I was going to run into you, I'd have brought you one of my jams. How about if I have Christof leave a jar of marmalade on your desk tomorrow?"

"That would be wonderful," I said. As apologies went, I'd take it. "Merry Christmas to you, too."

"If you see Sondra, tell her I hope she gets her dog back. She's probably missing him more than she's missing Jim."

A sad commentary, and probably very true.

"I will do that," I said.

Chapter 18

That afternoon when school let out, I finally got my chance to visit Aunt Peg. A small detour on the way home from Howard Academy brought me to her old, restored, farmhouse in back country Greenwich. The kennel building behind the house had once been filled with generations of Cedar Crest Standard Poodles, often more than a dozen at a time.

Now, however, Aunt Peg's full judging schedule keeps her busy many weekends of the year. As a result, her current Poodle population numbers only five dogs. All are black, all are adults, and they're all retired show champions. The kennel building is empty now; the Standard Poodles live in the house with Aunt Peg. They also serve as an attentive early warning system whenever a visitor arrives.

Faith had been to Aunt Peg's house before. She knew the drill. As I pulled the Volvo to the side of the driveway and parked, she was already dancing impatiently on the seat. When Aunt Peg opened the front door to her house and the pack of Standard Poodles came spilling down the steps to greet us, Faith was eager to hop out and join the fray.

I reached over and opened the door on her side. Head up, tail whipping back and forth, Faith went charging out of the car. As she mingled happily with her peers, I followed at a more sedate pace.

Aunt Peg had decorated her house for Christmas the previous week. Icicle lights dripped from the home's eaves. Evergreen roping spiraled around the porch railing. A holly-covered wreath adorned the front door. I paused and drew in a deep breath, reveling in the heady, enticing scent of pine that always signals the holidays' approach.

By the time I'd reached the foot of the steps, the Poodles had already dashed once around the front yard, then raced inside the house. Blessed with years of practice, Aunt Peg had deftly avoided being bowled over by the canine onslaught. Now she was waiting for me in the doorway.

"I need cake," I said.

Aunt Peg's sweet tooth is legendary. Over all the years our friendship have encompassed, only two things have remained constant and unalterable. There would always be Standard Poodles at Aunt Peg's house and there would always be cake.

Now as I climbed the steps and crossed the porch, my mouth was already watering. I hoped it would be mocha layer cake from St. Moritz, my favorite.

"Sorry," Aunt Peg said briskly. "You're out of luck."

The shock of her reply stopped me cold. "You're joking, right?"

Dodging the question, Peg waved me forward impatiently. "Come inside so I can close the door. You're letting all the cold air in."

I did as I was told. That's always a safe strategy where Aunt Peg is concerned. I'd barely cleared the doorway when she slammed the door shut behind me. The force she applied to the motion rattled the windows.

I wasn't the only one who was surprised by that. En masse, the Poodles came scrambling back out to the hallway to see what was up. Aunt Peg pointedly avoided all of our gazes.

I looked at the Poodles and shrugged. Their demeanor conveyed similar puzzlement. That made me feel better. Whatever was going on, at least we were all in it together.

"What's wrong?" I asked as I pulled off my coat and stashed it in the closet.

"Wrong?" Aunt Peg echoed innocently. "Why would you think anything is wrong?"

"When did you start slamming doors?"

"Last week. That door sticks."

Aunt Peg is usually quite an accomplished liar. But this time, I wasn't buying it.

"Doors stick in the summer," I pointed out. "Not the winter."

"So?"

There wasn't much I could say to that.

Outerwear dealt with, I started to head toward the kitchen. Aunt Peg always entertains with food. If she didn't have cake, surely there would be cookies. Or maybe scones, I thought hopefully. With lots of butter.

"Where are you going?" asked Aunt Peg.

Turning back, I saw that she meant to go in the other direction. She was facing her living room.

Okay, let's be clear about this. Family matters aside, Aunt Peg and I have been friends and cohorts for a number of years. And I can count on one hand the number of times I've ever been in her living room.

Peg never spends time in there. It's just a beautifully decorated, mostly unused, room that sits on the other side of the house, waiting for visitors whom Aunt Peg doesn't like enough to feed cake. Which is pretty much nobody.

"*Now* what's the matter?" she asked acerbically.

"I feel lost," I said.

"Well, snap out of it."

"*Me?*"

Aunt Peg stopped. She propped her hands on her hips and stared pointedly down her nose. "What is wrong with you today?"

"I want cake," I said softly. Even to my own ears, the plea sounded pathetic. I was a grown woman, for Pete's sake, not a child who needed to beg for a sweet.

But it wasn't only the lack of cake that was troubling. Now I wondered if that was just a symptom of a bigger problem. All at once I felt as though the foundation of our relationship was somehow crumbling beneath my feet. Everything seemed to be shifting and realigning around me and I had no idea why. Where was the Aunt Peg I knew and loved? And who was this stranger who was standing in her place?

"We have to talk," I said.

"I should hope so," said Peg. "Otherwise, why are you here?"

I grabbed her arm, turned her around, and steered her in the direction of the kitchen. The kitchen in Aunt Peg's house was what I knew. It was where I felt comfortable. It was where we *talked*.

"I'm having coffee," I said, directing her to a chair at the butcher block table. Aunt Peg refuses to buy a coffeemaker, but she keeps a jar of instant in the cabinet. It was close enough. "Would you like tea?"

"No, thank you. I'm fine."

I stared at her through narrowed eyes. Aunt Peg always wanted tea. And she was never *fine*.

"Am I on *Candid Camera?*" I asked. "Should I smile and speak toward a microphone?"

"Don't be ridiculous," Aunt Peg snapped. "You sound like an idiot."

"So do you," I shot back.

"I do not."

"You"—I leveled a pointed finger at her—"don't have cake."

Aunt Peg looked incredulous. "Really, Melanie? That's what your odd behavior is about? The fact that I don't have *cake?*"

"Precisely." I stood and crossed my arms over my chest. "Explain that to me. And it better be good."

She took a moment to gather her thoughts. "It's not good," Peg said finally. "Not good at all. I am on a diet."

Aunt Peg on a diet? The very idea was inconceivable. Peg was six feet tall and had the metabolism and energy of a Greyhound. In all the time we'd spent together, I'd never known her to worry about things like calories, or nutrition, or extra weight—unless her beloved Standard Poodles were involved, of course.

Aunt Peg ate anything and everything. And usually had seconds. And then dessert.

"Oh." A sudden burst of relief made me feel giddy, then weak. I sank down into a chair beside her. "That's great. Excellent actually."

Aunt Peg was not amused. "I can assure you," she said firmly, "it is not in any way *excellent*."

"Compared to the alternative," I sputtered, still somewhat light-headed. "You were acting so strangely, I thought maybe you'd been diagnosed with a terrible illness."

"Oh pish. There's no need for melodrama. I'm not dying. I'm just overweight. Fifteen pounds, to be exact."

"It happens," I said.

"Not to me!"

"Really?" I looked at her. "You've never gained weight before?"

"No. Why should I?"

Perhaps because you have the eating habits of a longshoreman and a voracious appetite for sugar, I thought. The sentiment seemed better off left unvoiced.

"I just saw you three days ago," I said. "You were fine then. What happened in the meantime?"

"I had my yearly physical on Monday. Apparently it's not unusual for someone my age to put on a few pounds. But fifteen pounds in one year was enough for my doctor to be a bit concerned. She would prefer that the trend not continue. I'm supposed to add more fresh vegetables to my diet. And do away with things like refined sugar, butter, and white flour."

"In other words," I said. "Cake."

Aunt Peg nodded. "It's only been since Monday," she said sadly. "I already want to strangle somebody."

"I could tell."

"Could you?" She peered at me across the table. "I thought I was coping rather well."

"Trust me," I said. "You're not."

"That's hardly my fault. It's not pleasant being hungry all the time."

Like that was news.

"Do what the doctor told you and eat your veggies," I said. "You like vegetables. And they're very filling."

"I like vegetables in their place," Aunt Peg corrected me. "In a small mound on the unimportant side of the plate. Not as the main event."

"I can't believe you went cold turkey," I told her.

"It seemed like a good idea at the time. Of course I was polishing off a Christmas strudel when I made the decision. I figured I should remove the last bit of temptation from the house before beginning the new regimen."

I got up from the table and went to put on the kettle. Under the circumstances, it sounded as though a strong dose of Earl Grey tea was definitely called for.

"Diets work better when they're not based on total deprivation," I told her.

"They do?"

"Sure. It makes sense, doesn't it? You can still satisfy your cravings but with a few bites rather than a whole cake. Then you're less likely to give in and overindulge later."

"Nobody told me that." Aunt Peg's expression brightened. "A sliver of cake sounds like a fine idea."

I thought it might. Except, of course, that we didn't have one.

"Also, it makes more sense to start a new diet after the holidays rather than before. You'll be less likely to cheat."

"*After?*" Aunt Peg was beginning to look almost happy now.

"You know, like on New Year's Day. You could make a resolution."

"I could at that," Aunt Peg said cheerfully. "This is all sounding much better. Perhaps I should have consulted with you sooner. How do you know these things?"

"How do you *not* know them?" I asked. "Everyone knows this stuff."

The kettle began to whistle. I got out two mugs and prepared tea for Aunt Peg and coffee with a splash of milk for myself. We both ignored the sugar bowl.

"I know dogs," Aunt Peg told me. "For the vast majority of my life, that has seemed like quite enough."

"As it happens," I said, rejoining her at the table, "that's why I'm here."

"Of course it is," Peg replied.

No false modesty around here.

"I've been to see Sondra," I said. "And I've talked to some other people, too. Did you know that Kiltie is going to Todd after the first of the year?"

"I didn't know that it was definite." Aunt Peg blew on her tea and took a cautious sip. "But I might have had an inkling that a plan was in the works."

"But here's the thing," I told her. "According to Jo Drummer, Sondra isn't the only one who made a plan involving Todd. Jo said that Todd's new special is an Afghan Hound that's coming over from England."

"Interesting." Aunt Peg pondered that. "I wonder if Sondra knows."

"I can't imagine that she does. She told me she's already lined up a whole bunch of advertising to announce Kiltie's new association with Todd. So how is that going to work if he has two top dogs?"

"If I know Todd, he'll make it work," Peg said thoughtfully. "There are a number of good, even great, professional handlers. But Todd has risen to the top by being the very best at two things. He always brings judges exactly what they want to see in their rings. And he knows how to keep his clients happy."

"Sondra seems like a tough person to please."

"She is indeed," Aunt Peg agreed. "Life has handed Sondra a lot of advantages. So many, that in most of her dealings she automatically assumes—quite correctly—that she has the upper hand."

I nodded. I could see that.

"But with Todd, the scales will be tipped in the opposite direction. He's offered more good dogs than he has time for. I'm sure Sondra approached him about adding Kiltie to his string and not the other way around. She's lucky to have Todd at the end of Kiltie's leash and Sondra will understand that. I'd imagine she'll behave accordingly."

"I should hope so," I said.

"And don't forget, Todd has two assistants both of whom are more than talented enough to be out on their own. So if he ever does end up with a conflict in the Best in Show ring, whichever dog he opts to hand off will also be in expert hands."

"Sondra is hoping to syndicate Kiltie," I mentioned.

Aunt Peg looked up, surprised. "I can't imagine why. She has more money than God."

"She said she wants the dog to have backers with serious clout."

"Oh pish," said Aunt Peg.

"You don't think it will happen?"

"It sounds to me as though Sondra has her head in the clouds. Once the dog is out with Todd, if he catches fire and really starts winning anything may be possible. But right this very moment, we're a long way from worrying about *that*. Especially since Sondra doesn't even know where her dog is."

"Which brings me to my next question," I said. "What do you know about the Tri-State West Highland White Terrier Club?"

"I've heard of them," Aunt Peg mused. "I believe they're based somewhere in Westchester. Am I meant to know more than that?"

"Apparently Sondra is a member, and I was told that she's been causing problems there recently."

"What sorts of problems?"

"She managed to get several fellow breeders expelled from the club."

"That doesn't sound good," Aunt Peg said with a frown. "You'd better talk to Meredith Kronen and find out what happened. If anyone knows the whole story, she'll be the one."

"Who's Meredith Kronen?"

"A lovely woman who used to breed Scotties. Now she judges terriers and she's beginning to branch out into the toy breeds. Meredith knows everyone in terriers and she's the kind of person who likes to keep her ear to the ground. There isn't a lot that gets past her."

"Do you have her phone number?" I asked.

"I can do better than that," said Aunt Peg. "I'll call and tell her you're on your way."

"*Now*?"

"Of course, now. Can you think of a better time?"

"Actually yes," I said. "Considering that I still have to pick up Davey and make dinner. How about tomorrow? You haven't even told me where Meredith lives."

"Rye." Aunt Peg gestured vaguely in the direction of the Merritt Parkway. "Right around the corner."

Only if you were speaking of a very large corner, I thought.

"Tomorrow morning," I decided. "See if she's free then."

Aunt Peg disappeared briefly. When she returned, she was holding a sheet of paper with an address written on it. "Ten-thirty," she said. "Meredith will be expecting you."

I got up and motioned to Faith that I was ready to go. Aunt Peg and the Poodle honor guard walked us to the door. I fastened my coat and wound my scarf around my neck. Then I stopped and sighed. There was one more thing I had to say.

"Now what?" asked Aunt Peg.

"I feel bad for Kiltie," I said. "I really do."

"So? We all feel bad for that poor lost dog. Why is that a problem?"

"Because the more I find out about Sondra, the less I like her. The way she behaves sometimes . . . I guess it makes me wonder why I'm even trying to help her at all."

"Because despite your faults, you are a kind and caring person."

Trust Aunt Peg to temper a compliment—one of the few I'd ever received from her—with an insult.

"*Despite* my faults?"

I wasn't asking for an enumeration. It didn't matter. I got one anyway.

Aunt Peg lifted a hand and began to tick off points, one by one, on her fingers. "Heaven knows you're too impetuous. And you're terrible about overscheduling. You never answer your phone. And on top of that, you're a slow driver."

Says the woman who treats most roads like her own personal Indy 500 strip.

"Considering that I'm slow and overbooked," I said, feeling more than a bit grumpy, "maybe I should call Sondra and tell her to find her own dog."

Aunt Peg opened the door and shooed Faith and me out into the cold December air. "Or maybe you should just buckle down and get the job done," she said. "Don't think about Sondra. Think about Kiltie. He's what matters."

What had I been hoping? That Aunt Peg would take my objection to Sondra to heart and let me off the hook so that I could go home and resume planning Christmas for my family? Apparently I should have known better.

With Aunt Peg, the answer was always the same. It was all about the dogs.

Chapter 19

Thursday morning, it was back to the Merritt Parkway again. Sam had work to do so this time I had Kevin as my companion rather than Faith. He and I were heading southwest toward Westchester County where Meredith Kronen was waiting for us.

"Go swim?" Kev asked from the backseat.

"No," I said. "Not today."

"Playground?"

"It's too cold for the playground. We're going to visit a nice lady."

"Nice lady." My son grinned happily. He likes everybody. "Fish?"

"Probably not," I told him. "She might have a dog."

"Poodle," Kevin said firmly. Since that's his favorite breed of dog, he assumes it's everyone else's, too.

"I don't think so," I said. "We'll see."

Meredith Kronen lived in a cute Victorian-style house at the end of a quiet, dead-end road in the village of Rye Brook. Since she was expecting us, I pulled off the road and parked in her driveway. As I was unfastening the buckles and clasps of Kevin's car seat, the door to the house opened. A middle-aged woman with frizzy red hair, thick, dark-framed glasses, and a wide, engaging smile, came out onto the porch to wait for us.

"You must be Melanie," she said as we approached. "I'm Meredith. Who's the young man?"

"Kevin," my son piped up before I could answer. "Do you have fish?"

Not surprisingly, Meredith looked taken aback by the question.

"I might have a can of tuna in the pantry," she told him. "Will that do?"

"Sorry," I said with a laugh. "We visited someone recently who had an aquarium. Now all Kev wants to talk about is fish."

"Ahh." She nodded in understanding. "An obsession. I get that. Everyone I know only wants to talk about dogs."

"I know how you feel. It's the same way at my house."

We walked up two front steps, crossed the narrow porch, and followed Meredith inside. As we dealt with coats and hats and mittens, I said, "Thank you for agreeing to talk to me today. I hope our visit isn't an imposition."

"Not at all, I'm happy to help if I can," Meredith replied. "Your aunt and I are old friends. And since she was recently instrumental in my gaining approval to judge Poodles, you might say that I owe her one."

Trading favors. The dog world revolved around that fundamental practice.

"I've brought some books and Matchbox cars with

me," I said. "Kevin can entertain himself while we talk, if that's all right with you."

"It's perfect. I put the dogs out in their runs so we won't be disturbed. Come on in and have a seat."

We got ourselves settled in a lovely living room whose Victorian-style furniture matched the design of the house. I sat down on a narrow upholstered couch. Kev was happy to find a seat on the floor at my feet. I unzipped the diaper bag and propped it open next to him so that he could look inside and choose his own distraction.

"Peg told me you wanted to talk about Sondra Mc-Evoy," Meredith prompted.

"That's right. You may have heard that her dog, Kiltie, was stolen?"

"I *heard* it." Meredith stopped and frowned. "I didn't entirely believe it."

"How come?"

"Because the entire story sounded farcical to me. That someone dressed like Santa Claus would abscond with Sondra's Westie at a Christmas bazaar? When I heard the news I assumed it was a joke. Or that someone was playing a prank of some kind. I'm afraid I didn't give it any further thought."

"It's no joke," I told her. "Kiltie's been missing for five days."

"In that case, I apologize. It appears I shouldn't have made light of what happened. Sondra must be beside herself with worry."

Irritated? Agitated? Annoyed beyond measure? Those were all adjectives I might have used to describe Sondra's reaction to Kiltie's disappearance. But beside herself with worry? Not really. In fact now that I stopped and thought about it, that was one of the things that had been bugging me about this whole situation.

"Aunt Peg offered my assistance to Sondra," I said. "She thought I could ask some questions and maybe help figure out what happened."

"Peg is good at conscripting people and bending them to her will," Meredith said with a laugh. "I believe she's signed me up for some duties having to do with the PCA Foundation. Are you good at finding missing dogs?"

"That remains to be seen," I told her. "But I am pretty good at asking questions."

"Have at it then." Meredith sat back in her chair and got comfortable. "What do you need to know?"

"I'm trying to find people who might have had a grudge against Sondra, or who were upset with her for some reason. And I heard that she caused some trouble recently at the Tri-State Westie Club."

"Who told you that?"

"If you don't mind, I'd rather not say."

"No, that's fine." Meredith dismissed her own question. "I was just curious, but I suppose it doesn't really matter. The story is hardly a secret. The entire membership of the club and half the Terriers breeders in this part of the country all seem to know about it."

"Are you a member of the Tri-State club?"

"Nope. Not my breed."

Her tone indicated that the answer should have been obvious. Which I supposed it was.

"But I have several friends who belong to the club," she continued. "So I heard all about what happened. You know how dog people love to talk."

I nodded happily. I did indeed. It was that fortuitous fact that often made my life so much easier.

"As you might imagine, a club that named itself Tri-State covers a pretty large area. There are members from western Connecticut, southern New York, and northern New Jersey. There's a big mix of personalities in that group, not to mention the inevitable differences in breeding programs and goals. Some members are very involved in club business, others not at all."

"Where does Sondra fit into the mix?" I asked.

"At one point, she was one of the VIPs at Tri-State. She held several offices, hosted club meetings at her house, and was co-chairman of the specialty show. But over the last couple years, her interest in the club and its activities has waned. I think her priorities have shifted. Having a dog as good as Kiltie has made her want to devote more time and energy to his career and less to all those club duties."

"Sondra must still care about what goes on there though," I said, "because I heard she got a couple of novice breeders kicked out. "

"Yes, she did. One breeder had her membership revoked by the board. The second one resigned in protest."

"That sounds pretty intense," I said, shaking my head. "The dog clubs I've known are always thrilled to get new members. More hands equals less work for everyone. So I'm assuming that the person must have done something pretty awful for that to happen?"

"It depends on who you talk to," Meredith replied. "And also, I guess, on who you choose to believe. The woman Sondra took exception to was a real newbie, both to the breed and to the sport. She had two Westie bitches and a young dog that she'd bought from three different breeders in other parts of the country. None of the three were finished, though she was trying with all of them." She paused, then added, "Not very successfully, I'm afraid."

"Owner handling?" I guessed.

"Yes. That was part of the problem. It wasn't all of it."

"I take it they weren't very good representatives of the breed?"

Meredith looked at me and sighed. "After all this blew up, I went back and looked at my notes. It turned out that I'd had occasion to judge two of the dogs. Neither did better under me than a low ribbon in a small class."

"Oh," I said.

"They weren't the worst Westies I've ever seen. But they certainly could have been better. In my opinion, the two I saw were barely show quality. And of course Rachel's inexpert grooming didn't do them any favors."

Westies are like Poodles in that learning how to groom them to advantage and present them in the show ring takes time and dedication. Talent helps, too. Both breeds are difficult for someone who's just learning the ropes to have success with.

"Everybody has to start somewhere," I said. Not that far from the newbie ranks myself, I might have sounded slightly defensive.

"Oh, I know that," Meredith agreed. "We all were beginners once. What Rachel needed was for someone to take her under their wing and show her how things ought to be done."

"But that didn't happen?"

"I'm sure it would have. In time. Rachel should have

just slowed down, taken a deep breath, and devoted herself to watching and learning. Plenty of dog people are willing to be generous with their expertise. I'd imagine she'd have found a mentor if she hadn't been in such a big hurry."

"What did she do instead?" I asked.

"Unfortunately Rachel got fed up with losing in the show ring. So she took the bitches and the dog home and bred them."

"To each other?"

Meredith nodded. "Somehow she seemed to think that the puppies would turn out to be better than either of their parents."

"She would have been better off placing those dogs in good homes and starting over with better stock," I said.

"I know that, and you know that. But as I said, Rachel was impatient. She wanted to be a breeder."

"What about genetic testing?"

"Whether it was due to ignorance or arrogance, I have no idea. But I gather that didn't happen either."

That was really *not* good.

"So Rachel ended up with two litters of pet quality puppies from untested parents that she needed to find homes for," said Meredith. "And being new, she had no waiting list or connections. But since she was a member of the club, she felt that she was entitled to place an ad for the puppies on the Tri-State web site. She also wanted to have her name added to the club's breeder referral list. And when Sondra found out about both those things, she threw a fit."

"It sounds like she might have had a good reason for that," I pointed out.

"For the initial objection, certainly. And Sondra wasn't the only one who felt that way. *None* of the Tri-State breeders wanted to put their reputations behind puppies of that caliber. But Rachel Bright wasn't a bad person. She was simply undereducated and somewhat misguided."

"The club should have taken her in hand and taught her what she needed to know," I said. That was what my local Poodle club would have done.

"Absolutely. And there were other members who realized that. Booting Rachel out the door was Sondra's solution to the problem. But if you ask me, it was a knee-jerk reaction. And not everybody agreed with her."

"What happened then?" I asked.

"The conflict caused a huge rift in the club. Some members backed Sondra because they thought she was right. Others backed her because they were playing politics and nobody ever wants to get on Sondra's bad side. But Rachel had her sympathizers, too. In the end, the decision was left up to the board."

"I'm guessing Sondra would have had plenty of influence there," I said.

"It wasn't just a matter of influence," Meredith told me. "Even though she has let some other club activities go, Sondra is still a board member. So she was one of the people making the decision, and I gather that she harangued the other board members until they agreed with her. Or at least until they didn't have the guts to vote against her. So Rachel was out.

"And then, when the news was made public, another breeder that Rachel had become friends with, resigned as well. The club was left with the worst possible outcome.

Two enthusiastic new members were lost to them and in the end, the only person who was happy about the way things turned out was Sondra."

"It sounds as though Tri-State could have found a much better way of handling things," I said.

"Of course they could have," Meredith replied briskly. "And they probably would have too, if Sondra hadn't gotten involved and forced the resolution she wanted."

"When did all this happen?" I asked.

"The ruckus started in October. The board voted late last month."

That would have been just a few weeks before the Christmas bazaar, I realized. Which might have left just enough time for someone who had a good reason to be furious at Sondra to plot and engineer a suitable revenge.

"It isn't hard to guess what you're thinking," said Meredith. "You're wondering if Rachel had something to do with Kiltie's disappearance."

"Aren't you?" I asked.

Instead of answering, Meredith glanced down and checked the time on her watch. "Rachel's a real estate broker for one of the major agencies. She works at their office in White Plains. I bet you could probably find her there this morning if you want to talk to her about it."

I did indeed. That was a no-brainer.

While Meredith looked up an address for me, I turned to Kevin. The toddler was sitting on the floor, leaning against my leg. A Richard Scarry book about cars and trucks was propped open in his lap. He looked up from the busy page to see what I wanted.

"Ready to go?" I asked.

"Ready, set, go!" he cried. It was close enough.

"Thank you for taking the time to talk to me," I said to Meredith as Kev and I paused in the hall to suit up again before heading back outside.

"I hope I helped," she replied. "Sondra McEvoy isn't one of my favorite people, but nobody deserves to lose her dog."

"Quick answer," I said. "Is Rachel Bright the kind of person who could have done something like that?"

"I probably don't know her well enough to say," Meredith admitted. "But I do know one thing. Rachel Bright was angry about what Sondra did to her. Really, really, angry."

Was it too much to hope that I finally had a real lead to follow? I wondered as Kevin and I made the short trip from Rye Brook to White Plains. After all the running around I'd been doing on Sondra's behalf, it would be about damn time. In the last five days, I'd turned up a lot of interesting information. But unfortunately none of it seemed to have brought me any closer to figuring out where Kiltie was.

The real estate agency Rachel Bright worked for was located on a busy midcity street. I was lucky to find a parking space not too far away. Sometimes Kevin possesses boundless energy. Other times— usually when there's something important I need to do—his little legs get tired before we've walked half a block.

As I opened the door to the agency, a buzzer announced our arrival. The outer office consisted of a single large room that was sparsely furnished. There were four work stations, one allotted to each corner. A spindly looking artificial Christmas tree was plunked in the center of the floor between them. Kev loves everything about Christmas and even he wasn't impressed. He barely gave the silver plastic tree a glance.

Only two of the desks in the room were currently occupied, both of them by women. The two agents looked up as I closed the door behind me.

"I'm looking for Rachel Bright," I said.

The woman at the near desk hopped up out of her chair and came quickly around to greet us. She looked enthusiastic, perky, and very eager to please. No doubt she was a good saleswoman. We hadn't even met yet and I got the impression that she was already calculating my client potential.

Too bad I was about to burst her bubble.

"I'm Rachel Bright," she said, hand extended. "How may I help you? Let me guess"—her gaze swept downward over Kevin, then back up—"I'm betting that you're looking for a home in a good school district."

"Not exactly," I replied. "My name is Melanie Travis. I was hoping to talk to you about your dogs."

"My dogs?"

Rachel's face fell. Then she swiftly recovered. I could almost see the wheels spinning as she remembered that houses weren't the only thing she currently had for sale. Instantly she appeared to be recalculating her chances of closing a deal.

"Of course," she said smoothly. "You must be looking for a puppy?"

Instead of waiting for my reply, Rachel hunkered down in front of Kevin. "Isn't that right, little boy? I bet *you* want a puppy."

"Have a puppy," Kevin announced. "Want fish."

Rachel opened her mouth, then snapped it shut again.

Go, Kev, I thought. It was nice to see *something* slow down the relentless barrage of sales patter.

"Maybe we could sit down for a minute?" I asked.

"Sure," said Rachel. "Over here."

She led the way to a pair of wooden chairs that were positioned beside a narrow table. Fronds from an oversized potted fern hung down over my shoulder as I sat down and pulled Kevin up into my lap. Giggling happily, he batted at the long, slender leaves.

Rachel waited until we were settled then said, "Why don't you tell me what you're looking for?"

Put like that, there was only one answer I could give.

"A missing West Highland White Terrier," I said.

"Missing . . . ?" Rachel sounded surprised. Then abruptly the other shoe dropped. Her expression shuttered. "You mean Kiltie."

"That's right."

"Did Sondra send you here?"

"No, she did not."

"I don't believe you."

"Nevertheless, it's true," I told her. "But considering the recent animosity between you and Sondra, I was wondering if you might know anything about his disappearance."

"If I did," Rachel said with a disgusted snort, "do you think I would tell you?"

I shrugged. "You might."

"Only if I was stupid."

"That sounds like a confession."

"Don't be ridiculous!" Rachel snapped. "It's nothing of the sort. I didn't take Sondra's dumb dog. But I'll tell you what—I'm glad someone did. Having Kiltie disappear from right under her nose? It serves her right."

"Sondra isn't the most popular person," I said affably.

Rachel refused to be placated. "And yet here you sit on her behalf."

"I'm here because of Kiltie," I told her. "And because even though you might have been mad enough at Sondra to want to lash out at her, I'm sure you wouldn't have wanted an innocent pet to be punished as a result."

"An innocent pet." Rachel blew out an annoyed breath. "I can't believe you just said that."

"You don't agree?"

"Not even close. So don't try to tug at my heartstrings to get what you want. Kiltie is nobody's pet. He's a competitor, a professional show dog who's shooting up the ladder of success. And Sondra McEvoy doesn't care who she has to shove out of his way to get there."

"Like you, you mean?"

"Hardly," said Rachel. "In the grand scheme of things, I'm a nobody. Sondra probably came down hard on me just for practice. You know, to keep her claws sharpened."

Sadly I couldn't disagree.

"Is there someone else Sondra has pushed out of the way recently?" I asked.

"You didn't hear this from me," Rachel said, leaning closer.

"Of course not," I agreed.

"Do you know who Todd Greenleaf is?"

I nodded.

"A friend of mine works in his kennel. She told me that Todd dumped a dog belonging to one of his long-time clients in order to make room for Sondra to wedge her dog into his lineup. The other client thought that Todd was going to be specialing his terrier this year, but it turns out he'll have Kiltie instead."

Rachel sat back and looked at me with a satisfied smirk on her face. "Except now Kiltie's gone. So maybe not. You know?"

Chapter 20

That was interesting.

I wondered if it was true. Obviously it was in Rachel's best interests to steer me in another direction. On the other hand, at this point I couldn't afford to discount any input that came my way.

"Why would Todd do that to someone he's had a long relationship with?" I asked.

"Are you kidding? For the money." Rachel shook her head at my naiveté. "It's always about the money."

There was that.

"Who's the other client?"

"A guy named Rick Stanley. He shows Cairns. Or at least he does when Sondra isn't throwing her weight around and screwing things up for him."

I knew that name, I realized with a start. Bertie had given it to me on Tuesday when I'd asked her about other exhibitors who'd been at the Christmas bazaar. I had called Mr. Stanley and left a message but he hadn't called me back.

It sounded as though it was time for me to do something about that.

"Not like that lady," Kevin said when we were back in the car and heading home.

"I know," I replied, glancing back at him. "I'm sorry you had to meet her. She doesn't seem like a very happy person."

"Not happy," Kev said with a firm nod. "No fish."

Kevin and I spent the afternoon at the Stamford Town Center doing some Christmas shopping. Fortunately, at his young age, Kev is easily distractible. Not only that, but the mall offers a cornucopia of interesting things for a toddler to see and do. I was able to select several presents for Sam and Davey, pay for them, and slip them quickly out of sight into shopping bags while Kev's attention was focused on other things. Every mother I know is adept at that particular sleight of hand. I'm pretty sure it's one of the basic job requirements.

Out in the parking garage, I'd just finished loading the car and buckling Kevin into his car seat when my cell phone rang. The caller's number looked vaguely familiar, but Caller ID didn't supply a name. I slipped into the front seat of the Volvo and fitted the phone to my ear.

"This is Jane Brew," a woman's voice said briskly. "I understand you want to talk to me?"

"Yes," I said. "It's about Kiltie."

"Who?"

Maybe we had a bad connection, I thought. Every other exhibitor I'd spoken to had known immediately who the Westie was.

"Kiltie," I said again. "GCH Westglen Braveheart?"

"Never heard of him," Jane Brew replied. "Are you sure you called the right person? Where did you get my number?"

I took a deep breath and started over. "You attended the Howard Academy Christmas Bazaar last Saturday."

"That's right. A friend and I drove down from Westport to get our dogs' pictures taken with Santa Claus. Is that a problem?"

"No, of course not," I said quickly. "A lot of other people did the same thing."

"Are you calling all of us?"

"No, I—"

"Then why me?"

"Because you show dogs."

"So what?"

Watching me from the backseat, Kevin tipped his head to one side and gave me a toothy grin. Even he seemed to know that I was fast losing control of the conversation.

"One of the dogs who was there that day—a West Highland White named Kiltie—was stolen from his crate at the bazaar that afternoon."

There was a brief pause, then Jane Brew said, "What does that have to do with me?"

"I thought maybe you might have seen something—"

"I didn't even see a Westie. I was busy with my own dogs. And minding my own business."

"That's too bad," I said.

"Are we done?" asked Jane.

"Umm . . . I guess."

Click.

I sighed and tucked my phone away. That, in a nut-shell, was why I preferred speaking to people in person. I'm not nearly as easy to blow off when I'm standing right in front of them.

"I guess," Kev said from the backseat.

Even though I knew he was merely echoing the last thing he'd heard me say, I still turned around and asked, "You guess what?"

"Christmas coming!" Kev cried. He pumped a fist in the air for emphasis.

This time of year, that child has a one-track mind.

When we arrived home, the house smelled wonderful. While Kev rolled around on the floor with the Poodles who'd met us at the door, I followed my nose to the kitchen. There I discovered that Sam and Davey were baking Christmas cookies.

I wrapped my arms around my husband, hugged him hard, and said, "I think I'm in love."

"I should hope so," Sam replied. He had oven mitts on both hands and a smear of flour down the front of his shirt.

"Hey," said Davey, talking around the warm sugar cookie he'd just popped into his mouth. "I'm helping, too."

That earned him a hug as well. Since he'd pretty much asked for it, Davey had the grace not to squirm out of my grasp too quickly. Even though he's opposed to parental displays of affection on principle, my son might have even hugged me back a little. It appeared as though the cookies were having a salutary effect on all of us.

I stepped back and gazed around the kitchen. Several dozen cinnamon cookies were cooling on racks. Two baking sheets were currently in the oven. Davey had been working on filling a third from a bowl of cookie batter on the counter.

"This all looks great," I said, helping myself to a warm cookie. "What's the occasion?"

Busy spooning batter into neat balls on the baking tray, Davey mumbled something under his breath. I turned to Sam for a translation.

"Christmas party at Davey's school," Sam told me as he checked the timer on the oven. "Davey volunteered to bring six dozen cookies."

"That was nice of you," I said. "When's the party?"

Sam and Davey shared a look.

"Tomorrow," my son informed me.

"They only gave you *one day's* notice to come up with six dozen cookies?" I asked incredulously.

"Not exactly," said Sam.

Oh. Maybe that was why Davey had allowed me an extra-long hug.

"How long have you known about it?" I asked.

"Couple weeks. I kind of forgot."

"I guess you did," I muttered.

"No big deal," said Sam. "Davey and I ran out to the market and picked up plenty of supplies. We've got everything under control."

"You're a lifesaver," I said.

"You know it." Sam grinned.

Kevin came charging into the kitchen with six Standard Poodles in hot pursuit. "Cookies!" he cried, his eyes widening as he looked around the room. "Want some."

"Me, too," I agreed. "Let's make lots of extras for us. You can help decorate."

I pulled off my coat, rolled up my sleeves, and went to work.

Friday morning, back to school. Walking down the semi-empty hallway with Faith upon our arrival, I wondered why we'd even bothered to show up. On this, the last school day before the start of Christmas vacation, it appeared as though half the student body had already gone AWOL.

In the teachers' lounge, the atmosphere was festive. The prospect of three whole weeks of vacation had put everyone in a good mood. Even Ed Weinstein looked cheerful. That had to be a first.

There was fresh coffee in the silver urn and a chocolate Yule log on the table. I hadn't planned to sit down but that cake was calling my name. I cut a sliver off the end and slipped into a chair beside Rita Kinney.

"Who baked?" I asked her. "You?"

"Are you kidding?" Rita laughed. "Who has time to bake? My mother sent it, and according to the box it came in, she didn't bake it either."

"Nice of you to share." I sectioned off a large bite and slid it into my mouth. "This is really good."

"Too good," Rita agreed. "If I hadn't brought it to school, I'd have eaten the whole thing myself."

"Your loss is our gain," said Louisa Delgado. She glanced down at her hips. "Literally and figuratively."

"Hey, Melanie," Ed said from across the table. "Did you find that lost dog yet? You know, the one that went missing from your bazaar?"

"Not yet," I replied, swallowing another bite of cake. "But I'm working on it."

"What's the hold-up?"

"Well . . ." I leveled Ed a look. "He's *lost*."

"I heard there's going to be a lawsuit over that dog." Ed paused for effect, then added, "A huge one."

With that pronouncement, every head in the room swiveled around to look at us. Probably just as Ed had intended. Too bad for him that I was tired of listening to his self-serving bluster. And that I was coasting along on a wave of cake-induced euphoria.

"I'm not surprised you're interested," I said brightly. "Since you were right there at the bazaar when Kiltie disappeared. What do you know about what happened?"

"What kind of question is that?" Abruptly Ed reared back in his seat. I found it interesting how quickly he'd gone on the defensive. "You're the one who blew it. Why should I know anything?"

"Maybe because you brought up the subject," Rita pointed out. "You're the one who wants to talk about it."

"Not like this," Ed grumbled. "Melanie has no cause to be snooping around me."

"Of course not, Ed," said Louisa. "Because, as usual, you don't have any idea what you're talking about." She reached over and nabbed his plate. "That's enough cake for you. I think the sugar's going to your brain."

Louisa stood up, walked over to the sideboard, and dumped Ed's remaining half piece in the garbage. A smattering of laughter came from around the room. Louisa smiled, extended her arm gracefully, and took a small bow.

Ed's face grew red. As the first bell rang, he stood up and left the room in a hurry.

"Way to kill the good mood," Ryan Duncan called after him. Everybody laughed again.

"That's my cue," I said, rising as well. As I exited the lounge and started down the hall, I realized that Louisa had followed me. I slowed my pace and she caught up.

"Do you have a minute?" she asked.

"Sure. What's up?"

"You know I have Poppy McEvoy for sixth grade math, right?"

I nodded. Louisa was a great teacher, but even she couldn't manage to spark Poppy's interest in math. The child loved words and hated numbers, which was why we had a weekly session together.

"Ed talking about that lost dog made me think that maybe I should say something."

I pulled over to the side of the hallway and stopped. "Go on."

"Have you noticed anything different about Poppy recently?"

"Define *recently*."

"I don't know exactly," Louisa said with a shrug. "Maybe a couple of months? It seems like something's going on with her. She's been distracted, even more so than the usual sixth grader. And maybe a little glum. I'm wondering if she's okay."

I leaned in closer, lowered my voice, and said, "Her parents separated not too long ago. Did you know that?"

"I had no idea." Louisa looked surprised. "Are you sure? Usually news like that is all over the grapevine. And I know I saw Poppy with both her parents at the Christmas bazaar."

"They were there," I agreed. "But at different times

of the day. Sondra told me about the separation herself. Poppy's father has moved out of the house."

"Poor kid," Louisa murmured. "No wonder she's been unhappy. Thanks for letting me know. I'll try to cut her some slack."

"And I'll try to bring Kiltie back," I said. "Maybe between the two of us, we can cheer her up a little."

By the time I reached my room, my first pupil was already waiting for me. Gordon Beck was a cheerful second grader who was new to the school that year. His recent dyslexia diagnosis was not only turning his academic performance around, it was also transforming him from a reluctant student to one who was now curious about his studies and eager to learn. I loved helping kids like Gordon; it was just one of the things that made my work at Howard Academy incredibly gratifying.

At the end of our tutoring session, Gordon opened the door to leave, then turned and looked back into the room. "Hey," he said. "There's a guy out here."

I'd been gathering my papers. Now I stopped and glanced up. "Who?"

"I dunno." Gordon shrugged. He shouldered his backpack and left.

The door pushed open farther and a man I'd never seen before came walking into my room uninvited. He was medium height and had a stocky build, along with bland features and grizzled gray-brown hair. He paused and shut the classroom door behind him, holding it in place until the latch clicked.

Security is pretty tight at Howard Academy. The school caters to a wealthy clientele and children's safety and well-being is paramount. Strangers don't go wandering around the campus unescorted. It isn't allowed and it doesn't happen. So even though there was nothing about this man that appeared even remotely dangerous, the situation was still unusual enough to put me on guard.

I lowered my hand to my side and snapped my fingers. Faith, who was snoozing on her cedar bed in the corner of the room, woke up and lifted her head. Sensing my abrupt change in attitude, she quickly got up and padded across the room to stand beside me.

Faith isn't a guard dog. She's never had protection training. But she's big and solid enough that her mere presence can act as a deterrent. *Better safe than sorry,* I thought.

Then the man surprised me. He glanced down at Faith and said, "That's a pretty Standard Poodle. She looks like a Cedar Crest dog."

My shoulders relaxed fractionally. Cedar Crest was Aunt Peg's kennel name. "She is a Cedar Crest Poodle," I told him. "Who are you?"

"Rick Stanley. I heard that you've been trying to get in touch with me."

Rick Stanley. All right. Not a stranger then. At least not entirely.

I motioned Faith back to her bed.

"You might have just returned my call," I said.

"I didn't feel the need." He walked over, pulled out a chair at my teaching table, and sat down. "But then I heard from a couple of people that maybe I should talk to you. So here I am."

"Who did you hear that from?" I asked.

"It's not important."

Maybe not to him, I thought. On the other hand, Rick Stanley's sudden appearance had generated so many other questions that I'd be silly to waste my time lingering over that one.

"This is a private school," I said. "How did you get in here? How did you know where to find me?"

"That part was easy," Rick replied.

I stared at him across the low table. I wasn't going to let him brush off this query so easily. If the school had holes in its security protocols, Mr. Hanover was going to want to hear about them.

"I don't think so," I said firmly.

"Look, it's no big deal. I'm a Howard Academy alum, okay? Class of eighty-eight. My brothers and I went to school here, kindergarten through eighth grade. I know every nook and cranny of this place. In fact, I bet I know this campus better than you do."

"Then you probably know that visitors are supposed to check in at the front office," I told him.

Rick just shrugged. "I didn't feel the need."

That was the second time he'd said that. I was beginning to get the impression that Rick Stanley was the kind of man who gave his own needs very high priority. I wondered where that left the rest of us.

"Hey, I was in the neighborhood so I stopped in," said Rick. "But I don't have all day. Do you want to talk about Kiltie or not?"

"I do." I pulled out a chair opposite him. "What do you know about his abduction?"

"Not a single blessed thing."

As if that was going to shut me up.

"You were at the Christmas bazaar from which he was stolen," I said.

"Just an unlucky coincidence. Like I told you, I'm an HA alum. I live in Greenwich and I like to support the school when I can."

"Did you see Kiltie when you were at the bazaar?"

"Sure, I saw him," Rick said easily. "So what? I'm sure lots of people saw him. Sondra's daughter was carrying him around. She had him at the photo booth at one point. I was there with Duffer."

"Where did he go after that?"

"How would I know? I wasn't keeping track. I was there to get my dog's picture taken. The girl finished and took Kiltie away and then it was my turn. That's all I know."

"Duffer's a Cairn," I said.

"Possibly." Rick chuckled. "Depending on your point of view. If you ask Duffer, he'd probably tell you that he's damn near human."

Been there, I thought. That shared connection made me warm to Rick Stanley just a little.

"I've heard he's a very good dog," I said.

"He is."

"Good enough for Todd Greenleaf."

"So that's where this is going." Rick's brief flash of good humor vanished. "That was supposed to be confidential. How did you find out?"

"It's not important," I said, echoing his words from earlier. Two could play that game.

"Fine, don't tell me. I can guess. Todd must be trying to make himself feel important by dragging me through the mud."

"No," I corrected quickly. "I've never spoken to Todd."

"Sondra then."

"Wrong again."

"I doubt it." Rick shook his head. "That woman's a bitch."

Among dog people, the word *bitch* doesn't have the

same connotation that it does in the real world. As a reference to a female dog, it's used all the time with impunity. But Rick's tone made it clear that he was aiming for the insult.

"You sound like you're very angry at her," I said.

"Of course I'm angry at Sondra. In my place, anyone would be. I've been waiting patiently all year for Todd to retire Horace. When he went home, it was supposed to be Duffer's turn."

"Horace?" I asked.

"You really don't know much, do you?"

This time the insult was aimed at me. I didn't even try to dodge it.

"Why don't you enlighten me?" I said.

"Horace is an Irish Terrier, GCH Runnymede Hot Stuff. You've never heard of him?"

I shook my head.

"Really?"

I decided that the question was rhetorical and remained mum. Rick just sat and stared at me. After thirty seconds of silence that felt endless, I gave in.

"I have Standard Poodles," I said.

"That's no excuse."

Indeed. Aunt Peg probably would have said the same thing.

"Horace retired in November, after the National Dog Show," Rick said. "I assume you've heard of *that?*"

"Yes."

"As soon as he was done showing, Duffer was supposed to be next in line. Imagine my surprise, then, to find out that Todd was also planning to add Kiltie to his string."

"In *your* spot," I said. We're dog people. We anthropomorphize.

"A spot I'd waited for *all year,*" Rick repeated in case I hadn't yet gotten the point.

"That was a rotten thing to do," I agreed. "You must have been furious with both of them."

"I was," Rick muttered. "And they deserved it."

Now he'd made me curious. "How did Sondra manage that?" I asked.

"Manage what?"

"To bump Duffer and get Kiltie put in his place. Why would Todd do that to a longstanding client? Is Kiltie a better dog?"

"Hell, no."

"Then what happened?" Rachel had told me that the incentive was money. I was curious to hear what Rick would say.

"I have no idea," he replied sullenly. "Maybe she's sleeping with him."

I snorted under my breath. I was pretty sure that Todd was gay.

"Besides," said Rick, "what does it matter? The important thing is that Sondra's in and I'm out."

"And that Kiltie is gone," I added. "Stolen from a Christmas bazaar that you attended."

"Along with plenty of other people." Rick dismissed my logic as unimportant. "I guess I should say thank you to you—considering that Kiltie disappeared while you were in charge."

Just what I needed. Yet another person trying to make me feel bad about what had happened.

"Not so fast," I said. "I'm hoping to get him back."

"I'm sure you'll understand if I don't wish you good luck."

"You wouldn't want Kiltie to reappear so that Duffer can beat him fair and square?"

"We're way past that point." Rick stood up and headed for the door. "And anyway, you know what they say."

I couldn't resist asking. "What's that?"

He paused to look back. "All's fair in love and dog shows."

Chapter 21

Rick Stanley, so careful to close the door behind him when he entered the room, left it sitting open when he walked out. Now I barely had time to gather my thoughts before a new caller came striding in through the open doorway.

I saw who it was, swallowed a sigh, and thought, *Damn*. The school wasn't even half-full that morning, so why did my room have to be the only place on the campus that was as busy as a souk on market day?

The headmaster stopped in the middle of the room, laced his hands together neatly at his waist, and regarded me with a stern expression on his face. "Are you entertaining visitors, Ms. Travis? On school time?"

"That wasn't a visitor," I said, thinking quickly. "He was a school alum."

Mr. Hanover considered that for a moment. "You will have to pardon me," he said, "if I don't see the distinction."

"We were talking about school business."

"Indeed. What business is that?"

Drat, I thought. Why didn't he stop asking questions? Otherwise I'd never be able to stop enlarging the progressively deeper hole I appeared to be digging for myself.

"It was Kiltie," I admitted.

"Ah yes, Kiltie." The headmaster nodded. "The canine who has gone astray. As it happens, I was coming to check on your progress with that regard. Perhaps in light of your recent conversation with the *school alum,* you have new information that you might want to share?"

I wish, I thought.

"Pardon me?"

Crap, I thought guiltily. Had I said that *aloud?*

"I'm still looking," I said.

"A week has passed. . . ."

Six days. I wanted to correct him. It hasn't been a whole week. Not yet anyway.

"I may be getting closer," I said instead.

I read somewhere that social white lies are acceptable under certain circumstances. Ones involving desperation. I was sure that this occasion had to qualify.

"I'm happy to hear that," Mr. Hanover replied. "We've received no further communication from Sondra McEvoy regarding her potential litigation. That is also good news. Nevertheless, the sooner we can wrap things up and put this whole unfortunate episode behind us, the better both I and the Howard Academy board of directors will feel."

I nodded. I could certainly understand that.

"What about Jerry Platt?" I asked.

"What about him?"

"I haven't seen any updates in the newspaper. I was

wondering if you'd been in contact with Detective Young. And whether you might know how the police investigation into Platt's death is coming along."

The headmaster looked at me thoughtfully. "Are you familiar with the phrase *Don't borrow trouble,* Ms. Travis?"

"I've heard it, yes." Unfortunately it was one of those pithy sayings that seldom seemed to apply to my life.

"After our initial interview, Detective Young has not felt the need to contact me again. I can only see that as a good thing. Under the circumstances, I feel I should exercise the same restraint with regard to the way he conducts his business."

"I see," I said.

"I should hope so," Mr. Hanover intoned.

There was no mistaking the subtext to his remark. But just in case I had, the headmaster said, "It appears as though Howard Academy has narrowly escaped becoming the focus of what one can only assume would be scurrilous and sensationalistic publicity. I would be extremely annoyed if that good fortune were to reverse itself for any reason."

"I understand."

"Keep your head down, Ms. Travis." The headmaster paused, then added, "You may find that your continuing employment at Howard Academy depends upon it."

The iron fist in the velvet glove. I could almost feel it wrapping itself around my throat.

"I'm not looking for a murderer," I said. "I'm just following the trail of a lost dog."

"Then we find ourselves in agreement. Kindly see that it remains that way."

"I'll do my best," I promised.

I hoped that it would be good enough.

* * *

On Fridays, Howard Academy has early dismissal. So it was only a few minutes after two o'clock when Faith and I found ourselves back in the Volvo, cruising down Lake Avenue on our way to Deer Park. I'd called Sondra before leaving the school and told her we were coming.

"You must have news for me," Sondra said. She'd sounded excited. "Do you know where Kiltie is?"

"Not yet. I'm still working on that. But I have a few more questions for you."

"Questions?" In an instant, Sondra's mood changed. "What kind of time-wasting idiocy is that? I don't need more questions! I need answers—"

I'd turned off the phone as she was still speaking. Sondra could rant and rave to empty air if she wished, but I was through listening to her complain.

"I hung up on her," I said across the front seat to Faith. "Sondra won't have liked that. Maybe she won't see us when we get there."

The big Poodle flapped her tail up and down in response. Faith likes everything I say. Either that, or she found the idea of skipping our visit with Sondra as enticing as I did.

"But here's the problem," I told her. "Even though I've talked to a bunch of people, I'm no closer now to knowing where Kiltie is than I was when I started. So I must be missing something."

Faith woofed softly. She agreed. Too bad she couldn't also tell me what it was that I had overlooked.

"So we're going to talk to Sondra again. We're going to ask more questions and see if we get different answers. And I want to talk to Jim, too." I flicked on my blinker and turned into Deer Park. "I've been thinking about my conversation with Louisa. There's trouble in that house. And it looks like Poppy is right in the middle of it."

Faith tipped her head to one side. I took that as a sign of approval.

That's one of the great things about talking to dogs. They make you feel like you're really smart. Even when you know you're not.

This time, Sondra didn't meet us at the door upon our arrival. Instead the maid opened the door and stared at Faith and me with a blank expression on her face. "Yes?" she inquired.

"I'm Melanie Travis," I told her. "I'm here to see Sondra. I believe she's expecting me."

"Please wait here. I'll check and see if she's receiving visitors."

The door closed in our faces. I looked down at Faith. "*Really*?" I said in a low tone.

Faith didn't bother to answer. She looked every bit as miffed by this turn of events as I was.

"Maybe we should go," I whispered. "What do you say? Want to make a run for it?"

The door snicked open again. Now Sondra stood in the doorway. Hands propped on her hips, she stared out at the two of us. "Who are you talking to?" she demanded.

"Faith."

The Standard Poodle lifted her tail in acknowledgment. Never let it be said that my dogs don't have manners.

"We were just passing the time," I said to Sondra. "While we stood and waited on your front step."

Sondra looked annoyed. Nevertheless she stepped aside. I took that as an invitation. I entered the house and Faith followed me inside. Once again we were directed to the library.

On our previous visit, we'd started with small talk. This time Sondra got right down to business.

"Maybe this isn't working," she said.

"What do you mean?" I sat down on a love seat near the fireplace.

"Peg told me you knew how to get things done."

"Did she?" I knew I sounded pleased. Compliments from Aunt Peg are as rare as horse feathers and this was the second one I'd heard recently.

"I haven't seen any evidence of that, however," Sondra snapped.

"You wanted me to talk to some of your fellow exhibitors," I said.

"And?"

"I've spent the last few days doing exactly that."

"With nothing to show for it apparently. Who did you see?"

I ticked off several names on my fingers. "Chip Michaels, Jo Drummer, Meredith Kronen."

"Meredith?" Sondra sounded surprised.

"She sent me to Rachel Bright."

"I hope you didn't believe everything that woman told you."

I ignored the statement and said instead, "Rick Stanley."

Sondra lifted a brow. "And what did *he* have to say for himself?"

"Rick's delighted that Kiltie's missing."

"He would be."

"It sounded as though he had a good reason to be upset," I said. "How *did* you get Todd to put Rick's Cairn Special aside and commit to Kiltie instead?"

"That's none of your business."

"But what if whatever strings you pulled had something to do with Kiltie's disappearance?"

"They don't."

"How can you be so sure—"

"Stop it!" Sondra said suddenly.

"Excuse me?"

"Stop badgering me."

"I am *not* . . ." I began. Then I let my voice trail away. Arguing with Sondra would get me nowhere.

I switched gears and tried again. "So what have you been doing since the last time we spoke?"

"Me?"

I nodded.

"I've been waiting." As I watched, Sondra's features rearranged themselves into a picture of dejection. "And hoping that my little dog will find his way home soon."

Last time I'd sat in Sondra's library, I'd been moved by her show of grief over the loss of her dog. This time, I wasn't convinced. Not only that but, in her place, I'd have been a lot more productive. Sondra had asked for my assistance in locating Kiltie, but I hadn't thought that would mean that she'd be abandoning her own efforts.

"That's *all?*" I asked.

"I'm a busy person." Sondra narrowed her gaze. "And I was counting on you to do *your* job."

"I'm a busy person, too," I said mildly. "And finding Kiltie isn't my job. I only got involved because I thought I could help."

"Well," she said, rising to her feet, "it appears that we were both wrong, doesn't it?"

Good manners dictated that I should stand as well. Instead I remained seated.

"I'd like to talk to your husband," I said. "Can you tell me how to get in touch with him?"

"No," Sondra replied firmly. "I don't want Jim involved in this at all."

"He was at the bazaar," I told her. "I saw him there with Poppy, early that morning. Maybe he knows something."

"He doesn't. Jim knows nothing about any of my dogs. He never has."

"Does he like Kiltie?" I asked curiously.

"That's rich." Sondra's chuckle sounded forced. "He doesn't even *know* Kiltie. He couldn't pick that dog out of a lineup if his life depended upon it."

"Even so—"

"I said I don't want you contacting Jim and I meant it. As you know, he and I are separated. We're currently in the process of working out a divorce. That means that my life and my dogs are no longer any of Jim's business. And that's exactly the way I want things to stay."

Reluctantly I realized that I probably shouldn't fault Sondra for taking that position. If I were faced with the task of unraveling all the bits and pieces of my life from those of someone whom I no longer loved, I might well have felt the same way.

"I think we're done here," she said abruptly.

As if on cue, Sondra's maid, Kalinda, appeared in the doorway to the library. She was holding my coat in her hands. I stood up. Faith did, too.

As we crossed the room, Sondra said, "Peg should have warned me about you. She never mentioned you had such a volatile temper."

"Excuse me?" I said incredulously.

I was perfectly calm. After all, it wasn't my dog who hadn't been seen in nearly a week. Which brought up another point. Kiltie had now been gone for several days longer than when we'd last spoken. Yet, curiously, Sondra appeared to be *less* willing to cooperate with me. I wondered why that was.

As she walked us to the door, I asked her. Reaching for the doorknob, Sondra went still. All at once, the atmosphere in the hallway felt oddly charged. I half expected her to lash out at me again.

Instead, Sondra slowly shook her head. "I'm just trying to deal with this situation the best way I can. Sometimes I think . . ."

"What?" I turned and looked at her.

"I just have to believe in my heart that things have a way of working out for the best."

I felt as though I left Sondra's house with more questions than I'd had when I arrived. I didn't like that feeling at all.

On the drive home from Greenwich to Stamford, I called Aunt Peg.

"Your friend Sondra McEvoy is very strange," I said.

"Surely you can't blame that on me."

"No, but I can blame you for getting me involved with her."

"Pish," said Aunt Peg. "That wasn't my fault either. You got yourself involved with Sondra when you misplaced her dog at your Christmas bazaar."

I bit back the first retort that sprang to mind and said

instead, "Sondra seems to think that I have a temper. She called me volatile."

"Considering the tone of this conversation, it occurs to me that perhaps she has a point."

I breathed in a sigh and let it out. Faith looked at me questioningly. I reached over and gave her a pat.

"Just once," I said.

"Melanie, what are you talking about now?"

"Just once, I would like you to stick up for me rather than the other person."

"I don't have any idea what you mean. I always stick up for you . . . on those occasions that you're right."

And therein lay the problem.

"Have you located Kiltie yet?" Aunt Peg asked, even though I was quite certain that already she knew the answer.

"No. And Sondra's reaction is bugging me."

"*Again?*" Peg's tone was arch.

I ignored that and said, "Why isn't she more worried about Kiltie?"

"I haven't a clue why you would expect me to know that."

"Sondra told me she believes that everything works out for the best."

"What's wrong with that?" asked Aunt Peg. "I hope she's right. Besides, you just said you thought that Sondra was strange. Under the circumstances, I have no idea why you'd be giving her philosophical beliefs any credence at all."

"Because she's Kiltie's owner," I said, calling on reserves of patience I didn't even know I had. "She's the whole reason I started looking for the dog in the first place."

"Nonsense. You're looking for Kiltie because he needs to be brought home. And because you want to help the child."

"Poppy," I said softly. Of course Aunt Peg was right. Again.

"Enough about you," Peg said briskly. "You'll be pleased to know that my diet is coming along quite well."

"It is?"

"I took your advice and loosened my restrictions. Even so, I've already managed to lose two pounds. It turns out that dieting isn't nearly as difficult as I thought it would be."

Said the only woman in the world, ever.

On the other hand, considering the current state of my own affairs, I supposed it was nice to know that things were going well for somebody.

Chapter 22

"How do you feel about divorce?" I asked Claire. She looked up from the thick pad of paper she was using to take notes and stared at me in surprise. "What a singularly odd thing to ask me two weeks before my wedding."

It was Friday evening, after dinner, and she and I were sitting at my dining room table. Claire had called and asked if she could stop by sometime to go over the arrangements for her upcoming nuptials. Delighted by the opportunity to turn my thoughts to something productive that didn't involve either Christmas or a lost Westie, I'd encouraged her to come straight over.

Sam had been as happy to see Claire as I was. But as soon as he'd heard the phrase "wedding plans," he had grabbed the two boys and all three of them had skedaddled from the room. Even the Standard Poodles were making themselves scarce.

Claire and I both laughed at that. She's the farthest thing in the world from a Bridezilla but I didn't see any reason to point that out to anyone. A bit of peace and quiet is a rare luxury in my life. And the possibility of conducting our conversation without constant interruptions from dogs and children suited both of us just fine.

Claire and Bob's wedding was designed to be a low-key affair. A small, interdenominational church on Round Hill Road in Greenwich would provide a delightful, understated setting. Guests were limited to family and close friends of the couple. Davey had been thrilled to be asked to serve as his father's best man.

Kevin, hearing that, had worked himself up into a pretty good pout until Claire came up with the idea of assigning him the role of ring bearer. The toddler had been practicing his duties for the last several weeks. Several times a day, he clutched a small pillow to his chest and marched around the house to music that only he could hear.

Considering that Claire had been responsible for planning much larger events during the course of her corporate career, I was quite certain that she had everything well under control. But if impending-wedding jitters made her want to run through the list of arrangements one more time, I was happy to serve as her sounding board.

"Sorry," I apologized now. "I didn't mean that the way it came out."

"I should hope not." Claire brushed back a strand of dark, silky, hair that had fallen across her face and frowned at me across the table. "If that's your way of telling me that you think Bob and I aren't right for each other, first of all you're wrong. And secondly, you might have thought about mentioning something sooner so we could have dealt with this issue and gotten it out of the way."

"Crap," I muttered, backpedaling hastily. "That wasn't

what I was trying to say at all. You and Bob are wonderful together. You're the best thing that ever happened to him."

Claire's frown didn't ease. Nor did she look entirely convinced. Since she was talking to Bob's ex-wife, I supposed there might have been a reason for that.

"You mean . . . excluding *you,* right?" she asked.

"No way," I said. "Not even close. Especially considering the whole divorce and all. Bob and I were not a good fit."

"Okay." Claire still didn't sound reassured.

"But maybe excluding Davey," I added. "Because he's pretty great."

That made Claire smile. "I'm happy to be in second place behind Davey. That suits me just fine. But now that we've got that cleared up, why exactly are we talking about divorce?"

Good question, I thought with a sigh. So much for taking a break from thinking about a lost dog.

"Actually," I admitted, "it's because of Sondra and Jim McEvoy."

"Who? I don't think I know that name . . . are they friends of Bob's?" For a moment, Claire looked puzzled. Then her fingers began to scramble frantically through the thick sheaf of notes in front of her. "Oh my God, are they coming to the wedding? When are they getting divorced? Do we have to change the seating arrangements? I can do that if I have to—"

"Wait!" I cried, holding up a hand. "Stop. Right now."

Claire looked up.

"Sondra and Jim aren't coming to your wedding."

"Well, that's a relief." She paused, then added, "I think?"

"It is," I agreed. "You wouldn't want them there."

"Who are they? Do I know them? Why are they getting divorced?"

And people told me that *I* asked too many questions. I had nothing on Claire.

"Do you remember the dog that disappeared from the Christmas bazaar?"

"Sure," she replied. "It was a little shaggy thing. Kilt-something."

"Kiltie. He's a West Highland White."

"Whatever."

Aunt Peg was going to have a new neophyte to train, I thought happily. And I would be delighted to hand over my protégée status to her. *Welcome to the family, Claire.*

"His owner is Sondra McEvoy," I said.

"Oh." Recognition dawned. "I remember her now. The woman who wanted to sue."

"Precisely."

"Well, thank goodness *she's* not coming to my wedding."

"I've been looking for Kiltie," I said.

Claire nodded. "I think Bertie mentioned something about that. Have you found him?"

The eternal question. Although this time I supposed I'd asked for it.

"Not yet," I said. "But recently it's occurred to me that maybe I've been going about things all wrong. I'm beginning to wonder whether I've been looking too far afield."

Claire set her papers aside and settled in to listen. She was very good at that. "What do you mean?"

"Kiltie didn't just run away from the bazaar," I said. "He was taken away on purpose."

"By our Santa Claus, right? That's what Bertie told me. The same man who later died."

"Correct. Then Sondra leaned on Aunt Peg and got me started looking for Kiltie. But now I think Sondra might have sent me in the wrong direction."

"That's utterly diabolical," Claire said with a sneer.

The reaction seemed a little strong. I looked at her questioningly.

"We don't like Sondra . . . right?"

"Not much," I admitted.

"Good," she said. "That's what I thought. I'm just trying to figure out which side I'm on."

"Mine," I told her. "You're on my side."

"Of course," Claire promised. "You don't have to worry about that. But if you don't mind my saying so, your story telling is a little convoluted. So let me cut to the chase for you. Where did Sondra send you?"

"The first time I spoke with her, all she wanted to talk about was the other dog show exhibitors who were mad at her, or the ones who had dogs that were always being beaten by Kiltie. Dog people with a grudge."

"Hmmm," said Claire. "That sounds promising."

"But that's just it," I told her. "It hasn't worked out that way at all. I've talked to a number of different exhibitors and none of it feels right to me. Mostly they tell me that they have no idea why someone would want to steal Kiltie, and it turns out that mostly I believe them."

"Good for you!" Claire declared roundly.

It was like having my own personal cheerleader, right there in the room with me. It was a shame I had to disagree with her.

"No," I said. "It's bad for me. Because none of the

looking I've done so far has gotten me any closer to finding the dog."

"Oh, I see."

"Suppose one of those exhibitors *had* taken Kiltie," I said, thinking aloud. "How would it benefit them?"

"I hope that's not a serious question," said Claire. "Because I'm sure I don't know. I don't even know what a West Lowland Whip is."

Oh Aunt Peg was going to have fun with her.

"Take Rick Stanley, for example. He had every reason to be mad at Sondra McEvoy. But when you stop and think about it, he had even more reason to be mad at Todd Greenleaf."

"Todd Greenleaf," Claire repeated dreamily. "What a great name. He sounds like a movie star."

"Close," I told her. "And then there's Rachel Bright. She has enough problems and too many dogs already. I can't see her trying to engineer the theft of another."

"If you say so."

"Chip Michaels needs better manners. Jo Drummer needs a flashier breed. And don't even get me started on Jane Brew."

"I wouldn't dream of it," said Claire. "It sounds as though you've been quite diligent."

"I have," I grumbled. "For all the good it's done me. Because basically I have diddly to show for all my efforts. Except there is one thing. . . ."

"What's that?"

"Sondra and Jim are getting divorced," I said.

"I know that," Claire agreed. "That's why they're not coming to my wedding."

"And Jim was at the Christmas bazaar."

"What a rat!" Claire cried. She awaited my approval.

When it wasn't forthcoming, she said meekly, "Wrong response?"

"Yup, sorry. Good try though."

Claire shrugged. That girl was game.

"And now it turns out that Sondra doesn't want me to talk to Jim."

"I get it," said Claire. She sounded relieved. "You want my blessing."

"Your what?"

"You want to talk to Jim even though Sondra told you not to. And you want me to tell you that it's the right thing to do. Okay, done. It's the right thing to do."

"Even if I have to go behind Sondra's back?" I asked.

"Even then," Claire confirmed. "Because apparently we don't like Sondra much anyway. So who cares what she thinks?"

"I think I love you," I said to Claire.

"Of course you do. I'm very lovable. Ask your ex-husband. He'll tell you. Now, can we *please* get back to what's really important here?"

"The wedding," I said guiltily.

"Of course, the wedding," said Claire. "The very least you can do is give my problems equal time."

"You're absolutely right," I said. "Go for it."

While I contemplated the best way to approach Jim McEvoy, Christmas drew ever closer. On the plus side: the house was decorated, the Christmas tree was up, and most of the baking had already been done. The minus: though I'd made extensive lists of presents I *in-*

tended to buy, I'd allowed myself to fall alarmingly behind in the execution of the actual shopping.

In the hopes of remedying that, Saturday morning Sam and I took the boys and went Christmas shopping on Greenwich Avenue. Clearly we weren't the only ones who'd had that idea. Even though we arrived early, we still had to park a couple of blocks away on Mason Street.

The avenue itself, the town's main thoroughfare and a popular shopping mecca for residents of both Fairfield and Westchester counties, was thronged with festive holiday crowds. By lunchtime, I'd already run into several children from school and a good friend from my old neighborhood in Stamford.

When Sam and Davey peeled away and ducked into Restoration Hardware, I leaned down and lifted Kevin up into my arms. With the sheer number of people jostling for room on the sidewalk, I was half-afraid he might get trampled by some overzealous shopper. As we waited for Davey and Sam to return, light snow began to fall. Carrying Kev, I edged over to the side of the promenade, out of the main flow of traffic.

Fairy lights hung above our heads. Christmas carols, piped out of the stores around us, filled the air. Kev clapped his hands and sang along. I was pretty sure he was making up the words as he went.

Above the din, I heard someone call my name. Turning to look, I saw Tony Dahl, his arms weighted down with holiday loot, making his way toward us through the crush of pedestrians. I gave him a cheery wave. Kev did, too.

"I'm glad I ran into you," Tony said as he drew near. "I've been meaning to call you. Hi, little guy."

"This is Kevin." I shifted my hip so that Kev and

Tony were face-to-face. The two of them shook hands. "He's a little overexcited about the upcoming holidays."

"I don't blame him," Tony said with a laugh. "Who could help it in a crowd like this? Hey, remember you asked me about my friend Hal?"

"Sure. Did you find him?"

"I did as a matter of fact. After I talked to you, I left a couple of messages on his phone and I checked in with some mutual friends. For a couple of days, I didn't hear a thing. But then last night, he called back and asked what was up."

"Where is he?" I asked.

"Baton Rouge. He's got family there. Went down for a holiday visit. He told me he'd had no idea that anything had gone wrong at the Christmas bazaar until the police contacted him in the middle of the week."

"Did you ask him why he had taken the job, and then canceled on us at the last minute?"

"I sure did. After the way things turned out, I wanted to know the answer to that myself. Hal said a guy got in touch with him right before the bazaar. Name of Chris Tindall. Does that mean anything to you?"

"That's the name Jerry Platt was using when Mr. Hanover hired him as Hal's replacement," I said.

Tony nodded. "I asked Hal what this guy had done to make him bail on us like that, and he said Tindall told him some long sob story about having a kid who went to Howard Academy that he never gets to see. Tindall and the mom aren't together anymore and he doesn't have visitation. So now it's Christmas and he's all broken up about it and all Tindall wants to do is surprise his daughter and spend a little time with her."

"I'm pretty sure none of that was true," I said.

"Probably not," Tony agreed. "But it doesn't matter because Hal fell for it. He thought he was doing a good thing for somebody and he let Tindall sub in."

"I assume Hal was reimbursed for his lost job?"

"You better believe it. He got two thousand dollars to make the switch."

"Wow." I whistled softly under my breath. "No wonder he was happy to help Tindall out. That's a lot more than we were going to pay him."

"That's what I figured," Tony said. "I asked Hal if that didn't seem a little suspicious to him but he said he didn't really think about it. All he knew was that someone was offering to pay him enough to take a week off and go fishing, so he jumped at the bait."

"Fish?" Kevin sat up in my arms. He hadn't been following the conversation but now, having heard his new favorite word, he wanted back in. "Who has fish?"

"Nobody, sweetie." I leaned down and kissed his forehead. "Let me talk to Tony for another minute. If you're a good boy, Santa Claus will bring you fish for Christmas."

"Fish for Christmas," Kevin agreed happily. "Santa bring."

"Cute kid," said Tony.

"Thanks." I smiled. What mother doesn't love to hear that? "And thank you for tracking down Hal for me. Do you have time for one more question?"

"Yeah, I guess."

"Jim McEvoy. Poppy McEvoy's father. You saw him at the Christmas bazaar, didn't you?"

"Sure I saw him. He volunteered to come in early and help out. He was on my crew."

Right, I thought. I'd forgotten about that.

"How did he seem to you?"

"I don't know." Tony shrugged. "Like a nice enough guy, I guess. That morning was the first time I'd ever met him. Jim seemed happy enough to be assigned to the unloading crew and he worked as hard as any of the other parent volunteers. Why do you ask?"

"I'm just trying to think things through," I said. "And maybe I'm taking a stab in the dark. You know that the Westie that was stolen later in the day belonged to his wife, right?"

"No, I didn't realize that." Tony sounded surprised. "I never made the connection. But by the time that dog went missing, Jim was long gone. He told me there was somewhere else he had to be that day. That's why he was on the morning crew."

Or maybe he'd arranged not to be at the bazaar later in the day in order to have an alibi elsewhere, I thought.

"Wait a minute," said Tony. "Did you say his wife?"

"That's right. Sondra McEvoy. She's Kiltie's owner."

"Geez." He stopped and shook his head. "I don't know if I should mention this or not."

"Of course you should," I encouraged him. "What?"

"It's just that that morning . . . well, there were a few times when he detoured away from what we were doing and went to hang out with another one of the parent volunteers. It's not like I could complain or anything considering that I work for Howard Academy and they pay for their kids to go to school there. But at the same time we had a job to do and my crew was pretty busy. And I was looking to keep everyone in line, you know?"

Standing there in the cold, I gave an involuntary

shiver. The hair on the back of my neck had begun to tingle. Jim was involved with a mother from the school. That was what Madeline Dangerfield had told me.

"Who was the other parent volunteer?" I asked.

"I'm not sure I should say. I mean, I probably shouldn't be gossiping about this stuff."

I wondered if I should point out to Tony that he was already gossiping about this stuff. And that it was much too late for him to have a sudden attack of scruples.

"Would it help if I told you that Poppy's parents are separated and heading for divorce?" I asked.

"I guess that makes things a bit better. At least it makes me feel better anyway."

"So," I prompted once again. "Who was Jim talking to?"

"Bradley Baker's mom. She was helping at the bazaar for most of the day. I think her name is Helen. Do you know her?"

Holy Christmas, I thought. I did indeed know Helen Baker. And I'd seen her at the bazaar, too. Helen had been a big help that day.

She'd been in charge of the raffle booth. The concession from which Kiltie had disappeared.

Chapter 23

"I have to go out again," I said to Sam.

After our busy morning in Greenwich, he and I had made the boys lunch, then put Kevin down for a much-needed nap. Now Sam and Davey were sitting side by side on the living room couch, engaged in a bout of virtual combat whose outcome appeared to be dependent upon some strategy, many explosions, and a great deal of body English, the latter being liberally supplied by both players.

"Okay," Sam replied. His gaze remained glued to the frantic activity taking place on the television screen. "See you later."

At least the Poodles were unhappy about my departure. Or at least they bothered to notice that I was leaving. I figured that had to count for something.

Helen Baker and her son, Bradley, lived in west Stamford, not too far from the hospital. When I'd called to ask if I might drop by to see her, Helen had sounded somewhat surprised to hear from me, but not entirely unwilling to talk. She'd told me that Bradley had swim team practice, and that she would be at the Stamford YMCA for much of the afternoon. We'd arranged to meet at a coffee shop around the corner from the Y.

I arrived first. I bought a cup of coffee at the counter and carried it over to a small booth near the front window. Five minutes later, Helen came hurrying in. She pulled off her gloves and scarf and tossed them down on the seat opposite me, then went to get her own hot beverage.

Unlike many of the Howard Academy mothers, Helen didn't look like she'd just stepped out of the pages of *Town & Country*. Dressed down for the weekend, she had on jeans and a chunky sweater. Her face was make-up and Botox free, and her blond hair was tied back in a ponytail. When she joined me in the booth a minute later, Helen greeted me with a friendly smile.

"Sorry I'm late," she said. "Bradley's coach had some handouts for the team parents to read through." She wrinkled her nose delicately. "To tell the truth, I'm delighted to have an excuse not to hang out at the Y all afternoon. I always leave that place smelling like chlorine. This will be much better."

"I'm glad," I said.

The questions I'd lined up to ask Helen would be tough. So it seemed like a good idea to start the conversation by making an effort to put her at ease.

"Is Bradley a good swimmer?"

"For his age group, he's great," Helen replied. "He's ten, and he swims in the twelve and unders. He's fast enough to beat some of the older kids, too."

"Good for him."

"It is for now," she said with a small laugh. "But I'm not kidding myself. I can't do much more than flail around in the water, so I doubt that my son is going to be Olympic material. Or even college scholarship material, unfortunately. But he's an only child so I like to keep him involved in as many activities as I can."

"Been there," I agreed.

"Really? Didn't you just get married a couple of years ago?"

Once again I was reminded just how close-knit a community Howard Academy truly was. The fact that everyone seemed to know everyone else's business made it all the more remarkable that—if my hunch was correct—Helen and Jim had been able to carry on a relationship right under everybody's noses.

"Second marriage," I told her. "I have a twelve-year-old son, Davey, with my first husband."

"I've met quite a few kids at the school," Helen said thoughtfully. "But I don't think I know Davey."

"You wouldn't have met him," I said. "He doesn't go to Howard Academy."

She peered at me over the rim of her cup. "How come?"

"When I first started teaching at HA, I was a single mother. I couldn't have dreamed of affording the tuition. Davey started out in the public school system and he's been thriving there. Plus that's where all his friends are now. So I haven't felt the need to make any changes."

"I know what you mean about the tuition," Helen replied. "There's no way I could afford that on what I make. But for all his faults, Bradley's father has at least managed to do one thing right. He's determined that his son should have the best education money can buy. And Howard Academy fits the bill."

"I take it you're divorced," I said.

Helen's expression was wry. "Does it show?"

"Little bit."

"It's been three years. I'm supposed to be over it by now."

"Says who?"

"Oh, you know." Helen shrugged. "Best friends, self-help books, lifestyle gurus."

"It sounds like you've gotten plenty of advice," I said with a smile.

"I've listened to what they all have to say, anyway. But unfortunately, none of the practical wisdom I've been bombarded with seems to stick."

"For what it's worth, I don't think you need to worry about anybody's time table but your own," I said. "I hated my ex-husband for years."

"And now?"

"Now we're finally friends again. Go figure. He's getting married on New Year's Eve. His fiancée's great. I'm helping her plan the wedding."

Helen chuckled at the idea. "Doug and I will *never* reach that state of equanimity. I'm absolutely sure of that."

"That's all right," I replied. "It's different for everyone. Finding someone new helps."

"I'm working on that part," Helen admitted.

"I thought you might be."

I watched Helen's brows lift in surprise. Her eyes narrowed fractionally. For a long moment, she didn't say a thing. Instead, her movements slow and measured, she paused for an extended drink.

On the other side of the booth, I sat in silence and waited her out.

"So that's why we're here," she said finally. "I don't know whether I should be annoyed or relieved."

"Relieved?"

"You know . . . that's it's not about Bradley. When you asked to meet with me, my first thought was that something might be wrong at school. That was why I agreed to see you."

"I thought it was because you didn't want to go home with your hair smelling like chlorine," I said.

Helen smiled reluctantly. "That, too, I suppose. So . . . how much do you know?"

"Enough to connect you to Jim McEvoy."

"Oh, that's right. I forgot." She tipped her head to one side. "You're Sondra's buddy."

"No," I said deliberately. "I'm not."

"Then why are we here?"

"It's about Sondra's dog, Kiltie—"

"Oh good grief." Helen snorted. "Seriously?"

I nodded.

"Sondra and her dogs. It's *always* about those damn dogs. If she spent less time worrying about those yappy little animals and more time worrying about taking care of her family, you and I wouldn't be sitting here right now."

"I guess that's what Jim told you," I said.

"*And* what I saw with my own eyes. Sondra's always been involved with her own interests. She neglected Jim. She didn't deserve him."

Nothing original there, I thought. Those rationalizations sounded like the same ones used to excuse away just about every illicit relationship ever undertaken.

"Trust me," I said. "You don't deserve that kind of trouble either."

"What does *that* mean?"

"After the Christmas bazaar last Saturday, a man died in Union Cemetery."

"I know," Helen replied shortly. "I read about it in the paper. So what?"

"His name was Jerry Platt. And he'd spent that day playing Santa Claus at our school. When he died, he had a picture of a West Highland White Terrier with him in his car. A dog just like Kiltie. It looks as though Sondra's dog didn't just disappear from the bazaar, he was purposely taken away. By Jerry Platt."

Helen sat back in her seat, pressing her slender shoulders into the cushion behind her. All at once she looked as though she wanted to put as much distance between us as possible.

"That has nothing to do with me."

"Actually," I said gently, "I think it does. Because when Kiltie wasn't with Poppy last Saturday, he was supposed to be locked inside his crate behind the raffle booth. You remember the raffle booth."

Helen's lips thinned. She didn't speak.

"That was your concession, Helen. You were the person in charge."

"You have that wrong," she said firmly. "Sondra and I were both selling raffle tickets, but she was the one running the concession. Do you think that if it had been up to me, that booth would have been filled with dog crates? Absolutely not. I don't even like dogs."

So she and Jim McEvoy apparently had at least one thing in common.

"Where were you when Kiltie went missing?" I asked.

"How would I know that?" Helen countered. "Sondra and I were in and out of that booth all day. Maybe she was keeping an eye on those crates, but I wasn't paying any attention to them at all. The first time I realized that something might be amiss was when you came by with Coco Silly."

"Lily," I corrected automatically. Then frowned. "If you weren't paying any attention to the dogs, how did you know the Cockapoo's name?"

Helen's cheeks flushed. "Someone must have mentioned it. You know, one of the girls."

"Which girls?"

"Poppy and . . . the other one."

"The one whose name you don't know. And yet somehow you seem to know the name of her dog." I stared hard at Helen. "Even though you don't like dogs."

"It's a memorable name—"

"Not really," I said. "Not unless someone had made a point of telling it to you."

"I have no idea what you're talking about," Helen sputtered.

Good try, I thought. The stammer was a nice touch. But I wasn't buying her denial for a minute. I was pretty sure that Helen knew exactly what I was talking about.

"I'm thinking that someone told you Coco Lily's name because you were going to be interacting with the dog yourself," I said.

"What kind of a crazy notion—"

"You're the one who opened Coco Lily's crate and turned her loose, aren't you?"

Helen pulled in a sharp breath. I could see her considering her options. She squared her shoulders and her gaze sharpened to a steely glare. When she spoke again, it was obvious she'd realigned her defense.

"So what if I did?" she asked. "Big deal. A little dog got out of its crate and ran a few laps around the auditorium. No harm done."

"Not to Coco Lily," I agreed. "But what matters is not that she got loose—but rather why it happened."

Helen lifted her coffee cup to her lips. The drink must have been nearly cold by now. She look a long swallow anyway.

"I have nothing to say about that," she said primly.

"That's fine," I told her. "I can't compel you to answer my questions if you don't want to. I imagine you'll be happier explaining what happened to the police."

Helen's mug landed back down on the tabletop so hard that our silverware rattled. "Why would *I* want to talk to the police?"

"I don't think it matters whether you want to talk to them or not. After I take this information to Detective Young, I'm pretty sure he'll be the one who wants to talk to you."

All right, maybe I was bluffing about that. Truthfully I had no idea whether or not the detective would be interested in hearing new details about Kiltie's theft. Or whether my information might be related to his own, much more important, investigation. But it was clear to me that Helen knew a great deal more about what had transpired that day than she was willing to share. And I was growing tired of our fencing match.

"Detective Young?" she repeated, frowning.

"He's the officer who's investigating Jerry Platt's murder."

"That had nothing to do with me."

"So you said." I made no attempt to hide my irritation. "All you did was open a dog crate, right?"

Glumly Helen nodded.

"And look the other way," I added.

"It was just supposed to be a small diversion."

"And it succeeded," I said. "Because while people were running around the auditorium chasing Coco Lily, Jerry Platt was able to slip Kiltie out of the bazaar."

"Why do you keep talking about this Platt character? Even if he was at the bazaar as you say, *I* never met him. I don't know the first thing about him or what he was up to. And I certainly had nothing to do with Sondra's little dog."

That last part I believed. Helen wasn't stupid. No doubt she'd made sure to give her lover's wife's dog a very wide berth.

"Who did?" I asked.

"Who did what?"

As if that evasion was going to work. It didn't even slow me down. I rephrased the question and tried again.

"Who arranged for Kiltie's theft?"

This time I hadn't even finished speaking before Helen began to shake her head. Her mouth was clamped firmly shut.

"All right, I'll make it easier for you," I said. "Forget about Kiltie altogether. Who asked you to open Coco Lily's crate?"

Again, only silence.

"Who asked you to create a diversion?"

"Nobody," Helen snapped. At least she'd gotten her voice back.

"Really?" I asked skeptically. "It was all your own idea?"

"You can't prove differently. No matter how many times you repeat the same thing."

Helen gathered up her coat and purse and slid out of the booth. I could see that I'd only have time for one more question. I needed to make it count.

"I know that Jim McEvoy must have asked you to open that crate," I said. "That's the only thing that makes sense. But here's what I don't understand. What did he hope to gain?"

Helen's motions were tight and jerky as she wound her scarf around her neck and yanked on her coat. "I'll be lodging a complaint with Mr. Hanover about your behavior here today," she said. "It was entirely out of line."

The warning was meant to intimidate me, to make me back off. Instead it had the opposite effect. Helen's threat made me mad.

"What happened last Saturday wasn't just about a dog or an unhappy marriage," I said. "A man lost his life. Surely that must mean something to you."

Helen had taken the first, hurried, step toward the door. But now she surprised me by pausing and turning back. For the first time, she looked uncertain. She glanced around the mostly empty café as if she was afraid of being overheard, then leaned down close to where I was still sitting.

"Ask your friend, Sondra, about the prenup," she hissed in my ear. "See what she has to say about that."

On the way to my car, I called the nonemergency number for the Greenwich Police Department and asked to speak with Detective Young. The desk sergeant informed me that he wasn't in and offered to connect me to the detective's voice mail. Instead I asked the sergeant if he knew when Detective Young would be back in, then waited while he checked the roster.

"He's off this weekend, but he'll be here bright and early Monday morning. If you want, you can leave a message with me and I'll make sure that he gets it."

"Thanks," I said. "That would be great. Could you tell him that Melanie Travis has some new information about the theft of Kiltie, the dog that Jerry Platt stole from the Howard Academy Christmas Bazaar?"

"Dog?" the sergeant repeated. "This is about a missing dog?"

"No," I replied. "It's about Detective Young's investigation into Jerry Platt's death. You know, last weekend?"

"Sure. I know about that. What's the information?"

Belatedly it occurred to me that both the new details I'd learned, and their significance to what had later befallen Jerry Platt, were probably too convoluted to explain in a short message. I didn't want the account's import to be lost in translation.

"It would probably be better if I talk to Detective Young in person," I said. "Maybe you could ask him to call me?"

"Sure. I can do that."

I spelled my name twice and left both my home and cell phone numbers with the desk sergeant before hanging up. On this hectic last weekend before Christmas, I could only hope that he wouldn't file the message in a lost dog folder and leave it at that.

Chapter 24

"What have *you* done *now*?" Aunt Peg demanded. I stared at the telephone I held nestled in my palm. My index finger hovered over the off button. I was tempted. Actually I was more than tempted; I was itching to sever the connection.

Unfortunately I doubted that that would deter Aunt Peg. She'd simply keep calling back until I answered the question and told her what I'd done. Which could be just about anything. I had no idea what transgression I was being blamed for at the moment.

It was barely eight o'clock on Sunday morning. Second week in a row, in case you're keeping track. At least this time, Aunt Peg had had the decency to call rather than simply showing up at my house unannounced.

I sighed and fitted the phone back to my ear. I supposed I might as well find out what the problem was this time.

"What are you talking about, Aunt Peg?"

"Sondra just called. She told me you've ruined *every-thing*."

Well, all righty then. I allowed myself a small smile. Apparently all my poking around had finally managed to hit a nerve. It was about time.

"What precisely have I ruined?" I asked.

"If I knew that, I wouldn't be calling. But whatever it is you've done, Sondra is mad enough to spit nails. She was so upset that I could hardly understand what she was saying. I think it has something to do with Jim."

"Indeed," I muttered.

"What's that?" Aunt Peg doesn't miss a thing.

"When I talked to Sondra on Friday, I asked her how I could get in touch with Jim. I told her I wanted to speak to him. Instead of helping, Sondra warned me off. She told me she didn't want me talking to her husband and that I was absolutely not to contact him."

"Apparently you didn't listen." Aunt Peg sounded pleased. There was nothing that made her happier than nurturing her relatives' subversive tendencies.

"Actually I haven't spoken to Jim yet. I didn't have time to get around to it."

"You didn't have time?" she repeated indignantly. "What about all day yesterday? Surely you couldn't have been busy the entire day."

I hoped that Santa Claus left a lump of coal in Aunt Peg's stocking. It would truly serve her right.

"As it happens I was tied up," I told her. I waited a beat, then added, "I was busy talking to Jim's mistress instead."

Luckily Aunt Peg couldn't see the satisfied smirk on my face.

"Oh?" she said with interest. "*That's* news."

"And there's more," I said. "Helen—that's the mistress—was also working at the raffle booth during the bazaar. She admitted that she was one who opened Coco Lily's crate and let her loose in the auditorium. She did it to create a diversion."

Anyone who knowingly puts a dog at risk is definitely not in Aunt Peg's good graces. I knew she would be annoyed by that and she was. "And under whose orders did she do such a thing?"

"That's the sixty-four dollar question," I told her. "But I can only come up with one name that makes sense. Especially since my questions upset Helen enough to make her threaten to file a complaint against me with Russell Hanover."

"Harrumph." Aunt Peg snorted into the phone. When it comes to Howard Academy, she's not without connections herself. "I'd just like to see her try."

"There's something else," I said. "Before she went storming off, Helen told me that I should ask Sondra about her prenup."

"Indeed?" Aunt Peg mused. "How very interesting. That might put a whole different complexion on things."

"In what way?"

"The reason Sondra called this morning was to demand that I tell you to back off and leave her family alone. She said the questions you'd been asking weren't helping. They were only stirring up more trouble instead."

I couldn't help that, I thought. It was what I did.

"Of course I was surprised to hear that." Aunt Peg didn't sound surprised. Instead, once again she sounded pleased. "I asked Sondra what she meant by that, but she wouldn't tell me. All she said was that from here on out, she intended to handle the problem herself. Sondra was very firm about the fact that your services were no longer needed nor wanted."

It took a moment for the import of her words to sink in. When it did, I suddenly felt giddy. "I've been *fired?*"

"Not so fast," said Peg. "Think about it. You know what this must mean. I bet Sondra has discovered where Kiltie is. She knows who has him and what she has to do to get him back."

Her reply had been intended to prick a pin in my budding good mood. Stubbornly I refused to let it go.

"But I've been fired. . . ." I said again.

Aunt Peg dealt with that insubordination in her usual fashion. She simply steamrolled right over my objections.

"I told Sondra that I'd stop by this morning so that we could talk. And now, with this additional information you've given me, I should think that we'll have plenty of things to discuss. Of course you'll want to come with me."

It wasn't a question. It was a foregone conclusion. I bowed to the inevitable and agreed.

"Let me guess," said Sam. He'd overheard bits and pieces of my conversation with Aunt Peg. "You're going somewhere again."

"Yes," I said. "But not for long. I'll be back in plenty of time to go to the Reindeer Festival with you and the boys this afternoon. I'm just going to run down to Greenwich and meet Aunt Peg at Sondra McEvoy's house. There are a couple of things we need to get straightened out."

"Still?" Sam quirked a brow. "I thought you got fired."

I guessed he'd heard more than I thought.

"So did I," I said glumly. "But apparently it didn't stick."

"Try to stay out of trouble, okay?"

I nodded, but I wasn't about to make any promises on that score. It was beginning to look as though trouble was exactly what Sondra McEvoy deserved.

An hour later, I met Aunt Peg at her house. We drove to Deer Park together in her minivan. Aunt Peg likes to get where she's going in a hurry. She drives with scant regard for speed limits and has an unerring ability to avoid traffic patrols. I wish I shared her gift.

During the drive, it became clear that Peg was still simmering from our conversation on the phone. She navigated up the McEvoys' driveway, hopped out of her van, and was striding determinedly toward the front steps of the large house before I'd even managed to undo my seat belt. By the time I joined her on the narrow porch, she had already rung the doorbell. Twice.

"That's odd," I said, when no appeared in response to our arrival. "Maybe Sunday is Kalinda's day off."

"Sondra was expecting me." Peg jabbed a finger at the buzzer again. "She knew I was on my way."

"Maybe she doesn't want to see me," I said. It occurred to me that this was the second time Sondra had engineered an end run around me by soliciting Aunt Peg's assistance.

"Don't be daft." She slanted a glance my way. "You don't think I told Sondra that you were coming, do you?"

I should have known.

"I have no intention of standing here all day," said Peg.

By my count, we'd now been waiting approximately

a minute and a half. Ever impatient, she began to rummage around in her ample purse. It didn't take her long to find her phone.

I stepped away from the door, turned around, and gazed out over the large yard. I was just as happy to let Aunt Peg take control. Besides, I was pretty sure she'd treat suggestions of mine as extraneous anyway.

Another minute passed. As Aunt Peg was discovering that Sondra wasn't answering her phone, I suddenly heard the sound of gravel crunching underfoot. It appeared to be coming from around the side of the house. Judging by the rapid succession of steps, whoever it was, was moving fast.

"Someone's coming," I said.

I hopped down the three stone stairs and followed the curve of the driveway in the direction of the garage. Rounding the corner of the house, I barely had time to register a brief flash of color and movement before something small and solid came crashing into me.

As I stumbled backward, I heard a sharp squeal of surprise. I was pretty sure it hadn't come from me. All the air seemed to have been knocked from my body with a sudden whoosh. Scrambling awkwardly, I lost my balance. My assailant and I went down together.

Reflex made me throw out my hands to break my fall. The gravel stung as we hit the ground. Luckily, even though I was on the bottom, my bulky parka protected me from the worst of it.

Then my head snapped down onto the hard surface. That hurt.

"Oww," I groaned.

Eyes still closed, I took a moment. Then I rolled to one side and dumped whoever had come careening around the corner, down on the driveway beside me.

"Ms. Travis!" a small voice cried. "What are you doing here?"

"Poppy?" I slid one eye open.

The sixth grader quickly maneuvered herself up. Fortunately she appeared to have survived our collision in one piece. Eleven-year-olds bounce, I thought. As opposed to adults who go splat. And since I'd been on the bottom, I'd broken her fall.

I resisted the temptation to groan again.

"Melanie, do get up off the ground." Aunt Peg came hurrying down the steps to join us. "Poppy, dear, what is going on? Where is your mother? She should have been expecting me."

As she drew near, Peg stopped and stared at the sixth grader. "Where is your coat, Poppy? It's freezing out here. What is Sondra thinking letting you run around in the cold dressed like that?"

Belatedly I realized that Poppy, wearing just a pair of jeans and a thin, cotton shirt, was clasping her arms over her chest and shivering. As I hauled myself to my feet, I unzipped my parka and pulled it off. Aunt Peg snatched it out of my hands and draped it over Poppy's shoulders.

"Thank God you're here," the young girl said through chattering teeth. Now that I looked more closely I could see how pale she was. Her freckles stood out like bright spots of color on skin the color of parchment. Her fingers twisted in agitation. "I need help. You have to come with me right away!"

"Where?" I asked, exchanging a glance with Aunt Peg. "What's the matter?"

"Back there." Poppy snapped out a quick point around the side of the house. Without waiting to see if we were following, she was already heading back that way at a run. "They're fighting. Somebody's going to get hurt. Hurry *up!*"

Aunt Peg and I both scrambled to catch up. "Where are we going?" she asked me.

"Sondra has a kennel in her backyard," I said. "She converted the pool house. I'm guessing that's it."

Passing the garage, we flew through an open gate and onto a flagstone terrace. Outdoor furniture, covered in winter tarps, was pushed up against the back wall of the house. Poppy veered left, heading toward the covered pool and the small, pale yellow building on the other side. Aunt Peg and I hurried along behind.

"It doesn't look like a kennel," Aunt Peg muttered. "Where are the runs? Don't the dogs ever get to go outside?"

Hell if I knew. Everything about this visit was proving to be a mystery to me.

Ahead of us, the young girl skirted quickly around the kidney-shaped pool. As she approached the smaller building, I expected her to go straight to the door. Instead Poppy bypassed the walkway, hopped over a low bush, and sidled over next to a window in the near wall. Clearly this wasn't the first time she'd spied on the occupants of the kennel.

But who was inside now? And what were they doing in there?

Curiosity propelled me to follow the sixth grader. Before I was even able to get a glimpse of what was going on, however, Aunt Peg took matters into her own hands. She stopped on the flagstone walk, delivered a withering glance my way, and announced in a loud voice, "I don't *think* so."

"Shhhh!" Poppy cautioned, pulling back from the

window. She looked like she was about to cry. "They'll hear you."

"I should hope so." Peg marched over to the door, turned the knob, and thrust it open.

Once again, I found myself scrambling to play catch-up. As the door flew inward, I heard the occupants of the room before I saw them. The sound of two voices, both raised in anger, was suddenly crystal clear in the sharp winter air.

Moving quickly, I managed to be right behind Aunt Peg when she entered the building. Poppy, hunched down inside my parka as if she hoped to remain invisible, trailed along behind.

"You've pushed me around for the last time," Sondra was saying shrilly. "I'm not going to let you control me anymore."

"You should be grateful I *am* in control," Jim McEvoy shot back. "Somebody has to be. Especially after the mess you've made of things."

A blast of cold air accompanied us into the small room. Even so, the battling McEvoys—facing off in front of a wire pen containing a pair of unhappy-looking Westies—were so intent upon each other and their own invective that they didn't even appear to notice our arrival.

"Daddy, stop it!" Poppy screamed. She lifted her hands and placed them over her ears. "Both of you stop it now!"

That got their attention. As Jim swung around in surprise, I realized that he was holding a third Westie in a firm grasp beneath his arm. The small, white terrier looked every bit as uncomfortable as the other dogs inside the pen.

"I don't know what's going on here," Aunt Peg said sharply, "but I think that's quite enough."

Jim's expression hardened at the interruption. He stared at Peg and me without the slightest shred of recognition. "This is a private matter between me and my wife and I'll thank you not to intrude. Whoever you are, please leave my property immediately."

I would have fallen back under Jim's malevolent gaze. Not Aunt Peg. She was made of sterner stuff. When she stood her ground, I did, too.

"Peg?" Sondra said uncertainly. "What are you doing here?"

"You asked me to come this morning, remember? We were going to talk."

Sondra looked dismayed. She gave her head a small shake.

Aunt Peg reached out a hand. She took a step toward her friend. "Is there something I can do to help you?"

"Yes, there is." As Jim intercepted the question, he moved to angle his body between the two women. His gaze skimmed briefly in my direction. "The two of you can show yourselves out. We are having a private conversation and you're not welcome here."

"Daddy, this is my teacher, Ms. Travis," Poppy piped up. Abruptly her fingers grasped the back of my sweater and held on tight. Her father wanted us to leave, but Poppy was equally determined to keep us in place. "You met last weekend."

"At the Christmas bazaar," I told him. I stared at the dog in his arms. "Is that Kiltie?"

Jim ignored the query and turned back to his wife. "Since these appear to be friends of yours, I suggest that you make them go away. If you don't, there will be repercussions."

It was much too late to avoid that outcome, I thought. The scene we were witnessing was definitely going to lead to repercussions. And none of them were likely to be good. Especially if that *was* Kiltie that Jim was holding in his arms.

Aunt Peg, whose eye for a good dog was much keener than mine, already knew the answer to that. "I see you've found your missing dog," she said to Sondra.

"Yes, I did." Sondra's gaze shifted away from us. Suddenly she sounded nervous. "Jim found Kiltie and brought him home. Wasn't that nice of him?"

I don't think any of us were fooled by that declaration. There was nothing *nice* about what was happening here. Finding Kiltie had been my goal, but his theft was one small part of a much bigger picture—one that had included Jerry Platt's death. Only an idiot wouldn't have foreseen that whoever ultimately turned up with Kiltie in his possession was going to have a great deal of explaining to do.

"How very fortunate for you," I said. "It must be a relief to know that Kiltie has been in safe hands all along."

"Yes . . . I mean, no . . ." Sondra stammered.

"Sondra, shut up," Jim hissed under his breath. "Don't say another word."

"But—"

Jim reached out with his free hand, grasped his wife's wrist, and twisted it. I heard Sondra gasp. So did Poppy. Aunt Peg started to react but Poppy was faster.

The girl slipped out from behind me and wedged herself into the small space between her parents. She tipped her face up to her father's. Her eyes were huge and swimming with unshed tears.

"Daddy!" Poppy shrieked. "You promised!"

A frisson of shock rippled through me. I saw Sondra's face go blank.

Jim's fingers opened and his hand fell away. Kiltie squirmed within his grasp, but Jim scarcely seemed to notice. He gazed at his daughter without saying a word.

I stared at the family tableau before me and felt my stomach lurch. Oh crap, I thought. I hadn't expected that.

This wasn't going to end well.

Chapter 25

"You *promised,* Jim?" Sondra's tone was low and menacing. Fingers rubbing her wrist absently, she backed away from her husband and daughter. "What did you promise Poppy? And what did she do for you in return?"

"Nothing," Jim replied quickly. He stepped back too, as if he wanted to distance himself from what had been said. "Poppy is mistaken."

"I am *not.*"

"Poppy," Jim snapped. "Not now."

"I think now is an excellent time," Sondra said, beckoning to her daughter. "Come over here and stand with me, honey. Unlike your father, I would love to hear what you have to say."

Uncertain what to do, Poppy looked back and forth between her parents. I was guessing this wasn't the first time Sondra and Jim had made her choose between them.

"Poppy," I said gently. "You don't have to say anything at all if you don't want to."

Aunt Peg reached over and poked her thumb in my ribs. The jab was hard enough to hurt. I jumped in place but held my ground.

"It doesn't matter." Poppy also moved away. Now we had three family members in three different corners of the room. "Nobody ever listens when I talk."

"I'm listening," I told her. I knew Aunt Peg was, too.

"I didn't want Kiltie to go away," Poppy said softly. "Daddy said he could fix it."

"Fix it?" Sondra's voice rose. Aunt Peg silenced her with a glare.

"Kiltie was going to live somewhere else so he could be a top show dog. Todd was going to handle him. He was going to be gone for a *long* time, maybe even all year."

Sondra looked surprised. "How did you even know about that? I never told you any of those things."

Poppy lifted her chin and stared at her mother. "I hear stuff. I pay attention when people are talking. Even when nobody bothers to notice that I'm there."

"Why you sneaky little—"

"Sondra," Jim said, his tone a warning. "That's enough."

"Oh no, it isn't," Sondra shot right back. "I think we're just getting started here. Keep talking, Poppy. Everybody's listening to you now. Why don't you tell us what you did?"

Poppy bit her lip hard. When she began to speak again, I hoped she wasn't tasting blood.

"Daddy told me if I helped him, he would keep

Kiltie safe and make it so that he wouldn't have to go away. I didn't want Kiltie to leave. So I did what Daddy asked me to do. I got Kiltie out of his crate at the bazaar and gave him to the Santa Claus outside. He was going to take Kiltie to Daddy and everything was supposed to be fine after that."

Poppy gazed at her father imploringly. "You told me everything would work out. You said if I helped you, everyone would be *happy*."

Surely I wasn't the only one in the room who heard the longing in the young girl's voice. Her parents had behaved abominably. How could they have been so callous as to pit her against each other and promise her happiness in return?

"Only a fool would believe everything your father says," Sondra told her daughter harshly. "He didn't care what happened to Kiltie. He only wanted him as a bargaining chip. He needed him for leverage."

"No, that's not right." Slowly Poppy shook her head. "I know what leverage is. Kiltie isn't leverage."

"You tell her, Poppy." Jim had the nerve to sound pleased by his daughter's denial.

"Oh really?" Sondra snapped. "Is that what you want? Then since we're busy *telling* things, why don't you tell Poppy about your affair with Helen Baker?"

"Hey!" I said loudly. That was way out of bounds. And since the squabbling McEvoys didn't appear to have an ounce of discretion between them, the teacher in me was suddenly itching to take control. "Both of you, cut it out."

I might as well have not even spoken. All three adults in the room ignored me. Even Aunt Peg, who should have been on my side.

"Here, Poppy," I said, holding out my hand. "Come

with me. Let's step outside and let your parents settle this on their own."

"No." The girl ignored my outstretched hand and crossed her slender arms over her chest. "I'm not going anywhere. Nobody ever tells me what's going on. I want to hear for myself."

No, she didn't, I thought. I knew what was coming . . . what had to be coming. And I was quite sure that Poppy didn't really want to hear it.

Jim seemed to have forgotten all about his daughter. Instead he rounded back to his wife. "Who told you about Helen?" he demanded.

"I didn't have to be *told,* Jim. I'm a big girl. I can figure things out for myself." Sondra looked as though she enjoyed inflaming her husband's wrath. "Do you think you were the only one who wanted leverage to bring to the negotiating table? We both signed that prenup in good faith and you can just forget about getting it invalidated. That's not going to happen."

"Oh, I think it will," Jim said with confidence. "I'm pretty certain you're going to change your mind."

As he was speaking, Jim slid his free hand into the pocket of his jacket. When he drew it back out, I saw that his fingers were cupped around a small black object. It took me a moment to realize that he was holding a taser.

Sondra glanced at the weapon only briefly. Her lip lifted in a taunting sneer. "What are you going to do, Jim, tase me?" When he didn't answer, she lifted a hand and gestured around the room. "Are you going to tase all of us?"

Aunt Peg took a prudent step back. I followed her lead and did the same.

My aunt is the bravest person I know. So now I was

surprised when she purposely angled her body so that it was half-hidden behind mine. Surely Aunt Peg didn't intend to use me as her shield?

Then all at once I realized there was a bigger problem. Poppy was by herself, alone and defenseless, on the other side of the small room. The only way I could get to her was to cross between Sondra and Jim, thereby drawing attention to us both. Under the circumstances, that seemed like a terrible idea. I could only hope that Jim wouldn't be so depraved as to think about pointing the weapon at his own daughter.

"I bet you don't even know how to use that thing," Sondra scoffed. She was so intent upon goading her husband that she didn't appear to care that the level of tension in the room was rising exponentially. "Where did you even get it from anyway?"

Jim lifted the taser and pointed it like a gun. I watched as his thumb slowly moved, sliding back the safety cover that hid the push button trigger.

"I keep it in the glove compartment of my car," he said. "For protection. It's been there for years. I always knew it would come in handy someday."

"You mean like last Saturday?" I asked. "In Union Cemetery?"

Jim spared me a brief glance. "That wasn't supposed to happen. Platt and I had a deal. The dog in exchange for the money. I was ready to pay him what we'd agreed but at the last minute he decided he wanted to renegotiate." Jim looked grim. "I don't like it when people do that."

"So you shot him," I said.

"I only meant to frighten him. Scare him enough to make him hand over the dog. I'd never even used a taser before. It just went off."

And yet he must have known enough to push aside the taser's safety cover, I thought skeptically. Just as I'd watched him do a minute earlier.

"I saw Platt go down," Jim said. "And I grabbed the dog and got out of there. I figured he'd only be incapacitated for a few minutes, then he'd get up and go home. I had no idea what happened after I left until I heard about it later on the news."

"Who cares about that now?" Sondra said impatiently. "It was an accident. It's over and done with."

If she truly believed that, I thought, she had to be the only one who did. But Sondra's focus was laser sharp. And she was only worried about one thing.

She stepped toward her husband and held out her hands. "Come on, Jim. Give Kiltie to me. We're done here. It's time for us to go in the house, sit down, and settle our differences like adults."

Jim raised his arm and brought the Westie forward. For a few seconds, I thought he was going to do as she'd asked. Then Jim repositioned his other hand—the one grasping the taser—and I realized how wrong I was.

Instead of pointing outward, the weapon was now aimed squarely at Kiltie's head.

"I wouldn't come any closer if I were you," he said.

Poppy's gasp sounded loud in the suddenly silent room. Her hand flew up to cover her mouth as Sondra abruptly stopped moving. I saw her swallow heavily. For the first time since our arrival, Sondra appeared to be unsure about what to do next.

"You can't tase Kiltie," she said. "That's animal cruelty. I know you wouldn't do such a terrible thing."

"I can do whatever I want," Jim replied. "This dog means nothing to me."

"But you said you wouldn't hurt him!" Poppy's plea ended on a strangled cry.

Jim spoke to his daughter, but his eyes never shifted away from Sondra's stricken face. "Get a grip on yourself, Poppy. You'll get your dog back—just as soon as your mother cooperates with me."

"Do it, Mom." The young girl sniffled. "Do what he wants. *Please.*"

"You bastard," Sondra swore. "I can't believe you would sink this low."

"Believe it," Jim said shortly. "We've been married long enough for me to know exactly what's important to you. So if this dog lives or dies, it's all on you. It's your choice and nobody else's."

"Just put the taser away, Jim. Okay?" Sondra's voice took on a wheedling tone. "Give Kiltie to me and we'll talk."

"We're talking now," Jim pointed out. "And our positions suit me fine. I brought some papers with me for you to sign. So you were right about one thing. We are going to settle our differences like adults. But we're going to do it my way, not yours."

"Jim, please, you have to listen to me—" Sondra stopped midsentence. She spun around and stared at the half-open door. If she had been a dog she would have pricked her ears.

A moment later I realized what Sondra had heard. It was the sound of sirens, at least two of them. They were wailing in tandem and growing steadily closer.

The McEvoys and I froze in place. Not Aunt Peg. Deliberately she stepped out from behind me. Staring hard at Jim, Peg lifted her hand and opened her fingers. Her cell phone was nestled in her palm.

"I called nine-one-one," she said.

"Shit."

Jim quickly snapped the taser's protective cover quickly back into place. He shoved the weapon into his pocket and thrust Kiltie toward Sondra. She barely managed to catch the little terrier before he fell to the floor.

Finally reunited with his owner, Kiltie squirmed and wriggled in Sondra's arms. As I watched the happy reunion, I realized that Aunt Peg hadn't been using my body to shield her from danger, but rather to hide her movements as she hatched a plot of her own. I should have known.

Jim turned to his daughter. "Poppy, come quickly and stand with Mommy and Daddy. And for God's sake, put a smile on your face. We'll tell the officers nothing is wrong. We'll convince them that the call was a mistake."

"I'm afraid you don't understand," said Aunt Peg. "I didn't make the call just now. The line's been sitting open with an operator on the other end for the last ten minutes. That's why the police are on their way. They heard everything you said, including the part about your accident with Jerry Platt. I didn't summon them. The police are coming here because *they* want to talk to you."

Jim's face went pale. Sondra's gaze flew wildly around the room as if she was looking for a means of escape. "Peg, surely you didn't . . . you can't mean . . ."

"*Sondra,*" her husband said ominously. "Shut the hell up. Right now."

For once she took his advice. Sondra snapped her mouth shut and didn't say another word. The glare she directed in Aunt Peg's and my direction, however, spoke volumes.

Jim wrapped his arm around his wife's shoulders. "Come," he said. "It will look better if we go out together to greet the police. Let me do all the talking. We'll present a united front, shall we?"

Sondra just nodded.

The sound of the sirens was almost deafening now. The squad cars must have already entered the McEvoys' driveway. Side by side, the couple walked out the kennel door. Neither spared a thought for Poppy. Eyes wide, the young girl watched them go.

"Ms. Travis," she said, her voice quavering. "What's happening?"

There was no good way to answer that question.

"The police need to talk to your parents," I said finally.

"It's about Kiltie, isn't it?"

"Partly. And some other things, too."

The child gazed toward the empty doorway where her parents had disappeared. Once again, her eyes were brimming with tears. "Am I in trouble?" she asked.

School rules be damned, I thought. I reached out and gathered Poppy into my arms for a long, hard, hug.

"No, honey," I said softly. "You're not in trouble."

After a minute she pulled away. Poppy tipped her head back to look at me. "Daddy did something wrong, didn't he?"

"I'm afraid so," I told her. "But it had nothing to do with you."

"I know that." Poppy sighed. "It can't be about me. It's *never* about me."

The girl's whole world was falling apart, and the two adults who mattered most to her were only concerned with their vengeful negotiations over a pile of money.

The McEvoy parents weren't arguing about Poppy's custody. Neither one of them had rallied to her side. It was as if Sondra and Jim's only child was nothing more than an afterthought, a remnant left behind in the scattered rubble of their unraveling marriage.

That had to be about the saddest thing I'd ever heard.

Chapter 26

With Christmas only a week away and Bob and Claire's wedding following shortly thereafter, I found myself spending the rest of December pondering the true nature of family. I reflected upon the significance of those innate bonds that hold us together—both the people we're born related to and those whom we choose to add later.

My own family's history is filled with its share of disruptions, deviations, and contentious behavior. Still there was something deeply troubling to me about Sondra and Jim McEvoy's careless disregard for their only child's feelings. Like Jim Platt, Poppy had gotten caught up in her parents' marital warfare and ended up as collateral damage. In my mind, that was unforgiveable.

And if that wasn't bad enough, I found out several days later that Poppy wouldn't be returning to Howard Academy after Christmas break. Mr. Hanover called me at home to tell me that the McEvoys had enrolled their daughter at a fancy boarding school a hundred miles away. She'd be starting there when the new semester began.

"Her parents wanted Poppy removed from the current disturbance," the headmaster told me. That man is ever handy with a euphemism. "They felt that sending her away was best for everyone involved."

"Best for them, you mean." I made no attempt to hide my displeasure. "Sondra and Jim barely paid any attention to her when she was right in front of them. Now they won't have to think about her at all."

I heard the headmaster sigh. "The decision is out of our hands."

"I know that," I retorted. "But it's still wrong."

"Ms. Travis," Mr. Hanover said gently, "I applaud your energy, your empathy, and your conviction. They are all wonderful qualities to bring to your job. But much as you might wish to, you can't save the whole world. None of us can."

I knew that. But I still felt utterly defeated. More than anything I wished that I'd given Poppy more hugs when I'd had the chance.

As for Jim McEvoy, he hired himself a terrific lawyer, the best that money could buy. He and Sondra have cleaned up their act—at least in public. They're still maintaining that all-important united front for the police, the media, and the judicial system. My cynical side is betting that Sondra is being compensated quite handsomely for her cooperation.

With Jim's legal team playing all the angles, it's beginning to look as though there won't be a trial, much less a jail sentence, for the man who caused Jerry Platt's death. While I'm relieved about that for Poppy's sake, the outcome does leave me wishing that the rules for acceptable behavior weren't different for the uber-rich than they are for everyone else.

Kiltie is back home with Sondra now. But since Jim has also moved back into his former house for the time being, I'm guessing that means that the Westie has been banished once more to the kennel. I've heard that Sondra now refers to that week-long period when Kiltie was missing and she was half-panicked about his disappearance as "a silly misunderstanding." According to Aunt Peg, Todd Greenleaf still expects the Westie to be headlining his roster of dogs after the new year.

As might be expected in a household with two young boys, our Christmas was a joyous, disorderly, and rowdy affair. Kev started the proceedings just after dawn when he came racing into Sam's and my bedroom, threw himself onto the bed between us, and shrieked, "Santa came! Santa came!"

Even Davey couldn't sleep through that. Within minutes, he too had joined us on the bed, bringing Augie with him. The rest of the Poodles could be forgiven for taking that as a tacit invitation. At that point there was nothing else for Sam and me to do but rub the sleep from our eyes and troop downstairs to see what kind of bounty Santa Claus had left behind.

Amid the pile of toys and games, Davey found a new tablet that he'd been craving since summer. Kevin was mesmerized by the large tabletop aquarium, filled with angel and rainbow fish, that Santa Claus had left for him on the sideboard.

"Santa brought me *fish*." Kev stared at the tank and exhaled an enraptured breath. "How did he *know?*"

"The same way he knows what a good boy you've been all year," I said, ruffling my fingers through my son's blond locks. "He cares about you very much."

"I love Santa Claus," Kevin announced.

Sam cast his eyes my way. "Me, too," he said.

Bob and Claire's wedding, which followed a week later, was utterly enchanting. Snow drifted downward through the crisp evening air. The church's tall white steeple, lit from below, pointed upward like a beacon toward the stars. Organ music stirred the soul and echoed out into the dark, winter night.

The sight of Davey, standing tall beside his father in front of the altar, made my heart swell with maternal pride. Bob's expression, as he awaited his bride, was wondrous with happiness. I hoped he and Claire enjoyed a long and happy marriage and I thanked the twists and turns of fate that had brought me to this place where I was able to wish only good things for my first son's father.

Thanks to some last-minute scrambling and a timely intervention by Sam, Kevin was still wearing his dark suit and bow tie when he preceded Claire down the aisle. Having aced the rehearsal, the toddler now decided to ad-lib the actual performance. He made it halfway to the altar at a decorous pace before taking off and running the rest of the way. Kev stopped just short of the communion rail, flung the satin ring pillow at Davey, and wrapped his arms firmly around his brother's legs.

Even though I was seated up front next to Claire's sister, Anabelle, and her nephew, Alexander, I could still hear the sound of Claire's delighted laughter coming from the back of the church. After a few seconds, Bob joined in. It seemed like a wonderful way to begin a marriage.

The ceremony was brief, but moving. I never cry at weddings but after the emotional whirlwind of the last two weeks, all my senses felt raw. I'd accomplished what I'd set out to do, but nothing had turned out the way I'd hoped. In the end, I'd still been left with the feeling that I hadn't managed to help nearly enough.

Sam quietly passed me his handkerchief and pressed his body a little closer to mine as we sat side by side in the pew. I appreciate the silent support. Sam got it. He always does.

Aunt Peg had arranged for the reception to be held at a nearby country club. She never would have done such a thing on Bob's behalf; the gesture was a sure sign of her fondness for Claire. My ex-husband realized that and I saw him thank her privately later. Aunt Peg brushed off his expression of gratitude but I knew she was pleased. Maybe there's hope for their relationship yet.

The mood at the reception was festive. I snagged a glass of champagne from a passing waiter and went to greet the happy couple. Claire and Bob were surrounded by well-wishers. A few minutes passed before my turn came.

"Welcome to the family," I said, holding my drink aloft in tribute to her intrepid act. "And hold on to your hat."

Claire didn't appear fazed at all. Instead she just grinned.

"I don't know about that," she said lightly. "Since you and Bob are divorced, we're not really related, are we?"

"Sure we are." Bertie came to join us. "Even if it's only in a step-something kind of way, it still counts. We're not going to let you get away from us that easily."

"Look what happened to Bob," I said. "He's still here. It must be our magnetic attraction."

"It's more like flypaper," Bob told his new wife in a loud stage whisper.

Unexpectedly I found myself sniffling again. "I got my first sister by marriage," I said, glancing Bertie's way. "And now I have a second. I couldn't have done better if I had chosen you both myself."

Sam came over, carrying Kevin in his arms. Davey was trailing along behind.

"This is the best Christmas *ever*," Kev announced happily.

I couldn't argue with that. I was surrounded by my family, the most precious people in my world. I wanted them to know how much they meant to me. I wanted to treat them with exquisite care. And I had no intention of taking even a single minute with any of them for granted.

Drawing Davey closer, I wrapped my arms around Sam and my two sons and held on tight. No member of my family was ever going to feel like they didn't get enough hugs. I would make sure of that.

"Mom, enough," Davey complained after a minute. "It's embarrassing."

"I know," I said, but I didn't let go.

It felt great.

Ever wonder what Melanie and Aunt Peg were up to before solving murders? Let's step back in time, when college-aged Melanie and her indomitable Aunt Peg were little more than strangers . . .

It's Christmas in Connecticut, and Peg Turnbull can't wait to spend her favorite holiday cozying up to husband Max and their clan of pedigree Poodles in Greenwich. But Peg's spirits drop when the family of Max's estranged brother Michael invites the pair over for Christmas dinner. Could her in-laws want to settle the long-standing feud over Nana's will? Peg isn't expecting any miracles, but it's been ages since Peg last saw her niece and nephew. Little Melanie must be out of pigtails by now . . .

When they arrive at the Turnbull's, Peg is not just surprised by how much Melanie has grown up. The family has spared no expense in preparing for the festivities—unusual, considering Michael blew his inheritance after years of financial troubles. Peg suspects there's an awful secret tucked beneath her brother-in-law's ostentatious good cheer, and she's determined to get to the bottom of it. Once she does, someone's ending up in the doghouse . . .

**Please turn the page for a
Laurien Berenson bonus novella!
A CHRISTMAS HOWL!**

Margaret Turnbull was a busy woman. She had a kennel full of Standard Poodles to care for, an article to finish writing for *Poodle Variety*, a litter of new puppies due after Christmas, and a big, wet, black dog lying on the grooming table in front of her waiting to be blown dry. What she didn't have was time for needless interruptions.

Unless they came from her husband, Max, whom she adored.

"Eileen wants us to do what?" she asked. Turning off the switch on the freestanding dryer to silence its loud whine, she tilted the nozzle away and looked up. Peg was quite certain she'd heard Max right the first time. Still, she wanted to hear him say the words again.

"Eileen and Michael have invited us to come for Christmas dinner," Max repeated.

Michael was Max's older brother. Eileen was his wife. The couple had two children, a boy and a girl. Those children had barely been teenagers the last time she'd seen them, Peg realized. Busy with school and friends, and everything else that young people got up to, neither had been present on the infrequent occasions Peg had seen her in-laws recently.

"I can't imagine what prompted them to do something like that." Abruptly her good mood vanished. A vague feeling of disgruntlement took its place.

Christmas, now just a week away, was her favorite holiday. Peg loved everything about the occasion, from the cheery decorations to the sound of Christmas carols to the holiday pastries and sweets. Just the heady scent of evergreen was enough to lift her spirits.

Christmas was supposed to be a time of joy and goodwill. Except, Peg thought unhappily, where her in-laws were concerned.

"Christmas dinner with your family," she said with a small frown. "What an odd idea. You and Michael are barely on speaking terms. And he and Eileen have never liked me."

"Don't be silly—" Max began.

"Oh pish." Peg's exclamation stopped him in his tracks. "We've been married for twenty-five years. We certainly don't need to rehash that old discussion. I am well and truly over the fact that your family disapproves of me for any number of reasons, not the least of which is that rather than producing a houseful of children, you and I ended up surrounded by Standard Poodles instead."

"You can hardly be held accountable for that outcome," Max replied with a twinkle in his eye. "Considering that the wedding present I got for you was the beginning of the Cedar Crest line."

"Lovely, lovely Laurel." Peg remembered their first Standard Poodle with enormous fondness. "A ten-week-old bundle of fluff and mischief with a shiny, black nose, beguiling eyes, and an old soul. I took one look and fell madly in love."

"You weren't the only one who was madly in love," Max said.

Peg slanted her husband a look. Her memories of their courtship were decidedly different. She recalled pursuing Max ardently—right up until the day she had let him catch her.

"Don't go mushy on me now," she said. "At this late date, I refuse to believe that you're really an old softie at heart."

Max just grinned. He knew full well that no one ever convinced his wife of anything that hadn't started out as her own idea.

"It's amazing how far we've come since then," said Peg. "And that here we are, so many years later, surrounded by Laurel's descendants."

She gazed around the tidy kennel with satisfaction. The area in which they were standing was part grooming space and part sitting room. Two walls were covered with win photos, eight-by-ten pictures taken at the variety of dog shows over the years where she and Max had handled numerous Cedar Crest Standard Poodles to their championships. A third wall contained an overflowing trophy cabinet. The fourth had floor-to-ceiling shelves, filled with the assortment of equipment needed to keep their dogs' coats in top condition.

Through a wide arched doorway, Peg could see the Poodles themselves. Two or three were sitting up and watching the activity in the grooming room. The rest were stretched out comfortably in their indoor runs. Currently she and Max had ten Standard Poodles, including Targa, the black male waiting patiently on the grooming table for her to resume his blow-dry, and Bonnie, who had finished her championship in the spring and was expecting her first litter of puppies shortly.

"Not entirely amazing," said Max, "when you think of all the hard work and dedication that's gone into what we've accomplished."

Reminded of the task at hand, Peg picked up a pin brush, turned the dryer back on, and repositioned the nozzle. If Targa's hair spent too much time air-drying it would begin to kink and curl. She needed the strands to lie smooth and plush, otherwise she would have to wet the Poodle down and start the job over. With nimble fingers and a practiced stroke, she began to work her way through the coat once more.

"Not to mention a little luck," she said, lifting her voice to be heard above the dryer's dull roar. "And plenty of good times along the way."

"Speaking of good times," said Max. "About Christmas . . ."

Peg sighed. She should have known that Max wouldn't allow himself to be sidetracked.

"Did Eileen happen to mention why she and Michael were offering this invitation out of the blue?" she asked.

"No. The question occurred to me too, but it seemed rude to ask."

"This is the first Christmas since your mother died," Peg mentioned.

"I know." Max nodded. "Even though it's been nearly a year, maybe the thought of having to celebrate the holiday without Nana made my brother want to reconnect with what little family he has left."

"Could be he and Eileen are trying to extend an olive branch."

"If so, that would be a pleasant surprise. And if it *is* the case, I certainly don't want to be the one to push them away."

"Nor do I," Peg agreed. Especially since she was the one who'd caused the initial rift between her husband and his family. Not that it had been her fault.

Right from the start, Max's relatives had never accepted her. Young and eager to please when they'd first met, Peg had found her attempts to cultivate a cordial relationship stonewalled by Max's close-knit Irish Catholic clan. Max's mother had made little secret of the fact she didn't feel that Peg was good enough for her darling second son. The more Max had stood up for her, the more his family had resented her influence over him.

Eventually she and Max had grown weary of the discord, and it had become easier for Peg to simply stay away. Over the ensuing years, except for the occasional family gathering to mark an important milestone, Max and Peg had limited their contact with the rest of the Turnbulls. They had had each other and their Poodles. That was all they needed.

Eleven months earlier, Peg had wondered whether Nana's death might draw the fractured family closer together in their grief. Instead it had only driven them farther apart.

And now this. An unexpected invitation to Christmas dinner.

Oh joy, thought Peg. She supposed she could suck it up and deal with her husband's relatives for one afternoon. Even if it meant sacrificing her favorite holiday for the cause.

Distracted by her thoughts, Peg let her fingers blunder through a snag in Targa's damp coat. The big Poodle lifted his head. His dark eyes looked up at her reproachfully.

"I know," she murmured. Gently she patted his head back down into place on the matted tabletop. "I'm sorry. That was my fault."

Max watched the interplay between his wife and the young dog. Peg had always had her own language for dealing with their Standard Poodles. She understood their thoughts and needs better than anyone else. Even better than him, and that was saying something.

Years earlier, he'd been forced to choose between the love of his life and the family who'd thought that if they made his life difficult enough, he would bow to their will. It hadn't even been a contest.

It still wasn't.

"It's up to you," he said now. "I know how you feel about Christmas. If you don't want to spend the day with my family, we certainly don't have to."

Peg didn't even hesitate. "Call Eileen back and tell her we'll be there," she said. "Find out if we can bring anything to help with dinner. I'm good with desserts."

Max nodded. He knew that. Peg's sweet tooth was legendary.

"And think of some presents we can get to take with us," she added.

"Me?"

"They're *your* relatives," Peg pointed out, "And besides, I'm busy. I have a dog to blow-dry."

Max went to make the phone call. He left the kennel with a smile on his face.

On Christmas Eve, Max and Peg were seated in their living room on either side of a roaring fire. They had lowered the lights, and the sole illumination in the room came from the twinkling bulbs on their plush, eight-foot Christmas tree. Both Max and Peg were sipping oversized mugs of marshmallow-topped hot chocolate. Both had a Standard Poodle draped across their feet.

Max's companion was retired show dog Champion Cedar Crest Salute. Beside him lay Champion Cedar Crest Bonaventure. Peg was keeping a close eye on Bonnie, whose first litter was due in only a matter of days. As the bitch rolled her shoulders, then stretched out on one side in an attempt to shift her large belly into a more comfortable position, Peg reached down and scratched behind the big black Poodle's ears.

Bonnie wasn't the only one who was feeling uncomfortable, Peg realized. And maybe even a little grumpy. Especially since it was her own fault for feigning a modicum of enthusiasm a week earlier when presented with the invitation to share Christmas dinner with her in-laws. Now that the day was almost upon her, Peg found that the only emotion she could muster with regard to the upcoming occasion was one of dismal resignation.

At least she was bringing the pies, Peg thought. That would help.

Max took one look at the expression on his wife's face, set down his mug on the table beside him, and said, "We don't *have* to go, you know. I can call Eileen in the morning and cancel."

"You'll do no such thing. It's much too late to back out now. I wouldn't dream of doing something that rude." Peg paused then added, "Even to your relatives."

"I can't imagine why." Max shook his head. "They've never treated you with the same courtesy."

"Nor you, recently," Peg pointed out. "When Nana was here, she was able to keep the peace between you and your brother. But once she was gone, it seemed like the two of you were immediately at each other's throats."

"Our problems started long before that."

Peg dipped her head in a small nod. For the most part, she purposely kept herself removed from Turnbull family business, but she could guess the event her husband was referring to.

"Three years ago," Max growled, "when Michael convinced Nana to place her investment account in his hands. Anyone could see that was a terrible idea. I tried to warn her, but she didn't listen to me."

"She didn't *want* to listen to you. There's a big difference. Nana knew exactly what she was doing. Michael was struggling. He'd just been let go from another brokerage firm. She wanted to help."

Max's body stiffened in annoyance. Feeling the sudden tension, Salute sat up and pressed his body against Max's legs, an offer of comfort and support. Idly, Max reached over and nudged his fingers into the Poodle's topknot. Salute tipped his head to one side and leaned into the caress.

"Nana wouldn't have had to help if Michael had been any good at his job," Max said. "It wasn't her fault that he ran through half the brokerage houses in New York like a stack of dominoes. Obviously he wasn't cut out to be an investment counselor. I don't know why he couldn't just accept that. If not for Nana's connections and the sizable account she entrusted to him, Michael would have been finished on Wall Street."

"Which is precisely why she stepped in," Peg said

smoothly. "Michael was her oldest son. She couldn't bear to see him fail."

"Nana's money was no different than any of the previous accounts he'd managed." Max's tone was bitter. "It ran through his fingers like water. I tried to stay on top of things. I could have intervened before the situation became dire, but Michael kept blocking my attempts to find out what was happening with the investments he'd chosen for her."

"And Nana let him do that," Peg pointed out. "She positioned herself between the two of you on purpose. Your mother was a smart woman. Don't think for a moment that she was Michael's dupe. I'm quite certain she knew exactly what she was doing. The most important thing to Nana was family unity—and she wanted her two sons to get along."

"Well, *that* didn't last," Max said unhappily.

No, it hadn't, Peg reflected. When Nana's will had been read, she had left the bulk of her remaining estate to Max. Their younger sister, Rose, who'd joined the order of the Sisters of Divine Mercy and taken a vow of poverty, received only a few family mementoes. The will had been explicit in its bequests. Michael, it stated, had already received his inheritance while Nana was alive.

"My brother had no right to be so angry when the will was read," Max said. "It was his own fault that things turned out the way they did. But Michael refused to see that. He was the oldest child. He'd always been Nana's favorite. He was brought up to believe he could do no wrong."

"And he found out the hard way that wasn't true," Peg replied. "That can't have been an easy pill to swallow."

"Michael wasn't the only one who had to deal with bad news," Max said with a snort. "By the time I got my hands on them, Nana's remaining assets were barely half what they should have been. Even accounting for Michael's losses in the last two years of her life, the estate was still much smaller than I had expected it to be."

"Perhaps Nana hid the full extent of her investments in Michael's career from you," Peg ventured.

"The thought has occurred to me."

"But you never asked him." It wasn't a question. Peg already knew the answer.

Max shook his head. "When she was alive, all Nana wanted was for Michael and me to act like brothers. I figured I owed her memory at least that much."

"Precisely," said Peg. "And that is why you and I will join Eileen and Michael and the children for Christmas dinner. If there's any possibility of a rapprochement between you and Michael, I have no intention of standing in the way."

She glanced over at Salute. Feeling her gaze, the black Standard Poodle opened his eyes, then stood up and stretched. Peg held out a hand and beckoned. Obligingly, the big dog stepped forward and positioned himself within easy reach.

"I was thinking I might take Salute with us tomorrow," Peg said, cupping the dog's long muzzle in her palm.

"Oh?"

"Now that he's retired from the show ring, there's not a lot of excitement in his life. I'd imagine he'd enjoy a day out."

"Of course he would." Max sounded amused. "Now tell me the real reason."

"It occurred to me that if I was going to spend the day surrounded by your family, I ought to have at least one friendly face to look at. Present company excluded, of course."

Max barked out a laugh. "I can't argue with your logic. Though Eileen might. She doesn't like dogs. Or pets of any kind, for that matter."

"*Truly?*" The thought was inconceivable to Peg. "I always knew there was something wrong with those people. How can you raise children and not allow them to have pets?"

"Don't ask me, I'm on your side. But before you go flying over there like a crusading avenger, I should point out that you're several years too late to help Melanie and Frank. Those two aren't children anymore."

"Really? The last time I saw Melanie, she barely came up to my chest. I'm quite certain she had pigtails." That might have been an exaggeration, thought Peg. But not by much.

"Well, she's not in pigtails now," Max informed her. "Melanie's almost finished with college. Not only that, but Eileen told me she's bringing her boyfriend to Christmas dinner."

"A *boyfriend* coming to a holiday dinner with the whole family? It sounds like that must be serious."

"I gather Eileen hopes not."

"She's already met the fellow?"

"So she said. The young man's name is Bob. He's studying to be an accountant."

"Oh my." Peg held back a chuckle. "He sounds deathly dull. What do we know about Melanie? Is she deathly dull too? Maybe they're a good match."

"I barely know anything more about her than you do. But I'm sure we'll find out tomorrow."

"I can hardly wait," said Peg.

She loved her husband. She truly did. That was why she waited until Max had looked away before rolling her eyes.

Salute stayed home.

There was no point in starting off the holiday visit on the wrong foot, Peg decided. And if taking the big Poodle along was going to upset Eileen, well . . . based on past experience with both her in-laws and her Standard Poodles, Peg was sure that her dog's easygoing temperament left him better equipped to deal with adversity than Eileen's uptight disposition ever would.

Peg bid the Poodles good-bye, gathered up her pies, and joined Max in the car for the twenty-minute drive to New Canaan. The grim smile on her husband's face looked every bit as forced as her own faux-merry demeanor. Before leaving the house, she'd stopped to pin a blinking Christmas tree brooch on the front of her dress. With luck, the tiny flashing lights might liven up the visit. Or at least give them all a good laugh, Peg thought.

One could only hope. Somehow laughter seemed like something that might be in short supply during the hours to come.

The trip eastward on the Merritt Parkway passed all too quickly. New Canaan was quiet on Christmas afternoon. It didn't take long to cut through the quaint town before heading north on Oenoke Ridge Road.

Max's brother's family lived in a lovely colonial home, set back from the road behind a stand of mature trees. The property was bordered by a low stone wall whose tidy appearance was reinforced by the neatly kept lawn. There wasn't a leaf or twig out of place.

The substantial, two-story house was painted dove gray and had dark green shutters. An electric candle flickered in each upstairs window. A double door, each side decorated with an ornate wreath, marked the front entrance. Low bushes on either side of the wide front steps had been covered with fairy lights. On approach, the entire vista looked festive and wonderfully inviting.

And, Peg thought, expensive.

"How do you suppose Michael continues to afford this place?" she asked curiously.

Max just shrugged. He steered the car to a parking area near the garage. "He and Eileen have lived here forever. They bought this house before the kids were born. Maybe he was flush back then. Or maybe it's mortgaged to the rafters. I'm certainly not going to ask."

Max was reaching for the door handle. He paused and sent his wife a meaningful look. "And neither are you."

Peg lifted a brow but didn't reply. Instead she busied herself with gathering up the desserts. She wasn't going to argue with Max. Not today of all days. But it was going to be an even longer afternoon than she'd envisioned if she had to spend the entire time watching what she said.

His own arms filled with presents, Max rang the front doorbell. He and Peg waited. After a minute, he rang the bell again.

"Do you suppose they've changed their minds about us?" Peg asked hopefully.

"I doubt it." Max freed up a hand and pushed the buzzer again.

This time, the chimes that sounded within the house brought a response. One half of the front door swept open. A young girl dressed in blue jeans and a holiday sweater peered out at them uncertainly.

She had to be Melanie, Peg thought with only the barest glimmer of recognition. Goodness, how many years had it been?

Max had said the girl was in college. If so, she looked young for her age. She had a soft, unmolded quality about her, as if experience had yet to sharpen her into the adult she would someday become.

Without thinking about it, Peg squared her shoulders; her posture was always impeccable. She couldn't help but notice that Melanie still stood a full head shorter than she did. Surely, Peg thought, the girl wasn't finished growing yet?

"Merry Christmas!" Max greeted the girl in a booming voice. He'd obviously decided it was up to him to set the proper mood.

"Merry Christmas," she parroted back, opening the door wide.

Max juggled the presents to one side and gathered Melanie into a hug. "I hope you were expecting us?"

"Yes, of course. Sorry about that! Everybody thought someone else got the door." The burst of words came tumbling out in a rush. "Mom's busy in the kitchen. Dad and Bob are watching football in the library. And Frank, well, you could spend all day waiting for him to do something useful. We didn't mean to keep you waiting. Please come inside!"

Melanie eyed the stack of incoming presents with evident surprise before remembering her manners and turning to Peg. "Aunt Peg?" The greeting came out sounding more like a question. "How lovely to see you again. Let me take your coat. Mom will be delighted to see those pies. Did you bake them yourself?"

"Yes, I did," Peg lied blithely. The pies had come from St. Moritz, the best bakery in Greenwich. But if Melanie didn't have the sense to notice the gold labels affixed to the top of the white boxes, she deserved to be misinformed.

Peg pulled off her coat and scarf and dumped them in Melanie's arms. Max's outerwear followed.

"Perhaps we could put these presents under the tree?" Max asked. Though they'd been invited into the house, they still seemed to be stuck standing just inside the front door.

Peg peered across the wide hallway into an expansive living room. Her Christmas tree at home was large, but it was dwarfed by the massive Scotch Pine that was the centerpiece of Michael and Eileen's decorations. Dozens of glass ornaments glittered in the soft light. Gold bows fluttered from nearly every branch. A fussy-looking Christmas angel graced the top of the tree. She was so high in the air that her gold halo scraped the twelve-foot coffered ceiling.

How odd, Peg thought, that with the entire family at home, the living room with its beautiful tree was empty of people. Why go to all the trouble to put up lavish decorations for the holiday and then not enjoy looking at them?

"Presents?" came a voice from above. "Did I hear someone say there were presents?" A lanky teenage boy with angular features and long, dark bangs that hid his eyes came skipping down the steps.

"Of course that would get your attention, Frank." He'd only just appeared, but Melanie already sounded exasperated by her brother. "Yes, Uncle Max and Aunt Peg brought us presents. Wasn't that nice of them?"

"Let me help you with those." Frank whisked the boxes out of Max's arms and headed into the living room. "And by the way," he called back over his shoulder, "Merry Christmas!"

"Same to you," Peg replied. She hoped the boy would prove to be more interesting than his bland sister.

"Don't just stand there, Mel," said Frank. "Go fetch the parents. Do they even know that Uncle Max and Aunt Peg are here?"

"We do now." Eileen appeared at the back of the hallway. Striding quickly toward them, Peg's sister-in-law pulled off an apron she was wearing over her dress and tossed it over the banister. "Honestly, you two, where are your manners? How long have Max and Peg been standing here?"

Eileen wrapped her arms around Max and kissed him on each cheek. "Teenagers," she said as she pulled away. "Other parents tell me they've survived this stage, but honestly I'm not sure it's possible."

She glanced at Peg as if she thought a handshake might be appropriate. Peg was having none of it. It was bad enough that she'd had to leave her Standard Poodle at home. She wasn't about to let her sister-in-law treat her like an interloper at Christmas dinner too. When Eileen shifted her way, Peg stepped forward with her arms out. The two women came together in an awkward embrace.

"Michael?" Eileen called as she stepped back. "Max is here!"

"He and Bob are watching football," said Melanie. "They probably can't hear you."

"Or they don't want to," Eileen muttered.

"I'll go." Melanie spun around and made a quick assessment of her looks in a mirror hanging on the side wall. Then she went scooting away.

Eileen looked after her and sighed. "Bob is Melanie's boyfriend," she said for Peg's benefit. She didn't sound particularly happy about that fact.

"So I heard," Peg replied. "Max has been bringing me up to speed."

"That's good, then. You'll know who everybody is."

She should hope so, thought Peg. Considering that she'd been related to most of them for more than two decades.

A minute passed in silence as they waited. When nobody appeared, Eileen wound her arm though Max's. "Maybe it would be easier if we went to join them," she said.

Eileen led her brother-in-law away. Left to her own devices, Peg trailed along behind like a lost puppy. Her nephew, Frank, seemed to have vanished again, she noted. So much for hoping for any entertainment from him.

"Dinner is in an hour," Eileen was saying. Her voice was high and chirpy. Peg wondered if it always sounded that way or if that was her holiday voice. "And of course you'll want a drink beforehand. Some eggnog to celebrate the day? Or Scotch? Michael has an excellent bottle of Chivas in the library. If you ask nicely, he might be persuaded to share."

Eileen laughed at her own joke. Max didn't look as though he thought it was particularly funny, but after a moment, he joined in anyway.

"I'll have eggnog," Peg said to herself. "Not that anybody cares."

"Of course you will," Eileen replied.

Peg wondered what that comment meant. She didn't dare ask.

The trio had nearly reached the library when Michael came striding through the open doorway. Peg hadn't seen her brother-in-law since Nana's funeral; the impression she'd had of him then still remained. Michael was a slightly shorter, slightly grayer version of Max. Both men had the same broad shoulders and long torsos. They both had kind eyes and smiled readily—at least when they weren't talking to one another.

"Merry Christmas, Michael," Peg said firmly, as if by stating the greeting she could make it true. Rather than stepping forward herself, she applied both hands to Max's back and propelled him toward his older brother.

Both wives watched with satisfaction as the two men shook hands.

"Merry Christmas, indeed," Michael replied heartily. "It was good of you to come."

"An invitation to a family gathering?" said Max. "Peg and I wouldn't have missed it. And this must be Melanie's friend, Bob?"

A young man was standing behind Michael, lingering just inside the room. Peg realized with a guilty start that she hadn't even noticed him until Max pointed him out. Usually her powers of observation were better than that. On the other hand, now that she was paying attention and had a look, there wasn't much to see. Everything about boyfriend Bob appeared to be perfectly ordinary. He struck her as the kind of average individual who would have gone unnoticed in a crowd of two.

At least he had some manners, however. Bob slipped

around Michael and extended his hand. "Bob Travis," he said to Max. "It's a pleasure to meet you, sir. Melanie hasn't told me much about her family."

Peg snorted under her breath. She could well imagine why not.

Then Bob was turning her way and repeating his name for her benefit as though she could possibly have missed hearing it the first time. "What a lovely brooch, ma'am," he said as they shook hands.

Ma'am indeed, thought Peg. Just how old did he think she was? Not only that, but the brooch wasn't lovely at all. It was a novelty knickknack, quite possibly the tackiest piece of jewelry she'd ever owned. It had been intended as a source of entertainment, not admiration.

The other three adults had continued their conversation. Bob, Peg realized, was still peering at the brooch intently. Perhaps, like a kitten, he was mesmerized by flashing lights.

"That's quite a lot of blinking," he said after a minute.

"It squirts water, too," Peg retorted.

"Really?" Bob leaned in for a closer look.

What an idiot, she thought. If the silly ornament really did squirt water, it would have gotten him squarely in the nose.

"No, not really," Peg said acerbically. "It was a joke."

"Oh, I see." Bob straightened and stepped back. "Humor." He made the word sound like a foreign concept.

Melanie came over to stand beside her boyfriend. "That's Aunt Peg. She's always joking around."

As if the girl had the faintest idea what she was likely to do, Peg thought with a sniff. She couldn't even remember the last time they'd seen one another. Honestly! This was like being surrounded by a pack of baboons. Peg could only hope that dinner was on the way. And that it would arrive sooner rather than later.

And then, of course, there would be pie.

That was a pleasant thought. Perhaps the first one of the day.

Peg tuned back into the adult conversation to discover that Eileen was in the process of taking drink orders and getting everyone organized. The plan taking shape seemed to imply that copious alcohol consumption would be expected to play a role in making the family occasion proceed more smoothly. Michael and the guests were to watch football in the library while Eileen and Melanie put the finishing touches on dinner. Peg offered to help out in the kitchen, a proposal that was politely but firmly rebuffed.

By the time dinner reached the table an hour later, Peg was working on a happy buzz. Unexpectedly, the eggnog had packed a potent punch. All four men had spent the intervening time staring fervently at the television in the library. Peg thought their attention level would have been more appropriate to the viewing of lifeand-death combat rather than a mildly interesting bowl game.

But at least that kept them from having to converse with one another, she realized. As long as all eyes were centered on the sporting event, everyone could pretend that they were getting along. Bored with that activity, Peg had passed the time browsing through the bookshelves in the room. She was delighted to discover an antique book of maps that had proven to be fascinating reading.

It wasn't until Melanie came to tell them that dinner

was on the table and the men stood up to go trooping into the dining room that Peg noticed that Michael was seriously tipsy. When her brother-in-law rose from his seat, lost his balance, then sat down again quickly, Peg caught Max's eye and raised a brow. He gave his head a small shake.

Yet another thing they weren't meant to talk about. Peg swallowed a small sigh. Her lips were going to be seriously sore by the end of the day if she had to spend the entire visit biting back comments that couldn't be made.

Frank and Bob, still talking about the game, went on ahead. When they'd gone, Peg leaned down and offered a steady arm to her brother-inlaw. "Perhaps you would be so kind as to escort me in to dinner?"

"I would be delighted, Peg. " Michael looked inordinately pleased as he levered himself up a second time. He glanced at Max with a sly wink. "Little brother, it seems your wife has indicated a preference. I'm afraid that means you're on your own."

"I think I can manage to find my way," Max replied imperturbably. "Maybe I'll just follow my nose. As I recall, Eileen is a wonderful cook. I'm sure she's prepared a feast for us today."

When they reached the dining room, Peg saw that Max hadn't been exaggerating. The meal that greeted them was indeed a feast. An enormous roast turkey held pride of place at the head of a wide mahogany table. An assortment of bowls and tureens held more side items than she'd ever seen assembled for a single meal. The first bottle of wine was open and ready to be poured.

They all found their places at the table. Brandishing a large knife and relishing his role as the center of attention, Michael managed to carve the bird without mishap. Plates were passed and helpings served. A round of wine was poured, followed by a second.

As the courses were served and cleared, conversation around the table ebbed and flowed. Happily occupied with the delicious food, Peg found that she was quite content to act as observer rather than participant in much of the family byplay. It didn't take her long to realize that the younger generation was more interesting to her than their parents. She'd known Michael and Eileen for years—perhaps not well, but certainly well enough. Melanie and Frank, however, were unknown territory. That was enough to make her curious.

Melanie appeared to be rather besotted with Bob, Peg mused. She hung on his every word, offered him the choicest morsels from each side dish, and leapt to refill his wineglass long before it was empty. Watching the pair interact, Peg was at a loss to understand what it was about the young man that merited such ardent attention. Bob certainly didn't seem to be anything special. Not only that, but his conversation consisted mostly of football scores and college anecdotes about people no one else knew.

Young love, thought Peg. What a crock.

She frowned and turned her attention to Frank. Surely, of the two siblings, he had to be the more appealing—if only for the fact that he didn't look as though he felt any happier to have been roped into this family gathering than she was.

"How old are you, Frank?" Peg asked across the table.

"Eighteen. I'm a senior in high school." For some reason, he sounded quite proud of that fact.

"So then you must be looking at colleges."

"Well . . . sort of."

Despite the fact that her attention was focused on the teenage boy, Peg couldn't help but notice the pained look that passed between his parents. "Sort of?" she inquired. "Isn't it time for you to be filling out applications?"

Frank speared a piece of turkey and put it in his mouth. He finished chewing, then swallowed, before replying. "I'm not sure I'm really cut out for college," he said finally. "I figured I'd take a gap year to think about what I really want to do."

"What you want to do is study," said Michael. "Get a degree. Make a start on a good career."

"No," Frank replied. "That's what *you* want me to do. I might have other plans."

"Like what?" Max asked with interest.

Frank shrugged. "I don't know yet. That's the whole point of taking a year off to find out."

"To goof off and hang around with your friends, you mean."

Eileen, seated at Michael's right, reached across and placed her hand on top of her husband's. Peg saw her squeeze his fingers gently. "Maybe we could save this discussion for another time. Christmas is a day to celebrate. To be thankful for our family and the things that we have and can share with others."

"Hear, hear!" Michael said heartily. "As usual, Eileen, you are absolutely right." He leaned across and kissed his wife's cheek, prompting a ripple of embarrassment among the three young people at the table. Then Michael disengaged his hand from Eileen's, picked up his glass, and raised it above his head.

"A toast!" he pronounced. "To family."

Six more glasses lifted. "To family," everyone echoed dutifully.

Max started to lower his glass. He paused and glanced at Peg uncertainly. She hoped he wasn't about to do something he'd regret. Judging by the expression on his face, he was hoping the same thing.

"To bygones!" Max said, raising his glass again.

All hands came back up. Bob looked confused, but he gamely joined in. "To bygones!" nearly everyone repeated.

Though Michael lifted his glass, Peg noticed that he remained stonily silent for the toast. That didn't stop him from taking a hefty swallow of wine along with the rest of the family.

"Speaking of family," said Melanie, turning toward the empty seat at the end of the table. "This is our first Christmas without Nana. Somehow I keep expecting to look over and see her sitting there with us."

"Me too," Frank agreed.

Abruptly Eileen's eyes darted toward her husband. She was looking for something . . . but what? Peg had no idea. Then as quickly as Eileen had sought Michael's gaze, she glanced away again. Peg wondered if she'd imagined that brief shimmer of tension between them.

"To Nana!" Melanie cried.

The girl's thoughtful salute was a well-meant idea. Everyone at the table should have simply raised their glasses in remembrance. But Peg saw in an instant that that wasn't how things were going to go.

Max had loved his mother dearly. But he'd also harbored a great deal of resentment over Nana's interference in his love life. Those feelings were only exacerbated when she'd later pushed him aside and turned to Michael for guidance and support. In the year since his mother's death, Max had worked to set aside his bitterness about the way Nana had allowed their relationship to deteriorate. But now, seeing the mocking smile on Michael's face as he turned to his younger brother and lifted his glass in salute, Peg felt Max stiffen beside her.

"To Nana!" Michael's voice was overloud. He rose to his feet and looked down upon them. "A wonderful mother who was most discerning about the people she kept around her."

Peg sucked in an annoyed breath. Michael was turning the blade deliberately. Of course, the insult was intended to strike out at her, too. That part she could brush aside. She'd been doing it for years. But she wasn't about to stand by and let Michael run roughshod over her husband's feelings.

Before she could say anything, however, Frank spoke up. The teenager appeared to be oblivious to the undercurrents that eddied in the air around them.

"To the best grandmother ever!" Frank seconded.

Max had been staring down at the creamy linen tablecloth. Now, his movements slow and deliberate, he lifted his glass along with the rest. "To Nana," he said softly. "I hope she knows how much we truly miss her."

"Some of us more than—" Michael began.

Eileen didn't let him finish. Instead she grasped her husband's arm and pulled sharply downward, guiding him back to his seat. "Wonderful toast, dear. I know we all share your heartfelt sentiments." Eileen paused to look around the table, her gaze resting on each face in turn as if daring them to contradict her. "Don't we?"

Frank and Melanie nodded together. Their mother had them well trained.

"Yes, ma'am," Bob said dutifully. He hadn't a clue what was going on.

Determined to smooth over the awkward moment, Eileen left a warning hand on Michael's arm as she turned and smiled down the table at her guests. From past experience, she knew the one topic that was sure to immediately engage her in-laws' interest.

"Speaking of Nana," she said to Peg, "did you know that she had a very good friend who competes in dog training like you do? Her name is Imelda Grissom. I wonder if you might know her."

"Dog shows," Peg corrected automatically. Then she stopped and thought about what Eileen had said. It was probably the first interesting thing she'd heard all day. "Imelda? Of course, I know Imelda."

That part was easy. Peg had devoted a large part of her life to her beloved Standard Poodles and to the dog show world. She knew everybody. "Imelda has Cavaliers."

Frank looked up. "She has *what?* Is that some kind of disease?"

"Cavs," Max informed the teen. His shoulders began to relax. "Otherwise known as Cavalier King Charles Spaniels. It's a breed of dog. They're quite charming, actually."

"Charming." Melanie sputtered a laugh. "A dog."

"Don't knock it till you try it," said Max. "You might be surprised by how lovable dogs can be. There are more than a hundred different breeds, one to suit every different job and owner personality."

"Not mine," Eileen replied. "All that dog hair and mess in the house? No, thank you."

"We know all about the different breeds," Frank said authoritatively.

Melanie nodded in agreement. "We watched Westminster on TV one year."

"We knew it was something that you and Peg were obsessed by," Eileen told Max. "So we watched to see what it was all about. We were trying to figure out the appeal."

"Oh?" Peg asked drily. "And did you?"

"No." Michael's tone was condescending. "It all looked rather silly to me. I have no idea how anyone could call something like that a sport."

"A bunch of froufrou dogs dancing around a big ring," Frank chortled. "And those silly looking Poodles . . . *they were the worst!*"

Eileen gasped. In the moment of horrified silence that followed, she looked as though she would have liked to disavow her entire family. Either that or slink beneath the table out of sight.

"*What?*" Frank asked, swiveling his head from side to side. "What's the matter? What did I say?"

"As it happens, Peg and I have Poodles," Max informed him. "Standard Poodles. The big ones. That's our breed."

"Oh." Frank gulped. His Adam's apple bobbed up and down in his neck. "I'm sure they're very nice."

"They are indeed," Peg agreed easily, deciding not to take offense. Seriously, did *every* aspect of this conversation have to be a minefield? "We have a very good dog right now named Champion Cedar Crest Target Sighted. We call him Targa. He's one of the favorites to win the variety at Westminster next year."

"So if you watch the show in February," said Max, "you might see him in the Non-Sporting Group ring with Peg handling. I can let you know the day and time, if you like."

"Don't go to any trouble on our account," said Michael. "I'm sure we'll be too busy to tune in for something like that."

Eileen forced a smile that looked more like a grimace. "But you'll have to let us know afterward how it all turned out," she said to Max in a conciliatory tone. "You can do that, can't you?"

"Of course," Peg agreed.

When pigs fly, she thought to herself.

Eileen and Melanie hopped up to clear the plates and serve coffee. Bob was conscripted to help. By the time everyone was seated once again at the table, the conversation had thankfully moved on. Melanie chatted about her studies. Frank, who was saving to buy himself a car, gave a detailed accounting of the makes and models he was considering. Bob added little, but managed to look politely interested in everything that was said.

In the annals of Christmas dinners she had known, Peg thought with an inward sigh, this was certainly going to go down as one of the worst. At least, mercifully, it was almost over. But that didn't stop her thoughts from returning to the question that had been nagging at her since the invitation had originally been extended.

Why had she and Max been invited to the holiday gathering? If, as Max had hoped, the occasion was meant to mend the long-standing family rift, Peg certainly hadn't seen any evidence of it. In fact, quite the opposite. Throughout the day Michael had treated Max and Peg with an air of careless disregard that bordered on disdain. Peg hadn't seen a single honest attempt to engage with his brother at all.

She looked around the lovely room and saw no genuine warmth or even holiday spirit among the assembled family group. Rather it seemed as though they were all—herself included— performing their roles like actors in a poorly written play. The only attractive thing about the whole occasion was the elaborate stage on which they'd all been brought together. The setting featured polished silver and gleaming crystal. They'd been served premium scotch and an expensive wine with dinner. Beyond the dining table stood an antique sideboard with a very good painting hanging over it.

Peg considered all that for a moment. She remembered the question she'd asked earlier when she and Max were approaching the house. Once again she found herself wondering how such an opulent display was within the means of a family whose finances were as precarious as she'd been led to believe. Clearly her in-laws had spared no expense in the staging of this Christmas celebration . . . but to what end?

As her gaze drifted aimlessly around the room once more, it came to rest on her brother-in-law. Seated at the head of the table, Michael was presiding over the gathering with all the hauteur and pompous arrogance of a banana-republic overlord intent on flaunting his dubious power and prestige.

Family resemblance or not, Peg thought, Max's brother was a nitwit.

Then abruptly she frowned as bits and pieces of disparate ideas began to tumble into place and form a more coherent picture. Finally something began to make sense. All at once, Peg was pretty sure she had the answer she'd been looking for.

Reconnecting with the conversation, Peg discovered that Bob was regaling the occupants of the table with a listing of the finer points of some arcane accounting system. Everyone was doing their best to feign interest in the topic. Delighted that they were otherwise occupied, Peg slid her foot sideways and kicked Max under the table.

He jumped slightly in his seat, then glanced her way.

"I get it now," Peg whispered.

"You get what?" Her husband scooted his chair slightly closer. His low tone matched her own.

"I know why Michael invited us today. It wasn't to mend bridges, it was to gloat. He wants you to see how well he's doing, even though you got the lion's share of Nana's money."

"Shhh!" Max turned and glanced quickly around the table. Thankfully no one was paying any attention to them. "For once, give that inquiring mind of yours a day off. It's Christmas, and it's enough that the family is together. We don't need to analyze everybody's motives. Can't we just relax and enjoy our holiday dinner?"

Peg lifted a brow eloquently. *Enjoying themselves? Was that was they were doing?* She didn't even have to say the words aloud.

"You know what my brother is like," said Max. "He's the quintessential oldest child. He always has to be the center of attention. That's all this day is about."

"No, it's more than that—"

"Leave it alone, Peg. Please?"

"But—"

"Now is not the time," Max said firmly.

He was right. Even Peg had to admit that. But something odd was going on with her husband's family. The more she thought about it, the more certain she was. Whether Max wanted to admit it or not.

With Peg on her best behavior, the rest of the afternoon unfolded uneventfully. Scarcely an hour passed before she and Max were finally able to make their escape.

Michael and Eileen walked them to the door. "I'm glad you could join us for our impromptu little gathering," Michael said as he showed them out.

Impromptu, my foot, Peg snorted. She'd been to formal weddings that weren't this well-orchestrated. Nevertheless, she hugged Eileen, thanked her for the lovely meal, and managed to keep the rest of her thoughts to herself as she and Max walked down the steps and climbed into their car.

Together they coasted down the length of the driveway in silence. It wasn't until Max had turned back out onto Oenoke Ridge—neutral territory, as it were—that Peg's shoulders rose and fell as she blew out a long breath. Beside her, Max finally spoke.

"That was interesting," he said.

The two of them looked at each other across the car's front seat. Both burst out laughing at the same time. Peg was positively giddy with relief that the visit was finally over. It looked as though Max felt the same way.

"Oh my God," Peg said on another exhale. Suddenly she felt as though she'd been holding her breath for hours. "That was terrible! What is *wrong* with those people?"

"Don't ask me." Max shifted his eyes away from the road and shook his head innocently. "How would I know? They're only my family." He tried to swallow his next laugh. Instead it escaped as a loud guffaw.

"I think that was the longest afternoon of my life," Peg said as they navigated back through downtown New Canaan.

"At least we were able to escape," Max pointed out. "The one I feel sorry for is Bob. That poor boy has no idea what he's getting into."

"I wouldn't worry about him. From what I could see, he and Melanie make a terrible couple. That will never last."

"He seems to think it will. I gather the announcement of an engagement might not be far off."

"Oh my," Peg muttered under her breath. It was a good thing the young couple didn't care about her opinion. "That's a mistake."

She and Max were once more on the Merritt Parkway and halfway home to Greenwich when Peg again broached the subject that had been bothering her all day. "How does Michael afford all that?" she wondered aloud.

"That's the second time you've asked me that."

"Because I really want to know. Your brother made hash of his career, and he squandered his inheritance. And based on past performance, I'm willing to bet that whatever job is keeping him busy now isn't nearly lucrative enough to support that kind of lifestyle."

Max pondered for a moment before answering. "On the one hand, I'm inclined to agree with you," he said finally.

"And on the other?"

"How and where Michael makes his money is none of my business."

"You can't tell me you're not curious."

"I don't have to be curious," Max replied. "You've always had enough curiosity for the both of us."

"But Michael's your family—"

"Precisely. And as uncomfortable as today may have

been, I'm still determined to look at his invitation as a step in the right direction."

"Pish," Peg said stubbornly. "I'm convinced that Michael only invited us so that he could rub your nose in his success."

"That's your opinion." Max's tone was mild. "It doesn't have to be mine."

"You're not going to let me get all worked up about this, are you?"

"Not if I can help it."

Peg sighed. "Sometimes I think you're just too nice a person."

Max gazed at his wife across the seat. "I thought that was why you married me."

"Because you were *nice?* Heaven forbid. I married you because you were hot."

"Hot?" Max sounded pleased.

"You still are, for that matter."

"I'm glad to hear that I haven't lost my touch."

"And you liked dogs," Peg said loftily. "That was a big plus."

"I'll bet."

"Your family," she mentioned, "was not an added inducement."

"No," Max agreed. "They wouldn't have been."

They'd talked their way around in a circle. Max and Peg completed the rest of the drive in a companionable silence. As they approached their house, Peg gazed at the lighted windows. After a moment, two black Poodle heads popped up into view. Two black noses pressed against the cold glass. Peg couldn't see the dogs' tails, but she knew that they were wagging madly.

The canine welcoming committee was in place.

"I'm glad that's over with," Max said as he pulled into the garage.

But was it? Peg wondered. She wasn't so sure.

The unanswered questions nagged at Peg over the next week. She knew that Max wanted her to leave things alone. He'd certainly told her as much. But leaving things alone was not Peg's style. Indeed, it could probably be said that she'd never left anything alone in her entire life.

And it was a life rather well lived.

No need to change her strategy now, Peg decided.

Just after the New Year, she called Imelda Grissom. The dog show community wasn't that large. At least it didn't seem that way to Peg, who'd been an integral part of it for years. She and Imelda competed at most of the same shows, they belonged to a common kennel club, they'd even served together on a committee or two. So it wasn't difficult for Peg to inveigle an invitation to drop by Nana's friend's house on a gray, overcast January afternoon while Max was at work.

What her husband didn't know wouldn't hurt him, she thought. And anyway, maybe her suspicions would prove to be wrong. If that were the case, Max need never know that she'd disregarded his advice. And if she was right . . . well, she would cross that unfortunate bridge when she came to it.

Imelda lived in Indian Harbor, a scenic area of Greenwich south of town along the water. The directions she gave Peg were excellent, and Imelda was waiting for her when she arrived.

"An entertaining visitor is just what I need to

brighten things up on a gloomy day like this," she said as she ushered Peg inside.

A trio of Cavaliers had followed their mistress to the door. The happy spaniels ran on ahead as Imelda led the way into her living room, where a comfortable couch and a china tea service were waiting. When Peg sat down, a lovely ruby bitch hopped up into her lap.

"Sophie, be good," Imelda said.

"Sophie is behaving perfectly," Peg assured her. Her fingers stroked the Cav's rounded head and scratched beneath her chin. "I hope you'll feel the same way about me when I tell you why I'm here."

"Is that so?" Imelda didn't appear at all perturbed by that confession. Instead she sounded intrigued. "Go on."

"I've come to pick your brain," said Peg.

"Perfect. I'm all yours." Imelda was vastly well-informed about all aspects of the dog show world. "Judges? Puppies? Westminster entries? Name your pleasure."

"Actually it's about a friend of yours."

"Gossip? *Moi?*"

Imelda's eyes gleamed. She was a woman who enjoyed trading information. The give and take of titillating tidbits was guaranteed to keep everyone in her vicinity on their toes—and especially Imelda herself. Peg knew she had come to the right place.

"Perhaps it would be more correct to call her a former friend," she said.

"That's the best kind to dish about. Are you going to tell me who it is or do I have to guess?"

"Sarah Turnbull."

A look of surprise flashed briefly across Imelda's face. Then it was gone and her expression sobered. "Dear Sarah," she said. "I miss her every day."

"Were the two of you close?"

Imelda took her time before answering. She poured two cups of tea, placed a delicate sugar cookie on the saucer of each, and handed one to Peg before saying, "Sarah and I were friends for years. We met at the Round Hill Club one summer when we were teenagers. Both of us were mad about tennis back then."

Imelda paused, then issued a correction. "Well, to tell the truth, we didn't really care about the tennis. We both had huge crushes on the club's pro. You've never seen two teenage girls take so many tennis lessons in a single summer. I think between the two of us we must have monopolized his entire schedule."

She took a moment to enjoy the memory. Then Imelda looked at Peg, cocked her head to one side, and said, "Sarah Turnbull was your mother-in-law."

"She was indeed," Peg agreed. She added, perhaps unnecessarily, "We were *not* close."

"No . . . I was quite aware of that."

"The two of you spoke of me?"

"Only once or twice in passing."

"I'm surprised it wasn't more often," Peg said bluntly. "Sarah seemed to have a lot to say about me, at least when I was listening. She saw me as the interloper in her perfect family. The hussy who'd had the audacity to seduce away her younger son."

Imelda permitted herself a small nod. "Quite so. Although I'm not sure I would have phrased it just that way."

"I'm hoping we can speak to each other honestly," said Peg.

'The most honest thing I know is that Sarah didn't like you very much."

"I'm well aware of that." Peg paused for a sip of tea. "She never made any secret of the fact."

"But now . . . Sarah's been gone for nearly a year. Surely this is all past history?"

"It is indeed," Peg agreed. "Actually I wanted to talk to you about Sarah's relationship with another family member. Obviously you know my husband, Max, who was her younger son. But did Sarah ever speak to you about her older son, Michael?"

"The one who stole her money?"

Peg swallowed a gulp of tea. It burned all the way down her throat. She coughed several times, then finally caught her breath.

"You said you wanted to speak honestly," Imelda chided. "So that's precisely what I'm doing. Bear in mind that if Sarah were still alive, I wouldn't have said a word about that. I'd have turned you around and sent you right back to Sarah herself. She could have answered your questions or not as she chose. But under the present circumstances, I don't see the harm in telling you what I know."

"Please do," Peg invited. She set her teacup aside. "I'd like to hear everything."

"As you may know, toward the end of her life Sarah wasn't a happy woman. She felt as though she'd failed as a mother. Both of her sons had disappointed her greatly."

"Max did so by marrying me," said Peg.

Imelda nodded.

"And Michael?"

"According to what Sarah told me, he appropriated a rather large sum of money from her."

"No," said Peg. "That's not right. Sarah gave him that money. It was to be invested on her behalf."

"In the beginning, yes, that was how it started. It wasn't how things ended, however. I believe Michael was in need of a new job."

Peg nodded.

"Sarah knew that he was struggling. Not much got past her. Plus, she made it her business to keep tabs. And Michael had a family to support. His children were Sarah's grandchildren. The only ones she was ever going to have."

Peg could scarcely overlook *that* fact. It had been a bone of contention for years.

"She felt it was her duty to step in and set him back on the right path. Sarah was sure that her intervention could make all the difference to Michael. She pulled some strings and secured another position for him. Her own investment account was included as part of the package."

"Michael lost her money by making poor investments," said Peg. "Dabbling in junk bonds and currency trading."

"That was what Sarah thought at first. That was what she had been told."

"Told by whom?" asked Peg.

"By Michael, her beloved older son." Imelda sighed. "He had convinced her to put the funds in a joint account. He told her that sometimes decisions had to be made quickly and that it would be better if the account was set up to allow both of them access. Sarah never questioned the wisdom of that. Michael was not just her financial adviser, he was her child. She trusted him implicitly."

"Dear Lord," Peg said under her breath. She was beginning to get an inkling of where this was heading.

"Some of Sarah's money was lost to bad investments,

but not all of it. The remaining funds simply . . . disappeared."

Peg sat up straight. "What do you mean?"

"They vanished." Imelda waved hand through the air. "Poof! As though they had never existed."

"Where did they go?"

"Your guess is probably as good as Sarah's. She suspected the Cayman Islands."

Peg was incredulous at this new twist. "Sarah *knew* about that?"

"Not at first. But eventually . . . yes. Your mother-in-law wasn't a foolish woman by any means. She understood finances. She knew how money could and should be made to work by those who had it. When a large portion of her estate went missing, she went looking for it."

"Did she find it?"

"Near enough," Imelda replied. "I don't think she ever discovered all the details, but there was sufficient evidence for her to reach a very unpleasant conclusion."

"Holy cow," said Peg. She'd come to Imelda hoping to find answers, but she certainly hadn't expected that one.

Then that realization was followed quickly by another: Max would be horrified by this information. He'd be appalled by his brother's betrayal. Even worse, he would most likely feel responsible.

Peg quickly cast the disturbing thought away. The most important thing now was to keep Imelda talking. "What did Sarah do next?" she asked.

"Nothing. As far as I know, she never said a word about it to either of her sons."

"I find that hard to believe."

"Think about it," Imelda said. "You know how much family meant to Sarah. She knew that revealing what she'd found out would tear everything she cared about to pieces. Accusing her own son of stealing from her? Even if he was guilty—perhaps especially if he was guilty— Michael would never have forgiven her."

"Even so," said Peg. "How could she just let him get away with doing such a despicable thing?"

"Sarah felt she had no choice. The disclosure would have pitted her two sons against one another. It would have ruined her grandchildren's lives. Ultimately she knew she couldn't allow that to happen. I'm quite certain that was why Sarah spoke to me about it. The knowledge was eating away at her. She *needed* to tell somebody. And there was no one else she could confide in."

Peg sat in silence for a moment, processing what she'd been told.

"I find this all quite shocking," she said finally.

"As did I," Imelda replied. "Not to mention Sarah herself. I know she subsequently made an adjustment to her will. Something to address the wrongdoing and restore the balance going forward, she said. She wanted Michael to know— even if it wasn't until after she died—that he hadn't gotten away scot-free."

Peg shook her head. She felt unbalanced, reeling from the scope of what she'd learned. It was as though she'd picked at one small thread and unexpectedly ended up unraveling an entire quilt. She lifted the ruby Cavalier and set her gently aside on the couch, then rose to her feet.

"That explains quite a lot," Peg said. "Thank you for confiding in me."

"It's what Sarah would have wanted me to do. Although quite frankly, I had expected to be having this conversation with your husband."

Peg had taken a step toward the door. Now she stopped and turned. "Excuse me?"

"Max," said Imelda. "After Sarah died, I thought I would hear from him."

"Why is that?"

"Sarah warned me it might happen. She told me that she'd left a private note for Max among her papers. She let him know that if he had any questions about the choices she had made, he should contact me for clarification. But he never did."

For a long moment, Peg simply stood still. She could hear the blood pounding in her ears. She and Max shared everything. She couldn't believe that he'd never said a thing.

"Max would have received that note almost a year ago," she said quietly.

"I take it he didn't mention it to you?"

Peg shook her head.

"Perhaps he was afraid you might take matters into your own hands."

As indeed you've done.

The thought hung in the air between them. Neither woman felt obliged to voice it aloud.

"Max should have told me." With effort, Peg tamped down her irritation. "We could have discussed the matter. Of course, I would have respected his wishes."

Even before the words were said, Peg realized they were a lie. Max *had* asked her to leave things alone. And yet here she was.

"You've given me a lot to think about," she told Imelda.

The other woman rose from her seat as well. Sophie

hopped down from the couch and the three Cavaliers eddied around Imelda's legs as she followed Peg to the front hall.

"Not all of it bad, I hope?" she said as she retrieved Peg's things from the closet.

"No indeed," Peg replied. "I asked the questions. I wanted to know. That was hardly your fault." She slipped on her warm, wool coat and deliberately changed the subject. "I assume I'll be seeing you next month at Westminster?"

"Of course," Imelda replied. "I wouldn't miss a minute of it. How's that specials dog of yours doing? Is he ready for his big day?"

"Targa." Just saying his name made Peg smile. "He's wonderful. Thank you for asking."

"See that he stays that way. I plan to watch the two of you win the Non-Sporting Group."

Peg gasped. She had always been superstitious. "Shush! Don't even *talk* to me about the group. Targa and I have to get out of the variety first. That's our first goal."

Imelda just laughed. "I've seen that dog of yours in action, and he moves like a dream. There isn't another Standard Poodle out right now that can touch him."

"Anything can happen," Peg retorted. "And at Westminster, it often does. I'm not going to count on winning that purple and gold rosette until I'm holding it in my hands."

"You're right," Imelda agreed mildly. "Anything can happen at that show. And I'll be there in the stands to cheer you on when it does."

* * *

Peg fully intended to drive straight home. And yet somehow—her thoughts whirling with new information and old recriminations—she instead found herself on the Merritt Parkway heading back to New Canaan. Perhaps she should never have started down this path. Had she possessed the knowledge earlier that Max had faced the same choice and deliberately turned the other way, Peg's decision might have been different.

But it was far too late for that now.

Having begun her quest for answers, Peg knew that she wouldn't behave as her mother-inlaw had done. She had no illusions about her ability to right the wrongdoing. But what she could do was prick a sharp pin in her brotherin-law's smug, self-satisfied existence, if only for the pleasure of watching his ego deflate.

It was mid-afternoon, and only Eileen was at home. That suited Peg just fine. Nana hadn't confronted Michael. Even angry as she was, Peg decided it wasn't her place to do so either. Instead she would talk to Eileen. Woman to woman, wife to wife. She wondered if her sister-in-law had any idea what kind of man she'd married.

Eileen drew open the front door in response to Peg's knock. She gazed out at her visitor uncertainly. "Peg," she said with a tight smile. "What a pleasant surprise."

"Not really," Peg replied. "Actually it's not pleasant at all."

Eileen raised her hand and braced it on the back of the door. "In that case, maybe I shouldn't invite you in."

"Do as you wish. You don't have to talk to me. I've recently learned some things that I'm trying to understand. I thought maybe you could help me with that. But I can speak with Michael if you'd prefer." Peg paused, then added meaningfully, "Or maybe Melanie and Frank."

Eileen stepped back. The door opened.

Peg strode inside. She unbuttoned her coat but didn't remove it. Somehow she suspected she wouldn't be staying long.

Rather than waiting for Eileen to provide direction, Peg walked across the hall and into the beautifully appointed living room. The Christmas tree was still up, she noted idly. It was still lovely. And it needed water.

Peg helped herself to a chair.

Eileen remained standing. "What's this about?" she asked. Now she sounded annoyed.

"Nana's will," Peg replied. "And her missing money. And your husband."

Eileen's eyes grew wide. She lifted a hand and touched it to her cheek. Her gaze slid past Peg and fastened on something in the far corner of the room.

In the time it had taken to drive from Greenwich to New Canaan, Peg had been determined to think the best of her sister-in-law. She had hoped that Eileen hadn't been aware of Michael's deception. But now she saw she'd been wrong.

"I see I don't have to explain why I'm here," she said.

Eileen remained standing. And mute. Peg knew she shouldn't find satisfaction in her sister-in-law's distress, but nevertheless she did.

"So here's my question. When Michael took the money that supports your lavish lifestyle— stole it not from a stranger but from his own mother—what was he *thinking?* Nana loved him. She supported him. How could he have done such a vile thing to her in return?"

"You're wrong," Eileen said quickly. She spun back

to face Peg. "Michael didn't steal anything. That's not what happened."

"Is that what he told you? If so, it isn't true."

"It's entirely true. The money Nana gave Michael was family money. It had been earned by his father. Nana inherited it upon his death, but it was intended to be passed on to the children when she died."

"But—"

"But nothing," Eileen interrupted briskly. "You, of *all* people, should understand. You who knew exactly what Nana was like. She expected everyone to obey her wishes, to adhere to her rules, to accept her standards of behavior as their own."

In spite of herself, Peg gave a small nod.

"Nana was a force of nature. And woe to the child of hers who fell short of her expectations in any way." Eileen nailed Peg with a hard stare. "As Max found out to his detriment."

By marrying you.

Eileen didn't say the words. She didn't have to.

"I believe we're discussing your husband," Peg shot back. "Not mine."

Eileen shrugged. "In their mother's eyes, both were guilty of terrible transgressions, were they not?"

"The two things weren't comparable at all," Peg snapped. "Not even close."

"And yet Nana never forgave Max for choosing you against her wishes, did she? Their relationship never recovered after that. And Nana certainly never accepted *you*."

"That hardly matters now," Peg said shortly.

"I think it does. Since you're the one who has the nerve to come into my house, and sit on my couch, and tell me what you think my husband has done wrong.

As if you have the mistaken impression that you *deserve* to have an opinion on the matter. No wonder Nana didn't think you were good enough for Max. Your actions today have proven it."

That complaint was an old one, ancient even. Peg told herself that the rebuke had long since lost its sharp sting.

"Those are fine words," she said. "Coming as they do from the wife of a thief."

"Oh please." Eileen flicked a hand through the air, waving the accusation away. "There's no need to be melodramatic. Michael helped himself to an advance on his inheritance, so what? He was Nana's oldest son. The money was his due. Nana wasn't hurt by that. At her age, she had plenty of money left to live on."

"If you think this is only about the money," Peg retorted, "then you're deliberately missing the point. How can you possibly believe that Nana wasn't hurt when she found out that she'd been betrayed by her own child?"

A fleeting shadow passed over Eileen's face. In the moment before her expression cleared, she looked uncertain. And briefly troubled. Was it possible, Peg wondered, that even now—after Nana's will had been read and her remaining assets distributed—that Eileen had been unaware of the true extent of her mother-in-law's knowledge?

Peg didn't have long to ponder that, however, because Eileen was already moving on. "You ask entirely too many questions," she said. "And I've already been too patient. You wanted answers and I've given them to you. If you don't like what you've heard, that's hardly my problem."

Eileen cast one last withering glance at Peg, then

turned and walked out of the room. Peg stood. She gathered her coat around her and followed.

"Why did you and Michael invite us here for Christmas?" she said. She wondered if her sister-in-law would reply, but Eileen just shrugged.

"That was Michael's doing. He asked me to extend the invitation. At first I was surprised by that. But then I thought about how stubborn Max is. Now that Nana is gone, he would never have made the first move toward a family reconciliation. It was up to Michael to be the bigger man."

"Oh pish." Peg snorted. "The bigger man indeed. Michael only wanted Max here so that he could show off what a success he was."

"So what if he did? There's nothing wrong with that."

Peg opened her mouth, then snapped it shut. She had nothing more to say.

They reached the front door together. Eileen placed her hand on the knob, but paused before turning it. "Earlier . . . when you arrived . . . you mentioned the children."

"I did." Peg wasn't proud of using that threat, but it had served its purpose.

"Frank and Melanie idolized Nana. And of course, they adore their father. If they were to hear of this conversation . . ."

"They might find themselves acquainted with the truth?"

"*Your* truth," Eileen said sharply. "Not ours."

Peg had always thought that truth was absolute. But apparently, according to her sister-in-law, it was open to interpretation.

"I'd rather you didn't tell them about this," said Eileen.

Even without the request, Peg wouldn't have. There was no need. Still she relished the small moment of power, perhaps the only one she'd ever had within this family.

"You want *me* to do *you* a favor?"

"What I want," Eileen said firmly, "is for you to behave like a responsible adult. Children process things differently. It's better to shield them from events that they're too young to think through for themselves."

More duplicity, Peg thought. Michael and Eileen were the perfect couple. The two of them deserved each other.

Interpreting Peg's silence as refusal, Eileen said in a snide tone, "Then again, since you've never had children of your own, you probably wouldn't understand what I'm talking about."

"I understand not wanting to hurt someone needlessly," Peg said quietly. She ran her fingers quickly down the row of buttons on the front of her coat and opened the door herself. "You don't have to worry about my disillusioning your children. They won't hear the truth from me."

Eileen placed a hand on Peg's arm. "Give me your promise." Peg lifted a brow. "Would it mean anything to you?"

"Just promise," Eileen repeated. "Please?"

And Peg did.

"You'll never guess where I spent the afternoon," Peg said to Max later that evening. They were sitting once more in front of the fire, both of them keeping a sharp eye on Bonnie, who was lying between them, panting.

The Standard Poodle had been growing increasingly restless all day. Despite the fact that a cozy whelping box had been set up in their bedroom for a week, Bonnie had been burrowing beneath the bed and trying to nest in the closet. It wouldn't be long now. Salute had been banished to the kennel for the time being, and neither Max nor Peg intended to let the black bitch out of their sight.

"Where?" Max asked. Truthfully, he was more interested in what Bonnie was doing than what Peg had to say.

"With Imelda Grissom."

"Don't tell me she's signed you up for another committee."

"No," Peg replied. "We talked about something else entirely."

Max lifted his gaze but didn't ask the obvious question. As the silence stretched between them, Peg realized there was a reason for that. He'd already guessed the purpose of their conversation. And why shouldn't he? Her husband had been sitting on his mother's last letter for a year.

"Nothing to do with me, I hope," Max said finally.

All evening Peg had wondered what she would say when this moment came. She'd gone looking for information because she'd been sure that knowing would make her feel better. But now that she had the answers she had sought, she found she only felt worse. Where was the justice in that? Where was the justice in any of this?

Peg wanted to share the story she'd unearthed. It *needed* to be told.

But Max's answer was unambiguous. His expression was clear. His eyes reflected the trust they'd built between them through the years.

And Peg had never been able to deny her husband anything.

"No," she said softly. "It was nothing to do with you."

When her Aunt Peg lands a gig as judge at a Kentucky dog show, Melanie Travis welcomes the opportunity for a road trip. Too bad a killer has planned a deadly detour . . .

For a dog lover like Melanie, the opportunity to attend the Kentuckiana Dog Show Cluster is not to be missed. Fortunately, the timing coincides with her spring break from teaching, so she heads for central Kentucky with her sister-in-law Bertie and Aunt Peg, who's accepted a week-long judging assignment. Once there, Aunt Peg reconnects with an old friend, Ellie Gates Wanamaker, a former Standard Poodle exhibitor and a member of a well-heeled Kentucky family. Miss Ellie has been out of the dog show world for more than a decade, but when Melanie invites her to spectate at the Louisville Kennel Club dog show, she's eager to accompany her.

Miss Ellie's presence at the expo center, however, provokes mixed reactions from exhibitors she hasn't seen in years, including some outright animosity. The following day Melanie learns that Miss Ellie has suffered a fatal accident while exercising her dogs. Aunt Peg, however, suspects foul play. Wishing to avoid any scandal, Miss Ellie's pedigreed family prefers to let sleeping dogs lie, but as Melanie begins to sniff around, she discovers Miss Ellie had many secrets, both in the dog show world and amongst her Kentucky kin . . .

Please turn the page for an exciting sneak peek of Laurien Berenson's newest Melanie Travis mystery LIVE AND LET GROWL now on sale wherever print and e-books are sold!

Chapter 1

I was moving fast.

The ground below me was little more than a blur. Scenery flew by with astonishing speed. I was running. . . .

No, not running . . . riding. I was on the back of a horse. I could feel the smooth motion of the muscular body beneath me. I could hear the creak of the leather saddle, and the steady, rhythmic sound of hoofbeats striking the turf.

Their pounding cadence pulsed through me. It drew me in and made me one with the motion. It propelled me onward, as if this heady race was the only thing in the world that mattered.

Where was I? I wondered. What was happening? Was I racing toward something—or was I running away?

I had no answers. All I knew was that I could feel the sharp bite of the wind on my face and a sensation of freedom humming deep inside my bones.

The feeling was heavenly.

It was addictive.

One thing I was sure of—I wanted more.

All at once a pale mist rose on the path ahead of us. Its silvery tendrils lifted and swirled, obscuring all view of what was to come. I found myself leaning forward in the saddle. I gazed in vain between the tips of two dark, pointed ears.

I could see nothing. The vista before me was still blank . . . and suddenly forbidding. In the space of a second, the breakneck speed at which we were traveling lost its appeal.

Frantically I reached for reins, but couldn't find them. My fingers felt thick and stiff. Useless. I screamed into the wind. I told the horse to stop but my words had no effect.

Then the mists shifted and drew apart and I saw that behind them lay only darkness. A void of nothingness. It looked as though my steed and I were racing toward the edge of the world.

Abruptly my stomach plummeted as the ground disappeared from beneath us. My hands flew upward, groping in the air, grasping desperately for purchase that wasn't there. My heart pounded with the sudden knowledge that I couldn't save myself. And then I was falling, helpless as I plunged downward and tumbled into the unknown below . . .

I awoke with a gasp and bolted upright in bed.

My heart was beating wildly in my chest. Mouth open, I was desperate for air. Fire clawed at my lungs. My insides still churned with the sensation of falling. Though my eyes were open wide I couldn't see a thing. Everything around me was black: inky and impenetrable.

I still had no idea where I was.

Clutching the bedcovers in frantic fingers, I swiveled my head from side to side. A moment later, my gaze alighted on the amber numbers of the bedside clock. Three-oh-two, it read.

Slowly my mind processed the number. With effort I made the connection to what it meant. Compared to my recent speed, I felt dull and sluggish as I worked to reorient myself. I gulped in a breath of cool air and shifted my shoulders, trying to ease their tension.

There was no horse. There was no wind. There was no yawning crater waiting to suck me down into its gruesome depths.

I'd been having a nightmare. That was all.

I gazed around again. My eyes had adjusted to the darkness now. I could see the familiar bedroom surrounding me. I could feel the slight dip in the mattress caused by the weight of my husband, Sam, who was sound asleep beside me.

Relief washed through me and I blew out a long breath. I was safe. I was home in my own house, with my husband, my two sons, and my six dogs.

I heard a soft creak and turned to see the bedroom door nudged slightly ajar by a long black muzzle. My Standard Poodle, Faith, the dog who understood everything about me and who knew my thoughts almost before I did, was standing silently in the doorway.

Faith always sleeps on my older son, Davey's, bed. But now in the middle of the night, something had called her to me. The big Poodle was so attuned to my emotions that she had sensed something was amiss. As I glanced in her direction, Faith tipped her head to one side inquiringly. Even in the murky darkness, I could see the gentle gleam in her eye.

As our gazes met, Faith padded silently across the room. She stepped beside the bed and pressed her nose into my hand, offering her own special brand of comfort. As the Poodle's warm breath filled my palm, I finally felt my heart rate begin to slow. I cupped Faith's muzzle between my fingers and rubbed my thumb over her lips and cheek.

"It's all right, sweetie," I said softly. "You can go back to sleep."

Faith acknowledged the comment with a low swish of her tail but she didn't look convinced.

"Really," I told her. "Everything is fine. It was just a dream."

Faith lifted one front paw delicately and placed it on the bed in silent inquiry. I glanced over my shoulder at Sam. Covers pulled up to his chin, head burrowed deep in his pillow, he was too deeply asleep to realize that his sleeping arrangement was about to become even cozier.

I scooched over toward Sam and patted the space beside me. "Come on up," I whispered. "There's plenty of room."

Faith leapt up lightly. She aligned her body next to mine, lay down on the quilt, and pressed in close. As I settled down beside her, the Poodle's warmth enveloped me.

I closed my eyes and finally slept.

"I had the strangest dream last night," I said the next evening.

The comment was delivered to a full house. It was our son, Kevin's, third birthday. In honor of the occasion, I had invited some of our relatives to dinner.

In most families a gathering like that would lead to convivial celebration. Not mine, however. My relatives are equally as likely to set the house ablaze as they are to coexist in peace. There's nothing boring about the extended Travis/Turnbull clan, especially when my provocative and ever-entertaining Aunt Peg is part of the assembly.

So far we'd managed to make our way through most of the meal without incident. Minutes earlier, Kevin's birthday cake, alight with festive candles, had been presented to the room with great fanfare. Kev had shrieked and clapped his hands, bouncing up and down in his seat with glee when it appeared.

My younger son was a little hazy about what the concept of three years meant, but he knew all about chocolate cake. When I set the dessert down in front of him, Kev's first impulse was to reach for it with both hands. Luckily his older brother, Davey—a gangly twelve-year-old, teetering on the cusp between childhood and adolescence—was there to quickly intercede. Cupping Kevin's small hands in his own much larger ones, Davey also help his little brother blow out the candles.

The layer cake was cut and served and everyone dug in happily. If I were to be honest I would admit that most of the evening's success was undoubtedly due to Sam's calming influence. When it comes to my relatives, my husband is smart enough and affable enough not to sweat the small stuff. Things that cause me to roll my eyes and rail about the general state of insanity just make him shrug his shoulders and chuckle under his breath.

Lucky man. I wish I knew how he did it.

Sam was seated at the head of the table. On his right

was my Aunt Peg. Now in the middle of her seventh decade, Margaret Turnbull is living proof that age is merely a state of mind. The woman possesses more than enough energy, ambition, and wit to run circles around me effortlessly. Unfortunately it's a circumstance she's not above exploiting to further her own ends. On the other hand, if it weren't for Aunt Peg I would never have discovered the intriguing appeal of the dog show world. Nor would I have Faith, or the other five Standard Poodles that currently grace and enrich our lives.

Completing the group seated around the table was my younger brother, Frank, and his family. For years Frank had been the feckless, thoughtless, bane of my existence. But now in his thirties, my little brother was finally grown up and married to one of my best friends, Bertie Kennedy. Their young daughter, Maggie, was seated between them. The child was keeping a beady eye on Kevin, seemingly determined to ensure that the birthday boy didn't get so much as a smidge more cake than she did.

Any minute now the sugar high was going to kick in, I thought as I gazed around the room. And then we'd really be off to the races.

And just like that I remembered my dream.

"I had the strangest dream last night," I said.

"Oh?" Aunt Peg looked up from her cake. "I read a book about that."

"About dreams?" Bertie asked. Her dark green eyes twinkled with amusement. "Or strange things?"

"Dreams, of course. Did you know that they're the way your subconscious works through problems while you're asleep?" Peg peered at me across the table. "Do you have any problems that need working out?"

She would ask that. There's nothing Aunt Peg en-

joys more than involving herself in other peoples'
troubles.

"Not that I'm aware of," I replied. "And certainly
none that involve a horse."

"A *horse?*" Sam sounded surprised. I couldn't
blame him. I felt the same way.

From across the table, Aunt Peg glanced at me
sharply. I wondered what that look meant.

"That was what was so odd about it," I said. "In the
dream, I was riding a horse. I've never done that in my
life. The horse was galloping, we were racing like the
wind. It's amazing how real it all felt."

"Real indeed," Aunt Peg muttered under her breath.
I waited for her to continue but instead she resumed
eating. Nothing could distract Aunt Peg from cake for
long.

"Where were you going?" Bertie asked curiously.

"I have no idea. Everything ahead was foggy. I
couldn't see a thing. We were just running."

"Maybe you were being chased by a zombie," said
Frank.

"No." I laughed. "I don't think so."

"Was it a flying horse?" Kev asked. He has a book
about Pegasus.

"No, just a regular horse. A very fast one."

"Maybe it was Willow!" said Davey.

Five years earlier, his father, my ex-husband, Bob,
had surprised Davey with a palomino pony named
Willow. Even though at the time Davey and I were living in a small house on a tiny plot of land, Bob apparently hadn't foreseen any difficulties with the care and
management of Davey's new pet. As ponies went,
Willow was lovely, but she hadn't lasted long.

"A pony," Kevin said with sudden interest. He had heard the story from his brother. "I want a pony!"

"Don't be silly." Aunt Peg sniffed. "Why would anyone want a pony when they can have Poodles instead?"

Poodles indeed. We not only had Standard Poodles, we were literally surrounded by them. And as Aunt Peg would have said, what was wrong with that?

Poodles come in three different sizes, but all share the same superb temperament. They're smart, they're endearing, and they have a superior sense of humor. Best of all, Poodles are people dogs. Wherever their family is, that's where they want to be.

Since the birthday celebration was taking place in the dining room, that meant that aside from the eight people sitting at the table, we also had six black Standard Poodles lying in attendance on the floor around us. Five of the six were even wearing party hats. The Poodles didn't look nearly as delighted about that development as Kevin did. In fact, judging by the expressions on their faces, they were feeling rather silly.

In my defense, the hats hadn't been my idea. Sam and Davey had snuck away and done the honors while I'd been busy greeting our arriving guests. But Aunt Peg's horrified gasp when she rounded the corner and saw the assembled crew—she being of the firm belief that Poodles are entirely too dignified to be treated frivolously—was gratifying enough to make me wish that I'd been a coconspirator.

All our Poodles are the Standard variety, the biggest of the three sizes. The top of Faith's head is nearly level with my waist, which positions her entire body within easy reach whenever she and I want to hold a conversation. That comes up more frequently than you might think.

Aunt Peg is Faith's breeder. Indeed she was connected in some way to nearly every dog in the room, her Cedar Crest line having set the standard for excellence in the Poodle breed since before I was born. A dedicated owner-handler in the show ring for decades, Peg had now scaled back her breeding and exhibiting commitments to concentrate on her burgeoning career as a dog show judge. As is true with many of Aunt Peg's decisions, that change in course has had the effect of keeping us all on our toes.

Faith's daughter, Eve, now lying beneath Kevin's chair in the hope there'd be spillage, was the second Standard Poodle I had brought to my marriage to Sam. He'd joined the union with two bitches of his own, Casey and Raven, both of whom were—like Faith and Eve—retired show champions. Sam was also the owner of GCH Cedar Crest Scimitar, also known as Tar.

Formerly an accomplished "specials dog," Tar had numerous Non-Sporting Group and Best in Show wins to his credit. Now, however, like the bitches, he was retired from the show ring and his long, plush black coat had been clipped off. He, too, wore the attractive and easy-to-care-for sporting trim, with a short blanket of dense dark curls covering his entire body.

Tar was a love. He was the sweetest, most well-meaning dog of the entire pack. But he was also the only dumb Poodle I'd ever met. Somehow, no matter what was going on, Tar always managed to be a beat behind the rest. Punch lines, along with other of life's intricacies, simply went right over his head.

Our newest addition and the only dog currently "in hair" was Davey's Standard Poodle, Augie. Davey was responsible for Augie's care; and with Sam's help, he was also managing the young dog's show career. The collaboration was a successful one as Augie was already halfway toward the goal of accumulating the fifteen points he would need to be named a champion.

In deference to his long and oh-so-valuable topknot hair, Augie was the only Poodle not wearing a party hat. He didn't appear to be upset about the omission. In fact, I was pretty sure I'd seen Augie sniff derisively in Tar's direction when he thought no one was looking.

Having heard Aunt Peg reference their breed, several dark heads lifted as the Poodle pack turned into the conversation at the table. Ears pricked as they waited to see what would happen next.

"Don't care," Kevin replied firmly to Aunt Peg. "Have Poodles. Want a pony."

"Ponies are too big," I told him mildly. "Besides, you already have fish."

Kev's aquarium, a cherished Christmas present, was visible through the doorway in the living room. My son refused to be mollified. He thrust out his lower lip and started to shake his head. Despite the date on the calendar, we clearly hadn't yet left the Terrible Twos behind just yet.

"And you have cake," I added.

"Cake," Kevin echoed. His expression brightened as Sam reached over and slid another sliver onto his plate. "I like cake!"

"Don't we all," Frank said heartily. He reached over and helped himself to a second piece. "That's why I came tonight."

"And also because it's Kevin's birthday." Bertie leveled a glare at her husband. "Right?"

"Sure," Frank agreed easily. "That, too."

"Has it occurred to you," Sam said to me, "that maybe the reason you were thinking about horses is because of

Peg's judging assignment at the Kentuckiana Cluster next week?"

"No," I replied. That thought hadn't crossed my mind at all.

Aunt Peg's upcoming trip to Kentucky had nothing to do with me. Bertie, who was a professional handler, was also making the trip to the Midwest. With four back-to-back dog shows scheduled to take place in Louisville, and several clients whose dogs were look-ing for majors, she had entered a sizeable string to show. But with spring break starting in just two days—two whole weeks of vacation from my job as a special needs tutor at private Howard Academy—I was look-ing forward to nothing more strenuous than sleeping late and reading several good books.

"Speaking of which," said Aunt Peg, "while we're on the subject, I have an announcement to make. . . ." She paused and looked around, waiting until she had our full attention.

"Which subject is that?" asked Sam. "Kentucky?"

"Judging," Bertie guessed.

"Cake," Frank contributed, speaking with his mouth full.

"Fish!" cried Kevin.

"Horses?" I teased.

"Bingo!" Aunt Peg turned and favored me with a small nod.

Horses? That was a surprise.

Clearly I wasn't the only one who felt that way. The whole table fell silent with nervous anticipation. With Aunt Peg, you never knew which way the dice were going to roll. She might have wonderful news or it could be something truly alarming. I'd long since resigned myself to the fact that life with Aunt Peg meant existing in a semiperpetual state of suspense.

"As it turns out, my trip to Kentucky has come along at a rather fortuitous time," she informed us.

"Why is that?" I asked.

"I have an asset in central Kentucky that I need to take a closer look at." Aunt Peg beamed at us all happily. "You are looking at the new owner of a Thoroughbred racehorse."